TAHN

A Novel

L. A. KELLY

 Revell
Grand Rapids, Michigan

Published by Fleming H. Revell
a division of Baker Publishing Group
P.O. Box 6287, Grand Rapids, MI 49516-6287
www.revellbooks.com

Printed in the United States of America

Library of Congress Cataloging-in-Publication Data
Kelly, L. A.
    Tahn : a novel / L. A. Kelly.
        p.   cm.
    ISBN 0-8007-5999-0 (pbk.)
    1. Good and evil—Fiction. 2. Middle Ages—Fiction. I. Title.
PS3611.E44965T34 2005
813'.6—dc22   2004018096

Scripture is taken from the King James Version of the Bible.

TAHN

With thanks to my literary agent, Alan Youngren, for believing in this story from the beginning; and to Emily and Jan and my pastors Terry and Debi Cain, for their continued support and valuable advice.

Soli Deo gloria

AUTHOR'S NOTE

One morning I woke up and just knew what Tahn looked like. I hadn't been thinking about this story previously. It was a whole new idea, and it presented itself to me in one big lump. I knew what the guy looked like. I knew what his life had been and how he felt about that. I knew the things he was going to have to do to survive and that he would be doing them not for himself but for a lady named Netta and a group of scared and dirty kids. It was huge. It consumed my thoughts. I grabbed paper and started trying to get down all the details that I could.

I knew how the story would start, with Tahn climbing up a wall by night to steal the lady out of her room. I knew where he would take her and why he would leave her to go back for the kids. That day, I began the story. For weeks it nearly consumed me. I took paper everywhere, even to the grocery store or the playground with my kids, and I struggled to put on paper all the things that were flowing through my mind.

I knew the story I was writing had a medieval sort of flavor to it, and yet it was unlike our real medieval history. I knew it might seem European, but it was taking place in no actual setting in Europe or anywhere else in our world. This was a story that was practically trying to write itself. And I was very aware that it claimed a place and time all its own and would defy every attempt to define it as truly "historical" fiction.

The characters in *Tahn* are very real to me because of the intense level of writing energy I experienced during the summer in which I wrote the rough draft. My heart pounded in the midst of suspenseful scenes, and I could feel the intensity all the way to my toes. I cried several times, laughed once or twice. I must have seemed a little crazy to some family and friends, but I knew it was a gift. I knew it was a story that had to be told, whether or not it was ever published and regardless of what it might be called if it was.

Tahn is special to me, though it is not my first book, because finally I accepted what I knew all along. I am a writer. And that is a calling I cannot deny. God has his purpose for me in it, even when I don't know what that purpose is. Partly because of my experiences with *Tahn*, I had the confidence to finish other books I was working on, as well as more ideas that I had set aside for so long.

I knew as I was writing *Tahn* that there was a message in it about the incredible mercy of our loving God, who reaches down to the lowest depths of humanity with his saving grace. But the story also speaks of the forgiveness necessary among men. Even when the peril of the story had lessened and the villains were no longer such a present and direct threat, I knew the story could not end until certain choices were made. Love or self-guarded preservation? Forgiveness or the bitter hate that hangs on so tightly and begs for justification?

It is my hope that readers of this story will think about such choices in their own life. I hope they remember *Tahn* and see past the surface of the next ruffian they meet. I hope they see a potential hero in every lost and wayward child and pray accordingly. Then *Tahn* and I will have done our jobs.

PART ONE

LIFE AND DEATH

I

Tahn crept up the stone wall like a reptile silent after its prey. Almost he hoped that the young woman was not in the room above him, he so loathed what was to come. But he knew she was there. He had seen the flicker of her candle and enough silhouette in the window to know it was her.

He stopped for a moment, almost three stories up, to take a breath and prepare his mind. Lady Netta would be terrified of a stranger taking her by force from her family home. And she would be even more terrified if she remembered the one time they had seen each other before this night.

But what choice did he have? She would not leave willingly. Not with him. And Tahn knew that if he did not steal her away this night, someone else would. Someone who cared far less for her dignity or her life.

He hoped she would not struggle too much, for the thought that he might hurt her pained his heart.

Everything was quiet. The nobleman Trilett and his kinsmen were sleeping in their regal manor, the pride of Onath, most blessed of all the towns of Turis. Cool wind rustled in the trees beyond the wall and gate, defenses in which the Trilett family had long placed far too much confidence. Guards should have been posted, many of them and not at the gate alone, to protect the lady and those she loved. By morning this grand home would be a shell emptied of its glory. And there was nothing he could do but try to ensure that none of the Lady Netta's blood would be shed there.

Her window above him was dark as he pulled upward toward it. Even his boots on the weathered stone made no sound. The lattice shutters were not difficult to push aside, and he was up and over the sill quickly.

He thought of another stone home in the Trilett hands, a different wall he had once climbed to a roof garden. Karll had been the young man's name. He had screamed to his bride in warning and had fought so valiantly.

Tahn shoved those thoughts from his mind. The Lady Netta. She lay on the bed here now, already sleeping. In an instant he was upon her. With one hand he squeezed both her wrists tight together. And with the other hand he pressed down firmly over her mouth. Even in the darkness, he could easily read the terror in her suddenly opened eyes.

"Do not scream," he ordered her. "Do not struggle, and I'll not hurt you."

But she struggled. She squirmed beneath him like a wild thing, but he was too strong for her and too good at anticipating her efforts. "You must cooperate with me tonight, or you will die," he warned. "Do you understand?"

His hand still pressed against her mouth, pushing her into the bed. The sight of her trembling nod made his insides burn. She would never understand. Her fear would be joined by so much more hatred when she realized who it was that had come to apprehend her. But he could find no alternative. Her family would never have listened to him. No more than a peasant could believe that a fox among chickens would protect them from the approach of wolves. He would have to get her out and hope that at least some of the Triletts would try to follow.

He rose from the darkness beneath the canopy of her bed, pulling her up with him. Clouds parted from the moon outside as the lady gained her footing in the middle of the room. He could not bear the look in her eyes. Did she know him already? Did she know that her black-garbed demon had returned?

"I will tie you," he told her quickly. "Because I cannot risk you escaping. But first I will let you gather warm clothing and whatever else you need. Without a sound. And very quickly, do you understand? If you wish to live, you must cooperate."

Slowly he released his hold on her. "Hurry," he commanded. "Or you will leave with nothing."

Feeling numb, Netta forced herself to obey the frightening intruder. How could this be happening? What might he do?

She pulled her warmest, bulkiest dress over her nightgown and laced on her shoes. Her comb, a sewing bag, and a few pages of handwritten script lay on the bedside table. She stuffed all of them into the pocket of her cloak and pulled it around her shoulders. Her mind was racing, hoping for a way of escape from this man. He'd surely kill her if she screamed or tried to run from the room. He'd already warned her of that.

She had no way of knowing what his intentions were. How did he even expect to get out of here without rousing someone?

She turned and stood as straight as she could, though her heart was pounding and the fear was like a sodden weight in her stomach. She would have to do what he said. He left her no choice.

Without a word, he took hold of her wrists and tied them tightly. Then he pulled a scarf from his pocket and gagged her. He had a long length of rope at his waist, and he knotted it carefully at the windowsill. When he had secured it well, he gave the end a toss through the open window. Then he grabbed her bound arms and looped them over his head.

"Don't scream," he told her. "Not till we get to the ground."

And they were suddenly out the window. Netta was dizzy with the terror of it. He scarcely held her at all. She simply dangled there on the neck of her kidnapper as he stole her away. Tears came unbidden and flowed in silent streams down her cheeks. When they were finally on the ground, he set her down in the dirt and picked up a stone. He looked up at the other windows of the great house. "Which is your father's room?" he asked.

She sat and stared at him. How could he expect her to answer that? She wouldn't. She wouldn't help this brazen villain. He might hurt her father. He might do anything.

"Point, Lady!" he insisted.

She shook her head boldly, defiantly, though inside her heart was quaking.

He hurled the stone anyway, at the one window that held a soft glow of candlelight. His aim was true and strong, and the stone went crashing into the room of Netta's Uncle Winn.

She tried to scream, and to her surprise, he reached and pulled the gag away from her mouth. "Yes," he told her. "Loud, now!" He grabbed her by the waist, threw her over his shoulder, and began to run. And she screamed, fearing for the reason he would let her. But maybe they would hear. Maybe they could do something before he got very far.

He was going to the back wall, farthest from the guarded gate. And she soon saw that he had prepared it for their exit. A long plank leaned against it like a ramp, and he was up like a cat without even slowing down. At the top, he held her with one hand and used the other to pull the board up until it leaned down the other side. He took the slope at a run and then kicked the plank to the ground at the bottom. She screamed again, hoping the guard from the gate would come, or her strong cousins, and stop this man before he could disappear with her into the night. But why, why would he let her scream and take that chance? Why would he tell her to?

He suddenly stopped and replaced her gag. She tried to fight him. She tried to struggle as he lifted her again. He was not a very big man, but there was little she could do in the strength of his grasp.

When they reached the woods, a horse was waiting for them. "This is Smoke," the kidnapper suddenly said. He lifted her to the horse's back and jumped up behind her. "Try to be calm," he told her. "I swear I will not hurt you."

But she did not believe him. It was like a horrible dream, to be planted in the saddle with the strange young man's strong arms ensnaring her. His clothes, his long hair, and his eyes were all black beneath the moonlight. She shuddered to think of another black-garbed intruder, on the roof of the springhouse, his sword dripping with the blood of her husband. She'd loved Karll so and had known him in marriage for less than a week when the fiendish killer took him away.

She glanced down at the kidnapper's hands holding tight at the reins in front of her, and she began to tremble. He was so much like that killer. Small and fierce and quiet. It had been three years ago, but she had barely recovered. And now the horror was back again. She could not control the sobs that broke over her.

"We will meet with company soon," he told her steadily. "I am sorry for it, but I have no choice. I will be rid of him quickly. He is a rough man, but I will not let him harm you."

He sat in silence a while longer as they rode through the depth of shadowy woods. And then he seemed to sigh. "Your father's home will be attacked this night, Lady," he said. "That is why I let your screams call them from sleep, once we were outside where they could not stop us. If they are already alert to a trouble, they are not so likely to be slaughtered in their beds. May they be elsewhere, searching for you with their weapons in hand."

The trees gave way to meadow. Netta's captor gave the horse a quick nudge, and the animal broke into a trot. When they slowed again for the return of dense black forest, he continued his talk. "The dark angels will burn your home. But Samis sent me to capture you separately, before the rest are assailed. He has plans of his own for you. The man we meet will have his orders where you are to be taken, but I have no intention of following them. I will hide you."

Netta listened with apprehension. Was it true, what he said? Her home attacked? She greatly hoped not. But he dared claim to be helping? By carrying her off like this?

"I mean you no harm, Lady," he went on. "You might think we should have stayed to fight for your family, but they would have had me away before the true enemy came. I know you cannot trust my word. And I alone would be too little help against the numbers tonight. I used the order to capture you as a chance to spare your life."

She sat silent in front of him. She feared there could be some truth to his words. She knew her father had an enemy in the Baron Trent, a rival for the throne left vacant for seven years as factions of their kingdom warred amongst themselves. The peaceful Trilett family were not crown-seekers, and certainly not mighty of arms, but they were highly favored of the common people, which was enough to incite the jealousy of greedier men.

But though she knew those dangers, she could not possibly trust this man. He was so much like Karll's murderer. Like the devil himself, who was also the father of lies.

She wondered that he seemed to be taking no precautions to avoid leaving a trail. Even when they reached a stream, he followed alongside it a great ways instead of going in.

"The cottage is just ahead," he soon told her. "His name is Darin, and he's an oaf. Try to do what he says, and it will be easier. I won't leave you alone with him." He turned the horse with a barely perceivable flick of his hand. "He will expect that I left your family sleeping. But if they are able to follow us here, I'll not fight them. My object was to get you away from there."

Tahn didn't speak again as they rode the rest of the way. It was just too hard, with this shaking young woman encircled in his arms. For a moment he almost wished he had sunk the dagger into his own flesh as he'd intended such a short time ago. But her life depended on him now. And the little ones depended on him too. Riding here from Samis's Valhal, he'd decided he could not leave them to face the torment he'd known. He could not die until he had them all safely hidden. The lady and the street urchins. Together. It was the only way he knew. Perhaps they could help each other. Perhaps they could even come to care about each other.

He thought of Lucas, bearing the master's summons, who had stepped into his room barely in time to stop him from thrusting the cold dagger into his own heart. But it was the summons that did the stopping. Because the new orders were against the Triletts, and only this compulsion to spare the lady could have given him the will to live on. Still, he wished he could have brought Lucas with him, because he had cared, finding Tahn so close to suicide. But Lucas was a dark angel the same as he was. He would have his own orders to contend with tonight, much as he would hate them.

A stab of pain bore through his heart with the memory of Lucas praying when they were little boys shut up in a dark room by night. Perhaps Netta Trilett was also praying right now. To the God of justice. And good.

But he must stop this foolishness, letting his thoughts wander so freely. He must concentrate on the task ahead. He drove Smoke on through the woods, carefully considering Valhal, Samis's stronghold, and how he could possibly breach it to bring the children outside. A miracle it would take, he knew that. And he could expect no favor from heaven.

***

Soon Netta saw the dim glow of a window ahead. Her dark-clothed captor dismounted soundlessly and stroked his horse's head for a moment as he looked at the cottage in front of them. He seemed to be whispering something to the animal he'd called Smoke. And then he pulled a long sword down from among the horse's bags and strapped it to his side.

Netta trembled. He was too familiar. Too like that killer from the springhouse roof.

He looked up at her soundlessly, and she could not help but think of Karll's brave struggle. Could this be the same man? Had he been the one to leave her lover bleeding to death in her helpless arms?

He'd come back like a nightmare to steal her from her home. Was there truth in anything he said? What could he possibly want from her? What mission of the devil was he about this night?

He said nothing, only turned his eyes away from her gaze and pulled her down from the horse's back. In his arms he carried her to the cottage door.

It was little more than a shack. The man inside whirled around at the sound of the door creaking.

"Already, eh?" the strange man taunted. "Well, you can get the job done, I guess. But you should be glad for that old door hinge, little man. You sneak up on the wrong person sometime and you'll have a knife in the throat." He smiled suddenly. "She's a pretty one, eh?" He stepped up and took Netta roughly from her captor's arms.

She squirmed, wanting away from this coarse man. He was huge, considerably more than a head taller than the stealthy one who had kidnapped her. And there was something abhorrent about the way he grasped her.

"What are the orders?" her kidnapper was asking.

"On the table," the man called Darin answered him. He plopped Netta down on a straw tick in the corner. "You haven't had time to touch her, have ya?" he asked with a smirk.

The kidnapper looked up at them, papers in his hand. Netta thought he looked so terribly young just then, certainly no older than herself. But it was hardness more than youth that she remembered in his features before. Was it the same man?

"She'll be needing a drink," he said suddenly.

"That can wait," the bigger man snorted. Netta was still bound but managed to scoot into the corner. Darin grabbed her by the leg and pulled her back. She kicked at him desperately, knowing his intentions.

"Business comes first," the kidnapper persisted.

Darin gave a disgusted groan. "There's a skin of good liquor on the back of the chair," he grunted as he groped a hand toward Netta's bosom.

"No liquor for her. Go get water."

Darin turned to face the smaller man. "You get it," he said. "I'm busy."

"No," her kidnapper insisted. "You will get it while I read the orders. Business comes first. We will have plenty of time for pleasure later."

Darin stared at him angrily then stomped out of the cottage with an empty skin in hand.

Netta sat up with relief at her temporary reprieve. Her captor had said he would help her, and he had. But it gave her small comfort—she didn't know what to expect from either of them next. He looked over at her briefly but turned his eyes back to the paper in his hand.

He had the same long and wavy dark hair. It was tied back the very same way it had been the night Karll was killed. He was even dressed the same, with the same sword. It was the man, she was sure, though she had not had such a generous look at him before. He was only about her height, with scant whiskers and a fearsome frown. His dark eyes were haunting in their depth. And she could not help but think of Karll lying before her, losing his lifeblood on the marbled tiles.

Tahn knew she was studying him, but he kept his attention carefully on the papers before him. Samis wanted her brought directly to Valhal, as though he considered the Trilett heiress some sort of prize. Anger churned in Tahn as he thought of the terrible fate of another woman Samis had brought to Valhal for himself. It must not be so for the lady.

He read the order that he was to leave her with Darin, return to the town, and torch the rectory where the Triletts were beloved. That being accomplished, he and Darin were to escort her together to Valhal. He grimaced, knowing the risk of what he would have to do. Netta Trilett was only one part of his crucial plan. He must somehow return to Valhal without suspicion. These orders, this trouble with Darin, could jeopardize any chance of freeing the children. But he'd had no choice but to stop here, or Samis would know already of his betrayal.

The big man stomped back in. He knelt in front of Netta, jerked the scarf away from her mouth, and poured the water at her gruffly. "There ya go," he said. "All satisfied." He set the water down and turned to Tahn with a smile. "You best be going. You got your orders."

The lady looked at them both with fear.

"I'm not going," Tahn told him. "You are."

"Can't," Darin replied instantly. "It's the order. You're not that much the fool, and neither am I."

"When I took this assignment," Tahn maintained, "Samis gave me charge concerning this girl, and I pledged my life over it, before any of us knew how wily she is. I will not risk failure at that charge by leaving her with some oaf who might let her escape for lack of watchfulness."

"Let her escape? I have far different things in mind."

"Indeed. But once you're satisfied, you ox, what shall keep you from rolling over to sleep in your bliss? I'll not take that chance."

"You will," Darin told him, "or face the wrath of Samis."

But Tahn shook his head. This had to work. "I cannot

begin another order until this one is completed. I must personally bring her to him."

"You will, idiot, after you torch the rectory."

Lady Netta gasped. And Tahn was saddened for her. A dreadful thing to hear, and better had she never known. "The wrath of Samis would be worse over the loss of his prize," Tahn insisted, "than it would be over a simple change of plan. Anyone can light a fire. But I will not trust anyone else with this wildcat. I told you she's wily."

"Don't seem so to me."

"She's resting."

"I won't change the order," Darin growled.

Tahn faced the bigger man with absolute determination. He drew his sword. "I'm changing it. I will explain the matter to Samis myself. He is not so unreasonable in the face of necessity. Now go!"

Tahn knew Darin had no desire to fight him. There were few now who would risk Tahn's speed and skill. He was barely bigger than the girl he'd carried in. But he was feared.

"All right," Darin relented. "It's certainly no part of the orders that we be fighting among ourselves. Let me help myself to the lady first, and I'll go and do your job for you."

But Tahn stepped forward. "I told you. Business comes first. You can have your fill when you get back. Make sure you are not seen."

Darin took his coat and his liquor and left the cottage with a curse.

Tahn knew that the lady was watching him in fear. But he was not ready yet to turn his attention to her. He sheathed his sword and stood by the window waiting. The big man's horse responded quickly to his impatient whistle, and then Darin disappeared into the darkness on his way to town.

After a silence that hung on the place like a heavy cloud, Tahn turned from the window toward Netta. Even in the dim light, it was obvious that she was crying. And no won-

21

der. Her life would never be the same after this night. He stepped toward her, and she backed to the corner again on her knees.

"Don't touch me."

For a moment Tahn stopped. Of course she would react this way. What else could he expect?

"Jesus," she whispered.

He shook his head sadly. "It is no wonder you are loved. You hold your faith in trying times. May you gain by it." Those were painful words to speak. Brutal to a heart without hope.

Netta scooted backward, trembling. What sort of creature was this? "Don't touch me," she pleaded again.

For a moment their eyes met. He took another step forward, and she had nowhere to go as he pulled a knife from his clothes. "I have to," he told her, "to do this."

He leaned forward and carefully cut the rope at her wrists.

The gesture surprised her. But the comfort of it was lost in her pain. "Why?" she screamed at him suddenly. "My family! The rectory! Why are you doing this?"

He didn't answer. He only leaned down for the skin of water and took a long drink. She bolted for the door. But he was ahead of her quickly, stopping the door with his boot.

"Don't, Lady," he said. "Please. If one of the others were to find you, it would not be well."

"What do you mean?"

"I mean that Samis will have you hunted. People know your name and your face. It would be hard to stay safe alone."

Safe? As though she could consider herself that now. This one was a killer. And the other would be back with an animal drive. She started screaming, hoping someone were near enough to hear.

He took her arm. "I doubt there's anyone close enough."

22

She started to struggle against him. "Let me go!" she cried. She kicked at him and fought like the wildcat he'd called her.

But he grasped both of her arms and shook her hard. "Listen to me!" he said and pushed her against the rough door. "Where would you go? Home? The soldiers of Samis are there by now, with swords drawn and torches ready. Darin goes to burn the rectory. And any friend who shelters you now has endangered his own life."

She sobbed violently and then sank to the floor. Could it be as he said? Was her world now gone?

She looked up at his face for a moment and could not read what she saw there. Her heart pounded with fear for her family and the good priest. "Lord, God," she prayed, "a building is but wood and stone, but spare the lives of those that dwell therein. Protect them from the violence of those that seek their hurt. Deliver them from the flames!"

Tahn stood over her, listening to the prayer. When she mentioned flames, he shook his head. Flames were the forte of this woman's God, were they not? The ultimate punishment. The fate of killers such as himself. More than anything else, that thought shook him. But he would not bow to it now.

Perhaps she needed some hopeful words that at least the holy persons in the rectory could be unscathed. "Darin won't be taking the time to lift his sword, Lady," he assured her. "And it may be that he will fail in his quietness as usual and give them ample time to save the place."

"What about my family?" she asked.

He knew he could give her no comfort there. But she had asked, and he must be honest, whether she believed him or not.

"I don't give your home a hope," he answered gravely. "Nor the family either, unless they are far and wide seeking you."

Netta bowed her head.

Horrible I am, Tahn thought. *Speaking horrible things.* He stood for a moment, knowing her turmoil. He had come into her life again, bringing pain and loss. But there was no helping it. He lifted her carefully and carried her back to the straw tick. She was so young and beautiful, with her rich, auburn hair and gentle features. She shook with fear at his touch.

"You should rest while you can," he said with a faraway solemnity. "We will ride again by morning, and it will be a hard day ahead."

He stretched himself out on the tick beside her but made no move to touch her again. They would only wait now until Darin came back, because if they left before that, Darin would run to the soldiers of Samis and tell of his treachery. The thought of what he must do burdened him, and he sighed. But for the lady, for the little ones, he had to try.

Netta sat tensely beside the silent young man. *Perhaps he will fall asleep,* she dared to hope.

"I know it's a hard thing," he said to her then. "But I'm all you've got, Lady. I can't let you go yet, do you understand? You don't know from what it is I'm trying to spare you."

She stared at him, knowing she could not believe him. He had told her he would not let the big man hurt her, but he had given the man permission to do all he wanted at the dread hour of his return. He had said he would not obey the orders when they came, but he had insisted to the man that they were foremost in his mind.

"You are a liar," she told him boldly.

"I am what you say I am," he answered her. "When I need to be."

Tears stung her cheeks again, and she rubbed her sore wrists. There seemed to be no answer here. Even unbound, she knew she could not escape him so long as he was awake.

"Water?" he asked.

She shook her head.

But he leaned for the waterskin and handed it to her. "You should drink. You'll be wanting your strength. Are you hungry?"

"No." She lifted the water and drank just a sip.

Tahn looked at her silky hair and thought about Karll and his new bride. It was the only time he had failed to have the surprise on any victim. And it was not his own fault. He knew he'd not been seen. He knew he'd not been heard. But he had noticed a burst of light above Karll's head, and the young man had whirled about as if warned by some unseen being. Otherwise, the Lady Netta too would have died that day. In buying time with his struggle, Karll had saved his bride.

Netta returned to anxious prayer. Tahn watched her lips move and the tears well up in her eyes. He could remember plainly her anguished scream. And her lover's last words: *"By Jesus, don't hurt her!"*

He shook his head. That night still haunted him, but there was no more sense thinking of it than of the flames.

He didn't sleep or even close his eyes. Instead, he rose to the table, knowing she wouldn't lie down as long as he was there. "Rest," he told her again. "And don't fear Darin. It is not bliss that awaits him here."

The night was well spent when the big man returned. Smelling of smoke and sweat, he burst through the door, and Netta jumped.

"Ho!" Darin laughed. "After tonight, the Triletts'll be nothing but an old story. You could see the blaze of their high and mighty place from the town!" Netta's heart pounded as he grinned and moved in her direction. "Awful shame for you, pretty lady," he went on. "Might as well set your mind to consortin' with us."

She rose to her feet, determined that she would not give in to this man, regardless of the consequences. But he looked down at her unbound wrists and laughed. "You two been havin' fun with the wait, have ya?" he chortled. "Fair enough. But it's my turn now. Don't ya be slappin' me, girl, or I'll make you well sorry."

Neither of them paid any attention to Tahn until he was directly behind Darin, his sword already drawn. Netta gasped in fear, but Darin failed to notice that her eyes were focused past him. Until he felt the cold tip of Tahn's sword against the back of his neck.

"You're little more than a slave to Samis," Tahn said. "Because of that, I will give you the chance to fight." He drew back his sword, and Darin turned around.

"*You* would call *me* the slave?" Darin laughed. He wiped his palms on his tunic before drawing his sword. "Where is your haste to leave and finish your orders, little man?" he taunted. "You only slow us down. Go out and talk to your horse while I take the lady, and we'll be on our way."

"I will not travel with you, Darin," Tahn said. "And I will never obey another order of Samis."

"You are mad."

"Then it is good madness and I claim it gladly. The lady is a praying one. Solicit her help while you can. You are leaving this world."

Netta shrank back against the wall. Perhaps they were both crazy. Perhaps they would forget her in their conflict. But so far they remained between her and the door.

"I will kill you first, devil!" Darin shouted. He lifted his sword and rushed forward. The smaller man easily parried. Swords clashed, and Netta edged against the wall. But the fight did not last long. Her kidnapper had forced the sword from his opponent's hand and thrust his own weapon into Darin's thick middle. Netta was so close now to the door,

26

but the small man whirled around and stopped her progress with the bloody sword point shoved to the wall just inches in front of her. Netta screamed and sank to the floor in broken sobs. The kidnapper grabbed her arm and pulled her up.

In the middle of the room, Darin was gasping for breath. Her captor brought his sword down again swiftly upon the big man's throat.

Netta closed her eyes and shuddered. That anyone could kill like that, without so much as a blink . . .

"Come, now," her captor said, interrupting her thoughts and pulling her to the door. His whistle was barely audible, but Smoke was in front of them in an instant. The kidnapper let his sword rest against the doorframe and lifted Netta to the back of his horse. He pulled a length of cord from a pack. "This will be the last time I do this," he said. "They know this cottage. We will have to gain distance."

He tied her hands together and then tied them to the peaked horn of his saddle. "I hate to take the time," he continued. "But I must be rid of the body." He took hold of Smoke's head and seemed to be whispering to him as he had before. Then he turned to Netta and actually smiled. "He's a good horse. He'll watch you for me while I dig. Relax yourself. Neither of us will hurt you."

He disappeared into the trees, selecting a concealed spot for a grave amidst the falling leaves. Netta struck her heels at the horse's side. If she could just get the animal to walk away, perhaps she could direct it somehow toward the Rhodes farm or that of any other good-hearted people. But Smoke would not respond to her urging. He would not move at all except to jump slightly in protest at her continued kicking.

"Would think you were a dog, you lousy beast," she sputtered. "What kind of a master can he be to you, anyway?"

She felt like screaming but doubted now that anyone would hear. Her captor had a mind for such details. Maybe if anyone did come, he would kill them like he had the big man called Darin. She kicked at the horse once more in her frustration, but he only turned his head to a stand of nodding bristlegrass near a tree. She was powerless, and it was a dreadful feeling indeed.

When Tahn finally had the grave filled over, he scattered fallen leaves and twigs across its surface to disguise it. In the same way, he covered the path where he had dragged the body to its resting place. It all looked again like undisturbed woodland. By the time he'd finished, the dawn light was edging its way above the horizon.

Tahn took a look into the cottage. There was no disguising the stain on its floor where the blood had seeped into the cracks of the rough wood. *Oh well,* he thought. This blood could not reveal its owner. Perhaps he could use it some way.

With a scarf from his pocket and water from the skin, he wiped the blade of his sword so it would not be sticky, and replaced it to his sheath. And he whistled, loud and shrill like Darin. The man's strong horse lumbered out from the brush. Tahn sprung to the empty saddle and drove the horse quickly toward the rising sun. His own Smoke instantly followed.

They traveled without a pause for what seemed like hours. Netta was growing desperately weary, but Smoke continued his pursuit of his master. Finally, the man slowed.

"We are near a horse trader who asks no questions. I will leave you with Smoke again so the trader cannot say he saw you." He patted the animal beneath him and sighed. "A shame to slaughter such a fine mount, but the trader will if I pay him to. For Darin to have run away with you, his horse will have to disappear too."

Netta had nothing to say to this man who cared more for horses than for the men who rode them. She did not even want to look at him.

He left her in a thick grove of trees. "I expect no one," he told her. "Though I know you would welcome someone to find you while I am gone. Should it happen, I wish you life. But if they are dressed as I am, scream with all the breath that is in you."

He had done his whispering to Smoke, and he rode away.

This time the horse did not follow. And once again, Netta tried in vain to get the animal to respond to her directions. Smoke simply ignored her and turned to grazing. Even at that, he would not move more than a few yards. She would not have thought it possible.

No one came, and the wait was torturous. She struggled against the cord, but it only made her wrists raw. She thought she should pray again, but the weight of despair seemed to crush her very heart into the dust. So she wept bitterly as the wind began to whip about her with an unwelcome autumn chill.

When she finally heard the approach of a horse, her heart pounded. *Let it be a kindly, common man,* she prayed, *who will have the conscience to help me.*

But it was the killer returning. He rode a different horse that was plain looking but strong. He gave a little whistle as he turned again to the northeast, and Smoke joined him gladly.

Tahn said nothing, but he saw the pain of his prisoner. He had wanted to push the horses and hurry on. He was desperate to move as quickly as possible. But he couldn't push Netta so. He knew she could not understand that what he did he meant for good.

He took them to a tiny stream that snaked through the dense woodland. When he unwound the cord from the horn of the saddle, he saw the angry red of her wrists. Her eyes were puffy and her face was streaked with the mixture of trail dust and tears. He lifted her down as gently as he could and led her to the water's edge.

29

He took her wrists and the cord around them into his hands and sought her eyes. But she turned her head away. "Promise me you'll not run," he said.

But she wouldn't. She just stared at the horses as they drank.

Though he'd gained no assurance, he helped her to sit, knelt in front of her, and carefully loosed the cord.

He could tell that the movement hurt her wrists, especially the right one, though she said not a word. She did not resist as he pulled her arms toward the cold water; she only shivered just a little as it washed over her wrists. But as he lifted his hands toward the scarf at her throat, she jumped to her feet with a cry. Quickly, he caught her elbow. "Wait," he said, pulling her down again. "I know what I am to you, and that we will never get past that, but let me help you. Please. While I can."

Netta could barely stand sitting still, but she knew it would do her no good to run. As he lifted his hands toward her throat again, she closed her eyes, her body tensing. But he only untied the scarf that still hung there, that had once been her gag.

He cut the scarf in two with a knife and swished both parts in the frigid, flowing water. Then he carefully wrapped the cold cloths around her aching wrists. "Let me get the waterskin for you," he said, "and fill it fresh so you may drink like a lady and not stoop like dogs and men." She didn't move an inch from her spot. He brought her the water, and she drank much. After their long ride she needed its cool refreshment.

Suddenly he was handing her a generous chunk of bread. "You'll not be hungry yet, I know," he said. "But try to eat, lest you become weak."

She stared at him, uncertain how to respond to his sudden kindness. He was not to be trusted. Of that she was sure. The man in the cottage had been an ogre, a horrible threat. But not so her Karll. There could be no good in the murder of that good man.

And she was not hungry. The anguish of heart over the fate of her family and friends was too great to think about food. But perhaps he was right. Eventually, he would have to rest. Then there might be some way of escape, if she were strong enough. She made an effort to down at least part of the bread.

He cupped water from the stream in his hand and drank, watching her. But he did not eat. "I would like to let you rest more," he said. "But we must go quickly. I will let you stay on Smoke, because I am not so sure yet of the new animal, good as she seems. I would not want her spooked beneath you." He sighed. "I'll not tie you, Lady. But don't spring from the horse's back. The fall could be of harm to you."

He stood and seemed to be looking far away. "We will ride the rest of the day and reach a cave tonight. There we will have shelter and rest. Then I must return to Valhal for the little ones. I would that you stay at the cave in hiding. By the time I am back, you will be sought far and wide. But I will not bind you there."

His voice had seemed as far away as his gaze. The little ones? What was he talking about? Where was Valhal? And who was the Samis they had talked about in the cottage?

She pushed those thoughts aside. If he were true to his word, she would be free of him soon. And even if he weren't, there would surely be some way.

2

The cave was a series of rooms connected by narrow passageways. He was obviously familiar with it. He led her inside and navigated easily by torchlight. The moonlight did not extend far into the interior, and the blackness made her all the more uneasy. This was the sort of place one could enter and never find the leave of.

When they reached a very large chamber, he stopped and released her hand. Netta could hear the continual sound of running water nearby. But her captor moved to the two leather bags he surely must have left here waiting for them.

One bag held candles. He lit five and placed them around the room before extinguishing his torch. The dance of shadows against the rock crevices of the cavern was strangely beautiful, and Netta was suddenly aware of being bone weary.

"I want you to eat again," he said quietly. "Then we must sleep."

He gave her the second bag. "It is yours," he told her. "Eat what you want now. The rest is for later. If you must leave, take it with you."

"I will go now," she dared to tell him.

"No, Lady. You are exhausted. You could not judge the woods or anything else aright until you have rested."

She did not relish the idea of a night with him in the cave's darkness. "I'll rest beneath a tree somewhere," she insisted. "You made me come in. Now please lead me out. You said you would not bind me here."

"I won't. But neither will I help you be foolish. There will be rain tonight. Accept the shelter. I will teach you the passage in the morning. Don't try to go out on your own. If you take a wrong turn, I might not be able to find you in these tunnels if you go too far."

That brought her up short. She knew she wasn't sure enough of the way out. She felt like screaming at him for the deception. What need to tie her if she were simply trapped?

She sat down in silence and pulled a piece of fruit from the bag. She had never known the kind of anger she felt for this man. He had taken Karll. And now he had separated her from her family with no way of knowing if they were alive or dead. He changed from kind to cruel like the shifting faces of a spinning coin.

She looked up, but he had disappeared. A line from Scripture leaped into her mind. "Love your enemies. Pray for them . . ."

The thought horrified her. It was the last thing she wanted to do right now.

She ate the fruit with some anxiety. She didn't like not knowing where he was. It was like being aware of a lurking beast, out there somewhere beyond your field of vision.

But she steeled her mind. Whatever he might do, she must keep her wits about her and be ready for the chance to get away from him. It was impossible to know what to expect, despite the things he said.

Suddenly he emerged from the darkness beyond the third candle, carrying something. If the passage had not been directly in front of her, she would not have known his presence. He moved like a ghost, without a sound, though he wore boots and the floor was solid rock.

He brought a pail of water with a ladle. "It is good and clear," he said, his voice so low she could barely hear it. "I will show you where the stream flows in the morning too, should you decide to stay."

He left the water at her side and retreated to the opposite wall. "Good night, Lady," she thought she heard him say.

The rock floor was hard and cold, but Netta didn't care. She was so exhausted that even her captor's presence could not keep her from rest. At first she lay on her side and watched him across the dim room. But he was motionless, and in a few moments, she was asleep.

Hours later, she was wakened by what sounded like some big animal. She jumped up with her heart pounding and looked around her. But the sound was gone. She noticed immediately that only two of the candles yet burned, and they had little height remaining. So she fished in the bag of candles and pulled out a handful. She lit three of them from the burning candle nearest her but nearly dropped the last one as the eerie sound came again and echoed through the chamber.

It was a dreadful wail, almost unearthly in its depth of pain. And it was coming from across the room. From her kidnapper, who lay on his back on the cold stone. She didn't know what to think or do. His body trembled from head to toe. Suddenly, he let out a piercing scream. She threw her hands to her ears. She wanted to scream too. This nightmare, instead of ending, simply rolled from one terrifying wave to the next. Surely she was sharing this cave with a madman.

Tahn screamed again in the agony of the flames. He could feel his body separate from himself, writhing and flailing about in pain. The nightmare had its hold, and he knew it for what it was, but he was powerless against it. He gasped for air but could only drink in the searing heat. There was no end of it, no escape. His body curled inward, and the shaking grew more violent. A piteous moan escaped him and then broke to choked sobs. In the midst of the flames, he saw the slamming door of his first night at Valhal. He

34

saw the screaming face of Samis, whip in hand. And he saw his own sword, dripping with the blood of someone named Karll.

⌧

Netta watched him fearfully. *He sleeps,* she realized. *God, what kind of a dream can it be?* He had moved several feet in his thrashing about. And now he rolled into a ball, his hands to his face, sounding more and more like a child in his desperate sobs.

"Dear Lord," she whispered.

He screamed again. He rolled toward her, nearer the candles, and she could see his face. The absolute terror written on it tore at her soul. She could not have imagined seeing such agony possess anyone, and she would have touched him then, to wake him, but she was afraid.

He lay shaking a long time. Finally he turned his back to her and drew his arms up over his head. He seemed calmer then. He grew quiet, and the shaking subsided. When at last he sat up, she was afraid to say anything. He didn't speak. He only disappeared into the dark passageway toward the sound of the water.

⌧

Tahn didn't consider going back to the lady until he knew by the ceiling's tiny sliver of light that it must be morning. He didn't know if he had wakened her with his dream, or how much of its effect she may have seen. He was loath to face her, but he knew that he must.

Above him the crack to the outside world grew dark and then light. He could hear the distant rumbling of a storm. He shook his head. What must the lady think of him? Killer. Kidnapper. And now weak. Or insane, perhaps. Driven mad by a dream. At least she had not tried to wake him. Long ago, Lucas had learned the danger of that. All Valhal knew. Perhaps they all thought him insane.

35

When he returned to the great chamber, his long hair was dripping wet, and he had a look of stone about him. "Let me show you the water," he said, picking up a candle.

Netta realized that he had traveled the dark passage with no light whatsoever, and wondered how he could stand it. But he made sure that she knew the route, making her get the feel of the stone passageway by hand.

Then he led her to the main chamber. "I have to go back for the little ones," he told her again. "I want to get you familiar with the cave quickly now."

"Who are the little ones?" she dared to ask, surprising herself.

"Just children," he answered. "I can't leave them there. I'm supposed to be their teacher."

When he said it, there was a remnant of pain in his eyes, and she was sorry she'd asked. She didn't want to know more about him and whatever he did.

But he continued. "If something happens to me, some of them may try to make it here on their own. I will tell them the way if I can. It is one reason, besides your safety, that I'd hoped you'd stay, to lead them into this room and the water."

"I—I don't want to stay," she protested.

"I know. And I understand. It is not your responsibility, and you do not wish to be my prisoner another day." He lifted the stump of the torch and lit it with a candle. "Come ahead," he told her. "I'll show you the way out."

She followed him with sudden anguish of heart. She wanted away from anywhere having to do with him more than she wanted anything else. Yet something about last night and now his words about children constrained her. *Oh, Lord!* she pleaded. *I want to run as far as I can! What should I do?*

As they neared the outside world, Netta heard the thunder. Rain was pouring hard at the cave entrance.

"I am sorry that I have to take the horses, Lady," he told her. "The youngest child is five, the rest not much more. I'll need the animals to carry the little ones over the distance. Keep the shelter, at least till the storm breaks. I would that you wait for us, and I'll give you your choice of the horses then. You may run out of food if there are problems to delay me. But I will bring more when I come. And here." He handed her a knife. "You may need this. It should be three days, but if I am not back in a week, you may assume I'm dead."

He bowed his head for a moment, and when he looked up at her again there was something deep and unsettling in his eyes. "Say a prayer for the children, Lady," he begged her. "They surely need it."

He gave a whistle, and Smoke met him at the flooded cave entrance. Soon they had vanished into the driving rain.

He rode hard in the storm, pushing himself and the horses. He knew he had no guarantee that his plan would work. It all depended on Samis believing his word. And Samis had never placed much trust in anyone.

Valhal stood on the side of a mountain, its high walls enclosing the home and training grounds of the self-dubbed dark angels and their savage mercenary leader. Unquestionably, Samis savored the notoriety of his men. He would send them out at the word of the baron or anyone else with wealth enough to pay them, to destroy and then return to their mountain retreat.

Valhal remained isolated. Most outsiders who knew of the place thought it was a cloistered monastery. Samis had designed it so. No one ever came but the rare merchant or young man fleeing life. And Samis could make good use of either.

Tahn approached boldly with his horses. He knew it

would not be possible to smuggle out seven children, most of whom did not yet understand stealth. He would have to do it openly, which would require Samis's permission, gained by deceit.

The sentryman yelled to him. "Dorn! You were not to return alone."

"I must see Samis!" he shouted back. "It is urgent. In the performance of my duty I have been betrayed."

Entering through the gate felt strange this time, as if he were somehow different. And he was. He was here as a lie; he was no longer part of this world.

Samis was waiting for him in the central sparring court. "Where is the Lady Trilett?" he demanded. He was old by the standards of the land, but his strength had not faded. He wore his black hair braided, and his confidence was such that he seldom wore his sword in the halls of Valhal. No one dared challenge him. Fear of the brutal consequences easily bested any detractor.

"I left the lady with Darin according to your orders, Lord," Tahn said, beginning his carefully constructed tale. "When the rectory was ablaze, I returned to them swiftly, but they were gone. Would that you had seen it well to leave her with me."

Samis's eyes narrowed, and Tahn knew it was because he had dared question the wisdom of an order.

"I looked for them," Tahn continued, "but lost the trail. It seemed clear to me that Darin wanted her for himself. But I fear he may have hurt her and been unwilling to own to it."

"Why do you think it?" Samis questioned, staring at him fiercely. Tahn met his eyes without hesitation.

"There was blood on the cottage floor, Lord." He waited, giving Samis time to think that over.

"You think Darin would defy me?" Samis shook his head. "He has not the courage to face my wrath nor the cunning to betray me."

Tahn freely acknowledged that. "Perhaps he will destroy himself," he suggested. "When he has done what he will with the lady."

"Where were they headed?" Samis asked.

"It seemed to be toward Tamask, Lord. I came to ask of you searchers. He has betrayed me as well as yourself. I wish to kill him when he is found."

Samis smiled. "Ah, Tahn. You are pleasantly bloodthirsty. What would you do with the girl?"

"If anything remains of her, I shall strap her to my horse and bring her here to you. I fault her none in it. I left her sufficiently tied. You will do what you will."

The older man nodded. "I will send you with the searchers you need. Rest yourself and your mount and be ready at first light."

"My lord, I prefer that you not wait," Tahn told him. "Send fresh men tonight ahead of me."

Samis looked at him in question.

"I doubt they will find his trail, considering the rain," Tahn told him. "There may be good fruit in searching the hills and the town nonetheless, but I have another plan."

Samis seated himself again on his woven chair. He was intrigued. "What is it?"

"Allow me to take my students. There is no better time for a first assignment. They are street rats, Lord. They know how to be unseen ears. Darin was not provisioned. He shall have to stop somewhere for that, and I expect it to be in Tamask. They know the merchants and every hiding place in that city. They can be useful to me."

Samis shook his head. "They have had too little training. There has not been time to build a loyalty. What is to keep them from slipping away from you themselves?"

"Fear, my lord," Tahn answered him. "They cannot hide from me. And they know what shall happen if they try."

"You remember well the hold of fear, then?"

"I do."

"I would not have expected you to implement my teaching style so nearly."

Tahn did not reply. So many times he had hoped there would one day be the opportunity to give this man the blade of his sword.

"You have a twofold purpose, then?" Samis was saying. "You wish to find Darin. But you also wish to give your students an active lesson they shall not forget?"

"Yes, Lord."

"And what if you lose some of them? You know you must kill them if they are too difficult."

"It is a small loss," Tahn told him carefully. "As you said, little training has been put into them so far. And there are street boys aplenty. However it goes, I shall return with the same number I parted with." Terrible words, but Tahn knew they were the right ones.

"You are cruel." Samis smiled.

"I had a good teacher."

───────

Tahn chose to leave before the night was through, allowing himself minimal rest. It was the sort of thing Samis would do, forcing the bewildered children out in the middle of the night, and Tahn knew it would please him. By the time he reached the children, they already knew that they were to be part of a search mission. The prospect frightened them, as did everything about this place. Only the youngest were sleeping when he lifted the bolt from their door.

"Wake your brothers," he commanded.

"We go now, sir?" asked a freckle-faced boy with a scar across his cheek. He was seven-year-old Doogan.

"Yes," Tahn told them as strictly as he could manage. "There will be no crying nor lagging behind. And you know the punishment for trying to run."

More than one of the boys looked anxiously at Tahn's sword. But only one child dared sniffle, the only girl among them, a tiny thing named Temas, also seven. She was dressed like the boys, her hair cropped short.

The two sleeping ones were roused, and the children were forming a line. But little Duncan, barely five, was stumbling on his feet.

"I fear he's not prepared for this, sir," the biggest boy said. His name was Stuva, and he was nine.

Tahn turned to look at him. The pleading in the boy's face made him want to pound the walls in anguish. But he betrayed no feeling at all. "You'll have to help him," he said.

Stuva jumped to put his arms around the younger boy, clearly relieved for the permission. They were brothers, and Stuva was always watchful for the little one.

"Carry your discipline proudly as we go," Tahn commanded the children. Eyes would be watching this unique departure, and Samis could yet call it off. Tahn could not tell the children his intentions. They must be clearly frightened to be leaving Valhal this night, not excited.

The young warrior and his ragged ensemble made their way toward the central gate.

"The Dorn's little soldiers," someone snickered.

Four young men were standing near the wall, sharing a vial of the powerful opiate so common to Valhal. "Think you can handle the brats by yourself?" one of them taunted.

"This many and the four of you as well," Tahn replied. They were teenagers but ruined already. It plagued him. He would have liked to take with him some of the bigger boys, especially thirteen-year-old Vari, who had never fit in. But the young men had already received so much of Samis's poison in their minds that Tahn couldn't trust them. And he had no authority over them anyway.

Samis was waiting at the gate. "You will be back in a week as we said?"

"Indeed."

In full sight of the children, Samis handed Tahn a whip. "You will know when to use this," he said.

It was not easy for Tahn to maintain his steel. But he could not fail. So he nodded. "Crybabies and shirkers," he said and affixed the cruel thing to his belt. Perhaps this was what he should afflict Samis with one day.

The children's fright was tangible. They stood all in a line, their wide eyes watching the teacher and his master.

Samis was supplying two more horses. Tahn had not known to expect that, and didn't know that he would keep the animals long. The extra horses would help them, surely, with the distance, but he wanted somehow to make their trail difficult to follow.

He tied a long line between each horse, with Smoke in the lead. And then he assigned places, Stuva and Duncan in the back, Tam and Briant, and then Doogan and Rane directly behind him. He would share his saddle with Temas.

Samis watched them leave. The tall man beside him shook his head. "Do you think they will do any good, my lord?"

"We shall see what they will do." Samis turned to the group of men at his right and called two of them by name. "Follow them," he ordered. "Make sure they are going to Tamask."

Then he turned from the gate toward his own chamber again, and the waiting bottle of wine.

For a while the children were quiet, just putting Valhal slowly behind them. Tahn did not take the time to make it easy for them. He was aware of two riders far behind, so he kept the horses moving at as quick a pace as was practical on the slope at night, almost ignoring his young charges. But the tension became too much for them. Little Rane began to cry, and it hit Tahn hard. Their torment had gone on long enough.

He slowed the horses and led them to a grove of trees.

"He's just tired, sir," Stuva spoke up in the little boy's defense. Only Duncan was his natural brother, but he was quick to claim the rest as well.

When Tahn stopped and dismounted, little Rane nearly dove from the horse in terror. But Tahn took hold of him quickly.

"I'll not hurt you, boy," he said. He took the whip from his belt and put it in the little boy's hand. "You can have it," he told him. He looked at all of their worried faces. "You will never return to Valhal. Never."

They were not sure how to react. What would he do with them?

"We don't understand, sir," Doogan told him, still afraid.

"Did you ever want to be there?"

"No, sir," Doogan answered quickly.

"What *do* you want?"

"Someplace safe. With food," Stuva answered.

"I will do my best," Tahn told them. "Though we will not be forgotten. They will hunt us, and we will have to hide."

Tam stared at him. "You're escaping with us?"

He barely nodded in the darkness, but they all saw it.

"But why?" Tam persisted.

"It is past time," Tahn told them. "I could not stomach another day."

"Nor I," Stuva said boldly. "I would not want to be as Vari."

Tahn turned to him. "Vari? What has been done to him?"

"They put him on the wheel."

"When?" Tahn asked, his heart sinking. He should have known this would happen. Peaceful Vari would not bear the sword for Samis. He shook his head.

"Not this night, but last," Stuva answered him, clearly stunned by the concern he was seeing.

Tahn looked into the boy's face but began thinking past

it. Vari might be dead already, depending on the position they'd started him in. But he might not be. And Tahn could not leave him, not knowing for sure.

"Stuva," he said. "I must go back. Everybody climb down."

He secured the horses in the trees near them and gathered the children in a tight circle. He had not expected this, and to try to rescue the boy would jeopardize them all, but he felt he had no choice.

"Stuva, keep together," he said. "If anyone comes, tell them I ordered you and you don't know where I went."

"Are you going to try to help him?" the boy asked, seeming unable to believe it.

"Yes."

"They'll kill you," Tam told him.

"It may be."

"Then what do we do?"

"Stay together. If I am not here by daylight, take the horses to Merinth and sell them there. Hide. You are good at that. But sneak away when you can. There is a cave east of the town, about six miles, under the third of four oaked hills. They know you are street rats and will expect to find you in a town. The wilderness there might be safer. And I'm hoping you shall meet a friend."

Temas started crying. "I want you to come back."

Tahn was not prepared for that. It had not occurred to him that they would actually want his presence, so soon, or ever.

He touched the little girl's cheek. "I will do my best. Remember, you are survivors." He pulled one of his knives from his shirt and gave it to Stuva. Then he gave another to Tam.

"There is food in the horse's bags," he told them. And then he left them on foot. He had a better chance of remaining unseen and unheard without the horse beneath him.

He could scarcely believe he was doing this. It was suicidal.

44

What would become of the children? If he did manage to get to Vari, the boy would be in no shape to travel.

Strangely, he wondered what Lady Netta would do when he failed to return. As if she would still be there. That was as unlikely as the idea that his rescue attempt could be successful. But wherever the lady was, surely she would be praying.

"God," he whispered as he ran over the rocks. "I know your hate for me, and I'll not argue. But have a mercy for Vari."

3

Netta was sitting in the cave, feeling frustrated and impatient. Still it rained. The downpour was such that she couldn't see the trees beyond the cave's mouth. The entry was flooded. She had retreated because of it and was feeling terribly helpless, not wanting to be in this place. She might have left hours ago, despite the rain, but feelings she could not understand had made her hesitate.

So she had prayed for the Lord to stop the rain if he would have her go. *Rain never lasts more than a few hours anyway,* she'd thought. But this rain had lasted all day and now into the night without so much as a letup. She felt like crying. She should not have prayed that way. She could not leave in the storm now without feeling guilty. And what would it avail her anyhow, when she wouldn't be able to see a path in front of her?

At least there was time, she comforted herself. Three days, he'd said. If he wasn't lying. She agonized at that thought. What if he was lying about everything? Perhaps no harm had come to her family at all, or the rectory. Perhaps no one hunted her but those two beastly men who had fought over her with a bloody result. She stood up, feeling restless and agitated. She had no obligation here. She must find out the truth. She should just go and take her chances.

But the way he looked, just before he left. The memory of it stopped her in her tracks. *"Say a prayer for the children,"* he'd said. *"They surely need it."*

He'd looked so worried. So . . . hurt. But how could it be? He was a murderer, and she should be glad to see him hanged. But he was telling the truth about the children, somehow she knew that. Whoever they were, they were young and precious and in grave danger. Odd as it seemed, there was one obligation she did have. She could not deny that request for prayer, no matter who it came from. She sunk to her knees and bowed her head. Perhaps now she'd be able to move on.

Tahn didn't take long to find the two riders who'd followed them. He sprang from a tree at the first one and knocked him easily from his horse. One thrust of his sword and the downed soldier was dead. Tahn hardly had time to think on it, except that these men would have no hesitation killing him or the children if they were caught in their deceit. Perhaps one day all of the bloodshed would end. For now it was survival. He turned to face the second rider.

But that soldier had no desire to face the Dorn in a deadly fight. He turned his mount quickly back toward Valhal, determined to tell of this treachery.

Tahn pulled his last knife from its place and threw it hard at the fleeing man's back. The soldier groaned with the sudden pain, slumped forward, and fell from his saddle.

Tahn killed him as quickly as the first man and was careful to retrieve his knife. He might need it. The jittery horse responded to his whistle, and he tethered it in the trees.

Now he could concentrate on getting into Valhal. There was always a sentryman on the wall and another at the gate. Both had a good view of the only path, and a signal horn ever ready. But would he have to go that way? Horsemen were so restricted, but he could hazard the rocks in any direction.

His feet moved fast as he thought it through. Vari was on the wheel, which was at the millhouse, where monks had ground their own flour back in the days when this forsaken place really was a monastery. The biggest of the waterwheels Samis had reconfigured. Vari would be there, still breathing,

Tahn hoped. One revolution of the thing could take a full three days before plunging a victim's head under the dark waters. But Samis did not always give them that long.

The millhouse was near the back of the complex. He could scale the wall near the water and—

Tahn stopped suddenly and smiled. The water. It went under the wall. Perhaps he could get in and out without ever setting foot on Valhal's cursed ground. He continued up the slope at a steady run, angling left away from the sentry's best vantagepoint. Soon he would need to use the rocks to hide himself as he edged toward Valhal's back wall.

The water's passage was small beneath the stone. But it was big enough. The stream was icy cold, but that was worlds better than flames. He took a deep breath and swam with the current under the wall. When he surfaced, the millhouse was ahead of him, and he could hear voices. He ducked back beneath the water and continued his progress. He did not surface again until he reached the outer wheel on the millhouse wall.

The water flowed beneath it and right through one huge inside room where Samis's wheel was mounted. He could see that the paddles of the outer wheel blocked his access through the wall. There was not space between them for a man's progress, though the hole was big enough. It looked like he would be crunched in the back with one before he could get all the way through. He watched the wheel for a moment as he listened for those voices. It seemed he would have to get out of the water and risk encountering opposition at the door.

But then he saw what he needed. One paddle of the old wheel had broken off. How long had it been that way? Perhaps it was God's mercy on Vari. He shook his head. The gap was edging downward. He dove beneath the water.

His timing was good. He surfaced in the millhouse, where the water flowed much slower. Vari was bound to the wheel, his body quivering, his head less than two feet from the water. No one else was inside. "Vari," he whispered. "Don't make a sound."

The boy's eyes popped open. He looked strange and wild.

Tahn cut the ropes one by one and caught the big youth as he fell. "You will have to do exactly as I say," he told him in a whisper, wondering about the paddle gap on their way out. The boy was not hurt. Just scared out of his wits and stiff. "We're going through this wall and the outer wall. I will take this one first and signal you."

But Vari was still shaking, and it was from more than the fear of his near death. Tahn recognized the problem as the boy spoke. "I need my measure," he said in a trembling voice. "Or I can't make it. Please."

The young warrior supported the youth with one arm and dug into a pocket. Heartsick for the boy's plight, he pulled out a small bottle. He was dependent already. Another complication. But perhaps it was well for this night, at least. The drug would dull him to all that was happening. But the icy water would surely keep him awake.

Vari drank what little remained of Tahn's opiate tincture and dropped the bottle in the stream.

"You have to make it now," Tahn told him. "Through the wall when I whistle. You understand?"

The boy nodded, but he looked confused. "I thought you'd come to put me out of my misery. Why do you risk yourself? Why would you help me?"

But Tahn only sank beneath the water to the hole in the wall. The paddles were difficult to judge on this side. And then he thought he heard the door.

It was Johns who faced Vari. He had come often, checking the wheel's progress for the exact moment Vari's head would reach the water.

"What the devil?" he exclaimed. "How . . . ?"

Vari dove beneath the water, fearing a knife or sword thrust.

"Come up, you little devil," Johns exclaimed. "Samis will surely be interested in such a clever skunk as you."

Johns walked toward the edge of the water. "There you are, you—"

He reached his big hands to grab the boy, but it was Tahn that surfaced before him suddenly. Johns's eyes had barely time to register the shock before the agile warrior pulled him in and dragged him under.

Tahn knew he would have to end this quickly before others could hear. He plowed his knife across the man's throat, and the water clouded red.

Vari had surfaced. "Same plan," Tahn told him, willing away a wave of nausea. "Let's go."

Tahn managed to exit with the paddle only scraping one boot, but Vari was not so lucky. On its next circle, the paddle struck his thigh, and for a moment he was pinned under water. Tahn had to fight the current's pressure on the wheel to release him.

"We have to keep moving," Tahn told him when they surfaced. It had to have hurt, Tahn knew, but Vari did not let on.

They swam for the outer wall, not stopping at the returning sound of voices. Vari was through the wall first. When Tahn came up on the other side, the boy was clinging to the reeds and panting.

"You all right?" Tahn asked him at a whisper. Again Vari nodded, and Tahn pulled him up by the arm to begin their rapid descent of the rocky terrain.

As soon as he could, Tahn pulled the boy into the shelter of brush and set him down to look at his leg. It was not as bad as it could have been. Still, it would be sore for days.

Vari was looking up at him. "Why?" he asked simply.

"To die that way." Tahn shook his head. "You're too good for that."

He pulled him to his feet again, and they made their way

through brush and rock down the side of the mountain away from the sentryman's eyes. Tahn was on edge. Vari's escape would be discovered soon enough, if it hadn't been already. He could not believe he'd gotten Vari out that easily. No one had ever penetrated Valhal before. But to his knowledge, no one else had known to try the water route.

By the time they reached the tethered horse, Vari was limping badly. Tahn helped him mount. Then he led them on foot to where he'd left the children. The dawn light was just taking its first peek above the horizon.

Vari watched in silence as they neared the ring of children. How could the Dorn have gotten them out? But all seven of the youngest trainees sat anxiously awaiting their teacher. Tam was the first to hear their approach. Other children might have cheered, but these obviously knew to fear such a display. But they all rose in greeting.

"It was a good thing you did," Stuva told the teacher.

"It was foolish," Tahn replied. "I risked all of your lives for his."

Vari looked at him but did not fault him any for the words. It was true, of course, and the children should know it. It was not the sort of thing a sensible soldier did. *But the Dorn is lucky,* Vari thought. *So he doesn't always have to be sensible.*

"We were glad you did it," Doogan said.

"We prayed for you," Temas added.

Vari smiled at that. Little ones could believe anything. And maybe God had helped. For the first time in a long while, Vari had done some desperate pleading of his own.

Tahn found it astonishing that no one had given chase. But he couldn't count on that to last for long. "Get mounted," he said gruffly. "Let's go!"

He loosed the horses from one another so they could maneuver independently. Then he charged ahead on Smoke toward another mountain stream that flowed downward to Alastair. Everyone at Valhal knew how he hated that town. So why not start off that way and then do something really stupid like double back? Lack of predictability could be a grand virtue. No one would expect him to be crazy enough to stay in the rugged wilderness for long with all these children, no better provisioned than they were. But there was dense pine forest past Devil Falls, and the men of Valhal were better fighters in civilization than they were trackers in the wild. Staying out of sight would be half the battle.

4

It was the third day since he'd left her alone. Netta was moving as quickly as she could through the wooded landscape. Finally the rain had stopped. It was a clear morning, and she fled farther from the cave, fearing she might encounter him at any moment. Surely there must be people nearby. *Lord, lead me to a house!*

But she traveled most of the day without a sign of anyone. Everything looked the same out here. The trees stood endlessly in all directions, and between them undergrowth rose as high as her waist. It was difficult travel with her dress snagging on the limb of a bramble every few feet. But she pressed on with a determined will. She must find someone. She must find out about her family. Surely they were all well, longing for news of their kidnapped daughter.

It was evening before she discovered an obvious trail. Anxiously, she followed it. But night came upon her, and it was hard to discern the trail. She was exhausted, so she stopped beneath a tree to wait for the morning light. She drew her knees up beneath her long ruffled skirt and hugged them to her bosom. All around her the darkness deepened quickly. She'd been so afraid of the dark as a child. But that was silly now. She was a grown woman, all of twenty-one. The cave hadn't been so bad. And neither was this. It was the sort of people who might be lurking about that bothered her.

Suddenly she heard a dog barking. Dogs meant people. But there were wild dogs too. So she stayed where she was and eventually fell into a restless sleep with her head on her arms.

She woke just before dawn. The fourth day. She was so hungry, but the bag of food was empty. Had her captor made it back to the cave? Whether he had or not, she was glad she had left. She looked around her. Surely food grew around here someplace. But there were only the woodland plants, most of them unknown to her.

She stood. It was a clear and cool morning. She pulled her cloak tight around her and set about following the trail again.

By midmorning, she heard a dog again, much closer. And she hadn't gone far before it sprang through the bushes at her, barking and growling.

"Stop, dog!" she cried, backing against a tree. "I mean no harm!"

But the dog kept at its furious barking, creeping toward her menacingly.

From somewhere through the bush a woman's voice reached them. "Socks! What you gone and found this time? Come back! Socks!"

The dog stopped its barking and cocked its head. Then, apparently deciding to obey the call, it turned on its four white paws and ran through the bushes the way it had come.

Socks the dog has a master close! Netta pushed herself up from the tree with a surge of relief. She parted the bushes to follow the animal.

A stream lay just ahead. As Netta emerged from the woods, she saw the woman there, washing clothes. The dog ran at her again, barking furiously.

"Socks!" the woman yelled in exasperation. But then she looked up. "Oh, Lord o' mercy," she whispered. "Socks! Leave the lady be. Go on now!"

The animal retreated to the edge of the water and watched her.

"Thank you," Netta told the woman in a trembling voice.

Before she could say more, the woman spoke on. "You look like you been through something fearsome, Lady," she said. "You couldn't be the young Trilett they're looking for, and made it all the way out here, could you?"

Netta didn't know what to say. What did this mean? Were all the things that killer had said really true?

The fear and questions must have been plain on her face.

"Lord o' mercy," the woman repeated, eyeing Netta's once-fine dress, now torn. "My husband was to Merinth yesterday, and he came back telling me—"

"What?" Netta cried out, her heart pounding. "What has happened?"

"You are her, aren't you?" the woman asked. She seemed afraid now too. She was looking suddenly at the bushes around them.

"Yes," Netta told her. "Please tell me what your husband said."

"He said some of the baron's men came to Merinth asking if anyone had heard tell of you. Are you alone?"

"Yes."

"You run when they burned the place and got this far?" she asked incredulously.

Netta sunk to her knees. *Then it is true? Oh, dear Lord!* "What about my family?" she begged. "Did your husband hear anything about my family?"

The woman lowered her eyes. "They say they're gone," she answered. "But they're searching. Could be some made off like you."

For a moment, Netta just stared, almost unwilling to believe her. Her home was burned? Her family scattered? And the treacherous baron was seeking them? She shook her head, the shock of it washing over her.

The woman rose from her laundry to approach her. "I'm sorry for you, dear lady," she said. "Yours was a good family. I'm praying there's more of you in the woods somewhere." She sloshed across the stream. "They say the baron's about to claim the throne now. The beast! He's the one done the awful deed, isn't he?"

Netta couldn't answer. Somewhere there was a mysterious man named Samis. The dark angels who had clashed in the cottage had given him the blame. May God judge him.

She thought of her father's careful efforts toward peace, and her eyes filled with tears. It was so unfair.

The woman handed her a handkerchief. "You must be hungry," she said.

Netta dabbed at her eyes, her hunger forgotten.

"I want to help you, Lady," the woman continued. "But we've so many young ones. I beg you to understand we can't keep you here. For the sake of my babies."

Netta nodded numbly. "Bless you your prayers," she managed to say.

"They'll continue with you, dear one. Let me get you food packed, a blanket, and a water bag. I'll not bring you to the house, though, lest the little ones see you. They're altogether too honest. Should anyone come searching, better they know nothing at all."

The woman was up and gone, calling the dog to follow her.

Netta sat alone and stared into the water. What to do now? Surely some of her family had survived. There had to be a way to find out for sure. There must be a way to find them. But where could she go? She wiped at her tears again and looked at the gathering clouds.

When the woman finally came back, her arms were full. "Stay away from the towns," she said. "They're asking after you, like I said."

"Have you heard anything of the rectory at Onath?" Netta asked.

She nodded sadly. "My husband said there was a fire there too. Same night. Such a shame." She took hold of Netta's hand and pulled her up. "I brought you some twine," she said. "You tie the blanket on your back and the bags over your shoulders, it'll be easier traveling." She proceeded to decorate Netta's slight frame with the provisions.

"God be with you," the woman said. "You know about where you are?"

"No, ma'am."

"Merinth lies west. You're a length o' ways from Onath to the south and west. Joram is the closest town east. And then there's Alastair up north. Don't be telling me where you're going. Just be safe at it and godspeed." She gathered up her laundry and turned quickly back to her house, as if she were afraid to linger a moment longer.

Netta turned from the stream and walked slowly back into the forest. Sudden darkening clouds now hid the sun. It looked like it could rain again. It was surely midday. And it could not have seemed more dark and dreary.

When night came, she didn't know how far she'd gotten. She wasn't even sure in which direction she was headed. It was miserable walking through the mud and brush, but she didn't feel like stopping. Then the rain began again in earnest. It was a hard, soaking rain, and she was quickly drenched. She looked around her for anything resembling a shelter and ran for a huge tree with low sweeping branches. But she could not see the ground in front of her in the darkness. She tripped on a root and went tumbling down a slope into the soggy ditch at the bottom.

Netta cried out in pain and pulled her ankle toward her. It was throbbing from the bad twist of her fall. She looked through the rain around her, wondering what to do. Everything looked so hopeless. Her ankle hurt terribly, and she had no idea how to get help, or even where she was. The location of the cave was a mystery now. A crushing despair hit her as she thought of her family facing the torches and swords of deadly men. The woman at the stream could have no reason to lie. So the kidnapper had spoken the truth. The Trilett home was destroyed.

But they were such good people, such decent people. Did

nothing make sense anymore? She turned her face to the sky, the pain like a tormenting flame in her soul. "Why?" she screamed at the black clouds above her. "Oh, God, why?"

Sobs broke over her, uncontrollable now, but there was nothing to answer her but the pounding rain.

5

Tahn knew the caves. He had hidden the children in a tiny one in the cliffs beyond Alastair and set off alone for the town by night. He would steal what they needed. He had no more money, and he would not take the chance of being recognized in that town he detested, anyway.

A bag of food and a bottle of the tincture were the bare necessities for survival right now. He knew Samis was looking for them. But his hiding had been effective. No one knew now where to look. Once he returned, he would rouse the children, and they would begin to wind their way down to the bigger cave, where they could winter if necessary.

He would give the big cave to the children, he decided. Let them claim it if they chose to. He would stay around if they wanted him to, just to make sure they were all right. He had to do that much.

But he would not get close to them. He would never give more than the rare touch on a little head. And when the children slept, he separated himself as far as seemed practical and slept alone. Whether Lady Netta had witnessed his nightmare, he might never know, but he would not take the chance of it happening again. The nightmare would return; it always did, and he did not want the children to see it.

At the smaller cave Vari was sitting on a rock, cutting up a fish that he'd gotten himself very wet to catch. Some of the younger ones slept. The rest were watching him.

"You suppose the teacher'll be back soon?" Briant asked him.

"Real soon," Vari assured them.

"Is he our papa now?" Temas asked.

"No," Vari said, giving her a strange look.

"He's the teacher, same as before," Briant told her. "He's not old enough to be a papa to all of us, anyhow."

"But it's not the same as before," the little girl maintained. "We're kind of like a family."

"No, we're not," Doogan put in. "A family has to have a mama. I know. I had a mama once."

Temas looked at him. "I only had a papa. But he wasn't good. Not like a family."

"Family is blood kin, mama or not," Vari said. "Like Duncan and Stuva."

"Then what are we?" Briant asked.

"I don't know," the bigger boy said. He'd gotten the meat from the bone and was cutting it in strips. "Call us whatever you want. Make up a word, for all I care."

He pushed a piece toward each of the three who were awake. It would be easier if they could just accept things, he'd decided. It was useless to think of mothers or fathers. There would be no one but themselves to even care, except maybe God.

He shook his head. God seemed awfully far away. He took a bite of the raw fish and leaned his back on a rock. Tahn would watch out for them, and that would have to be good enough.

"Does that taste good?" Doogan asked.

"Better than grass," Vari told him.

"We won't eat grass, will we?"

"No." Vari laughed. He could have confidence in that. "The Dorn, he's liable to bring roast duck for all we know."

Doogan smiled, and the other children sat in silence. Vari looked out over the rocky terrain toward Alastair, where he knew Tahn had gone. He would be back soon enough. The teacher had gotten them this far. And he would continue to take care of them, no doubt.

6

On her sixth day alone, Netta rediscovered the cave with some dismay. She limped her way toward it slowly, turning everything that had happened over in her mind. She was afraid to face the man again, but she knew she needed help. Perhaps he might let her rest here till her ankle was stronger and then give her directions out of these troublesome woods.

No sound came from the cave. That wouldn't be unusual for him, of course. But he had said he would bring children. They must be deep inside.

The water standing at the cave's entrance had drained away. She leaned against the rock wearily. It was hard to be back here. Just because the man had told the truth about her family didn't mean he could be trusted. What about Karll, an innocent man?

She looked long into the mouth of the cave, wondering if she should hurry away while she still could, before her presence was known. But how far would she get? And which way?

There had been nothing easy about the past few days. Even with the woman's provisions, she'd had a pitiful time in the elements, and it wasn't likely to get better. So with a sigh, she ducked her head to enter the cave. "Lord, give me strength," she prayed.

The passage was dark, and she didn't like it. But shortly, she expected a candle glow ahead. She followed the narrow passage by touch, careful not to make a turn in the wrong place. But there was no glow. For a moment she feared she had turned wrong, but then she felt the peculiar hump in the wall that the man had shown her, and she knew she'd gone the right way. She went on farther with dread in her heart. Even when she knew the great chamber was just ahead, there was no light. There was no one here.

She sat on the floor of the cave rock in the depth of darkness. Her throbbing ankle demanded rest. What had happened? Was he dead? What about the children he'd been so worried about?

"Lord, I don't understand!" she cried. "I can't find you in any of this. I feel so alone!"

She just sat for a moment, letting the blackness soak over her soul. There was no one to help her. No one. Tears filled her eyes, but she wiped them quickly away. It would do no good to cry. She would have to find her way to safety again somehow.

She got on her knees and began to crawl for the entrance, unable to bear the darkness any longer. She knew there was a bag of candles in there somewhere, but without the flint the kidnapper had carried, she had no way to light them. It would be useless to stay inside.

"Lord Jesus," she spoke as she crawled out. "The children he was talking about, do help them. What kind of life could they have with a killer for a teacher?" She sighed. "I don't understand him, Lord. He seemed a dreadfully hard man. Why is he concerned for little ones? How can such opposite things rest in the same heart?"

When she was close enough to the entrance to see the fading light of sunset, she stopped and watched the darkening sky. It seemed strange to be so alone. She wished there was someone by her side, if only to take her mind off her own hurts. She thought of her mother, who had been dead for more than five years. She'd always said, "Seek a way to help someone else when you are troubled, and it will better you every time."

So in the evening's quietness, she curled up on the cave

rock and prayed for her cousins by name, one by one, until she fell asleep.

It was sunny when she woke, a warmer day than it had been before. How good it would feel to have an opportunity to wash. If she'd had light inside, she might have gone into the cave's running stream. Or if her ankle had felt better, she might have sought a stream out here somewhere. She'd have to do something eventually. It certainly would do her no good to sit and wait for someone to happen along and find her. Especially not that killer.

But she thought of the days that had passed and was fairly certain it had been a full week. If he was not here by now, he wasn't coming. That's what he'd said.

The thought gave her sadness, but she refused to accept that it was for his sake. It must be for those unknown children. And for herself as well. It was hard, feeling so helpless and lost.

She hung the blanket and her cloak over bushes to air out. She was nearly out of food, with no idea how to get more. The woman with the dog had all but begged her to leave. She'd been kind enough but afraid for her children. And anyone else she managed to encounter might be the same way. Or far worse.

"Help me trust you, Lord," she said aloud, "that I will be reunited with my family soon." Her eyes misted, but she willed the tears away. To rest her ankle, she sat against a tree near the cave and gazed up at the vivid blue sky. Today everything looked so crisp and clear. How could a world of such cruelty be so beautiful?

When she looked down again, there he was, standing in front of her. The kidnapper and killer. His long hair was tossing about in the autumn breeze.

"I am glad that you stayed," he said quickly.

He was alone. No little ones by his side. Had he lied about that after all?

"Has anyone been here?" he asked her.

She shook her head. She couldn't speak to him for the lump in her throat. Fear and uncertainty overwhelmed her again.

"Do you deceive me?" he suddenly asked, a touch of anger in his voice.

"No!" she cried out. "What do you want from me?"

He pointed to the blanket on the bush. And then she understood. It hadn't been here before.

"No one was here," she stammered. "I—I tried to go. I found a farm a long way from here. A woman gave me the blanket and food but was afraid to let me stay. I got lost. I hurt my ankle. I found my way back . . ." She watched his eyes. What would he do if he didn't believe her?

He walked to her side and pointed down at the leg she held straight out in front of her. She nodded, and he knelt and pulled her skirt back enough to examine her ankle. When he looked up at her again, the anger was gone. He eased her shoe off and then stood up. "Have you seen anyone else?"

"No."

He whistled. She was expecting Smoke to come bounding out of the underbrush, but he didn't come. After a moment, the leaves began rustling, and then a dirty face appeared out of the bushes. And then another. And another. And then the rest all at once, eight of them in all. Stunned, she just stared.

"Is that our cave?" a child asked.

"Indeed," the warrior answered.

"Can we go in?" There was excitement in the voice but with reserve unusual in a child.

"When I get the torch lit."

They all appeared to be boys. One of them walked up to Netta with wide eyes. "You're pretty," the child said.

"What's your name?" Netta asked.

"Temas."

The child ducked his head shyly. Or was it a *her*? Netta couldn't be sure.

They were all filthy, which, she reminded herself, she was as well. They were also a skinny lot, without a smile among them.

When the dark warrior had the torch prepared, he moved to the cave entrance, and all of the children followed him in. But Netta didn't move. She knew she must think about this. She must pray. She didn't want to stay. But she didn't want to go.

After many minutes, he came back for her. "I have to leave them," he said. "I'll be back by daylight tomorrow. I would that you rest inside with them."

He didn't wait for an answer. He just picked her up and carried her in, holding her until he had to set her down to navigate the narrow passage. "You can walk?" he asked.

"Yes."

He took her arm anyway, as if he wasn't so sure, and led her the rest of the way to the main chamber. It was lit again with candles, and incredibly, the children all sat in a circle, as silent as the stone around them. He pointed at each of them in turn, saying their names. "I have told them we shall have a lesson," he said. "And then they must rest."

He lifted the water pail and turned toward the sound of running water. "Vari," he said. "Let me show you the stream."

The biggest boy rose to go with him. Vari was almost as big as the man but definitely younger, and he walked with a barely perceivable limp.

None of the rest of the children moved an inch. Netta was amazed by that. No questions? No exploring? They were so young. What kind of hold did he have on them that they should not even act like children?

When the strange man returned, his hair was dripping wet. He held the pail of fresh water. Vari was behind him, his hands studying the cave passage.

Their teacher brought the pail and set it in the middle of

65

the circle. "From the youngest," he said, and all the children rose to take a drink in their due order.

Netta could see fear in their faces. Was he hard to them? Why were they with him at all?

As soon as they had all drunk, he separated them into pairs of unequal size. "You who are the smaller, you have been traveling a long time," he told them. "Suddenly a threatening stranger appears. You who are taller, the stranger is you. Now, traveler, what do you do?"

"Am I alone?" Briant asked.

"Good question," the teacher responded. "You are alone and unarmed except for a knife. Your opponent is armed likewise." He pulled eight short sticks from a pocket and tossed one to each child.

Netta was horrified but said nothing. What could she possibly do?

"He's so big," said Temas, who was paired with Stuva. "I don't wanna fight. Can I scream an' act like there's somebody close?"

"Worth a try," the teacher replied. "But your adversary has been watching you. He knows there's no one."

"I'll throw my knife at 'im," little Duncan said with a vehemence that shocked Netta. *What is he doing to these children?*

"Only throw if you know your mark and your opponent without a doubt. If he dodges, you are unarmed."

"I'd tell him I just wanna pass, and he'd be wise to be on his way," Briant said, sounding like a teenager at seven.

"But he attacks," the warrior told them. "Go ahead, strangers."

All four of the bigger children moved on the smaller ones, and they were suddenly sparring roughly. It was hard for Netta to watch. They fought like it was real, and the man walked among them, shouting encouragement or criticism. After the separate battles, all four of the younger ones were conquered, Temas and Duncan easily. But Rane had bitten his opponent and nearly squirmed away, and Briant had moved handily with his stick before finally being bested by the much bigger Vari.

"Better," their fierce teacher told them. "One of these days, you'll be surviving. Now, why did I wait before calling you up to the cave?"

They were all quiet until Stuva spoke. "You were checking to make sure it was safe."

"What did I find?"

"It was safe," Doogan said.

"No. I waited. Why? What did I see?"

They were thinking, all but Vari, who smiled and waited.

"The lady," Temas said, "an' her things outside."

"Yes. But I waited. Why?"

"You saw somethin' that wasn't here before?" Stuva asked.

"Indeed." Tahn nodded his head. "I want you to remember that. Whenever you go out and come in, look. If anything has changed, do not come in as usual. Why? What would it mean?"

"Somebody else has been here," Doogan said. "Maybe not a friend."

"That's right. Remember that." He glanced over at Netta. "That's enough for now," he told them. "Drink what you need. From the youngest."

He walked over toward Netta. "They will need to rest now," he said. He turned to leave.

"Sir," she called out, and he faced her.

She quaked inside, wondering how to address this. Why couldn't she just let it go?

He stood in silence, waiting, and she forced herself to meet his intense eyes. These were children, and for their sakes she must speak boldly.

"I saw that you can read, sir," she began. "Are you teaching it to them?"

"I haven't gotten to that yet," he answered with no excuses.

She swallowed hard, searching for the words. "You do agree that it's important?"

"I suppose so, yes. But first things first, Lady."

"*First* they should be children! You're supposed to teach them, you say. But you hurt them, and they hurt each other when they act this way! It is letters they need, and a decent chance to develop a moral strength. Don't you consider such things?"

He looked at her in a way that she found impossible to discern. And then he nodded. "I would be grateful," he told her, "if you would choose to begin while I am gone."

He called to Vari to follow him, and then he turned and walked out.

Netta wanted to scream at him. How could he act as though he could just snatch her and take over her life? He had no right to expect her to do his bidding, no matter what his reasons were. She was angry, but then she turned and looked at the children. They were all staring at her as if waiting for something. She couldn't just walk away.

They were so quiet and solemn, with a look in their eyes that told her they had seen more than their share of suffering. He had said they would need to rest. A shame not to have decent beds. "Are you all very tired?" she asked.

"No," Tam answered, looking at her with his face scrunched up. "Are you going to stay with us?"

"A little while," she told him. "Until my ankle is strong, at least. But I need to find my family when I can."

"But our teacher said your family is dead," Stuva told her.

The words were like a blow to Netta. *Surely not. Not all of them!*

"It's all right," six-year-old Rane added. "We don't have family either. We make it all right."

"We've got each other, though," Briant said. "We're a shayleelay."

"A what was that you said?" Netta asked.

"A shayleelay. Since we're not a family," the boy told her.

"But what does that mean?"

"It's just what we are. Since we stay together and all."

"Where did you hear that word?" she asked.

"I made it up. Vari said I could."

Vari was returning to the chamber just then and laughed. "I didn't know you'd take me seriously." He was carrying Netta's belongings that had been by the entrance, and he set them down beside her.

"The teacher said to bring these in," he explained. Then he gave Netta a long look. "You shouldn't be so upset. He's the best."

She thought of Karll once more and could barely squelch the tears. "He's a killer," she said quietly and then immediately wished she hadn't spoken. She was still unsure of this boy, or even the smaller ones. But her words didn't seem to bother any of them.

"Yes," Vari acknowledged. "We know. But he's the best. He's quick and he's quiet. He don't brag, just gets the job done."

Netta was certain that she read admiration in the boy's eyes. "Surely you don't wish to be like him?" she asked, unable to hide her horror.

But he was looking at her oddly. And he sighed. "Not completely like him, I guess," he finally answered. "I never wanted to be a killer, nor much of a fighter neither. And he respects that."

Netta stared at the boy in front of her. He was as big as she was. With wild hair and wild-looking eyes, he truly looked like he could be dangerous. What he said had surprised her. But especially what he said about that frightening warrior. Hadn't he just been teaching them, even the littlest ones, to fight?

Vari must have seen her doubt. "You can be sure none of us'll hurt you," he said. "We'd fear the Dorn over that, indeed. And *he* won't hurt you neither, ma'am. He's taken with you, perhaps. I don't know."

His words hung in the air for a moment, and she felt a knot in the pit of her stomach. Taken with her? The thought stirred a churning discomfort in her, but she brushed it aside quickly to grab onto something else Vari had said. "The Dorn?" she asked. "Is that what you call him?"

"Sometimes."

"What does it mean?"

"Don't know. It's his name. Tahn Dorn."

"You said you would fear him. Would he hurt you? Does he?"

Vari laughed. "I suppose he'd do what it took if one of us was trouble, but otherwise I don't suppose he'll hurt us none. You never know for sure, I guess. But I don't expect it."

Little Duncan crept up beside her and sat down. "Don't worry," he said, his big sad eyes looking up at her. "We'll mind him good. There won't be no trouble."

Netta felt like crying. A flock of children pledging allegiance to a killer and afraid to do otherwise. "You don't have to stay with him, do you?" she ventured. "Don't any of you want to leave?"

Temas slipped forward toward Duncan, shaking her head.

Nine-year-old Stuva spoke up. "Where would we go? Back to the streets to freeze next winter or starve if we can't steal enough? Or maybe get caught and beat to the bone?" The memory was noticeably intense in him. He was almost trembling. But his face was set, not willingly betraying the emotion. "Or we could go back to Valhal," he continued. "And be locked up and beat on, if they don't kill us for leaving. We're not like you, Miss," he said. "None of us ever saw no fine house. Most of us don't remember no family to mourn over. All we ever been is hungry and scared, till Samis. Then not so hungry but scared lots worse."

She looked around at their dirty and solemn faces. So many of them were nodding in agreement. Were they all orphans? Or abandoned in the streets?

"What's moral strength?" Doogan suddenly asked.

"Yeah," Tam said. "Something we gotta learn?"

Netta smiled. "Everyone needs it, yes. But sadly, some never find it."

"Is it hard?" Rane asked.

"No." Netta looked around at them. "It is simply knowing right from wrong and the proper and godly thing to do whatever your situation."

"It sounds hard," Temas remarked.

"I'm hungry," Duncan said.

"Shut up," Tam whispered to him urgently. "No complainin', now."

Netta looked at them both and took the smaller boy's hand. "If you're hungry, dear one, it's all right to say so." She looked up at all of them. "I don't know what he has told you about that. But with me, if you need something, just say so, and we'll do the best we can and ask the Lord to make up the difference."

"But we only got one loaf left, Miss," Stuva told her. "And he said that was yours. He'll be back soon enough bringing more for us."

Netta shook her head. "Not for quite a while, I'm afraid." *So that's where he went in such a hurry. Without even allowing himself rest.* "Let's share what we have in the meantime, shall we?" she suggested. "Fetch the bread for me."

She reached in her own bag and pulled out the two remaining apples and the knife Tahn had left with her.

But all of the children were reluctant to eat, hungry as they were. "Come on now," she told them. "If it is mine, I can do what I wish with it, can't I?"

71

Rane smiled at her, and it was good to see that from one of them. "I guess so," he said.

She cut the apples and bread till there were eight pieces of each. It was so little for so many, but she didn't want to be troubled about it in front of them. Let them learn that God shall provide. "Is it all right with you if I bless the food?" she asked.

"You mean pray?" Rane said with wonder.

"Of course she means pray," Vari said impatiently. He turned his eyes toward Netta. "Do what you want."

She said her brief thanks and passed around the meager meal.

"None for you?" Temas asked.

"No. No, I don't need it," she told them. "I'll eat with you tomorrow, Lord willing."

Vari looked up at her with a strange expression.

"What does 'Lord willing' mean?" asked Doogan.

Netta paused. Did they know nothing about God? Perhaps not, with such a background and such a teacher. But she couldn't leave it that way. She would have to tell them all she could in the time she had with them. "I mean that we can trust God," she began. "He is our provider. I thanked him for this food, and I know he will give us more. He may use Mr. Dorn to bring it, but he will provide, one way or another."

"What if he's unwilling?" Vari asked, the challenge plain in his face.

"He could not be unwilling," Netta assured them. "God loves his children. He will provide for us." But she sighed. This was a test of her trust as well as theirs. Never before had her future been so uncertain. "Let's not worry," she said. "Go ahead and eat."

All of the children obeyed her, but Vari met her eyes and mumbled, "I've known many days when he was unwilling for me and I had nothing."

"No," Netta insisted. "He is always willing to provide for

72

us. This world can be terrible sometimes. But it's because of men who don't do as they should. For each of you, the times you were hungry, I'm sure God was willing for you to be fed. He loves you. But there was a person somewhere who was unwilling to do the right thing or all too willing to do the wrong."

"I understand that," Doogan told her. "I always tried to beg first, and only stole if I had to. Sometimes I could see 'em thinking it over, but often as not they'd turn me away anyhow."

"How do you know God is real?" Stuva asked. "Especially if he can't make people do what he wants?"

"I know it can be hard to understand," Netta explained. "Especially when people are cruel. But God does not want to *make* people do anything. He wants us to choose to do right. We can ignore him if we wish, and many people do. But he would have us to love one another."

"Samis said there's no God," Tam said in a voice barely above a whisper.

"Maybe no one has told him. God created this world. He sent his Son, Jesus, to teach us about his love. Wicked men killed Jesus, but he rose from the dead. And he is with us always."

"Does the Dorn know you're a Jesus teacher?" Stuva asked with concern.

"Of course he does," Tam maintained.

Netta nodded in affirmation. "He does," she assured them.

"Then it must be okay," Briant assented.

"But you're supposed to be a letters teacher, right?" Stuva questioned again.

"That too," Netta told him, feeling unnerved by the idea. She'd been too taken off guard by all these children to insist that her kidnapper help her find her way. But now the little ones were all looking at her with such expectation. She could think of no solution. Perhaps she should accept the charge, at least for the day, and do everything she could for them while she was here. She looked around at their dirty faces. "Are you anxious to start?"

"We're done eating," Stuva answered. "We might as well. Maybe we should do that first and talk about Jesus after."

"Well enough with me," she replied. "Does that suit everyone?" There were nods from all the children except Vari.

"Do any of you read at all yet or know any of your letters?"

"No, Miss," Temas answered for all of them.

"I do," Vari told her with a sober look. "But the rest weren't to Valhal long enough."

The second mention of Valhal filled her with questions. Where was this place? What was it? And who was Samis?

But she had other business at hand and an idea of how to begin. "You can be my helper then, Vari," she told him, suddenly considering that if she were to gain their confidence as a teacher, perhaps she could draw them away from the fearsome man she could not trust. With that in mind, she carried the water bucket over to the wall and set candles close. Then she wetted her finger and carefully drew an A on the rock wall. The water darkened the rock just enough to make the shape visible.

"Can you all see that well enough?"

Every head nodded.

"It's the letter A," she told them. "The first letter of the word *apple* and many others like *and*, *able*, and *amen*. I believe our floor is dusty enough for you all to give it a try with your fingertips, if you wish. Draw it just like I did. Two lines leaning on each other, and another line joining them in the middle."

It was to be the first of many lessons with "talk about Jesus after." And then they all chose their places to sleep for the night. The children clustered together on the hard floor as though they were used to such conditions.

Netta slept too, but she woke before day, lit new candles

from the few nearly burned out, and looked long at the faces that surrounded her. All of them, even Vari, slept huddled against at least one other child. For warmth, she surmised. They looked like angels in their sleep. She covered the smallest ones with her blanket and cloak and then knelt to pray for them.

"You persist in your faith," a voice suddenly said.

She wheeled about, and there was the Dorn, as the children called him, standing less than ten feet away. He was like a phantom, to navigate the cave chambers and approach her like that without a sound.

"It's all right," he told her. "Pray all you wish. It may surely help you." He set down a bulging sack next to the one that held the unused candles. "Have you slept?"

"Yes." She got up just to increase the distance between them. She was afraid of him again, knowing that the children were likely to sleep on for a while.

Much to her surprise, he addressed her fear.

"Rest yourself. If I had wanted to defile you, I would have done it when we were alone."

"I learned your name today," she ventured, now wondering about this man and what drove him. "Where—where are you from?" She didn't expect him to answer, but again he surprised her.

"Alastair."

"You have family there?"

"No."

"But you have a home there?"

He looked at her with a strange emptiness. "I don't remember if I ever did, Lady."

She glanced toward the sleeping boys, and his meaning sunk in immediately. "Do you mean that you were like them? A street orphan?"

"As far as I know."

To think of him as a helpless child made Netta uncomfortable. He certainly wasn't helpless anymore. She met his dark eyes squarely. "But now, now you are teaching them to be like you, whatever you've become?"

He turned from her gaze and stared at the wall. "No," he said. "Whatever I am, I do not teach it. I teach them to fight because their lives are in danger."

"And will you teach them to kill people?"

He hung his head. "If need be."

She could not bear it. "Look at them!" she cried. "They are children. They're not made for fighting and killing. They're just *children*! They should be loved and protected, not trained for blood. It's barbarous. Have you thought how you will care for them? In this cave? With winter coming?"

"We would all of us prefer it to what we've had," he answered. "They will eat. And the depth of the cave does not freeze."

"Then you will stay here?"

"Maybe. Right now I will sleep. If they wake before me, food is in my sack. Let them eat all they want."

He turned from her and began to walk into the dark cave depth. *He has such a child's face,* she thought. *But tonight, the way he walks, the way his shoulders hang, he looks almost ancient.* "Mr. Dorn, sir," she called after him.

He turned slowly.

"May I ask you . . ." He looked so tired that she hesitated. "May I ask you . . . how old are you, sir?"

"Twenty, perhaps," he answered quietly. "Since it was about sixteen years at Valhal. But it never really mattered to me." He stood looking at her, as if waiting for something.

Only twenty? Could that be possible? She looked down at the sack he'd stuffed full. He'd been needy once. Was he trying to help these children because he'd been there? Or was there more to it than that? "You were gone so long tonight . . . where did you go?" she asked with timid voice. "What did you do?"

Tahn frowned immediately. *She asks it with suspicion,* he thought. *I am a monster in her eyes. She expects that I have gone and killed again. And with good enough reason. It seems I cannot do otherwise, even when I want to.* Abruptly he turned away from her and disappeared into the darkness toward the sound of the water.

Netta sat down against the cave wall, puzzling over him. Sixteen years at Valhal? Stuva had said Valhal scared them more than life in the streets, something about being locked up and beaten or killed for leaving. So the strange young Tahn Dorn was right about the children's lives being in danger, and his own. And not just for helping her.

She thought back to the first terrifying night she'd spent with him in this cave, and how troubled he'd been in sleep. She had never seen anyone thrash so, nor cry out in such desperation. It was as though he had experienced a measure of hell and was carrying it with him every day, behind the hardness of those youthful eyes.

"Lord, give him rest tonight," she prayed and then gasped to hear the words from her own mouth. He who had killed her husband. And now she prayed for him? She could never forget precious Karll. What would he think of her now, willingly remaining in his killer's lair? Tears filled her eyes, and she pushed the thought away. "Protect these children, dear Lord," she pleaded. "They have so little. And they need so much."

She looked at the two sacks at her feet. There were plenty of candles. It would not hurt to take one to navigate the passage out. Perhaps she was simply foolish and cowardly to stay here. Perhaps she should slip away now before the children woke. She rose to her feet.

But little Temas was suddenly behind her, pulling at her waist ribbon. Netta twirled around, almost expecting to find the hauntingly silent Tahn Dorn again, and she sighed with relief. "Child!" she exclaimed. "You mustn't sneak up on me like that."

"I'm sorry," the little girl said. "I didn't wanna wake the others. But I was wondering, since we're both girls and all, can I sleep next to you?"

Netta touched the child's shoulder. She wasn't sure it was a good idea to let any of them get too close to her, but she couldn't deny this simple request. They were likely all starved for any affection. "I don't think I'll sleep any more," she said. "But you may snuggle beside me if you wish." She sat down, and Temas was at her side immediately.

"You didn't know I was a girl, did you?" the child asked.

"No, dear one, I wasn't sure," Netta answered. "Do you always dress just as the boys?"

"Yes, ma'am."

"Is that your teacher's wish?"

"He lets me be a boy, ma'am, but I acted like that before I ever come to Valhal. He was the onliest one there, except the little boys, that knew I was really a girl."

Netta was silent for a moment, thinking about that. But she decided that if Temas wanted to explain further, she would.

"I like your dress," the little girl said.

"It needs washing frightfully," Netta told her. "Have you ever had one?"

"Yes, ma'am. When I lived with my papa. That's when I found out it's better to be a boy."

"I don't understand, child," Netta said. "Why?"

"Men don't do the same things with you." Temas looked up at her.

And Netta understood. Too well. "Oh, dear." She hugged the child to her breast. "It is not always like that. Certainly not all men—" A sudden horrid thought stopped her. "Your teacher . . . does he . . . ?"

78

"He treats me just like the boys," Temas told her. "I like that. He told the others he'd thrash 'em if they told anybody at Valhal I was a girl. He said some of the men would be like my papa."

"Then he's never hurt you?"

"Not except in a fightin' lesson. But that's a lesson for you."

Netta stared at her for a moment, and then she hugged her again. It seemed their teacher had some good in him at least, but there was need for so much more.

"That feels good," Temas said of the embrace. "I was cold."

Netta rubbed the little girl's arms. "Perhaps it will be sunny again tomorrow," she said and sighed. She had but one blanket and her cloak. It seemed Tahn Dorn traveled without them. He had said the cave wouldn't freeze, but it was chilly, and how much more of that would the winter hold for these little ones? None of them had a coat or even a simple change of clothes. And no bedding. She felt like crying for them. Did not their teacher think of things like that?

Then she remembered Tahn's words. Sixteen years at Valhal. And perhaps he was twenty? He had said he'd been a street orphan in Alastair. He might have been even younger than Duncan then, fending for himself. But what had happened? How had they all gotten from the streets to that dreaded place called Valhal?

Temas was curling up beside her. Netta sighed. She could not leave them now, whether or not her ankle was better and she knew her way. She could not bear to leave them till the children were provided for better than this. Perhaps Mr. Dorn himself knew nothing of comfort. Perhaps he had never learned what a child might need beyond simple survival. But she would make sure he knew before she left. Better yet, she would find a home for the children elsewhere.

"Miss?" Temas asked shyly.

"Yes?"

"Did you have a mama?"

"Yes."

"Was she a good mama?"

"Yes. Very good."

Temas cuddled even closer. "Will you be my mama?"

"Oh, child." Netta sighed.

"Please, Miss, please! The boys have all got each other. They're my friends, but I've never known me a woman up close before."

Netta lay back against the wall. She could not possibly answer. She just stroked the girl's short chestnut hair until she fell asleep. And then Netta looked up at the cave ceiling with an aching heart. *Why, Lord?* she questioned in her mind. *What can be done for these children? What do you want from me here?*

The children had been trail weary, and they slept long. Then they woke hungry, anxious to see what Tahn had brought them.

Netta expected him to sleep long too, considering what little rest he'd had. So she encouraged them all to be quiet as she laid out the food and spoke again about God the provider. Only Vari wasn't interested in eating. With shaking hands, he insisted on going down the passageway that led to Tahn's inner room, despite Netta's protest. He was gone for quite a while. And when he returned, he kept to himself, and something about his eyes looked different.

The rest had eaten their fill and divided themselves into two groups for a game they called "nimbles" when Tahn joined them in the main chamber.

"Circle for a lesson, brothers," he said, and all the children, including Vari, ran to obey him.

"Mr. Dorn," Netta interrupted him. "They had such a day yesterday. They need time just to play and be children."

"Well enough. When we finish." His look was stern with

determination. "I will advise you to move now toward the entrance and enjoy your morning," he told her. "I wager you'll not like this."

"Why wouldn't I?" she demanded. "Unless it is wrong, and you know it is?"

All of the children stared at Tahn. What would he do about this strange woman who dared to question him like that? Would he send her away? Or worse?

But he did nothing. "Think of a storm," he told the children.

Netta shook her head in dismay. He had such a hold on them that they all stood straight as sticks in rapt attention.

"Just air. But there is strength in it that you can't see. And there is strength in each of you." He had locked eyes with the little boy named Briant and quickly stepped the distance between them, pulling out his long sword.

The boy was clearly frightened, but he stood as still as he could as the sword drew ever nearer, until Tahn had rested the blade of it against his chest.

Netta shuddered. The man had been right. She did not like this. "Mr. Dorn!" she cried out. "Please—"

But the words stuck in her throat as he turned toward her. She didn't see the childlike face then, nor the sagging shoulders. She saw the hard eyes of the dark angel who had killed her beloved Karll with that same sword.

"Go!" he commanded her.

But she shook her head, not knowing where the boldness was coming from. "You terrorize them," she said. "If they must be prepared to fight, at least let them know safety now! There is a great strength in peace of heart as well."

"Sit down," Tahn ordered. All the children obeyed. But Netta stood, still facing him. He moved toward her, sword in hand.

Inside she trembled, wanting desperately to run from this man and anything having to do with him. But she knew she shouldn't, for the children's sakes. As he got closer and lifted the sword, the picture in her mind was Karll, the blood pouring without remedy from his severed throat.

"Jesus," she said, just as he laid the sword against her chest as he had Briant's.

"Were they other children," Tahn began, "your words would be well enough. But they are now targets of he who taught me the craft of the kill. You don't understand what that means. Most of the battle is mind, and I must prepare them. One thing they must conquer, and conquer now, is the paralysis of fear."

Somehow she was able to meet his eyes without wavering. "There is only one way to do that truly," she said. "Trust. In the God who holds our lives in his hands."

She knew she'd struck a nerve with him. For a fleeting moment she saw in his eyes the torment of that horrible dream they had not discussed.

"I heard about your lesson," he said. "And I will not interfere, however you see fit to teach them. But you will not interfere again with mine. You will join our circle now in silence, or go as I said. Pray if you wish. But you will leave us alone."

It was not a challenge. It was a simple statement of the way it would be. Netta knew she could not press the matter further. She also knew that somehow she had made her point. She took her cloak and a fresh candle and walked toward the cave entrance.

They were much longer at their lesson than they had been the previous day. She sat beside the opening in the cave's first room, pulled the pages of script from her pocket, and read what she could of the epistles of Saint Paul. She prayed for whoever remained of her family, wherever they might be, and for the saints who loved the rectory and had stood in danger because of it. Then her heart returned to the matter of Mr. Dorn and the children with him. What should she do? They couldn't just live like this forever.

It seemed like an eternity had passed when Stuva emerged from the chamber toward her. "You're welcome now," he said. "We're returning to nimbles." He watched her carefully replace the worn pages to the pocket of her cloak. "Why didn't you just leave us?" he asked. "You can walk all right. You could've been a long way by now. Are you afraid of the men seeking you?"

"More than that," she told him. "I could not be satisfied leaving you behind. I need to know that you will be all right. I need to find a way to help."

"You are helping, Miss," he said. "Strange as you are. But the Dorn helps us too. An' you did a foolish thing today. He might've killed you." He turned and went back into the cave tunnel without waiting for her. She was surprised how quickly he moved, being as new to the cave as he was.

Tahn had disappeared. The younger children played their strange game, and then Netta read to them from her pages of handwritten script, part of her father's collection and his father's before that. And she was thankful that Benn Trilett had had the heart to educate his daughter as well as Trilett sons.

When she was finished, despite her displeasure with it, the boys all took to sparring with one another. Netta had been noticing the rips in some of their clothes. Since they were plenty warm with all the activity just then, she had them pull off their shirts, and she took the needle and thread from the sewing bag in her pocket and sat down to mend. She was glad she had brought it, and glad her mother had insisted she learn such things for herself and not just rely on the servants.

Much to her pleasure, Temas sat with her and watched her mending in fascination.

Soon enough, the boys were hungry, and Netta waved them on to whatever they wanted from the food bag. Had any of these children ever had a hot meal? Perhaps one day she could see to that. She said a silent prayer that the Lord help her find a home for them. But she knew of nowhere for certain that it would be safe to go.

Vari didn't eat as much as the others, despite his size. Soon he was on his feet and headed once again down the passageway toward Tahn's chamber.

"The Dorn told him to come after he ate," Temas told her.

"Why?" Netta asked.

The little girl just shrugged her shoulders. "Can I do that?" she asked and ran her finger along Netta's freshly sewed seam.

At first Netta hesitated, but then she thought that such a perfectly normal activity would be a wonderful thing to share. So she placed the needle in Temas's hand and began to guide her in a simple stitch, using the hem area of her now soiled scarf.

The girl learned quickly and was soon making some decent little edge stitches. But Netta kept wondering about Vari, why he acted strangely, and what drew him alone to Tahn's chamber early in the morning and now again. She stood up.

"I will be right back," she announced.

"You shouldn't follow him right now," Stuva said, somehow knowing her intention.

"Do you feel as though Vari is your brother?" she asked him.

"Yes," he answered without hesitation.

"I'm beginning to share some of that feeling myself," she said. "So I must follow. I'll be right back, as I said."

She took a candle with her and began to navigate the long narrow passage. After considerable distance, she could hear Tahn's voice.

"I would rather I had no need of your help tonight," he was saying.

"I understand," Vari answered softly.

As quietly as she could, Netta approached them, snuffing her candle. She followed the voices through the darkness toward another candle's glow.

They were sitting on a rock. Tahn held what looked like a tiny bottle in his hand. "You understand what you'll have to do?" he was asking.

"Yes, sir."

Tahn took a drink and handed the bottle to Vari. "Just a little sip this time," he cautioned the young man. "You need to be in your senses tonight."

From the darkness, Netta came upon them just as Vari was taking his sip with shaking hands. "What is that?" she demanded.

Tahn jumped to his feet and whirled to face her with fire in his eyes. "Never," he said, sounding almost breathless, "never, Lady, should you creep up on—"

"I asked what that is you gave him!"

For a moment he stood silent, meeting her gaze with defiance. But then he sighed. "It is an opiate tincture."

"Opiate?" she fumed. "And you share it with a youth? You care no more for the children than that? Instead of blankets you bring them drugs?"

As soon as she said it, she was sorry she had. The change in his eyes was frightening. There was anger. But there was also a hurt that was deep and raw. He took a step forward, and she found herself backing up, unsure of what he might do.

But he turned to Vari solemnly. "You can manage it tonight?"

Vari nodded.

"I will be at the archway at midnight," Tahn told him. Then he brushed past Netta and walked away without meeting her eyes. Early as it was, she knew he would be leaving the cave for another night without giving her any further opportunity to talk.

Now it was Vari looking at her angrily. "You're not fair to him!" he shouted.

"How long has he been giving you that drug?" she asked, unwilling to acknowledge what Vari had just said.

"Only a week," Vari told her, the anger still evident in his voice. "And it's because I begged him! I'm addicted, Miss, and it's not his fault. Samis started that when I was ten."

Ten? Netta was appalled by the world of these children.

"If he hadn't gotten it for me," Vari continued, "I'd be fit for nothing before long. And I can't go through that right now. Not till we're better settled."

It was plain when he said it how scared he was. She sat down beside him. "Is Mr. Dorn addicted too?"

"I don't know," Vari answered honestly. "I've seen him take a sip now and then like he did today, but I don't know how much of a hold it has."

"Any of the others?" Netta asked.

"No. They weren't there long enough. When you first get to Valhal, they rule you with fear. It's later, when you start to get a little size and fighting ability, that they give the drug. To everybody, I guess." He looked at her with what seemed to be a bottomless sadness. "Don't talk to the Dorn like that again," he said. "He *does* care. He risked his life to come back and get all of us out of there. I was already on the wheel. I would be dead now if it weren't for him."

"The wheel?" Netta asked.

"It used to be a water wheel for a mill. But Samis made it over. It's real slow. When he's given up on someone, sometimes he has them tied to it. When they go head down they drown."

"My Lord," Netta whispered. "Vari, I'm sorry. He . . . he saved you from that?"

"Yes, ma'am. Should be him you tell the sorry to. You act like he's a villain. But he's not. He's our friend." He stood up with a sigh. "But he's gone again for now. Nothing we

86

can do about that. So we oughta go back to the youngsters, Miss. They'd benefit from another lesson."

He walked away, and Netta sat for a moment staring at his back. He had told her such horrid things almost without emotion. It seemed all of the children shared that emptiness of expression much of the time. Did that awful place, Valhal, take away one's ability to cry?

7

Vari went to Merinth that night just as Tahn had requested. And after only two hours there, the youth drove his horse hard through the timber to put the town behind him. His hands braced the reins so tightly they hurt. He sucked in a breath of air and swallowed hard at the lump that crowded his throat. He was glad to be leaving Merinth. He was even glad to leave Tahn there, rather than have him at his side right now with the blood fresh on his shirt and the fire still in his eyes.

With his gut churning, Vari kicked at his mount, still seeing the panicked face of the fat man Tahn had killed. Blood had gushed from the man like a fountain, desecrating his pristine robes.

"We're here to save a life," Tahn had told him. But instead, they'd ended up fighting for their own. Swords were clashing, but Vari couldn't seem to move. The dead man's eyes held him in their anguished stare.

He'd pulled himself away and ran past another body in the hallway. He'd followed the sound of Tahn's voice and reached a large room in time to see his friend struggle with Britt, one of Samis's best swordsmen. Vari had to help, knowing that Britt could be nearly as brutal as his trainer. He picked up a candlestick from the vespers table and threw it at the dark angel Tahn fought, just to call the man's attention away. And Tahn took full advantage. His first blow brought his opponent to the floor, and the second nearly severed the curly head.

Vari closed his eyes, but the scene wouldn't leave him.

Every step of his mount was jarring him, as though his insides would tear loose and spill on the ground. The horse stumbled suddenly over a stream, and Vari clutched his stomach and cursed himself for being so weak. He pulled the reins and clambered to the ground. A sickening heat spread down his spine, and he lost what little he'd eaten onto the stream bank. *God!* his mind screamed. *God, make it go away!*

He thought of the children sleeping in the cave and the Lady Trilett, who'd tried very hard to stop him from leaving. She'd wanted him to tell her Tahn's plans, but he would say nothing of where he was going or why. Tahn had said it would hurt her too much if they weren't successful, that if her kinsman were killed, it would be better for her not to know he'd been so close.

They had not been able to rescue the man, so Vari was glad he'd kept Tahn's confidence. He had obeyed, and he knew he would do it again. But now he lay on the rocks, breathing hard and feeling like he'd have to heave all over again. Why did it have to be like this?

Tahn had saved his life. Tahn understood him better than anyone—how he couldn't bear the thought of killing, how he hated even the fight, no matter how necessary it might be. Tahn knew that. He knew it all. But he'd asked him anyway. Tahn had killed anyway. And he'd had no choice.

It was a trap they were in. A huge and terrible trap that encompassed everyone and everything they knew. Even the lady, with all her talk about a God who provides, was trapped in this bloodshed and pain. She might not ever know her loss. Tahn had forbidden him ever to tell her what he had tried to accomplish for her in Merinth tonight. But she would bear the loss just the same. It seemed that God had provided nothing but death for the Trilett name.

He sat up and brushed the hair back from his face. *God, we just want to be safe! We just want to be left alone! Can't you see that? What do you want? Why does everything have to be so hard?*

He plunged his hands into the icy stream and brought them up dripping to his face. "I wasn't supposed to live like this," he said aloud. "Mama prayed over me every night." He shook his head. Mama had taken fever, and it had killed her quickly. What had her prayers ever won for her?

He could still picture her kneeling by her bed, her gentle voice reciting the Lord's Prayer.

"Keep your faith," she'd urged him. *"We may be poor, but God will provide."*

Netta Trilett seemed so much like her. So much so that he didn't even want to go back to the cave. There was such a tightness in his head, such a heat. Maybe he should just lay back down here and soak up the night's coolness.

But Tahn had said to go straight back. Straight back, no delay. Vari looked up at the starry sky, knowing Tahn would be in Merinth gathering food for the children and making sure no one followed them. He pulled himself to his feet, still feeling a gnawing ache in the pit of his stomach.

He would die for me, Vari reasoned. *There should be someone willing to do the same for him.* He grabbed at the horse's reins and struggled back into the saddle.

His mother's words jumped into his mind. *"Jesus died for you."* She'd said it only the day before she left this world forever. She'd spoken with such certainty. And he'd been so young. Only eight. But she seemed to expect him to understand, to take away the message just like that and never stray from it.

"You don't know where I've been, Mama," he said to the stars. "You don't know what life is like for me now." He gave the horse a gentle kick, and they moved slowly through the trees. "I can't help it," he whispered.

It would hurt Mama to see him now. It wasn't easy, thinking of her. It always made him sad, knowing he was failing her so miserably.

He rode on, wondering if the lady would be up watching for him. It was a wonder she stayed around, considering what Tahn had told him. She was a strange one. Noble born. It was a wonder she didn't despise them all.

The cave was quiet as he neared it. He slid from the horse slowly, still feeling weak in the knees. Maybe they were all asleep. Maybe he wouldn't have to talk to anyone.

He leaned on the rock at the cave entrance and took a deep breath. He couldn't think of any way this night could have been different. *God help us!*

He felt his way in carefully, shaking his head at himself as he went. What right could he have to pray? Leave that to Lady Trilett, or someone else who was sure what they believed.

As he entered the cave's large chamber, he immediately saw the lady sitting beside a candle, praying. Just like Mama. It angered him, and he wasn't even sure why.

"Vari?" she said quietly.

"I need to sleep," he answered her abruptly. His hands were shaking, and he fumbled with a pocket. The little bottle. Tahn had left it with him. He drank and lay back against the cave floor. It'd been a long time since he'd had a mother, and he'd certainly never asked for another one. What business did she have waiting up like this?

"Vari?" she tried again. "Is everything all right?"

"Leave me alone."

Netta sighed. The thought of him with that bottle in his hand plagued her. Just a boy. She spoke to him with a quiet voice. "I told you about our Savior, that he heals. He can heal inner hurts too. Even your dependency."

He closed his eyes. "The world is full of hurts, and he's the one who made it. Maybe he *can* heal, Lady, but he doesn't for us."

Thirteen, and he looks like he's thirty! her mind exclaimed. And Tahn, just past a child himself, seemed almost an old man sometimes.

"Vari," she persisted. "I believe he's willing. But he wants us to want his help."

He rolled to face her. His eyes looked so strange. "You don't know what I've wanted, do you? God should know, but I don't think he's listening."

She was quiet for a moment, unsure how to address the level of pain she was seeing. "Vari, he loves you."

"You can't know that for sure."

"Yes. I can. His holy Bible tells us God loves us."

Vari sighed. "I partly believed Samis, that there's no God. I don't guess God would be well pleased in that. But what does he expect? There've been times I prayed, Lady. And God didn't care to pay much notice."

She took a deep breath. "Did you pray on the wheel?"

He looked at her with angry eyes. "Yeah. Wouldn't you?"

"You're alive, Vari. Because God listened."

He sat up slowly.

"God wants to help you," Netta continued. "He wants to heal you. He loves you so much, Vari! All of you."

"Are you sure, Lady?" he questioned, his eyes looking deep and tormented. "Does God love the Dorn?"

Netta stared at him for a moment, feeling almost as though she'd been slapped. But then she nodded assent. "Yes. He does. You must understand that God does not always like what people do. He does not like the killing. But God loves the people anyway. Even the Dorn." Saying it was powerful. She felt the bitter hurt in her beginning to wash away. Tears filled her eyes.

"He told me tonight that he killed your husband," Vari said solemnly. "He told me that you would hate him forever, and I just need to understand and accept that. But he'll let you stay with us as long as you need to. He wants you to be safe."

She bowed her head. Tahn Dorn was a strange man indeed. With a depth of soul she hadn't seen at first. "I—I don't hate him," she said. "I wanted to once, but I can't. Not when I know how God loves all of you. Please, Vari, give God a chance to help you."

He was quiet for a very long time, thinking about Mama kneeling by the bed. She would want him to pray. If she were here, she would agree with the lady. She would say it was time he tried again. Slowly Vari nodded and somberly began her prayer. "Our Father, which art in heaven . . ."

Netta was clearly surprised but quickly joined him in his flawless recital of the Lord's Prayer. "Where did you learn that?" she asked when they finished.

"From my mother. Back in another world. I didn't believe in God's love much after she died, but if you and God don't hate the Dorn, maybe it's real. And maybe I got a chance too."

She touched his shoulder gently. "He never turns away those who call on him. When did you lose your mother?"

"A long time ago," Vari answered quietly. "I was mad at God then."

"Maybe you should talk to him about it."

"Maybe. But I'm not sure how."

"Do you want me to help?"

Her question made him quiver inside, and he knew he should respond quickly. He should be a Christian, like Mama wanted. He couldn't deny that God had helped her. She'd had more peace than anyone he'd ever known.

He swallowed hard and looked into Netta's eyes. "Do you know a lot of prayers?" he asked. "I need one that'll tell him I'm going to trust him again. He wants me to claim him, and I'm going to try. We need God to take care of this mess we're in, don't we?"

"Yes," she told him. "And I thank God for giving you a faithful mother."

Vari bowed his head. "I don't understand him, you know," he said quietly. "Not at all. But that's not important, I guess.

93

Mama just trusted." He looked up at the lady but thought of his mother somewhere, perhaps smiling down. "Go ahead and pray, Lady. I think I need this now."

An hour later Vari finally slept, looking so peaceful. Netta couldn't help but thank God for what he'd done.

But then she remembered how Tahn had looked when he left. God had used him, that was clear, to save these children and give them a hope. She'd accused him of not caring, but Vari had been right. There was more care in him than she'd imagined, or he would never have attempted to take on these little ones and their needs.

She lay down against a cool rock, thinking of the night Tahn had stolen her away. He could be so fierce. Had the Dorn ever known a mother's love? Or was that godless Samis the only guide he'd ever had?

Just before sunup Tahn returned. Once again, he made no sound. Maneuvering the narrowest part of the passage with a bag over his shoulder and a bundle under one arm, he hoped no one was awake yet. He was so tired.

But he wasn't surprised to find Netta sitting up. He'd come to expect it. But this night, the fewer words between them, the better. He walked just close enough to set his bundle of blankets down at her feet.

"I'm sorry there are only two," he said without looking at her. "I will get more tomorrow." He set the bag down. "The food," he explained and turned quickly toward his tunnel to the cave depths.

"Mr. Dorn?" she called after him.

He stopped and stood still in the darkness. *What will it be this time?* he wondered with a heavy heart.

"Thank you."

He turned to her slowly. "For what, Miss?" he asked. He avoided her eyes.

94

"For the blankets," she said. "And the food. Trying to help these children. Saving Vari's life. And mine."

"It was all needful," he answered simply. "Like I said, I'll get more blankets tomorrow. For now, they'll have to share. Thank you for sharing yours with the little ones." He turned away.

"Wait!" she called again and then hesitated. "I need to know, Mr. Dorn," she said with her voice suddenly quivering. "I . . . I need to know . . . Why did you kill my husband?"

This time when he turned, he was too far into the darkness for her to see his eyes. He looked like some sort of specter lingering there in the tunnel.

"I was told he was an enemy. I had orders."

"He was a decent man," she protested. But she saw Tahn shift toward one wall and knew he was watching her closely. It had been three years ago. Could he really have been only seventeen? "What would have happened had you disobeyed?"

"Whatever Samis decided," he said with a solemn voice. "More of his punishment. Or I might have been killed."

"The wheel?" She shuddered inside. It was hard to ask him these things. It was hard to see the killer who had torn her life asunder as a victim himself.

"Maybe," he answered her with a sigh. "But you would be right to think that I should have let myself die back then. Sometimes I am sorry that I did not."

A silence hung between them for a moment. She didn't know how to respond to that. But there was something else she wanted to know.

"Mr. Dorn . . . please, who is Samis?" she asked at last. "He sounds like the devil himself for cruelty."

Through the darkness between them, she could see him lower his head. "Not far removed, I suppose." He turned away again.

"Will you tell me about him and Valhal?" she persisted, stepping toward his tunnel.

"Not tonight, Lady," he said wearily. "And do not follow a dark angel into the darkness. Stay with the children. As long as you choose to be with us, I thank you for your help with them."

She caught another glimpse of him before he disappeared into the blackness, and those shoulders suddenly seemed to be carrying the weight of the world.

8

In the morning, Netta was determined to do something about the filth in which they were living. But it would have to wait until Tahn Dorn woke, since the water and his separate chamber lay in the same direction. She would not risk disturbing him in sleep. He seemed to get far too little of it.

She ate with the children and began another lesson in letters. It did not seem so chilly today; perhaps she could wash the children's shirts. They would dry quickly outside in the sun. She would ask first, of course. Things always went more smoothly that way.

They were just finishing the lesson when Tahn appeared. Without his shirt, strangely.

"Mr. Dorn," she said. "I would like to wash clothes today. If you permit me to have the children's shirts, I'll do the best I can with them in the stream below."

Little heads turned and eyes looked at her as though they'd never heard of such a thing.

"They'll all be needing bigger shirts soon," Tahn said. "Would help to have a change for us all, as well. I must see to that."

Netta was glad he noticed such things. She'd been think-ing she'd have to approach the subject soon.

"Give the lady your shirts," he commanded the children. "Then circle for a lesson, brothers."

He turned to Netta again. "I have set mine to soak in the water already," he said. "You needn't touch it."

She was rather surprised he'd had the same idea. "Mr.

Dorn," she inquired further. "Is the stream safe for bathing? There are no holes or such?"

"Yes, Miss," he said. "It is a pleasant bath. I am sorry I hadn't told you."

"When your lesson is through, might it be well with you to bring the children to bathe?"

"Indeed," he answered. "Good thought for them, Lady."

She gathered the children's shirts with her cloak and dirty blanket and headed for the water, pleased with Tahn's agreement. He sent Stuva with her to help her set candles enough to see by. "Remember," she told the boy when he turned to go back, "I will come when I am finished. You all wait until then."

"We shall be busy enough, Lady," he answered.

She would bathe first. The water would be cold, but how heavenly, nonetheless. Then she would put on her dress only, and wash the nightgown she'd worn beneath it all this time. Then, when the nightgown was dry, she'd wear it and wash the dress. Oh, for more clothes! The thought of being seen in her nightgown troubled her, but she could stand the dirt no longer.

She bathed quickly, for despite the agreed upon arrangements, she was ill at ease unclothed. It was not pleasant to put the dirty dress back on, but there was little choice.

She set about the task of washing the clothes vigorously, hoping they wouldn't fall apart in the water. She scrubbed all the little shirts, her own gown and cloak, and then the blanket. *Where is Mr. Dorn's shirt?* she wondered. *I might as well do him the favor. He said it was soaking.* But it wasn't in sight of where she'd bathed or washed. She followed along downstream a short way with two candles. There it was, in a tiny pool beneath a sliver of light in the ceiling.

Outside light. A wonder he hadn't told her this, either. It would have been easier to see to do the wash here, rather than where they set up the candles. Oh, well. There was still Tahn's to do. She took it in her hands and started to scrub.

No wonder he'd wanted to wash it. The front seemed full of stains that weren't there yesterday. Something must have happened while he was gone. If the candles had not been so few and dim last night, she might have noticed stains like this, even on a shirt so dark.

She lifted the shirt to look more closely. The water running off it was tinted red. It was dripping over her hands and into the flowing stream. Blood! She dropped the shirt onto the rocks and jerked away.

The dark swirls trailed through the water and disappeared. She washed her hands quickly and then stepped back from the stream. Tahn's tainted shirt lay in a heap, and she would not touch it again. Had he killed someone last night? Did he kill for the food he brought, or the blankets, or what? Surely he was not following orders now.

"Father God!" she cried. "I was beginning to trust him, to think he had done foul only when his life was forfeit! But what is this? What sort of a man is he?"

She tried to steady herself. Perhaps he had encountered someone searching for them. Perhaps he'd had to do whatever he'd done, for the children's sakes. But no. He had wanted Vari to join him, and the youth still would not speak of it. Whatever the Dorn had done was planned.

She tied the other clothes in the blanket. That and a candle made a cumbersome burden, but she didn't ask for help even when she reached the large chamber. "I'm finished there, whenever you need it now," she told them all as she walked through to take the clothes to the bushes outside. She'd carefully avoided looking at Tahn but could feel his eyes on her just the same.

There is no point, she thought, *in any confrontation in front of the little ones.* If only there were some way to get to someone who might help. Perhaps a priest. And then she remembered he had promised her a horse. She could scarcely believe she had forgotten that, though her mind was full of prayers for her family and concern for these children.

She had almost finished laying the clothes across branches in the sun when he came out behind her, alone.

"You found the water pleasing?" he asked.

"The water, yes."

"Temas asked me if you were angry at something."

She turned to face him. "What did you tell her?"

"That I didn't know."

"I want the horse you promised me. I want to leave today. Surely a priest would shelter me. Is there not one in Merinth?"

He bowed his head. "Miss, I am sorry, but you must not."

"Why? You swore to me I would be free to go!"

"It is not safe for you in Merinth."

"But the priest—"

"He is dead."

She looked at him in horror. "How do you know that?" she demanded. "Tell me how you know that!"

<hr/>

Tahn tried to turn away from the accusation in her eyes. How well he knew it by now. Always in his dream, there were decent people, angels, or God himself, looking at him that way, right before he was cast to the flames.

"No," Netta stopped him from his retreat. "I want you to talk to me! I saw your shirt. Did you kill someone last night?"

"Yes, Lady." He turned toward her again, but she backed away.

"Why? There is no one threatening you!"

Almost he couldn't speak. "We are threatened every day." He had to turn his eyes from her. "Were Samis and the Baron Trent both dead, we would all be safer."

"But last night, why? Who was it? Why?"

"I would prefer not to speak of it with you, Lady."

"I don't care what you prefer! You must tell me the truth or I shall leave on foot and take any of the children who will come with me. I'll not stay here with a cold-blooded killer. I have given you a chance to tell me you are not that. Can you?"

With much effort he met her eyes again. He knew it would have been easier for her if she never knew. "I had heard of a relative of yours, Lady. I tried to find him. I had heard the baron's men had him and would be passing through Merinth. Last night I would have freed him, but he was already dead."

Netta sank backward against a tree. "Who? Do you know?"

"They said his name was Winn."

"Uncle Winn." Her eyes clouded with tears. "It was his window where you threw the stone. He must have been seeking me."

"I am sorry." It was hard for him to bear her tears. If only he could someday be the source of someone's smile.

"Then you killed—trying to prevent them?" She was crying freely now.

"No, Lady. It was too late for that. I killed the dark angel who performed the deed, the baron's captain who paid him for it, and the priest who met with them for money and agreed to lie about what was done."

Netta stared at him as it sunk in. Three men? Because of Uncle Winn? She shook her head. It wasn't right, no matter how wrong those men were. "My family never asked you to do them vengeance," she told him. "It is wrong."

"They were looking for you, Lady. Because they knew your uncle was. Almost I had convinced them that Darin had killed you. Now they are not so sure."

Something about that made no sense. "The priest was looking for me?"

"He agreed to. Through his people. For money, good lady. The baron is buying favor. They say he shall be king before the feast of your Savior. And he and Samis seek us far and wide."

"Then you killed these men to protect me?"

"Yes, Lady, as well as ourselves. Vari and I were seen. Even if we had escaped them, they would have followed and killed all of you. We had no choice."

"At least for me, please, sir, not again."

"I cannot make that promise."

She shook her head. "Why is it so important to you to save my life?"

He was looking far past her into the vastness of sky. "The angel," he said.

She turned around, following his gaze, but there was nothing. "What angel?"

"The day I killed your husband, I would have killed you too. That was my order. But your husband saw something, a light above him, that warned him of my presence. Because he yelled and fought so hard, I hadn't time to get to you before your men came up. But before I left, I saw the light again, in front of you. It was an angel between you and me."

Netta had no idea what to make of that story. She had only seen the attacker and the terrible fight. "Have you seen other angels?"

"Only in dreams."

"But why does it cause your concern for me now?"

"You are the only one that lives, Lady, of all my orders."

She still didn't understand, but something of what he was saying sunk in. "How many?" she asked. "How many people have you killed?"

"I cannot tell you, Lady. I have stopped the counting. Three last night. Three the night I went for Vari. Eight years of orders. They all flow together."

"You started when you were *twelve*?"

"Indeed. Samis used me often. Especially when there might be climbing. Some I know were asking for the sword by their deeds, as Darin did. Others, like your husband, may have been good men."

Until that moment, she hadn't seen the turmoil inside him over so much death. His face was ashen, and once again, he would not meet her eyes.

"I know you would wash your hands of me, Lady," he said. "But wait, please, till things are quieter in Merinth and round about. For your angel. And the children."

He turned from her and began to walk away into the trees. But she saw in the bright sunlight what she could not see earlier in the cave's dimness. His shirtless back was riddled with scars; even the skin beneath them was waxy and pale. What tortures had he known?

She thought she should call out to him, but somehow she couldn't manage it. So she only watched him disappear into the timber. In a moment she heard a whistle and knew he'd gone off on Smoke.

The rest of the day she could not stop thinking of Uncle Winn. And home. And strange Tahn Dorn. God had been right to tell her that first night to pray for her enemies. It was right that someone should pray for Tahn Dorn. What must he have inside him? Fury and pain and the horrible nightmare she had seen. She could not imagine what it would be like to have lived in his world.

***

Just past nightfall he came back in a different shirt, with two more blankets and a bag of clothes. It plagued her that he was probably stealing, but she had no remedy for that until she could step forward and reclaim what had been her family's wealth.

Oh, she lamented, *if I had known before of Temas, Duncan, and the rest, what I could have done for them! We had so much!*

Netta washed her dress as she had planned, and the children's pants, now that there was something else to put on them, poor fit or not.

103

When she was finished, Tahn again separated himself from them, going into his own chamber. Netta read to the children as they helped themselves to a block of hard cheese.

"Why doesn't the Dorn spend as much time with us as you do?" Tam asked.

"He has much on his mind," she told him. "He must think about food for tomorrow, other things we might need, plus your lessons and protecting you."

"He doesn't hug like you," Temas said.

"Perhaps he can't," Netta suggested.

"Why not?" asked Rane.

"Well, none of you hug very much. Almost never, in fact. But perhaps the more you are hugged, the more you are able to give hugs."

"Has Teacher ever been hugged?" Duncan asked.

"I don't know," she replied. "But I rather doubt it. You seem to have had very little of that where you've been."

"You're right," Stuva said. "He lived at Valhal an awfully long time. You suppose he remembers anything else?"

"He remembers Alastair," Vari told them. "Someone he knew got hanged by the crowd. And then they all chased him and poured hot water down the hole where he was hiding."

Netta gasped, thinking of those scars. But he would have been such a small child in Alastair. His earliest memories were of something like that?

"What'd they do to make everybody so mad?" Briant asked. "Steal stuff?"

"Nobody seems to know," Vari said. "He don't remember that part."

Doogan was shaking his head sadly. "I don't think he got hugged much."

Netta turned to look at the boy. Such a past Tahn Dorn carried! Doogan was surely right that he'd not been hugged much. "Let's make that a project, shall we?" she suggested.

"Tomorrow let us see which of you is brave enough to be the first to try it."

"You mean hugging the Dorn?" Stuva asked, incredulous.

"I don't think that's such a good idea," Vari added.

"We won't know that for sure," Netta said. "Until we try. He does need to know that you appreciate what he has tried to do for you."

"You really want one of us to do that?" Vari asked, still unconvinced.

"We should also pray for him. You agree, don't you, Vari?"

"Yeah," he said. "That can't hurt."

<hr />

Netta soon had the children tucked beneath blankets. It never took them long to fall asleep. She sat up for a while, thinking of Uncle Winn again and praying for her father. *Lord, let him be alive somewhere.*

When sleep finally came to her, it was filled with dreams of her childhood home, relatives and friends gathered for the blessed holy day of the Christ's birth. But sleep was interrupted in the wee hours of morning by Temas's urgent tugging.

"What was that, Lady? What was that?" The girl sounded frightened.

Netta sat up. "What, child?"

But Doogan answered her. "It sounded like an animal."

It wasn't long before she heard it. It did sound like an animal, somewhere deep in the cave. An animal in pain.

"Does something live in here?" Doogan was asking.

But Netta's heart pounded, remembering her first night in this cave with the Dorn. The sound was coming from the direction of the water.

She didn't know that it was him. But when the sound came again and rose to a scream, she was sure. It was muffled by the cave walls and did sound like some distant animal, but Netta knew Tahn was somewhere there in the darkness, shaking in torment.

She stood up. She hadn't woken him before, but surely she could now. It must be the same hideous dream. She couldn't bear to know it was going on, even at a distance.

"All of you wait here," she told the children who were awake. "There's nothing to worry about. I shall be back shortly."

She took a fresh candle and started down the passageway as the screams rose again.

Vari sat up quickly. "No, Lady, don't," he said.

But Netta didn't hear him.

"Mr. Dorn?" By the time she reached Tahn, he was curled on his side in violent tremors, his arms covering his head.

"Father God," she whispered. "We sorely need your help." She set the candle on a rock in the middle of the room. How did you best wake someone in the throes of a ghastly nightmare?

"Mr. Dorn," she said again, approaching him slowly. She leaned and gently touched his arm. He shrank back like a caged animal, looking wild and wounded. For a brief instant, their eyes met, but he wasn't awake. The hell was all over him, and she knew she'd made a mistake. But it was too late.

He sprang at her, and she landed hard on the cave floor, his hands suddenly clutching her throat.

"Tahn, stop! It's the lady!" Vari cried as he rushed out of the black passageway.

But Tahn didn't stop. He couldn't.

"Stop!" Vari cried, running desperately at his friend. He grabbed at Tahn with both arms. The warrior released Netta long enough to wrench loose from the boy's grasp and throw him halfway across the room.

Then he turned again to Netta. She had jumped up and backed against the cave wall. "No, Mr. Dorn," she said. "We mean you no harm. Lord, help him come out of this!"

Vari had gotten up and grabbed the candle. He crept forward between them, holding out the flickering light like a weapon.

"Vari, no," Netta whispered. Tahn did not look so much like an animal to her now. He was a child, terrified and in pain.

But Vari stood fast. "You can't get to her," he said. "The flames are between you." He brandished the candle in Tahn's direction.

And Tahn shrank from it. He retreated to the far wall, where he sank to the floor, covering his head again. He let out a wrenching cry.

Vari set the candle down and stepped toward him.

"No!" Tahn screamed.

Netta couldn't bear it. "Lord, deliver him!"

Tahn put his head down to his knees. He was trembling still. Vari sat down, watching him.

"Whether a dream or demons hold you," Netta said, "the Lord would have you in your right mind again, Mr. Dorn. No one harms you here."

He looked up at them, and it was as though it were little Duncan sitting there. But he stood and turned away from them.

"Tahn?" Vari said. "Are you all right?"

He didn't answer. He just walked away into a black passageway that neither Vari nor Netta knew.

"Well." Vari sighed. "Let's go back to the youngsters."

"Are you sure he's all right?"

"No. But I'm sure I'm not going after him. When he comes out, he'll be all right."

107

9

Tahn sat alone in the blackness. He wasn't sure of everything that had happened, but he knew it was the dream, and they had come, and he had fought them.

Why didn't they know to leave him alone? But in a cave full of children, how long might it be before it happened again? How long before someone got hurt?

He must not let himself sleep here again. He would find another place, somewhere in the woods. But he knew that was no solution. Were his screams loud enough, they still might find him.

No, it seemed he could not sleep at all without endangering those he wanted to protect. And what good was a protector who must be feared?

He sighed deeply. What good was he to anyone? He did not wish to face the children again. *Lady Trilett is right,* he thought. *I terrorize them. I terrorize her. I even terrorize myself.*

He thought of the knife he always had with him. Perhaps it would be best to slash his throat now and not wait another day to make those flames his home.

He stood, wondering where best to leave his body. Further into the cave tunnels, surely, where it could not be found.

But he stopped. What would they do? He had brought another bottle for Vari. He must give it to him and tell him where to find the man who could supply him with more. He must see that the children knew the way to the towns and how to find food. He could not leave them yet. Not so unprepared. And he must not leave his body in the cave depths at all, lest they search for him and become lost. No, he must just ride away one night and never come back. But business first. He must leave them able to survive on their own.

When Tahn finally returned to his chamber, Vari was waiting. For the opium, Tahn decided. He was needing it so often.

He pulled the bottle from his pocket. "I want you to come to town with me again," he said. "So you'll learn where to find what you need if I am away."

Vari was just watching him and said nothing.

"Has the lady resumed her lessons?" Tahn asked.

"Yes."

"Good. When they are finished, we'll take two of the other boys with us. They need to know the towns and how to get there."

"Tahn . . ."

The warrior turned to look at the youth. Then he held out the bottle in his hand.

But Vari didn't take it. "Tahn, sir," he said. "I . . . I pray for you."

Tahn bowed his head. Somehow, from Vari, that was not really a surprise.

"I appreciate what you did for me," the youth continued. "Anyone else would have let me die."

But Tahn was not able to address his gratitude. "Take the bottle, Vari," he told him. "Get it done while we are alone so we can attend to business."

Vari stared at the bottle and then the haunted eyes of the man who held it. And he made a decision on the spot. "I don't want it anymore."

Tahn was quiet as he thought about what that would mean. "Vari," he said. "It will hurt."

"I don't care. I'm sick of it."

Tahn looked down at the bottle in his hand. Vari was a youth of courage. For so long, he'd been sick of it too. But what might be happening around him in the span of time needed for the drug to leave his system? "I can't be out of my senses for three days," he said quietly. "I must think of the little ones."

Vari nodded his head. "There will be a time for you."

"You'd best not ride to town today," Tahn told him. "You always drink in the morning. You'll be shaking for it by noon."

"I prayed with the lady night before last," he said. "I trust God will help me."

Tahn remembered his own prayer for Vari on the mountain, and something broke within him. *Vari will know God and the peace of God the rest of his days! Would that it might have been possible for me!* He turned away, suddenly unable to bear the boy's presence.

Netta was dismayed by the look on Tahn's face as he brushed past them. She had hoped he would be all right when he came out, as Vari had said. But he wasn't.

Little Temas had seen it too. She jumped up and ran toward him. "Mr. Dorn, sir—"

Tahn turned around slowly, unable to ignore the child's call.

She hesitated for an instant and then clung at his waist in a huge hug.

Tahn patted the girl's head with a shaking hand and closed his eyes for a moment. When he opened them, everyone was looking at him. "Return to your lesson, girl," he said and turned from her quickly to go outside.

Netta followed him with her eyes.

"I don't think he liked that," Temas said sadly.

"Don't think that," Netta told the girl. "You did the very best thing you could have done."

She looked at all the children and their carefully drawn letters in the dust. Vari was just coming up from the other chamber. "Jesus said we are to love one another," she told them. "You mustn't hesitate. You need it from each other dreadfully. But I fear your teacher has never known such things. He will need help learning to receive them for his own."

She glanced toward the passage out. "Vari," she asked. "Can you continue for me?"

"Yes, Lady," he told her, glad that she would ask. It pleased him that she would take her leave of them so quickly and run to follow the Dorn.

Tahn was in the trees, brushing Smoke's side, when the lady found him.

"Had I wanted your company, I would have stayed within," he said.

"I understand, but I wanted to talk to you, please."

"I told you never to follow a dark angel into the darkness, Lady. I might have killed you last night." His face felt tight.

"You are not a dark angel, Tahn Dorn," she said. "You are a child and a man, both hurting terribly."

He looked over the horse's back.

"How long have you had such dreams?"

He didn't want to talk about it. He would rather mount and ride, go now and never come back. But he knew he wouldn't. "Years," he answered finally. "I was a child."

She nodded. "A child with scars from burning water and the cruelty you could not escape?"

He looked down at the ground, putting the two together in his mind for the first time. The horrible hellfire waiting for him, and that terrible time so long ago when he'd screamed without remedy at the burning pain. How could she know?

"Mr. Dorn, you have carried your weight of pain all your life, but it need not continue so."

"You're wrong," he said suddenly. "It can do nothing but continue! You ask me of my dreams. I know from them

111

what the future holds. For years I have known! It was the dreams more than Samis that ruled me. The hell flames kept me obedient to him, because I knew how surely I would meet them were I not."

He looked so desperate. Netta wanted to reach for his hand, but she couldn't. "You do his evil deeds no more," she said. "It does not rule you now."

He sighed. "I have learned the folly of delay. How is it better to put off for a few hours or days what is inevitable? I shall die and I shall burn, all in a matter of time."

She was struck by the absolute hopelessness of his words. She had never before met anyone so utterly convinced of hell who was not running for the remedy. "You believe in God, do you not?"

"I was taught not to," he said. "But I know better." He slapped Smoke's rump, and the animal walked away.

"Then why do you not turn to him?" she asked.

"Turn to him?" He looked at her with fear in his eyes. "Lady," he said, "I have no great longing to hear his rebuke." He left her quickly and disappeared into the trees.

Her heart pounded. Had he never heard, never, about forgiveness? Nor the mercy of God? He must not go on with such a burden! "Mr. Dorn!" she cried, running after him.

Suddenly he was before her. "What do you want?" he raged. "Haven't I said do not follow me? Do not ever follow me, for your safety's sake! You can't change what's mine. Sow your seed where there is hope. In the children."

"There is always hope," she said softly. "For you as well. God knows what you've done. But Christ prayed for the forgiveness of his murderers. Do you think he would not forgive you?"

"Please." Tahn turned away. He couldn't bear this. Better never to see a treasure you can't touch, never to hear of its unreachable goodness.

But she grabbed his arm. "Mr. Dorn!" she pleaded. "Listen to me! You know the judgment of God is real. But the Satan who hates you does not want you to hear of God's mercy! Jesus died as the bearer of your penalty. You need not carry such torment when Jesus has torn away the chains of hell by his blood. Have you not heard that God so loved the world that he sent his only Son, that whosoever believes in him shall not perish, but have everlasting life?"

He stared at her. She was the widowed Trilett heiress. How could she speak to him so? "How could you believe these things for me?" he asked. "How can you not wish me the flames for the sake of your husband?"

"I have forgiven you," she said. "But God prepared a way for that long before I was able. Do not fear him, Mr. Dorn. He has always loved you and shall not turn you away."

It couldn't be as she said. Could it? He was afraid to reach for such a hope lest it be dashed away. He whistled for Smoke. "I need to go."

"No," she told him. "We have food enough for now. I will leave you alone to think, if that is what you need truly." She turned again toward the cave. "God be with you, sir," she said. "Remember, when you are able, how much the little ones respect you and long for your company."

He didn't look at her and didn't try to answer. He only stood in silence with a weight on his heart as she walked away from him and went back inside.

10

Vari was not shaking by noon for lack of the drug. He seemed to be bearing no ill effects of his decision. Tahn took him and Stuva, Tam, and Briant exploring in the countryside around them. The following day he took Stuva and Tam into Merinth.

All the way there and all the way home, Tahn instructed the boys in things they might need to know about their location, its resources, and winter survival. They returned with more clothing and an abundance of food.

Tahn had been in a hurry to get back, to know if it had gotten more difficult for Vari. The first thing he did when he returned to the cave was look around for him. "Where's Vari?" he asked.

"He took Doogan with him to the stream you were at yesterday," Netta told him. "He was determined to catch fish."

"You shouldn't have let them go," he snapped at her. "He should not be in the water right now."

"He seemed fine. The Lord has smoothed his path."

He turned from her and left to find them, muttering to himself about people without a common measure of sense. She just didn't understand, that was all. Vari might have seemed fine then. But in ten minutes all that could change. He knew how Vari fished, underwater and by hand. It worried him. Doogan was a good swimmer but maybe not strong enough to help someone so much bigger if they were foolish enough to choose a deep pool.

He hurried Smoke along, though the horse hadn't rested.

He would go to the stream's closest point and follow it upstream the way they'd gone yesterday. But suddenly he heard hooves. A running horse. He pulled the reins, jumped from the saddle, and led Smoke into the bushes for concealment. But it was Doogan who came crashing from the brush on the horse Tahn had left behind.

"Doogan!" Tahn yelled, his heart suddenly pounding as it never had before. Something was wrong or Doogan would not be alone.

"Sir!" The boy seemed amazed to see him out there. "Vari sent me for help!"

"Did you leave him in the water?" Tahn asked, pulling Smoke forward.

"Yes, but—"

"Just lead me! Move! Go!" They charged the horses forward as fast as the underbrush would allow.

You smoothed his path, did you, God? Tahn raged in his mind. *Delivered him, did you?*

When Doogan stopped, Tahn leaped from the saddle and flew toward the water. But he stopped on the bank and stood, stunned.

Vari was sitting on the opposite bank, holding the head of a dripping wet teenage girl. "She's breathing all right now, I think," he said. "I can't believe you got here so fast."

Tahn crossed the stream to them, grateful for the cool flowing water to calm the pounding fire that had been in his chest. "What happened?" he asked as he knelt beside them.

"I think she fell from up there." Vari pointed to where the bank rose steeply just past them. Mud had been giving way along the bank, creating a newly precarious drop-off. At the bottom of it, at stream's edge, lay an overturned basket.

Tahn looked carefully at the girl. She had a cut on her face, and what would become some nasty bruises on her cheek and one arm. But Vari was right that she seemed to be breathing well.

"You pulled her from the water?"

"Yes," he answered. "She must've hit her head. She wasn't making it good at all. We heard the splash."

Tahn looked at him closely. He seemed to be more sound than he'd ever been. Maybe God *had* delivered him.

The girl was starting to stir. She opened her eyes slowly and looked up at them with trepidation.

"Rest yourself," Tahn told her. "You fell. We're here to help."

She seemed confused and was looking around.

"Do you live out here somewhere?" Vari asked her.

She nodded. "Upstream," she managed to say.

"A farm?" Tahn questioned.

"Yes, sir." She closed her eyes again.

Tahn looked at Vari and Doogan. "We'll have to find it and take her home," he told them. "I'll carry her. I'll have to hold her in the saddle."

"Why don't you take Doogan?" Vari suggested. "Less weight for Smoke after the trip. I can manage her all right."

Tahn looked at him in question. But why not? He had rescued her. If he wanted to carry it through till he saw her home, let him. He smiled. Vari and his God. Perhaps this young man could do anything. If Tahn were as certain of the strength of the rest of the children, he would have no fears for them when he was gone.

They rode through the trees, following the stream. Tahn was not particularly anxious to meet a family of strangers. The girl woke again, and Vari whispered, "Be home soon. It's all right."

She leaned her head against Vari's chest and watched the trail ahead of them. Tahn shook his head, thinking it strange that she should feel comfortable with them. Soon he could hear a dog bark.

"That's Socks," the girl said. "We're home."

A teenage boy was the first to see them. "Papa!" he

116

shouted. A man came out from the humble cottage, followed by five children and a woman with a baby.

"Leah!" the woman gasped. She gave the baby to a girl about Stuva's size and ran toward Vari and her daughter. "Lord o' mercy!" she cried. "What has happened?"

Vari handed Leah down to her father and brother. "Mud slide on a slope, I think," he said. "She fell in the stream. Struck her head solid."

The man was looking at him. "Did you pull her out, son?"

"He did, Papa," Leah answered for him.

"God bless you," the man said. As he took Leah to the house, the woman turned to Tahn.

"Won't you get down?" she said. "Let us give you something for the trouble. We owe you all such thanks."

"No, ma'am," he told her. "You owe us nothing." He looked over at Vari. "He did what a man should do."

"You traveling?" she asked. "You got no bags. Can we give you a meal? Roy Lin! Get a chicken!"

"Really, ma'am," Vari said with a smile. "You don't have to."

"You can eat it here or take it with you," she said. "Papa! Is she all right?"

A voice came from the house. "Yes, Mama, she seems to be fine. Bunged up and shook."

The woman smiled with relief. "We'll give you something, truly. Would you rather have a goose?"

The man looked out the door of the house. "Come in," he said. "I would that you sit a while."

It wasn't a big house or in any way rich. But Tahn could tell that Doogan was fascinated by all that he saw. There had been a lot of things at Valhal. But that was different. This was a home. Two little girls asked if Doogan could come and see their puppies.

"Go ahead," Tahn said when he saw the boy's eyes light up as never before.

Leah's father insisted they stay and eat. He kept Tahn and Vari at the table with him to talk while his wife was busy cooking.

He introduced himself as Kert Wittley. "You from around here?" he asked.

"Yes, sir," Tahn replied.

Mr. Wittley accepted that without a word of explanation. "We'll have a new priest before long," he said, obviously welcoming the opportunity to talk a while.

"Merinth?" Tahn asked.

"Yes, God rest the last father. But Lord forgive me, I'll not miss him."

His wife turned around from her pot. "Kert! What a thing to say! And in front of strangers!"

"They're not strangers, Abby. Leah says this boy saved her from drowning. That makes him the same as blood kin. That's what my father used to say."

Tahn and Vari looked at each other. Neither of them had been in a situation like this before.

"Besides," Mr. Wittley continued, "the Lord'd have us tell the truth. And that last priest did God no service in speaking in favor of Baron Trent as he did."

"We can't stay long," Tahn told them in discomfort. Perhaps it was good to acquaint Vari with these people, in case he ever needed help quickly. But this was not a safe subject.

"Oh, your wife'll give you no grief when she sees what we send you home with," Wittley declared. "Men need to share news, so we know what to do and how to pray. The two of you brothers?"

"Yes, sir," Vari answered. Tahn could figure what he was thinking: If Vari were blood kin to Leah, then he and Tahn must be that indeed.

"We don't favor the baron around here," Wittley talked on. "Don't know how you feel, but I don't fear to say so. I pray God he doesn't claim the throne. He's no Christian man, though he would have us believe it to be so. You are God-fearing people, aren't you?"

"Yes, sir," Vari answered for them again, glancing up at Tahn.

"I thought as much of you. Be glad to have you come by any time. What brought you to the Lindy stream? Come out often?"

"Fish," Vari told him.

"Good fishing here, true enough." He turned his eyes on Tahn. "You never told me, you don't be favoring the baron, do you? With all that's happened?"

"We do not." Tahn's discomfort was leaving him. An instinct told him the man was sincere, and perhaps he could be helpful. He allowed himself to be drawn into the conversation willingly.

"'Course you don't." The man smiled. "He's rich as King Solomon, but despite all that, he can't get the favor of the people, for all his trying. Not now, especially. We all know he's responsible for the slaughter of the Triletts. But he's heard such an outcry on that, he's seeking him someone else to blame."

"Who else *could* he blame?" Tahn asked. He knew the baron had hired Samis for the deed. That was, after all, what Samis did—sell the services of his killers. But such work would not be possible if there were no men like the baron to finance it.

"There's talk of a mercenary trainer in the mountains," Wittley told him. "A hard sort. The baron would like nothing better than to make the deed his fault and make of himself a saint."

Betrayal, Tahn thought. *Perhaps the two shall slay each other.* "May they meet at night," he said aloud.

The farmer looked at him oddly, recognizing the common saying. "You think the baron would be so foolish as to duel a fighting man?"

"One can hope."

The man was shocked. "You've a bold tongue, young man. I know men who would be pleased to meet with you. Christian men who don't wish to bow to a murderer on the throne."

Abby Wittley turned and looked at her husband with alarm, but he waved her back to her cooking.

"Oh, there's not so many," he went on. "And we've no schemes against anyone, I promise you. But we'd do what we have to, to protect our families, at least. Tell me. You've no love for the baron. Who would you have on the throne?"

"I care not," Tahn answered. "So long as it's not him."

"Ah, my heart exactly!" the farmer said. "Except that I pray for a Christian. We do well to do that."

***

Tahn was content with the discovery of these neighbors. In a desperate situation, the children and the lady might get help from Kert Wittley and his family. A grateful friend was a wonderful thing for them to have.

After the meal, he and Vari rode home with a goose and two loaves of fresh bread. *Now I know that the children would survive,* Tahn told himself, *if I were to die tomorrow.*

II

That night, Tahn stayed with the children in the main chamber as they ate. He watched Netta's lesson but remained across the room from them, leaned against the far wall.

He was thinking how little he was a part of what Netta and the children seemed to have. She had taught them a hymn, and they sounded like angels singing it together. She was doing what he'd told her and sowing her seed of faith in them.

The lesson in letters went quickly, and Netta pulled worn pages from the pocket of her cloak. But she did not seem to be reading as she spoke to the children in a solemn voice. "The prophet Isaiah said, 'Who hath believed our report? And to whom is the arm of the Lord revealed?'"

At first her words made no sense to Tahn. His mind warred so that after just a few more lines he was ready to get up and walk out. But she continued, and before he could rise to his feet something powerful in the words stopped him and held him.

"Surely he hath borne our griefs, and carried our sorrows: yet we did esteem him stricken, smitten of God, and afflicted. But he was wounded for our transgressions, he was bruised for our iniquities: the chastisement of our peace was upon him; and with his stripes we are healed."

It stuck in his mind so that he scarcely heard the rest of what she said. Suddenly she had stopped, and Stuva was asking a question.

"That's about Jesus, isn't it?"

"Yes," Netta answered. "Remember he shall justify many. That means we can have peace with God, knowing his mercy has washed away our blame." She glanced at the children. Tahn knew she was aware he was still listening, but she wouldn't look at him. "Let me read a little on that," she said.

She turned to her pages of Scripture and read from Romans 5. "God commendeth his love toward us, in that, while we were yet sinners, Christ died for us. Much more then, being now justified by his blood, we shall be saved from wrath through him."

Tahn stared down at the rock floor. Her words were tearing a hole in his soul. But she just kept going.

"For if, when we were enemies, we were reconciled to God by the death of his Son . . ."

He could take no more of it. In an instant, he was on his way outside. He drove Smoke at a fierce pace through the wooded hills, not even sure what he was trying to distance himself from. Vari's words were echoing in his mind. *I pray for you.* It hurt Tahn to think about it. The children would expect their teacher to share their trust. They just didn't understand.

When he finally stopped by a mound of rocks, he was tense with emotion. "I know how you feel about me!" he shouted toward the sky. "I have heard you say it in my dreams. I am worthless to you." He left Smoke at the base of the mound and started climbing. "Burn him, you always say! He is not worthy of life!"

He stopped on a rock and looked out over the valley. "I am glad for Lady Trilett," he said slowly. "She gives the children hope. Perhaps one day they'll be able to do more than hide or fight. She'll make of them proper gentlemen, and a lady, given the chance."

He pulled the bottle of tincture from his pocket and looked at it. "If I were a child at her knee, it might be that hope I'd be drinking in, instead of this." He took a long swig of the stuff. Too much, he knew, but he didn't care.

"She says you would not turn me away. She doesn't know, does she? She doesn't know all the blood that feeds those flames. She couldn't wash away the blood of one night, God! How can she expect you to wash away a lifetime?"

He stared at the bottle again. Why wasn't he feeling its warming lull?

"I envy you, Vari," he spoke into the night. "To have never dreamed, never killed—"

Suddenly he stood and hurled his bottle into the moonlight. Far away it crashed against the rocks. "What need do I have of it further?" he said. "I am no good with my life as it is. I'll bear it one night more, God, and in the morning give myself to the flames unless you show me I can have a hope in what the lady speaks."

He started walking slowly down the mound. He hadn't slept since Netta and Vari were put at risk of his dream. He had drunk so much of the tincture that it should be making him tired. But it wasn't.

He whistled. *I'll just ride tonight,* he thought. *I'll find a pretty place, by water, to greet the sunrise and give my head a last cool dip. Then I shall part this world as so many have, by the blade in my hand. I can't see the lady or the children again, God. I can't hear any more of it. I am eaten up with longing for what I can't touch.*

Smoke was beside him, and he mounted quickly, still brooding. *Each day adds fuel to the flames, doesn't it?* But he smiled. *I can't be sorry. If I had not lived this long, each of them sitting in that cave would be dead or in torment.*

He sighed and looked at the stars above him. "Thank you, God," he whispered. "For giving me that much. It was worth it, I think. Please care for them. I can't do it anymore."

He rode at a walk for at least a mile as Netta's words tossed about in his mind.

"Surely he has borne our griefs and carried our sorrows . . ."

"When we were enemies we were reconciled to God . . ."

"He was wounded for our transgressions . . . bruised for our iniquities . . ."

"Being now justified by his blood, we shall be saved from wrath through him . . ."

All the things she said were tugging at him. He drove Smoke to a run but couldn't get away from his thoughts. What was happening to him? Instead of the opium lulling his mind, God was reaching for him, clutching at his heart.

In his dreams, God rejected him. But Netta had said God would not turn him away. God so loved the world that he sent his Son, Jesus—the One who prayed for the forgiveness of those who killed him.

Tahn swallowed hard. The Son of God had prayed for killers. Murderers like Tahn Dorn.

A peculiar sensation began to spread through him, and he stopped, shaking, at the bank of a stream. He could not explain what was coming over him. He only knew it was God and it was an awesome, fearsome experience. God was all around him, possessing this forested plain and the incredible sky stretching above it. God, far past his mind, was taking a deep hold on his scarred and wounded heart.

Suddenly he could not contain himself. Tears blurred his vision, and he was shaking even more fiercely. He knew he could not stay in the saddle. So he tumbled down to his knees and wept beneath the open sky.

"Lord God!" he cried. "Would you forgive me? Could you indeed?"

He could not have stood to his feet then if he'd tried. The pain of his soul seemed to be floating away with the water beside him. He had never cried this way. He had never felt such a release of the torment inside him. It was not the blood of a thousand dark nights that God chose to see, but the blood of his Son, breaking the hold of hell forever.

"Will you have me, Jesus?" he stammered. "Have you such a mercy? I don't deserve it, Lord God! I thought I could never know what your love is like. You've a right to hate me, I know that! Would you give me your mercy? I don't understand, Lord, but I want it more than life. Forgive me! Please forgive me! I have been the servant of Samis and Satan, but Lord, let me be your servant instead. I shall be indebted forever for such a Master—such a mercy!"

He could not continue for a moment, the tears so overwhelmed him. And when he finally could speak again, it was with a peace he had never known. "Help me, Lord," he said. "I want to be in your hands to use now. You could have turned me away. But I thank you, God! I never thought I would be loved. I never thought you would give me a moment's mercy. Lord, I thank you! You have freed me from the terror that held me. I know it, as surely as I live!"

He lay on his face, and suddenly he was laughing the spontaneous laugh of a soul set free. There would be no more nightmares. There would be no more hopeless dread. There could be peace.

He was on his feet before he knew it, leaping and shouting. He had never known this kind of joyous excitement, not even as a child. He jumped about on the rocks, leaped over a bush, and then stood laughing with his arms extended and his face toward the sky. Such a weight was lifted! Who knew how light a man could feel?

He stood there for the longest time, drinking in the first joy he'd ever known. When he finally looked around him, the world looked new and somehow crystal clear. *I will never be the same,* he realized. *Nothing will ever be the same.*

Smoke stood patiently, watching him.

"Thank you, Lord!" Tahn cried out. *I need to tell them,* he thought immediately. *I need to tell Vari what has happened to me.* "Smoke," he said. "They will not know what to say. Who could have thought Tahn Dorn could ever be happy like this?"

He bent to drink from the stream. Such beautiful, God-given water. He dunked his head into it and came up shaking the wetness from his long hair. "Smoke," he said. "God is good. Can you believe it? He has saved me! Do you understand?"

He drank again, but this time, he began to feel an odd tingling in his spine. Something was wrong; he knew it. It was as though a voice was suddenly shouting inside of him, "Get out of here!" He stood and looked at the hill beyond him.

There, standing tall in the moonlight, was a black-garbed dark angel, sword in hand.

"Come on, Smoke," Tahn said and mounted quickly. He knew he'd been seen. But thanks be to God that the Lady and the children weren't with him.

Knowing he'd be followed, he rode into the cover of trees, away from the direction of the cave. *The man won't be alone,* Tahn was thinking. *And I can't lead them to the others. God be with the little ones! God protect them and provide for them, because now there can be no going home.*

12

It worried Netta that Tahn was not back before the children woke. That was almost a routine for him. After breakfast, she led the children in prayer and began another lesson. But she was distracted by her worry. And she wasn't the only one.

"Do you think the Dorn was upset with us last night?" Stuva asked.

"No," Netta answered. "He had to think. Sometimes that's very important."

"What did he have to think about?" Temas asked.

"About God, dear child. And his love for us."

"Are you sure?" Stuva asked skeptically. "He didn't look too happy with all your Jesus talk."

"It's kind of hard to tell," Doogan told him.

"I don't understand him," little Rane admitted. "I can't tell if he's mad or not."

"He's just the Dorn, that's all," Briant explained.

"Don't worry about it," Vari told them. "He'll be back with a bagful of something soon enough. Let's get done and go fishing."

But Tahn didn't come back. When fish were caught and the day was old, still he didn't come. Netta got the children to sleep that night with no answer to Temas's timid question. "When is Teacher coming home?"

In the wilderness to the northwest, Samis camped with a group of his men. He had hired a tracker, but Tahn was slippery. He stayed ahead of them and out of sight. *If it is possible*, Samis thought, *I have taught him too well. But he has a fatal flaw that did not come from me.*

"It's just a matter of time," said a tall mercenary at his master's side. "He will have to rest, and then we will cut him down with our swords."

"No," Samis maintained. "You will not catch him that way. Even if you do get close enough."

The slender soldier scowled, insulted by his leader's assessment. "You know I am a match for him, Lord," he said. "More than a match."

"You deceive yourself," Samis told him. "We need only the proper bait."

"What bait will draw the Dorn?"

Samis did not take long in explaining. "He likes children," he said. "We will give him one. Go get me a child. I don't care where and I don't care its age, so long as it can scream like a demon."

The following night, Tahn and Smoke reached Pearl Mountain east of Tamask. He knew he was still being followed. And that someone was tracking very well.

"I'm glad you're with me in this, Lord," he said. "I don't know why my life continues, but I know now that it's not mine to take."

He stopped beside a stream. "We'll have to rest, Smoke," he said and silently dismounted.

He thought of Stuva, Temas, and the others. He knew that with God's help, surely Vari and the lady would do well for the little ones. He could trust for that. But he was sorry he could not share it. "God, I pray for Netta Trilett to find a husband like herself," he said, "strong in faith and kindness. For Vari, the life he has dreamed of, to marry a girl and raise strong children off the bounty of the land. For Temas, Lord, the mother she longs for. And for the boys, the chance to become men of honor and honest means. For all of them, God, I pray a life of safety."

He drank of the cool stream. "Let the wrath of Samis be spent in his pursuit of me," he prayed, "that he forget the children. Lord, let him never murder another soul!" He looked down at his own hands and shook his head in dismay. "Help me, God! Help me, that I not spill blood again."

Smoke had wandered off in his grazing, and Tahn sought out a secluded spot in the bushes to try to get some sleep. *It is strange,* he thought. *Now that there is peace in dying, I don't wish to. I would rather that you make a way, Lord, that I can go back to them.*

In the morning, he crawled to the stream to drink again. He was hungry, but he was so used to the feeling that it was easy to ignore. He had never slept so well in all his life, and he felt strangely happy despite the precarious circumstances.

He was about to leave when a scream suddenly broke across the quiet valley. Tahn stood and whistled softly. "Smoke," he said. "You be ready, boy."

He mounted quickly and began to ride away from the sound, but it came again, followed immediately by another scream, louder.

"That sounds like a child," he said with a sigh. He knew such screams from his years with Samis. Somewhere not far away there would be a terrified child, perhaps hurt. Someone should take pity and respond to those cries.

Another scream rose in the distance behind him. He knew he was still being hunted. The mercenaries on his trail might even be the cause of those screams. It would not be unlike them. But even so, he should help.

"Have a mercy for the little one, Lord," he said and turned his horse toward the sound.

Marc Toddin prided himself on being the best at what he did, and he didn't mind being paid well to help catch a killer. He rather enjoyed it. But this with a child, this was different.

He went to broach the subject with Samis, but before he could say a word, the older man said, "We will not need your services any further, Toddin. You may as well go home."

"But what about the girl?" he asked.

"That is not your concern," Samis told him, his eyes narrowing.

Toddin looked long at him and knew better than to say anything more. He had been told the man was an expert with a sword.

But Toddin was not a man to ride off and leave a girl's screams behind him. He had three daughters. What sort of a person would kidnap a girl? Even for such a purpose? It made the hunter worse than the hunted.

He left Samis and went to his horse. One of the young mercenaries was standing nearby. "On your way?" he asked.

"Yes," Toddin told him reluctantly. "Samis tells me you won't be needing a tracker anymore."

"I hope he's right," the soldier said. "He thinks the Dorn will just come to us now. I'm not so sure. Seems foolish to me."

Toddin had been considering the same thing. Much as he'd like to, he didn't know how to get the girl away from the armed men. Why would a killer like Tahn Dorn take such a chance?

"When you are all finished with your sport," Toddin asked, "what will you do with the girl?"

"I hope we take her with us," the young man replied. "It's been a while since we had a girl up there."

Toddin frowned, but he mounted his horse without a word lest he betray his anger. He didn't know what could be done, but he couldn't just trot off and forget about it. Who were these men who had no more care than this for an innocent child? And why would a killer care if someone screamed? He'd been deceived. If Samis could be so sure his prey would come to them for the sake of the girl, then he hunted a man far better than himself. Angry inside, Toddin rode quickly away. He could do nothing against so many men. He left the mercenary camp behind him, but he knew he wouldn't be able to turn his horse for home.

When Tahn was close enough, his heart ached for what he saw. Would it never end? In the middle of a wide clearing with a single tree, two of Samis's men had a girl of ten or eleven tied by her wrists to a thick, low branch.

"This is a trap, Lord," Tahn whispered. "Had they taken her for her own sake, they would be riding for Valhal now, or to some dark corner. They would not be waiting here in the open."

The girl was sobbing, and one of the men struck her across the face. Tahn shook his head. "If I ride away, they will keep her, sure as I'm born." No bushes or rocks were in the clearing for cover, just patches of meadow grass stretching out from the ancient tree. Samis and his men had chosen their spot well. There was no way to come at them unseen. And only two of them? Surely there were others, hiding in the surrounding trees, ready to descend when he showed himself.

He knew what Lady Trilett would do first, and he knelt down beside Smoke. "Lord, I don't want to do this," he said. "But I have no choice. They will use her and then kill her, you know that. Help me give her a chance. Help me, Lord, just to get her away from them."

He thought of Netta and the children and how he longed to see them again. But he shook his head and turned his face to the sky. "My life is in your hands," he whispered, then stood and took Smoke's reins in his hand.

He rode in fast, low to the saddle and straight for the tree. When he was close enough, he leaped from the horse's back to a branch of the ancient oak and cut the ropes quickly.

"Get on my horse," he told the girl. But he knew she was hurt and shaken, so he jumped down to help her. Both mercenaries stood ready. Tahn took the girl's arm to hurry her to the horse, but an arrow from the trees sunk deep into Smoke's back, and the animal jumped wildly at the pain.

"Run for the woods, girl!" Tahn screamed. He drew his sword to cover her trail, but the two warriors were backing away. Tahn turned to run after the girl, but an arrow sunk swiftly into his upper leg and brought him to his knees. The girl stopped and looked behind her.

"Go on!" he shouted to her. "Run!" She disappeared into the first cover of trees as a second arrow pierced Tahn's back and felled him to the dirt.

"C'mon girl, over here," Marc Toddin called out as he saw the girl running into the woods. He pulled the girl up to the saddle behind him and glanced back at the fallen man. The soldiers of Samis were already descending on him like vultures. Nothing could be done for him now. "God rest him," he whispered and kicked his horse forward to a run with the girl clinging to him desperately, surely hoping that this ride was for home.

"That's enough!" Samis was shouting to the archers. "I want him alive!" He walked to his captive with gloating satisfaction. No one had ever successfully turned coat from him. No one ever would.

Tahn lay on his side, fighting for breath through the pain. Samis looked down at him with a cool smile. "Ah, Tahn," he said. "A good fool is a fool nonetheless."

13

It had been four days. Netta was tense with the uncertainty of what to do next. The children had never been so quiet since the first day they'd come. She had gone to the stream with them—fishing seemed to be one of the happiest diversions they had. But no one was happy today.

Finally Temas voiced the subject troubling everyone. "Is Teacher coming back?"

"I pray that he does soon," Netta answered. Had he found trouble? Or had he simply had enough of them?

"Do you think he's still mad at us?" Doogan asked with a worried expression.

"He wasn't mad at *us*," Stuva maintained. "He was mad at the lady."

"He wasn't mad at nobody," Vari insisted.

Netta turned and looked at him. Something in his voice sounded broken.

"Do you think he got tired of us, then?" Briant asked sadly. "People do that."

"You're an idiot!" Vari shouted. "You don't know him at all!" He ran from them, up the hill and away from the stream.

"Vari!" Netta called after him. "Stay here," she told the rest, and followed the youth.

She found him sitting on a rock, his back to her. From the sag of his shoulders, she knew he was on the verge of crying. But he must have heard her behind him.

"He wouldn't do it, Lady," he said. "He wouldn't just go without telling us."

Netta sat beside him. "He is a loner, Vari. A man we cannot predict."

"No. Something happened." He stood and stared down at her. "He's worked so hard for us, he wouldn't just leave!" She had never seen tears in any of the children before, but Vari shed them freely now. "I've got to find him!"

Her heart broke for him. "I would gladly agree," she told him, "had we any idea where to look. But Vari, we don't know which direction he went, or how far. I'm afraid it is not safe. You know even the weather could be unpredictable soon. I wish I could tell you something different, but you can't leave the little ones. You know better than I do how to provide for them right now."

He looked down at his feet, wishing she weren't right. But Tahn could be anywhere. There was no way of knowing.

Far away from them, Samis had his man but was still furious. Some of his own warriors were whispering that the old man had been bested. Tahn Dorn had deceived him, stolen away the children and Netta Trilett too. He had dared to violate the walls of Valhal in defiance and rescue one ordered to die. They were even saying that Tahn could never have been caught without the trap, that Samis himself feared to face him with a sword and so had hidden in the bushes and used arrows.

Even though he now lay unconscious and in chains, Tahn still posed the greatest threat to Samis's power that he had ever faced. Tahn had shaken the simple belief that the master was invincible. Without that, the fear would fade away, and Samis's power would eventually crumble.

Samis hated Tahn for that, hated that he must now prove himself unmatched again in the eyes of his men. Tahn must pay, and pay openly and powerfully, lest the bloody kingdom Samis had woven for himself begin to unravel.

He stood watching as Tahn began to stir. They had snapped the arrow shafts short, but no effort would be made to dig the tips from his flesh. *Let him carry them to his grave,* Samis thought. *And it shall not be long in coming.*

When Tahn opened his eyes, he was not sure where he was, only that he had been moved. He saw first the face of his old teacher, and then behind him the interior walls of a modest building.

"Where is the lady?" Samis demanded.

Tahn closed his eyes again. His leg was numb, but the wound in his back hurt terribly. He had never felt so weak. But there was no fear in it, no worry. He did not bother to answer.

Samis had never been a patient sort, but this night he was in no mood to be ignored. He grabbed Tahn by the jaw with one hand and drew out his dagger.

"Where is she?" he yelled, pressing the point of his weapon at Tahn's neck. "You know I meant her for myself! Where is she?"

"You may as well kill me," Tahn told him. "I will never tell you."

"You will tell me all I require, fool, or I shall make you sorry you ever saw the light of day."

But again Tahn did not answer him.

"You will do what I tell you," Samis insisted. "You will help me find the lady and the children. You know you dare not disobey me again. You know what I will do to you." He pushed his blade at Tahn's neck until he'd drawn blood.

"No," Tahn told him. "Your dagger will gain you nothing from me."

"What if I brought you flames, Tahn?" Samis asked cruelly. "What would you do then?"

"It doesn't matter what you do. Because it can't last forever." It was such a comfortable, beautiful thought that he couldn't help but smile. "Thank you, Jesus!" he exclaimed, noticing the chains for the first time as he tried to lift his arms.

"You've gone mad," Samis said. "It is no wonder you dared challenge me. You're a raving lunatic."

"I am saved by God."

"You are dead, and no god can save you."

Tahn was surprised at how little he feared what would come. It truly did not matter. Only a few hours or a few days, and all of Samis's tortures would be gone. He'd be free forever, welcomed by God. Blessed thought!

Samis pulled the dagger up and raked it across Tahn's left cheek before sheathing it again.

"I have appreciated your talent," he said. "But now I shall make of you a grand lesson for any other proud young fool who thinks he can scorn me." He lifted a farrier's mallet from the table behind him.

"You could have been my successor one day," he said.

Tahn closed his eyes, expecting a blow. It came swift and hard to his stomach. He cried out. But Samis hit him again, in the side of the head, and this time the room spun fiercely and then suddenly slipped away.

"Excuse me, my lord." A soldier stepped in and called Samis's attention. "A messenger has come from Baron Trent."

Samis scowled. What could the baron want now? The traitorous devil. He tried to skin him before the people to save his own neck. How dare he petition for anything?

He looked down at Tahn, who now lay so still.

He should have been glad for what I did for him, Samis thought. *He should have been proud that I trained him to be the best assassin money can buy. I would have made him the next leader, but he's chosen to be nothing but a treacherous disappointment. I should have left him to die in Alastair.*

"Sir?" The soldier at the door interrupted his thoughts. "What shall I tell the baron's captain?"

Samis turned toward the young man. "You will tell him nothing! I will confront the baron's fool myself. You will stay here." He reached down again and slapped at Tahn's cheek. "Tahn! Look at me!"

But there was no response. Was he already unconscious? *No matter,* Samis decided. *He will still be alive when I bring him before my men. And I will make him pay dearly for what he's done.*

"Stay with him," Samis commanded his soldier again. "If he wakes, you give him nothing. No water. Do you understand? He will curse the day he chose to cross me."

Samis went to meet the baron's representative. And the young soldier stood in the doorway just looking at Tahn. The master had him chained hand and foot, though he'd lost a lot of blood from his injuries and there were men both inside and out. *Samis is getting old,* the young man thought. *That's why Tahn Dorn is such a threat.*

Tahn moaned and tried unsuccessfully to roll. He opened his eyes slowly and met the gaze of the soldier barely older than he was.

"Thought he'd beat you senseless," the man said.

The room still spun, and Tahn's head throbbed wildly. *Samis will be back,* he thought. *It's just beginning. God help me.*

"You should have stayed invisible, Dorn," the soldier told him. "You know he'll take you apart."

Tahn just closed his eyes again. Better not to listen to him, not to think about this. He should try to pray. That's what a believer would do. God be with Vari. God be with Stuva, Doogan, and the lady . . .

Without a word from his lips, he slipped from consciousness again, and the young soldier stood by the door shaking his head. It was not going to be a pleasant thing to watch the Dorn die.

Far away from them, in the Church of Our Holy Redeemer at Onath, an aged priest knelt before the cross at the front of the sanctuary. He prayed long for the peace of the kingdom, for the souls of his parishioners, and for the missing Netta Trilett. When he had finished, he took fresh oil, a flask of wine, and loaves given to him by a neighbor. He began to descend into the darkness beneath the old church to an underground passageway, known only to a succession of Onath clergy, between the church and the fire-damaged rectory standing nearby.

Moments later, without his bundles, he stepped from the church door, greeted passersby, and then walked to the rectory to inspect the work of the craftsman charged with the supervision of repairs. The clergyman and the craftsman ate their modest meal together.

"They are well?" the craftsman asked with a quiet voice.

"Well enough considering their pain, Tobas."

"When will they show themselves? Our town does its labors with a broken heart. The Triletts are our soul, Father."

The priest shook his head. "We have lost far too much. We cannot risk what little is left to us. You must be quiet."

Tobas bowed his large head. "Is there any way to know the murderers for certain?"

"It is in God's hands," the priest replied. "The psalmist wrote that the wicked is snared in the work of his own hands. It shall be so, son. And we shall be satisfied."

14

Samis stood face to face with the baron's grim-faced Captain Saud.

"We have worked together for so long it is natural for our men to share knowledge," Saud insisted.

"Natural for you, perhaps," Samis said coolly. "But my men report only to me. You will tell me which of them told you of my prisoner or—"

"I neither know the man's name, nor care!" Saud roared. "But you should thank him for the favor he has done you! The baron is prepared to offer you a generous sum for the true traitor in your midst."

"Tahn Dorn is not for sale."

"To a man like you, Samis, anything and anyone is for sale."

Samis stared angrily at the baron's captain, who stood before him so boldly. "Why should I not demand a price for your return instead?" he asked. "Why should I not send my men upon the proud baron as I did the house of Trilett, to destroy him? He dares to speak of me to the common people, to rest on me blame for what he hired. He should have known there would be an outcry. He's a fool, but he shall not make me pay for his ignorance. Why shouldn't I slay him as he sleeps? Why shouldn't I strike you down now and any other who dares come to me in his name?"

But Saud stood his ground. "The baron understands your anger, sir. But he is also aware that he is your greatest financier. A war between our regimens would be inexcusably costly to both. Especially now, when our union could become so profitable. He therefore offers you not only a generous sum but a solution to your problem and his among the people."

Samis shook his head. "I cannot see what profit can remain in working with a man who so stupidly sabotages his own ends. I did my job, but he was the worst kind of fool to think the murder of Triletts would help him gain the throne."

"It will yet do just that, if you will sell your prisoner. And it is a generous offer indeed, considering the job was never finished."

Samis scowled. He was very aware of the missing Trilett problem. He also knew that something had stirred the Triletts that night, and crucial surprise had been lost. The Trilett men had been awake, armed, and scattered about, ready to fight. If they had not been so greatly outnumbered, more of them would have survived. Surely Tahn was responsible for that too. He was the only one who had been there early. It was imperative that an example be made. This must never happen again.

"I have told you," Samis said to the frustrated captain, "Tahn Dorn is not for sale."

"What can you do with the treacherous devil except kill him?" Saud asked. "And what good is he to you, quietly dead? Let the baron kill him for you publicly where all men may look on and either cheer or fear."

Samis stroked at his graying beard, newly intrigued at those words. Perhaps it would serve him to hear the details of this plan.

<hr />

When he returned to Tahn's side, he was wealthier and well satisfied with a plan to which he could add his own purposes. He was pleased to find his prisoner awake.

"I had thought to burn you alive at Valhal, Tahn," he said. "With my men looking on. It would have been an appropriate end. But you already know the flames, don't you? You will do better than that for me."

Tahn turned his face away, and Samis slapped him viciously. "You forget such an early lesson?" he chided. "Look at me when I speak to you, boy!"

When Tahn met his teacher's eyes, he could see the cruel confidence in him. Not long before, there had been a fear in Samis, as though he knew his world might topple. But it was not there now.

"I have today to do with you as I will," Samis was saying. "But in the morning, you belong to the people of our fair kingdom to do what is fit to the murderer of Triletts."

Tahn stared at him, and his stomach knotted. *Surely not, Lord! I am prepared to bear what will be for what I have done, good or bad. But for what I have not done?*

Samis smiled. "You must have thought you'd won. That you had brought doubts about my leadership and the security of Valhal. That you had sabotaged my stainless record of jobs perfectly finished." He leaned and slapped him again.

"You must have thought you had sown the seeds of my destruction. But Tahn, what a fool you are! You and your students might have inherited Valhal one day. You were that good. But instead, you will be cursed and despised, surrounded by crowds who ask for your death. Think of it, Tahn! None will trouble me when they have such an opportunity to satisfy their lust for revenge. They who love the Triletts shall call me a hero and the baron as good as prince for delivering to them the guilty party for public execution. You shall be to them the man who gathered men to the task. May you burn in hell forever!"

The weight of his words was like another blow. Angry crowds? Like his first memories at Alastair. God have mercy. "I shall be scapegoat for the both of you, then," he said.

"As well it should be," Samis laughed. "It fits you. You have been profitable to me in life and in death."

"The Lord be my help," Tahn said in a quiet voice. "Thanks be to him that I shall not know that hell forever."

Samis laughed. "You shall hang, Tahn. You shall suffer what the crowd sees fit to give you. Let God help you if he can. None can save you from the righteous hatred of a people mourning their beloved Triletts. They shall be doing God's service to destroy you." He knew he'd made Tahn squirm, for just a moment, and it was enough to delight him.

"The women shall dance in celebration!" he continued his tirade. "We shall parade you through villages before the day, so that all may know who you are and what you've done. It is my special hope that your street rats show themselves for the event. It would please me to gather them all and cut their tiny throats. And let the lady show her face! I relish the thought. She shall make a fine slave to me, as I first intended. I imagine her to be warm at night, am I not right?"

Tahn had turned his eyes and his mind away from Samis's ranting. There was something the lady had told him once. A Scripture verse. It had stuck in his heart the night he was so wondrously saved. *Being now justified by his blood, we shall be saved from wrath through him . . ."*

He knew he need not fear the wrath of God or of hell now. Blessed Savior! Couldn't God also save the lady and the children from the wrath of Samis? For that, he had perfect trust. But what of himself and the wrath of a misguided crowd?

He could scarcely dare to hope it.

Netta prayed alone at the cave's entrance on a sunny morning. There was a lot to concern her. The responsibility for these children that Tahn had once told her was not hers now rested solidly on her shoulders.

And she still had no idea of the fate of any of her family except Uncle Winn. She continued to pray desperately for them, refusing to give up hope.

Then there was Tahn himself. He was such a complex

sort, and she'd never been entirely comfortable with him. Still, Vari could be right. Tahn had worn his concern for the little ones like a coat he could not take off. That he would just abandon them did not seem to fit with all he'd done before.

And the provisions. Tahn had left them with a lot of food, but after a week, it was almost gone. It troubled Netta greatly that someone would have to go to one of the towns for more.

Vari was anxious to search for Tahn, and Netta was concerned about the trouble he might find. But Vari was as aware of the need as she was, and found her just as she'd turned to come back into the cave. "I'd better ride to Merinth this morning," he said. "We've got to get more food."

"I want you to stay," she told him. "I'll go."

"You?" he questioned. "You can't. You don't even know the way."

"I'll take Stuva with me," she said. "Vari, the others need you here. You can fish, you know the plants better than I do, and you've befriended the neighbors. If something should happen to one of us right now, better that it be me."

He was looking at her skeptically. "What do you think would happen?"

"I can't explain," she told him soberly. "I just don't feel right about you going. There is trouble of some kind, perhaps."

"And you think you could handle that?" He shook his head. "Lady, I'm sorry, but you're a lady. You don't know ten beans about trouble."

"I would stay on the outside of it, Vari," she said. "But if you had the slightest suspicion it might concern the Dorn, you would be in the very midst."

There was anger in his eyes, but his voice did not betray it. "Then you admit he would not leave us willingly."

"We can't be sure, but I expect not."

He sighed with a depth of sadness almost tangible. "Lady,"

he told her, "I think Tahn would agree with you. I think he'd want me to make the little ones my priority. If it weren't for that, you couldn't keep me here. I respect you, but I can't understand how you could know he was in trouble and walk away. Of course I'd be in the middle of it! How could I do anything else?"

She put her arm around him and was surprised that he didn't pull away. "Vari, I respect you too. Especially for your love for him. But I didn't say I would walk away. If he needs our help and it is possible to give it, I couldn't refuse that. But he wouldn't want any of you to imperil yourselves. Now let's look into those clothes Tahn brought you and fit me up as a proper poor boy."

Vari gave her a quizzical look and then laughed. "A poor boy? You?"

Netta smiled. "If I wear this dress, dreadful as it has become, I will gain attention. My father gave me too much, and it was once finer than most can afford. In Onath, my face is known, but in Merinth, dressed as a youth like yourself, perhaps I'll not draw glances."

"Lady," Vari voiced his skepticism, looking at her womanly figure and silken brown hair, "you don't have the look of a boy."

"You will help me, then, Vari. Perhaps in loose layers with my hair tied back as the Dorn does his, I could at least blend in a crowd."

"Are you sure about this?"

Netta sighed. "You are so like an adult, I will be as frank with you as I can. I need to do this. I need to know I can leave this cave and not be bound to it as a slave to what has happened. I need to listen for word of my family. I need to know you will be right here safe. I don't want to be left wondering if you shall disappear as Mr. Dorn has. How could we survive, only me and the little ones? Vari, I must learn my way. I must learn how to handle trouble, if need be. A lady or not, I cannot stay helpless!"

"Fine," he conceded. "I'll help you. You'll go. But there's something you need to know first." He paused, taking a deep breath and watching her closely.

"Tahn told me the night we tried to save your uncle that he'd stand against the whole world for you, that he'd give up his life if he had to. He said there'd be no price too high for some way to make you smile, instead of disliking him so. He never said he loved you. I don't think he could. But I don't know what could be so close, even though he had such a struggle knowing how to handle the way you talked to him."

Netta stared at him. That the Dorn cared about the children, she admired. That he would save her life for the sake of an angel, she greatly appreciated. But this? "No, Vari."

"Just listen," he said. "I know you've got to be proper, like a lady should. You might never admit it. You probably can't. But you love him too. I've seen it in you."

She didn't say a word. What could she say to a thirteen-year-old that thought he knew such things?

"Now don't get mad," Vari told her. "I know you have to act like it's all a matter of what makes sense for the children. But you stayed for more than that. You saw what he was going through with the nightmares and all, and—"

"Vari," she said sternly, "that's enough of such talk. We all do what we must for one another and ourselves. If I knew where to find my family, you know I would have gone."

He looked down at his boots with a sigh. "All the same, Lady," he told her, "if you see him, you won't stay on the outside. You won't be able to."

Netta and Stuva were soon mounted and ready to go.

"Stay together and don't talk to anybody much," Vari was telling her. "And listen to Stuva. He's got a good enough head on his shoulders."

Netta just nodded. *How much like my mother Vari seems today,* she thought. *A shame there is so much responsibil-*

ity on him, young as he is. "Vari," she said. "Stay close to the cave."

He laughed. "You think I'll hide from you? If we're not here, we'll be at the stream."

In a moment they were gone, the lady and the nine-year-old, looking like peasant brothers together on the old trail to Merinth.

"I don't figure you ever had much chance to learn stealing," Stuva told her. "You better let me do it."

Netta shook her head. "I was just now praying that the Lord would provide another way."

"Don't worry over it," the boy said. "Someday you'll be rich again, and you can pay it back."

"That's a wonderful idea. I'll remember it for all that's been taken so far. But still we should believe that God will provide other means now."

Stuva gave her a sideways glance. "You're the strangest person I ever met."

She didn't answer. The strangest person she'd ever met was Tahn Dorn. And when she'd known the depth of his pain, she had wanted to help, just like Vari said. Thinking about it made her wish her mother were here to talk to. For the first time she was almost glad her mother had gone on to heaven before her beloved home was burned. But how precious her advice would be right now!

It made Netta uneasy to realize that Vari wasn't all wrong. She knew she'd come to care about what happened to the Dorn. She wanted his safe return almost as badly as the children did. She rode in silence, thinking that only God could put a caring heart in a man like Tahn. And only God could have brought her to see it.

When they got to Merinth, Netta knew it was not just an ordinary market day. It all looked normal enough as they came into the town, but she could feel a strange tension. Down one street she heard shouting and looked in that direction. But Stuva was turning the other way. "Mostly liquor and hard goods that way, brother," he told her. "The food vendors are over here."

"Stuva, God be with you to find us food," she said solemnly. "I will meet you right back here."

"Remember what Vari said," he told her with concern. "Where are you going?"

"I will tell you later," she said. "If I'm not here to meet you in an hour, you can go on home. I remember the way now."

Stuva looked at her for a moment with his brow furrowed. She was glad he didn't argue. "I don't know what you want to do," he said. "But if you're not here, I'll wait. I don't think Vari would want us traveling back alone."

She nodded, and Stuva obediently rode toward the open market food vendors, looking back once or twice. She could tell he was worried for her to be alone.

Finally he disappeared into the crowd. With heart pounding, Netta turned her mount the other way to follow the distant commotion. Stuva had been too intent on the food to pay it any attention, but amidst the far-off shouts she'd heard the word *killer*. Other people might think of someone besides Tahn Dorn when they used that word, but she had to know for sure. The closer she got, the more tension she felt. Soon a growing crowd was just ahead of her.

"He'll be hanged, that's what they say," someone was saying.

"If he be the one slaughtered the Triletts," someone else said, "that's too good for him! They hang any common criminal. Let him be flayed first!"

She felt as though her heart would jump through her throat. He who slaughtered the Triletts? To be hanged? She moved the horse forward.

Two soldiers were gesturing to dismiss the people. "Go on now!" one of them shouted. "You've seen his sorry hide. But we can't let him out to you. We're bound to get him to

Onath for the execution. Come there if you'd watch it. The baron would be proud to show his honor for the memory of a noble house."

Onath? The baron showing honor? That did not make much sense to Netta.

Some of the crowd was dispersing, but others were savoring the fervor of the moment. "Murderer!" someone screamed. Someone else was picking up rocks and throwing them at the wagon behind the soldiers. The entire back of it was enclosed with heavy bars. A cage on wheels. But Netta could not see the hated criminal.

She dismounted carefully and tied her horse at a post in front of the nearest shop. Then she pushed her way through the crowd, praying that the people, and especially the baron's soldiers, were too absorbed to pay her much attention. More people were gathering, and more were throwing rocks through the bars of the cage. There was so much shouting. And more soldiers. She knew she shouldn't be here and shouldn't be doing what she was doing. But she couldn't help it. She had to see who was in that wagon.

She forced her way toward the front of the crowd. Finally she squeezed past a large man with a cane and got her first clear view of the prisoner.

It can't be! her mind screamed as panic rose in her heart. It was Tahn. The man who had tried to give them a fighting chance. Caged and condemned.

He looked like he'd been beaten severely. His face was cut and swollen with bruises. The back of his shirt and one pant leg were drenched in blood. They had chained his hands above him to the top of the little cage. He was sitting, but the weight of his upper body hung from those chained wrists. He did not look conscious.

Lord God! They can't do this! her mind cried in protest. *It can't be this way! He tried to help us!*

Netta pushed her way closer. There were soldiers in front

of the wagon and on both sides. But at this moment, she didn't care. She wanted to reach him. She had to.

She saw the broken wooden shaft protruding through his bloody shirt, and her eyes filled with tears. *An arrow in his back? This is honor?*

"Killer!" screamed the woman beside Netta. "You've stolen the heart from us! May you burn in hell!"

Netta had no idea what to do, but she knew she must do something. She could not let this crowd continue to harangue him. She could not let the soldiers just take him away.

She was about to speak. But Tahn opened his eyes to look at the woman who had just screamed out. And then he saw Netta.

She could scarcely bear the look he gave her. The tears flowed in silence down her cheeks, and her mind raced for what might be done to help him.

Two more soldiers were coming from the nearest shop, liquor in hand, and Tahn seemed to know what she was thinking and the danger it would put her in. With painful effort, he took a deep breath and struggled to speak, still looking her in the eyes. "Just let me go," he said. "It's all right now."

Her breath caught in her throat. She understood his meaning, and she had to obey him, much as she didn't want to, as much as it broke her heart. She felt like she was choking, but she nodded to him and then turned and pushed her way back through the crowd toward her horse. Condemned he was. Beaten near dead and now to be executed, but he was still thinking of her safety.

"Fool!" a man shouted at him. "They'll let you go to swing at the end of a rope!"

Netta mounted and turned to ride toward her meeting place with Stuva. The soldiers joined the man in chiding Tahn for what they thought was a plea to be released. But Netta knew what he'd meant. There was no way she could do anything against so many soldiers. There was no choice but to let it go, though her heart cried against her mind at it.

Then she thought of what she'd seen in his eyes. It was pain, yes, and a dreadful weakness so unlike him. But there was a peace behind it he'd never had before, a peace far greater than any circumstance this world could allow.

"It's all right now," he'd said. And she suddenly realized what else he was telling her. Though there might be no way Netta could save him, God already had. Surely Tahn had wanted her to know that he had no more fear of hell, that his eternity was secure.

The knowledge of it brought the tears back. She wept for the joy and the sorrow in it all, and rode quickly from that street as the wagon began its move in the opposite direction.

15

Stuva wasn't at their meeting place. Netta dried her eyes and tried hard to compose herself, but she couldn't stand the wait. What sort of things might happen to a child alone in this town where the people threw rocks and cruel words at a man given no chance for justice? She was almost sorry she'd sent Stuva on, though she knew he would not have been able to bear the sight of his teacher without endangering his own life.

She directed the gentle mare toward the food vendors and began searching for the boy in the crowd of the open market.

"Big brother!" someone called.

Netta turned her head. It was Stuva, all right. He was sitting on a cushion behind a giant array of vegetables, looking quite important. She'd never seen him with such a smile.

"Big brother, look!" he exclaimed with excitement. "I'm tending to these goods! I've made three sales! I never had a job before!"

She dismounted and tied the horse at the nearest post. She wiped at her eyes quickly, hoping he wouldn't see the horror that must still be there. She couldn't tell him about Tahn. Not now. If she did, they might not leave this town alive.

"His name is Guston," Stuva was saying. "Just as I came past, his wife came yelling for him. I don't know what was wrong, but he left in a hurry. He said I looked like an honest boy. Imagine that! He said he'd pay me to make sure no one stole his things, and extra if I made him money!"

Netta smiled for him, knowing it was an answer to her

prayer, and that it had made an enormous impact on the young boy's heart. But she couldn't quite share his joy. She felt like sinking to the ground beside those rosy peppers and crying her eyes out.

He was looking at her strangely. "What happened?" he asked her, his voice more sober.

"It is not a good time for me to talk about it," she answered, not entirely able to hold back the tears.

Stuva nodded and glanced at the two women in bright clothing who had stopped to look over his bounty.

"It's all right, big brother," he told Netta with a remarkable empathy. "I miss the folks too."

One of the women glanced at Netta and Stuva and then whispered something to her companion. In a few moments, the women had bought as much as they could carry and paid for it generously.

"I think they thought we're orphans," Stuva told her.

"We are," Netta answered quietly.

"God answered your prayer," he said, trying to cheer her. "I guess he really does care. Things'll be all right."

But Netta turned away and stared at the rooftops. *I thank you, God, for Stuva's sake,* she silently prayed. *But God, please! You give us a blessing, but what about Tahn? You must care for him! Spare him, Lord. He never wanted to be a killer. You know it. He doesn't deserve this.*

The man called Guston returned with the news of a grandchild born unexpectedly early. He was greatly pleased with Stuva's earnings and paid them well.

They rode home with their bags full of food, but Netta could not shake her sadness and refused to talk about it on the journey. She needed the time to pray. How could she tell the children? She must somehow, but it might be the hardest thing she'd ever done. How would they react? Every day the little ones prayed for their teacher's return. And Vari. God help him! What would he do?

When they finally reached the cave, no one was there. The stream, of course. That's where Vari said they'd be.

"Might as well go meet them there, Miss," Stuva said. "Don't you think? Maybe they're hungry."

"Yes," she agreed. "We might as well."

"I'm sorry for whatever bad news you got today," Stuva said suddenly. "You really loved your family, didn't you?"

"Yes," she answered quietly, not wanting to talk about it.

"I love Duncan too. But he's not all. If something was to happen to any of the rest, or to the Dorn, or even to you, Miss, I'd be sore bothered."

She swallowed the lump in her throat. "I know you would, Stuva," she said. "You're a brave and good boy."

"I worry about the Dorn now," he was continuing. "He's been gone so long. Doesn't it worry you?"

She looked down at her lap, afraid to meet his eyes lest she break down and weep in front of him again. "Stuva," she said, "it worries me greatly. You must pray for him, please. And when we can, I must speak to you and Vari about it."

"Let's go get Vari now," he said and turned his horse for the stream at a trot.

All six of the younger children were near the stream, along with a boy and a girl Netta had never seen before. They had a fire going, and the smell of roasting fish greeted Netta as she and Stuva neared. When they dismounted Temas came running toward them, ready with a welcoming embrace.

"Where's Vari?" Stuva asked right away.

"He went walking with my sister," said the big boy coming toward them. "I'm Roy Wittley, ma'am. Your little brothers have been telling us about you."

Netta recognized the name of the neighbor family whose daughter Vari had saved. "Pleased to meet you," she said and then looked past him to the little wide-eyed girl by the fire.

"My sister Muriel," Roy told her. "You sure got a big

family. 'Bout like ours. Only we still got our folks. When will that big brother o' yours be comin' back? Papa's been hopin' he'd come round again."

Netta didn't even try to answer.

"Where'd Vari and that girl go?" Stuva persisted.

"She went showin' him the herbs," the boy explained. "We gather them for the healer in Merinth. He gives a fair price for our time, and your brother was well interested in that."

"Well, he needs to get himself back," Stuva said with a measure of disgust. "He's supposed to be watching for the youngest."

"They'll be back before long," Roy said. "There's nothing out here to trouble us. Besides, he knew I'd be right here cookin' the fish."

"And me," Tam spoke out. "We're doing fine. They came fishing too, and we threw in together."

"Muriel's seven like me and Briant and Temas," Doogan was saying with enthusiasm. "They've got poles they made themselves, and they let us use them. Now *we're* going to make some!" He was up quick as lightning to grab one of the poles to show Netta.

It was all so normal for children that she could hardly take it. *Why, Lord?* she questioned. *Why can't they have the normal lives they want and need?*

Temas was tugging at Netta's clothes, and Netta leaned down to the girl. "That big girl was kissing Vari," Temas whispered. "We saw them."

Oh, Vari, Netta thought. *I hate that I must burst reality upon you this way! If only your family fantasy could be true and Tahn could just ride back as though nothing had happened.*

She sunk to the ground, and Temas was quick to sit beside her.

"You must be awfully poor," Muriel was saying, "for you two not to have no dresses."

"I know you're tired," Stuva was telling Netta. "But I think I'm going to go find Vari. We've got more important things to do than visiting."

He looked so grown up, and so burdened, that Netta wished she hadn't told him anything. Now he was nearly as anxious as she was, and he didn't even know what she had to say. Perhaps it wasn't right that she should tell them. What could they possibly do but go and get themselves killed? Maybe it would be better for them never to know.

But they could hear the sounds of someone's approach. Netta heard their voices before she could see them.

"Maybe he got away from them," a young girl was saying. "Maybe he's all right."

"No," came Vari's choked reply. "Somehow I know he's not."

They broke through the bushes toward them with a painful urgency. Vari, with an agonized expression, was leading a badly limping horse. Smoke.

Vari saw Netta and directed his words to her. "Tahn's horse," he said. "Look at him! Been arrow shot. Looks like it's been days. I told you he didn't leave us willingly! I told you something happened!"

"It must have been bandits," the girl, Leah, offered. "Maybe somebody helped him. He might be on his way back before we know it."

Vari turned to Leah. "Perhaps you should go home now," he said gravely and then looked at Roy. "Take the fish. You caught most of it anyhow."

Roy Wittley shook his head, looking around at Netta, Doogan, and the others. "You keep the fish," he said. "Plenty more where they came from. And it's the least we can do when you got news like this. Come on, Muriel, Leah, we ought to go home, like he said. Sometimes a family's got to manage things on their own."

But Leah didn't want to go. "If we can help you," she told Vari, "to search or anything, we will, just tell us!"

"Pray for him," Vari told her. "Please, Lee."

Netta knew how the children were affected by the sight of Tahn's mount so badly wounded. Yet none of them said anything until the Wittley children had gone.

Netta put her head down on her hands, feeling the hurt and the questions in the circle around her. *Lord,* she prayed urgently, *did you lead Smoke back here? I might have carried this horror alone and the grief of it until it crushed me to the dust, but now I have no choice! God help them! It is too much, Lord, that children must bear this.*

She began to cry, helpless to stop it, though she was very aware that they were now looking at her.

"I think she might have something to tell us," Stuva said quietly.

"Was it Samis?" Tam asked.

"They couldn't catch Teacher," little Duncan said bravely. "He must be hiding."

"He must be," Temas agreed. "He's the best." But she leaned against Netta's side, and Netta knew by the little girl's shaking that she must be crying now too.

Netta lifted her head and wiped at her face with one sleeve. "God have mercy," she whispered and looked up at Vari's stormy eyes. "I saw him," she said quietly. "He was a captive of the baron's soldiers. They are telling the people that he killed my family. They plan to execute him."

Most of the children were shaken to a pained silence. But Vari and Stuva were angry.

"He was in Merinth?" Stuva yelled. "Why didn't you tell me? We might've done something!"

Vari's look was like daggers. "If you had let me go, Lady," he said, "I could have helped him. I wouldn't have left till I did!"

"Listen to me!" She raised her voice in answer to their blame. "He saw me too. He told me to go! I saw at least seven armed soldiers. There may have been more, plus an angry crowd! Would God there could have been some way

156

to save him! But there was nothing we could do. Thank God none of you were there, because you surely would have been killed! He knew it. That's why he sent me away."

The tears broke over her again. "I am so sorry!" she cried. "God knows I didn't want to leave him like that!"

Vari had grown very quiet. "Is he hurt?"

She nodded.

"I don't understand how they could ever catch him," Doogan said with a sniff. He put his arm around Rane, who was suddenly trembling.

Netta swallowed hard and squelched her tears. God only knew what these children had already seen. She might as well be ready to tell them anything she could, hard as it was.

"Think he's strong enough to escape?" Vari asked.

"No," Netta said gravely. "He has an arrow in his back. He was beaten severely. One of his legs is bloody. I have scarcely seen anyone so weak."

Vari was staring past her, his face as pale as the swirling clouds in the sky behind him. "When do they mean to kill him?"

She knew what he was thinking, and her heart was torn at the thought of it. Oh, if only they could save him! But what of these precious lives? "I don't know when," she answered. "They say they will go to Onath."

Vari looked then at the faces around him. "I've got to go to him," he said solemnly. "Maybe I can't stop them, but I've got to try like he did for me."

"I'm coming too," Stuva said.

No! Netta's heart cried, but before she could say anything, first Doogan, then Duncan, and then all the others were voicing their agreement.

"You can't!" she cried, terrified beyond words for their young lives.

"You can't stop us, Lady," Tam said. The boy's face was set with a determination mirrored in all the others, and she knew he was right. There was no way she could stop them.

Lord, what have I done? she wondered. But then from somewhere deep within her came a strength she did not expect. *No weapon formed against you shall prosper.* She knew it was a Scripture verse, and it gave her hope and resolve. If she could not prevent these dear ones from leaving, then she must do everything she could to help them.

"Vari," she asked. "Your friend offered her help. Might she and her family be trusted?"

"I think so," he said. "They don't know who we are, ma'am. But they are no friends of the baron, and they are good people."

"Let us go to them and beg a wagon," she said. "I fear the Dorn is not able to sit the saddle, and we may need a wagon for our journey."

"You're coming?" Stuva asked in surprise.

"I am," she said and rose to her feet. "You are like my own children," she told them. "I love you all, and I fear for your lives. But you are right. We can't just let him die alone. I pray God that even if we fail, we might let him know we've counted him worthy that we should try."

"You're brave," Briant told her.

Netta shook her head. "No. I'm not. But he is accused of destroying my family. I wouldn't be a Trilett if I let that lie stand."

Vari almost smiled. "You know Onath, don't you?"

"Like the back of my hand," she answered.

"Then let's go."

Leah's mother was outside and saw their approach. Netta could tell that she recognized her immediately, even in the boy's clothes. "Lady, I didn't know you were with these children," the woman said. "But God be thanked you've survived."

Kert Wittley was right behind his wife. "Lady?" he asked.

"It's the Lady Trilett," Mrs. Wittley told him. "The one I gave provision for."

158

Roy, Leah, and the other Wittley children looked at them with surprise.

"Forgive us," Mr. Wittley told Netta, "for not sheltering you then. My wife was afraid." He looked hard at the children's faces. "Roy and Leah tell me the young man's horse came back to you arrow shot."

"Yes, sir," Vari said. "We aim to go and find him. We need your help, if you will. We need the loan of a wagon."

"Before I do anything," he said, "you tell me who you are, boy. You can't all be Triletts, surely, but Leah says you claimed to have an older sister. Was it the lady you were talking about?"

"I claimed her as such," Vari admitted. "But it's not so." He dismounted. "I'll give you the truth, as God is my witness. Then God judge you for what you do with it."

"Vari!" Netta exclaimed. But the look in his eye as he turned to her was so deep and resolute that she held her peace.

"This is the Lady Trilett as sure as we breathe," he said. "We don't know whether or not she's the last of her house." He gestured suddenly to the children. "All of us—we were the captives of the man who carried out the slaughter. We were to be the same as slaves to him, sir, killing when he bid us. That's what he would train us up for. And my brother—I call him that because he saved my life—he took us all out of there and was careful to hide us and see to what we needed. And he saved the lady too, by snatching her out of her home before they could lay a hand on her. But now they took him and are blaming him for what's happened. They'll kill him at Onath, sir, unless we get there to stop it."

"I heard they caught the villain," Kert Wittley said, his eyes still on the faces of the children. "Didn't know who they meant."

"It's a lie, what they say," Vari continued. "He had no part in what was done."

"It's said he's a known killer." Wittley sighed. "One of

159

those grim mercenaries that shows up out of nowhere. Who is he really?"

Vari looked down at his feet.

"He is a Christian man, sir," Netta spoke up. "He was one of these." She reached to touch Duncan and then Briant. "He was a captive child, raised by a demon of a man to do unspeakable things. He was numbered among those mercenaries unwillingly, and he turned from them at great peril to save our lives."

Vari looked at her with appreciation. He had not known how to respond.

"Now please, sir," Netta continued. "We beg your help. I would that you spare us a wagon, and if I cannot pay you for its service, then God shall reward you the more. And I plead with you both—" she looked over at the man's wife, "keep the youngest so their lives are not at risk in what we do."

"No!" Duncan protested. "I want to come with you!"

"Listen, please," Netta said, now looking at Vari. "I have watched you all. I know how brave you are. But I also know the smallest among you are not prepared to face what might lie ahead."

Temas started crying.

"Please, Vari," Netta continued. "Help them to understand. You know what I am saying."

***

Vari was quiet for a moment, remembering the sparring of Tahn's lessons. Never yet had the smaller four ever managed to survive their imaginary attackers. Sometimes Stuva, Tam, and Doogan fared better against him or even the Dorn. He turned to Mr. Wittley. "Would you favor us so?" he asked.

It was Mrs. Wittley who answered. "Child! How could we not? You can't take babes against soldiers. Haven't any of you got family somewhere?"

"No, ma'am."

"Roy Lin!" Kert called his oldest son. "Ride to Dole Briggs and tell him I need to meet with the men. They can come here."

Roy jumped to obey.

"You'll need help, boy," Kert told Vari. "I can try to persuade my friends."

"How long would it take?" Vari asked.

"Be tomorrow before everyone's got the word. What they'll answer to it, I don't know. Every one of 'em would fight for his family, and they're good men. I wish I could promise you they'd go to Onath for a stranger—"

"But you don't know for sure."

"I can't answer for 'em, much as I'd like to. They've got families to consider. Maybe if you stayed and spoke to 'em—"

Vari shook his head. Maybe wasn't good enough. "We can't lose that much time," he said. "Not a whole day. He could be dead. Rane, you and Duncan and Temas, you stay here. Briant, you too. Keep them in line. You do whatever these good people tell you and help them with things. We'll be back for you as soon as we can."

"It's not fair, Vari," Briant said. "We love the Dorn as much as you do."

Vari sighed. "We've got to do what makes sense. They'll be looking for eight street urchins such as ourselves. If they don't see the right number, they might look elsewhere. Besides, I need you all to tell the men about the Dorn and what he's done for the lady and us. If they want to come then, you'd have done us a service."

"But you said he might be dead by then."

"And he might not. We don't know how fast they're traveling or what they're going to do when they get there. We can't take chances. We'll do it both ways. You've got to stay here and get the job done."

Briant looked down at his bare feet. "All right," he said. "We all got our place."

"Good man," Vari said. "Now the rest of you mind the Wittleys."

"Let me get you that wagon," Kert Wittley told him then. He shook his head. "I hope you return safe. I admire the fire in you. You're better'n a man."

Before they left, Leah ran to tell Vari good-bye.

"Remember what I said, Lee," he told her. "Pray for him."

"I will pray for all of you," she pledged. "That God be with you and that those who have hurt you may never hurt another."

16

There was no prison in Onath, and there hadn't been an execution there since Netta was Stuva's age. They entered the town at night, and it seemed deathly still.

"Where would they take him?" Vari asked Netta.

"I don't know." She was sure they'd said he would be killed at Onath. But she wasn't sure the reason for the choice. Why wasn't the baron's prisoner taken to the baron's own hometown? "Follow me," she said and led them through the quiet streets.

Everything was dark, and little had changed. It was strange to her, coming back into town this way. It made all the familiar places seem beyond her touch. Until they came to the church.

That building stood tall and proud at the center of town, and Netta was relieved to see that it had escaped damage. The rectory nearby was still standing, and Netta thanked God for it, though she could see some signs of the fire's ravage.

"We should go in the church," she told the boys.

"Are you sure?" Vari asked. "Why?"

"I need to find the priest. And you all need to rest. In the morning we'll find out where Tahn is. I trust there'll be no execution without a crowd and a lot of commotion in the daylight."

"Then we should find him now and get him out at night," Vari protested.

"He's not in this town," Netta told them. "Not yet."

"How do you know?" Tam asked, mystified.

"They will come with a lot of noise and a cage on wheels.

163

There will be soldiers everywhere. They will send someone ahead to stir up the people first. It is too quiet now. He's not here."

"What if he's already dead?" Doogan asked.

"I don't think there's been time," she replied. "If they follow the old custom, he'd be hanging three days with a bonfire nearby and a guard to see that whatever people do, they don't take him down." She drove the wagon toward the stable house behind the church, surprised that she could talk to these boys as though they were men.

"People make me mad," Tam said quietly.

"I understand," Netta told him. "But I fear you haven't seen the worst, of a crowd at least. This town has loved the Triletts. They shall hate what is claimed against Tahn."

She thought about that for a moment. Surely that must be why the baron had chosen Onath for the execution. The soldiers had said the baron would honor a noble house. How better to court favor than to become an avenger by such gruesome means? What better place to make oneself a hero than before Onath's grieving crowd?

Father, give me strength, she prayed. *Give Tahn strength! What he must be enduring right now!*

"Are you sure the church is safe?" Vari interrupted her thoughts.

"I trust it," she told him. "They are my friends."

They brought the horses and wagon into the stable house next to the animals and carriage already inside. Netta patted the nose of one of the horses in the stable.

"Cherub, you are still here," she whispered. She turned to the boys. "If Father Marc Anolle is still here as well, I know we are safe. This is his horse. He will help us."

"I don't like your 'if,' Lady," Vari told her.

"Trust me," Netta told them. "What choice have we, till we know where to find our Dorn?"

Netta pulled open the huge sanctuary door and urged them inside. But they all seemed afraid.

"We're not supposed to be in here, are we?" Tam said, looking into the dark hall with its vaulted ceilings and recessed walls. The moonlight that filtered through the stained glass windows created shadows that made the place look truly cavernous.

Vari pushed past them. "Find a place to lie down." But he stopped in the middle of the aisle. "Lady Trilett," he said, "God would not fault us using his house this way?"

"He has prepared it for us," Netta told him. She looked around anxiously. "Father Anolle!" she called. "Are you here?" She went toward a door at the back of the sanctuary and called again. "Father Anolle?"

There was no response.

"I've never been in a church," Doogan said. "It feels strange."

"We need to be here," Stuva maintained. "We need God's help tomorrow. He'll hear us for sure in here."

Netta was walking back to them. "He hears us always," she said. "But Stuva is right. Let us ask for his favor and guidance."

They sat in a circle in the aisle, and she led them in prayer and told them the story of David and Goliath. When she was finished, the boys lay beneath the pews and soon were asleep.

But Netta could not rest. This was almost like home, and her heart stirred within her for her family.

They had passed the ruins of the Trilett estate as they neared the town. Her home was heaps of stone and ashes now, and she'd had to put the sight of it behind her quickly. *Where are they?* she wondered. *My father, my aunts, my cousins—what has become of them?*

"All of my world has changed, Lord, except this place," she whispered and then glanced over at the sleeping boys. They'd needed the rest, but she could not wait a moment longer to know if Father Anolle was all right. Might he be in the rectory? She hadn't expected that because of the damage, but he was not in here. She had to know whatever he could tell her about her family. And she had to pray with him for the Dorn.

She slipped from the church quietly and ran across the moonlit churchyard. The rectory was dark and quiet, with scaffolding over a third of the back for the repairs. She ran to the door at the front. *If he's not staying here, where would he go? If he were in the church, surely he would have heard us.*

She pounded on the door, but there was no response. The rectory too was empty. "Lord God, where is the priest?" she cried. "Show me!" But she returned to the sanctuary without answers.

She fell to her knees at the altar and began praying, but she stopped suddenly. She'd heard a sound, so faint and far away. Voices.

"Father, where are you?" she called. She rose up and found her way through the dark to one of the back rooms.

"Father Anolle, are you here?" she called again, but only silence answered her. "I know I heard someone!" she said. "Help me, God!"

She peered out the window over the churchyard. The rectory stood stark and silent, just as it had minutes before. But now a faint glow appeared and passed before a window. Soon the rectory's side door opened, and a tall figure emerged holding a flickering candle.

"Father Anolle!" she cried. She could not wait for him to cross the churchyard. She ran out to him and fell at his feet.

"What is it, child?" the priest was asking. "Who are you? For what have you come?"

He leaned and took her arm, but she did not rise when he tried to pull her upward.

The priest set his candle down carefully and knelt beside her in his long robes. "Who are you, child?" he asked again. "What brings you here so late at night?"

166

"Father Anolle," she said.

He stared at her for a moment, but then he pulled her into his arms. "Netta, dear child!" he said. "Thank God you're alive!"

But he broke from the embrace suddenly and took her arm again. "Come," he said with some urgency. "Come with me now."

He led her into a back room of the church and by the dim candlelight rolled away a rug from along one wall. Then he lifted a concealed door to reveal the dark tunnel going down into the depths. "There are steps," he told her. "Come with me now." He took another candle from a table and lit it for her.

She stared in surprise. "Father—" she began, meaning to tell him she was not alone.

"You must have feared that all were lost," the priest broke in. "And they feared for you beyond measure."

Her heart leaped in her as she realized what he meant. Someone was alive! Somewhere beneath this church, in this hole black as pitch, someone in her family was alive!

"Follow me closely," the priest was saying.

Netta followed him down the dark steps, but he turned a corner and seemed to disappear.

"Father?" she called out.

"Lord above! Netta?" another voice answered.

And Netta gasped, unable to believe what she thought she had heard. "My father?" Hurriedly, she followed the priest around the corner and into a room.

"Netta? Truly?" The voice of the nobleman Lord Bennamin Trilett reached cautiously across the darkness.

"Father!" Netta cried. She dashed forward toward his voice, but he was there to meet her before her third step and pulled her to his chest in a crushing embrace.

"God be praised!" he cried. "Great God be praised!"

"It was her we heard in the church," the priest explained. "She came running out to me as I reached the courtyard."

"We thought you were lost the night your screams woke us, cousin," another voice said. A young man stepped from the shadows toward her.

"Jarel!" Netta said. "I thank God for your lives!" It was Winn's son, the awful tease she'd avoided as a small child. How glad she was to see him now! But she grew quiet. "Are there any more?" she asked them. "What about the others?"

Her father took both of her hands in his. "Dear girl," he said softly. "They are with your mother now, God rest them."

She choked down a sob. Dear Aunt Mara, her cousin Anton, and—

"Netta," her father said. "Are you all right? Really?"

Her mind whirled. For a moment it was hard to think past the sorrow. But there was so much to tell them. So much to ask. God help them understand.

Her father was leading her to a cot. Jarel lit a pair of oil lamps with the priest's candle, and suddenly the room seemed almost a cozy living space. "We've no idea what you've been through, child," Benn Trilett was saying. "Rest now. Sleep if you can. We will talk when you are ready."

"No, father." She stumbled over the words. "I have with me . . . friends . . . They are upstairs . . ."

Immediately the priest moved to the dark stairway. "Who are they, Lady?" he asked with concern.

"Children," she told them. "They are sleeping, I think, beneath the pews."

"Children, you say?" the priest asked in amazement. "They should not be alone. They would not be too frightened if they found me upon waking?"

"I shall go back up to them, Father Anolle," she said. "But first, have you heard of the execution soon to take place?"

"Indeed," the priest told her. "It shall be right outside the churchyard. I was told the scoundrel was taken by the baron's men as he sought a young girl's harm."

"He's the one who led the men to destroy us, Netta," Lord

Trilett added. "And one of the baron's men told Father Anolle it is the same devil who killed your Karll! I thank God you are here to know his punishment."

"No!" she cried out. "No, Father! He's no devil. That is why I came here. Father, we have to stop it! He saved my life in taking me away. He saved yours by letting me—telling me—to scream as I did. Father, I shall tell you everything, but please believe me, he's no devil. I pray that we may save him!"

Her father held her. "They say his name is Dorn, child. You tell us he is innocent?"

"Yes, Father. The children upstairs, and others, he spared from the true villain, a trainer of killers whose name is Samis."

"I don't understand, Netta," Jarel said. "If the man meant no harm, why did he take you away? Why did he not speak to us of the danger instead of only having you scream? It would have gone far better for us. First they slaughtered those who stayed praying, then they rounded up whoever they could find as we searched for you."

Netta bowed her head. "He said it would be that way," she whispered sadly. "That only those seeking me would have a hope to survive." She looked up at their faces, knowing how hard this must be for them. "We would not have listened to him," she said. "We would have run him off without trusting his words. Or perhaps worse. Because truly he is the one who killed Karll."

"Child!" her father exclaimed. "How can you say he is innocent, then? Did you leave with him willingly?"

"No, Father, but he did not harm me. He meant it to save some of us."

"Cousin," Jarel said, shaking his head, "I've heard it how a woman can be swayed by a captor till she see no more the wrong—"

"You don't understand!" she insisted. "I will explain it. All of it! But you know me, and you know the love I had for

169

Karll. If I didn't know the very truth before God about the man, I would wish him dead. But he *is* innocent, Father! He didn't know how to do it perfectly, but he did save my life and yours. He risked his life for the children. And I believe with all my heart that he has given his soul to the care of our Savior!"

"You speak inconceivable things, Netta," Lord Trilett told his daughter.

"I—I should go back upstairs before the boys wake and find me gone."

But it was too late for that. Vari had stirred against a pew and then sat up in the dark. "Lady?" he called. "Are you awake?"

He found Doogan beside him, and Tam and Stuva nearby. But no one else.

"Miss?" He stood, and the shadows seemed to dance around him. Where could she have gone?

He was walking toward the altar when he heard a man's voice and saw the faint candle glow. He ducked into the darkness beneath the nearest pew.

"They are orphans," Netta was telling someone. "I told you of the villain, Samis. They were in his capture, and Tahn Dorn saved their lives."

"Did you see this rescue?" a gentle voice was asking.

"No. The children told me about it."

"How do you know they are not with him to deceive you, child?"

Vari had heard enough. Netta clearly didn't consider this man a threat, but the man obviously didn't respect them. The youth jumped to his feet. "Let a man who calls me a liar at least look on my face first," he said.

"Vari!" Netta called to him. "It's all right!"

A tall man entered the sanctuary and lit the candles above the altar. Netta immediately followed, holding the hand of another man.

170

"Vari!" she said again. "My father and cousin and Father Anolle are alive and well!"

But Vari could not brush aside the accusing words so easily. Behind him Stuva was stirring. "Vari?" the boy called out sleepily.

"Get the others up, Stuva," Vari told him soberly.

"I meant you no insult, young man," Lord Trilett said as Netta pulled him to Vari's side.

Netta spoke quietly. "My father is a good man, Vari. And Father Anolle is a priest of God. We are safe with them. But you know the Dorn better than I do, and I trust you can believe that it will take more explaining for them to understand."

"We may not have a lot of time, Lady," he said gravely. "Do any of them know where he is?"

From the wall where he had lit more candles, the priest moved to join them. "The man who came to inform me of the coming execution was a captain of Baron Trent, and he said they would be bearing the prisoner through several towns before they came. He wished me to ask my parishioners to tell it publicly and to prepare the yard before the church not for this morning but the next."

"The next?" Netta asked in dismay. "Do you know at all which towns?" She hated the thought that Tahn could be another full day and night in the pain and humiliation she'd seen.

"No, Lady," the priest said with what seemed like real sadness. "I know not, except that what the baron has set in motion will take an act of God to stop."

Stuva, Doogan, and Tam were all awake now but kept their distance, watching the newcomers.

Netta took the clergyman's hands suddenly. "I have hungered for your prayers, sir," she said. "Please, pray for him."

"Pray for my cousin, Father Anolle," Jarel said from the doorway behind them. "She is kidnapped by this man called Dorn and now returns with his gang to loose him from law. Even she dresses like them."

"Jarel!" Netta exclaimed. "There has been no real law in our land since the death of our king. Each man with men under him is a law to himself. Tahn Dorn is not convicted by any law but the baron's. And can you really believe *him* to be your friend?"

"A valid consideration," the priest said. "It has been the baron's men along with the dark-garbed strangers seeking you all these days."

"He throws the blame from himself," Netta added. "To court the people."

"We're not a gang," Doogan put in. "We just want to help the Dorn."

The priest turned his head to look at the child. "Come closer, young man," he said. "All of you."

The boys didn't move but looked to Vari, and he nodded his head.

"Would you wish to join us as we pray for your friend?" the priest asked them.

None of the boys answered, but they came closer. Father Anolle began to pray aloud for the protection of the innocent and for justice to be done.

"It'll be daylight soon," Vari said when he finished. "I want to go and find the Dorn." He turned to the priest. "I thank you for your prayer. God is with us, I know it. But I would thank you to tell me their most likely road into town."

"What do you expect to do?" Netta's father asked.

"I won't know until I see them," Vari answered. "But it doesn't matter how many soldiers or people. And it doesn't matter, sir, what you think of us. Nothing will stop me from trying to help him. I would die for him if I could."

"How old are you?" the Trilett lord asked him.

"Thirteen. Old enough to know the foolishness of your words. What would we gain in deceiving your daughter?"

Bennamin smiled at Vari's stroke of stubbornness. "Forgive me, young man, for speaking without knowing you."

"Let me feed you," the priest told them. "Then I will help

172

you find how far they've gotten. But promise me that you will allow me to petition God before you act. Your friend shall be surrounded by soldiers. I would that we find a way that will not endanger such courageous and loyal friends."

Jarel was staring at him. "You will help them?"

"They have come to me, and I will do what I can," the priest said.

"I would hear your story, Netta," her father said. "If the man is as you say, we cannot let him bear the weight of such an accusation against him."

Jarel turned to him in disbelief. "Would you risk your life for him, Uncle?" he demanded. "We could be attacked as soon as we venture out of here!"

"If we are not willing to come out for an innocent man," Benn asked his nephew, "what is the use of hiding? We've always represented the truth. If we do nothing but survive, we've lost our purpose."

"She said he killed Karll!" Jarel continued to protest. "How could he be innocent?"

Lord Trilett sighed. "I must know more, of course. I understand your concern. But now he is accused of destroying us. If he tried instead to spare even one of us, I am obligated to act."

"Oh, Father!" Netta cried. "Thank you!"

"He has promised nothing," Jarel reminded her. "Except to hear you out."

Netta's heart pounded within her, but her mind was torn. Now that she had found her father and cousin alive, she was putting them in danger. But she saw little hope in any other way. *Lord God, we are all in your hands!*

17

The cool night faded into dawn and the dawn into mid-day. The movement of the heavy wagon, though painful, had lulled Tahn into a half sleep. As the miles passed, he was scarcely aware of anything, until they neared the next town. It was Jura, Onath's closest neighbor.

"Here they come!" someone yelled.

More people, Tahn thought. *More rocks, eggs, curses.* He grasped the bars above him where his chained hands hung and pulled himself to sit up straight. A sharp pain shot from his back to his side, and he groaned.

One of the soldiers driving the wagon glanced back at him. "You're always wakin' up to enjoy this," he said with a smirk. "Right stupid if you ask me."

"I'll be glad when we get the mangy dog hung up," another soldier said. "I'm gettin' tired of lookin' at him."

"Keep your eyes on the street then, Raulon," the first soldier told him. "Make sure we don't plow nobody under goin' through the crowd."

He stood on the front of the wagon and shouted, "Make way for the killer of Triletts, bound to die at Onath!"

The villagers were scurrying about. Women grabbed their children and hurried them away from the spectacle. But others stayed, pressing forward.

Someone threw the first handful of rocks through the bars of the cage. "Hang him! Hang him!"

As the shower of rocks continued, Tahn looked over the heads of all the people at the cloudless blue sky. "Thank you, God," he stammered through labored breath, "that this cannot go on much longer."

A large rock hit the arrow shaft in his back, and he cried out with the new intensity of pain. *I will be glad to die,* he thought. *Lord, receive me.*

On a hill past a row of shops he saw a young man seated on a horse, solemnly watching. Vari? His heart pounded. *No! Go home!* He wanted to cry out. *Just go home!*

But as suddenly as he'd been there, the young man was gone, and Tahn could not be sure it was Vari at all. *Keep them away, Lord,* he prayed. *Keep them away, please!*

"Make way, now! Make way!" someone shouted. Tahn turned his head and saw a woman coming toward him with a huge steaming pot.

It was a punishment reserved for scoundrels. The boiling water, tossed by an angry crowd, and his memory of it was clear. The ravaging burn that soaked over clothes and lingered, it seemed, forever. "Oh, no," he said, a tremble in his voice. "No." Almost he could feel it already.

The woman rushed forward with the pot held between two towels. But just as she prepared to fling the steaming water, a yapping dog darted between her heels, and she nearly lost her balance. The metal pot clanged against the back of the wagon, and most of its burning contents was lost to the ground.

He could cry for the relief of it. "Oh, thank you! Thank you, Jesus!" Only his boots had been splashed. It seemed to him the greatest miracle he could ever see.

The wagon rumbled on down its slow course through the streets, and the woman stared after it, shocked at his prayer.

There would be no more steaming pots. But the shouts continued, and the rocks, from the mob around the wagon. The woman watched as some of her neighbors pulled away and let the assault go on without them. *They heard what*

I heard, she was thinking. *They heard the blessed name from his lips. Is he truly a killer? Or a Christian?* It was inconceivable that a man could be both.

She slowly stooped down and picked up her pot from the mud. She had seen condemned men before, and they had been horrid creatures who either cursed their captors or moaned pitifully for mercy though they themselves had given none. She would have expected this one to be the worst. Like the devil, they'd said, with such hatred for a noble Christian house.

"Antia!" the coppersmith's wife was calling her. "My husband has said we shall go to Onath to watch him die. Surely you would join us!"

But Antia was still staring at her pot. "Not a drop touched him."

"Don't trouble yourself," the other woman said. "You know the Lord shall punish him. Come ahead, now, before they are too far ahead of us."

"'Twas the Lord he thanked." She twisted the old dishtowels in her hands. Watch him die? It was no longer a happy thought. But she would go with them, she decided. Across the street, the weaver was returning to his shop with his teenage son. "Did you hear him honor the Holy Savior?" she called, knowing the weaver's family to be far more religious than her own.

"God be with him," was his solemn reply.

They heard, Antia thought. *They know what my mother told me, that the pain of death brings out the heart of a man.*

"We would not have expected the baron to avenge them," the coppersmith's wife was saying. "There is a good about him we knew not."

"A good," Antia echoed. "Or a bad." She ignored her friend's stare and started off after the wagon, her bare feet moving briskly over the dirt street and her pot now abandoned in the still-warm mud.

Soldiers were sent ahead to Onath, and the crowd following him did not cease. *It will be the sunset,* Tahn thought, *and not the sunrise I see when I die.*

He looked at the faces following behind the cage. *Keep the children away, Lord!* he prayed again. *I want them all to grow and become wise, wiser than the people who so blindly trust the baron's schemes.*

He swallowed hard and licked at his parched lips. *Indeed the thirst could kill me before I see the rope,* he thought. *But there will be no relief of that until I am plunged in the river of God.*

The streets of the Triletts' hometown were lined with more people than he had ever seen gathered in one place. The familiar shout had already started and seemed to be bouncing off every wall. "Hang him! Hang him!"

He closed his eyes. *Once before, I heard this,* he remembered. *Such a long time ago in Alastair. He was a big man, at least when I was so small. He told me to run, but I couldn't. Not until they left him swinging and turned their wrath on me. Lord God, I still don't know what I did wrong. Perhaps I was a killer even then.*

It suddenly seemed fitting that a hanging, his earliest memory, would also be his last. He grasped the cage bars above him and looked out at the people. "Dear Lady, they love you. They just don't know how I have loved you too."

His own words gave him pause, and he thought that if he weren't as good as dead he would scorn himself. *What does Tahn Dorn know of love? The lady would be appalled at such a thought. She needed a gentleman. Someone like Karll.*

He caught a glimpse at a boy on a horse between two buildings. *No.* He turned his head for another look, and the youngster raised his hand and dipped his head in salute. Stuva. Giving him a victor's honor.

There was a good in seeing him, but his heart neared panic over it. He would have screamed at him to leave Onath, except for the attention it would cause. And if Stuva was here, he would not be alone.

Tahn was suddenly pelted from all sides with sticks, eggs, and a volley of stones. But a nearby voice rose above the din. "May the Lord look down upon us this day," a man was saying. "May the Lord have mercy on his soul."

It was a large man on a large horse decorated with gold and scarlet. A cross hung at the animal's neck, the chain of it woven into its mane. But the rider was no priest. He wore a common man's clothes with a craftsman's hammer at his belt.

"It is Father Anolle's horse," some woman was saying. "He would have us remember our religion, even with a killer."

"Pray for him, if you wish," a man scoffed. "God's favor is to punish him just the same!"

"Death to the murderer!" another man shouted. The fearsome call was echoed over the crowd until it gave way to other shouts.

Where could all of these people have come from? Tahn wondered. Hundreds. Loud and angry. It must have been the entire town of Onath and a good share more besides. If things had been different, such crowds might have carried the Triletts to the crown. But now they did the baron's bidding.

The big man on the clergyman's horse still rode alongside the wagon, repeating the same prayer again and again as they neared the grounds beside the church. "May the Lord look down upon us this day. May the Lord have mercy on his soul."

There seemed to be soldiers everywhere, and Tahn knew the clothes and stance of Samis's mercenaries among them. *They have all come,* he thought. *The baron's men and the dark angels under Samis. And most of them young men, like me.*

178

It had never occurred to him before that he could pray for them, and it certainly seemed to be a strange thought now. But perhaps there could be good in it. *If there are any that want out, Lord God, let them find a way. Let them see their masters today for the men they are.*

There were two poles erected beside a platform across from the church. The noose end of a thick rope hung over a wheel suspended between them. The other end was wound around a turn crank guarded by the baron's burly captain. Soldiers lined the platform and the space around it, and centered among them stood the baron himself in noble finery.

The wagon stopped, the drums began their low rhythm, and the crowd began to still.

"Bring him to face the people!" the baron commanded.

One of the soldiers leaped up and loosed the chain that held Tahn's wrists above him. But Tahn did not have the strength to hold himself upright without it and collapsed immediately to the cage floor. The soldiers opened the heavy door and dragged him out. One soldier stood ready to re-shackle Tahn's arms behind his back. But as he started, Tahn glanced up at the tall turret of the church, which stood so stately behind the people. And there he saw the lady.

It was more than he could bear. She was too close. Stuva was too close. He wanted to scream at her. *Don't let them see you! There are too many! Just too many! There's nothing you can do!* He tried to turn, afraid he might see some of the others exposing themselves to this danger. But he realized too late that the soldier with the chain in his hand took the movement as resistance. The big man swung the shackle down hard with a blow across Tahn's face.

At just that moment, the church bells began to ring. The sound of it created a tense stirring among the people.

The baron fumed. *What the devil is this? I asked that priest to stand on this platform and bless the people and our function. I asked him to eulogize the Triletts for the people's ears. I never asked for this!*

The people were beginning to turn toward the church, and it made the baron furious. The priest would pay for this. Church bells, usually for holy occasions or the funerals of the faithful, were hardly appropriate for an execution. Whatever that mad priest could be thinking, it was time to draw attention back to the purpose at hand. Dorn must die.

Baron Trent rapped his long golden staff against one of the hardwood poles. "This day we are called of God to avenge the murder of our precious countrymen!" the baron shouted to the crowd. The bells stopped. Now he could be certain he would be heard. "This is the man known to have burned the Trilett home!" he continued. "He called his men to the slaughter of the family we have loved. It is right that he die for his crimes."

"No!"

The voice rang out loud and clear over the heads of all the people. Netta Trilett, at the balcony of the church tower. The baron stood stunned. *She dares to show her face—now?*

Just as he was about to speak, there was movement behind her, and the words stuck fast in his throat. Bennamin. The noble Trilett lord, suddenly at his daughter's side.

"He is innocent!" Netta shouted. "Tahn Dorn saved my life! Let him go!"

There was a roar in the crowd, and the baron could not discern it. The people were happy to see living Triletts? Well enough, but now he knew where they were, and they would not escape the church alive. He signaled his soldiers to bring Tahn forward. This must not change things. He had waited long enough. Tahn Dorn must die. Surely the people would see it to be so.

"You are mistaken, good lady!" he yelled to her. "He has deceived you. You know not the terror he caused while you were hidden away. He is a known killer, and he must bear the price."

180

Some of the soldiers shouted their agreement, but there was a strange silence among the vast crowd as they looked from the one side to the other.

Bennamin Trilett was lifting his hand, and all eyes turned to him. "He will not bear the price for the crimes of another!" his clear voice rang out. "I fault him for nothing against my family. He is innocent before our God."

This is too much, the baron thought. *This will soon be out of hand. But there are only two Triletts and a priest? I have the strength of my soldiers! I will have my way by that strength alone.* "This villain must die!" he shouted to the people, and then he called to his captain. "Go to the church!" he commanded. "Bring them out!"

Soldiers were dragging Tahn onto the platform toward the waiting rope, as other soldiers ran for the church doors.

"Let him go!" Netta shouted again. The silence that had fallen over the crowd was shattered. Blood-angry for the sake of the Triletts, they now turned in defense of them. The church doors were blocked, and the soldiers were beaten back.

Other soldiers drew their swords and attempted to hold back the press of the crowd toward the platform, but they found themselves faced with stones, bottles, staffs, and anything else the angry mob could get their hands on. So many, swarming at them. It was a tide impossible to stop.

"Keep them back from me!" the baron screamed.

"Don't kill him!" Bennamin shouted, but his voice was lost in the din of the crowd.

The baron looked around him. His own men strove with the people, but where were those accursed mercenaries who were supposed to be so skilled? He could see they had abandoned him when they saw the turn of the crowd.

Some of his men brought horses. "Keep the people back!" he cried again. Tahn lay unconscious on the platform, abandoned now by the soldiers fighting back the mob. The baron knew there would be no time for a hanging now. He yelled to his closest man with drawn sword and pointed his long finger at the Dorn. "Kill him!" he shouted, and then he ran for the nearest mount, leaving his men behind him to face the crowd alone.

As the baron's soldier turned to Tahn with his sword upraised, the strong hand of the craftsman grasped his arm and pulled him back. Vari pushed his way through the crowd from the church wall where he'd waited till the Triletts revealed themselves. Finally, he reached the platform, leaped onto it, and rushed to Tahn's side. *Thank God he's still breathing.* But he looked so still.

The craftsman still struggled against the soldier's sword, so with his fists together, Vari struck the soldier in the back of the head. The swordsman slumped to the ground, and the crowd broke forward over the platform. Some of the soldiers fought on, but most were fleeing now. Stuva and Doogan drove their borrowed wagon toward the frenzy at the platform, and Vari and the craftsman together carried Tahn to meet it.

When they had him safe in the rough wagon, the tall craftsman jumped in with them.

"Tahn?" Vari called out but got no response. He shook his head. "He's hurt bad. Let's get to the church."

Stuva drove the wagon around to the back of the building as the bells started ringing again. Then Bennamin Trilett began to address the people, and the roaring din was soon stilled so his voice could be heard.

"Teacher won't die, will he?" Doogan asked.

Vari looked up at him and swallowed hard. "Where's Tam?" he asked suddenly.

"He went with you. Didn't he?"

He shook his head. "Oh, Lord," he said. "Please get Tam back here safe. The Dorn'll be awful upset if he wakes up and one of us is gone."

They drove as close to the back door as they could, and

two women rushed out to meet them. Vari looked at them and then at the tall craftsman, who was already lifting Tahn from the floor of the wagon. "You'll take good care of him, won't you? I've got to go find my little brother."

The craftsman gave him a reassuring smile. "You can trust us."

Vari glanced down at Tahn and then at Stuva and Doogan. "Stay with him," he ordered. "Don't leave him for nothing. He needs us right now." Then he ran back toward the crowd.

Baron Trent fled down the streets on horseback with some of his men. *Accursed town! You were supposed to hail me! Accursed Triletts! You were all supposed to be dead! That is the mercenary's fault. He has ruined me with his failure to complete an order. I told him he had to kill them all! He has made me a laughingstock!*

He looked around him. So few were following, compared to the numbers of that crowd. Most of the people, no doubt, would stay right there until it grew too dark to catch another glimpse of their beloved Triletts.

They are so few now, the baron considered. *When the people have all gone home and have forgotten to be watchful, I shall have another chance at them. But it will take quite a scheme to turn the public favor after this.*

Almost they had left Onath behind them when a horseman broke from behind a nearby building. The baron spurred his own horse faster, but the other rider's arm flew out, and he could feel the sudden pain of a knife shaft sunk into his thigh. He screamed out curses and turned his face to his attacker. A boy! Just a scrawny little boy!

"Get him!" he shouted at his men. But he sped on, even though only one of his men turned in obedience. He would not linger another moment at Onath, lest some other insane peasant throw a blade.

It didn't take Vari long to realize Tam had taken a horse. He mounted quickly and set out after the child.

Only moments later, Tam's horse came charging down the middle of the street with a young soldier in close pursuit. Vari turned his mount directly at them. Tam sped past, looking pale and angry.

The soldier tried to turn his animal when Vari blocked his path, but Vari leaped at the soldier like a cat, and they fell together to the ground. Vari was on top quickly, and they fought in the dirt.

"Give up!" Vari shouted. "Go home!"

But the young soldier hit at him and struggled for the chance to draw his sword.

"Kill him, Vari!" Tam was shouting.

The streets were quiet. Everyone else was either racing toward the baron's estate or in the churchyard listening to Benn Trilett.

Vari looked down at the soldier. He looked to be maybe as old as Tahn. Maybe not. "Give up!" he shouted again. "I don't want to hurt you. But I can't let you hurt my brother."

The young soldier stopped his struggle for a moment and stared up at him. "You're the Dorn's kids, aren't you?"

"Yeah!" Tam shouted. "And we should kill you for what you did!"

The soldier shoved at Vari, and they struggled again.

"No!" Vari yelled at the man. "Just give up and get out of here before the crowd hears us!"

But he wouldn't, and Vari had to hit at him again. Finally he fell back, and Vari pulled the sword from the dazed soldier's sheath and stood over him with it.

"You can kill him, Vari," Tam said again.

"Get up," Vari commanded the young soldier, who obeyed him with angry eyes.

"I know what it's like," Vari told him. "You got this job and maybe nothing else. But it's not worth it. Just look at what happened. If you've got anywhere to go besides back to the baron, go there. Because his trouble with these people is not over."

The soldier stared at Vari for a moment in surprise. Then something in his eyes softened. "I've got kinfolk in Tamask," he said.

Vari breathed a sigh of relief. "Your horse is waiting."

The young man looked down at his sword, which was still in Vari's grasp.

But Vari shook his head. "I'm keeping this. You wouldn't trust *me*, would you? Get out of here before the crowd spots you."

The soldier just nodded, turned to mount, and rode away.

When he was gone, Vari threw the sword down and turned to Tam.

"What got into you? We weren't supposed to chase after them!"

"I put my knife in the baron, Vari! In his leg!"

"You could have got us killed!"

"I had to! We can't let them get away!" Tam was shaking, the tears suddenly bursting over him.

Vari stepped toward him and put his hands on the younger boy's shoulders. "We did our job. The rest is up to God and the people."

But Tam shoved Vari away. "You should have killed him! You saw what they did to the teacher!"

Vari reached for the boy's arm again, but Tam swung out at him with both fists.

"You could have killed him, but you let him get away! You should have killed him, Vari!" His face was fiery red, but his eyes plainly showed his terror and pain.

Vari grabbed him brusquely and held him close. "Listen to me! I had to fight him. But I'll never kill unless I have to.

Do you hear me? Neither will you! It's not always going to be this way. We're going to be safe, you hear me?"

The little boy was still trembling with fists clenched. Finally, he buried his face in Vari's shirt and cried in his arms. "What about the Dorn?" he choked out between sobs.

"He'll be okay, Tam. You'll see."

"Are you sure? I—I thought he was dead."

"He's not dead. Come on and I'll prove it."

At the church, Netta waited as her father finished his words to the people and told them to return to their houses. They were not quick to go, though the sky was now darkening. Certain of the townsmen declared their intention of setting a watch outside the church in case the baron's soldiers returned. Others wanted the nobleman's favor for attacking the baron directly, in retribution for his misdeeds.

Netta stood against the doorframe, listening to her father speak peace to the people. She wanted to rush down to Tahn and the boys, but Jarel prevented her until they could go down together. When the crowd finally began to depart, Benn Trilett leaned at the rail for a moment, watching. When he turned slowly around to Netta, she thought he looked older than she had ever seen him.

"Love and hate," Benn said. "They are so closely linked. I think I did not understand until today what power I have had for the baron to be jealous over."

"He is a fool," Jarel declared. "He would kill us for something he could gain by goodness."

"I thank God his blood is not on my hands."

"Father?" Netta took his hand. "I am sure Mr. Dorn is hurt badly, but I want to see him. Would you meet him?"

"Indeed, child. I would speak to him when he is able."

They went down together. The craftsman, Tobas, had already removed Tahn's shackles and Vari and the younger boys were all safely clustered about.

The priest and the devout women he had summoned were

nearly finished bathing Tahn's wounds. A man named Amos Lowe was with them, considering the best way to remove the arrow shafts, starting with the one in his back. Tahn gave a wrenching cry at the touch of it.

"You youngsters may wish to be elsewhere a while," Amos told them.

But Stuva crossed his arms and sat tight. "We're not going anywhere."

Netta walked up and put her arm around the boy just as Tahn cried out again.

"Lady Trilett," the healer said. "This may become unpleasant."

"Already it has been that."

Tahn moaned and tried to roll over.

"Lay still," the healer told him with a soft voice. "Don't try to move."

Tahn opened his eyes and saw the strange man beside him.

"He's a friend, Tahn," Vari hurriedly explained.

"You're in my church," Netta added, hoping to put him at ease. She was not sure how he might react to strangers in a strange environment.

Tahn turned his eyes toward her. Oh, his face! She wanted to cry. So cut, bruised, and now swollen. "I told you to let me go," he said between gasping breaths.

"You are not sorry that we couldn't. Are you?"

He shut his eyes for a moment. "Are you . . . all . . . all right?"

She smiled and her eyes misted. Still the Dorn did not think of himself. "Yes," she answered him. "We are all right."

"Vari . . . the little ones?"

"They're with the Wittleys, Tahn. We're safe." Vari touched Tahn's arm. "I think the healer man will have to cut on you some. Can you make it?"

Tahn only looked up at Netta again. "Please—don't watch this."

Vari turned to Stuva. "Take Tam and Doogan, will you, and go with the lady. Keep her company and get some rest."

The younger boys started to protest, and the healer stopped and looked at them.

Tahn turned his head, struggling to see the boys. Every movement hurt him. "Go on," he told them. "Do . . . what . . . you're told."

"Yes, sir," Stuva answered. "I'm glad we found you, sir."

"I'm . . . glad I . . . found you."

Netta could see the surprise in their faces. The Dorn had never said anything like that before. All three of the boys stood up.

"Come with me," she told them. "Father?"

She had expected Bennamin to step out with her and meet the Dorn at some easier time. But he sat on the floor beside Vari.

"I wish to stay," he said. "You go on, Netta. Get them something to eat."

Tahn looked for the source of the strange voice.

"It's the lady's father," Vari told him.

He could not help but smile. *A Trilett. Alive. God be praised!*

"Don't move now," Amos told him. With his sharp blade, he started cutting around the arrow point. Tahn cried out again, and Vari took his hand. He squeezed it for a moment as Amos continued, but in his weakness, Tahn could not bear up under the pain. Vari saw him slip from consciousness, and it scared him. "He can't die," he told the healer. "The little ones could never take it."

"I don't think he'll die," Amos said. "Seems like a strong one to me."

"How bad are the wounds?" Benn asked.

"Enough to keep him down for a good while. Been beaten fiercely. And these arrows didn't happen today. He's a lucky

188

one not to have it sore infected." He gave a grunt as he pulled the arrow tip clear from Tahn's back. "There's the nasty thing."

"When will he wake up again?" Vari asked.

"Can't say, boy, but rest easy. Best thing is for him to go out as he did. Makes it easier for both of us." He looked at one of the women. "Rema, take a cloth now and press on that like you're holding him down to the floor." As the woman obeyed, he glanced at Benn and then turned his attention to Tahn's thigh. "Lord Trilett, I'm well thankful to find you alive," he said. "And I'm honored to be of some service."

"I am honored to have your help," Benn told him. "I would thank you to do everything you can for this man."

"Will you gather men against the baron?" Amos asked. "It would not be hard to find volunteers, and no one would doubt your justification."

"I just spent a sermon convincing the people that it would be wrong. There would be much spilled blood among them. I don't want that."

"But if he comes back?"

"He is a stubborn man. But I believe God that he will not."

"Did God talk to you?" Vari questioned.

"Through his Word," Benn told him. "He said he would bless those who bless us and curse those who curse us."

Vari considered that for a moment and shook his head. "It oughta be that easy. But things just don't work fair. I know the Dorn's killed on orders and all of that, but he's been better than kin to me, sir, and he's never had much of anything but curse. And look what happened to your family! It wasn't right! So how do you know it'll be all right now?"

Benn sighed. "You trust," he said quietly. "You pray to God, son, and then you have to trust him."

"I'm not very good at that sometimes." Vari took a cloth and touched it to Tahn's cheek where movement had renewed bleeding. "It's not just the baron I'm concerned about," he admitted. "It's Samis. He won't never stop. Not till we're all dead."

"He would kill the younger children?"

"In a minute. And he'd enjoy it too."

Amos held up the second arrow point.

"Don't any of you have family, boy?" Benn was asking.

"Temas's father was alive last she knew, but she's never going back to him."

"The rest of you?"

"Duncan's got Stuva. I guess we all got the Dorn."

Bennamin looked down at Tahn. What sort of a man was he, to take on such a responsibility? And to win Netta's trust?

"Soon as he's well enough to travel," Vari continued, "we'll go back for the little ones. The lady knows how to find us at the cave, if you ever need—"

"Young man," Benn interrupted him. "You expect to live in the cave?"

Vari swallowed hard. Had it been a mistake to tell him that? Maybe it was stupid to trust him so soon. "I . . . I suppose Tahn'll be deciding that. When he's up to it."

"Then I will have to talk to him."

Vari nodded. *Oh, Lord,* he prayed in his mind, *you've got to help us, please. There's the baron and Samis. And people knowing where we are. And Tahn looking true awful. But I already promised Tam things'd be okay. You've got to come through for us!*

He looked up at Bennamin but could not read what he saw in the man's sober expression. The Trilett patriarch held the bloody dressing on Tahn's leg while Amos turned to preparing his bandages and herbs.

18

Samis stopped his horse beside a stream to drink. Onath was the worst fiasco of his life. How could a man be so completely stupid as to set himself up in the Trilett stronghold that way? Oh, the baron and his good ideas! He should have killed Captain Saud when he came with the message. *Should have killed the baron too,* he thought, *and had it done with. Then I could have lit the night sky with Tahn's flames. And my men would not have soon forgotten those screams.*

He looked over at the two riders with him. They had hidden with him at Onath and watched the debacle. Now they were both strangely silent.

"Lucas," he called. "Go to Linesk where the others will be gathering. Tell them to meet me at the ruins outside Jura. The baron's ignorance is not ours. We will not be letting Tahn escape us."

Lucas looked at him. "It would appear safer to let it go, sir," he said.

"You dare to question me?" Samis roared.

"He's charmed," said Dothe, the second rider.

"He's a traitor! And he's injured. Are you such cowards?" Samis was fuming. If these two dared question him to his face, what might the others be thinking? The walls of his power were crumbling once more. He could feel the furious pounding of his heart in his chest, and it was giving him a headache. Perhaps he should teach these two a lesson on the spot. He put his hand on his sword.

But Lucas saw his action. "My lord," he said, "when shall I tell them you will be at Jura?"

"It will be daylight. I will go first to the baron and teach him the consequences of the trouble he has caused me."

"Is there anything else?"

"No! Just go and make sure they do what I say. Mattius is watching the church. He will know if they leave. Getting to Tahn will be a simple matter when the crowd is not assembled. We should have set fire to the church before, instead of just the rectory."

Lucas looked down at the ground. Had Samis forgotten? Hadn't Tahn been ordered to burn the rectory? It was still standing. Surely the church would have been, too.

"Go on!" Samis ordered him, and Lucas obeyed. The mercenary leader then turned to Dothe. "You will come with me," he said. "We will visit the baron."

Dothe was yards away, across the flowing stream. "He will have men guarding the gate."

"Of course he will. And we shall tell them we have a brilliant plan for his ears."

"Have we?"

The question set off Samis's anger again. "Of course we do, you idiot! We will kill him and take care of the Dorn ourselves!"

"Sir—"

Samis scowled at the young warrior and spat on the ground. "If you wish to argue, you may as well step from your horse and face me now."

Dothe met his gaze. "It's over. That's why you hate the Dorn so much. Chase me down if you think you can. You've no arrows to take me with." He spurred his sleek horse and disappeared into the trees.

Samis spat again and cursed. Almost he began pursuit, but he thought better of it. No one could run or stay hidden for long. Dothe could be dragged out at a more convenient time. His men would be hearing from Lucas that he had gone to visit the baron. It was a lesson they needed.

They will know I am still capable of the grandest of kills, even alone. I will challenge him. Such a prideful man will not back down in front of family and friends. I have heard he is angry with me. Well and good! And none can fault me the victory in a fair fight.

Lionell Trent was pacing in the courtyard of the baron's estate, listening to the shouts of protest from the group of citizens who had followed his father to the gates. He had already learned from a soldier what had happened at Onath, and he was incensed by it. His father's precious plan for power had backfired in an outrageous way. How could the House of Trent save face now that the people openly accused the baron of war on the Triletts?

It created a danger even from other noble houses who might fear that the baron's mayhem could spread to them. There had been only rumors against the baron before. But now? Any of the other noblemen might claim justification to rise against the Trents!

Lionell quivered with anger. *For his own greed, Father has endangered my future! Almost I could kill him for that. People will not honor me now. They will not bow when I grace their village streets. More likely that they toss their rotted vegetables with a shout of death to the House of Trent.*

How could his father have been so stupid? He must have known there would be Triletts alive somewhere. He deserved whatever came against him. But the rest of the Trents? They were cursed to have the baron as their head.

He watched his mother hurrying past with her nurse toward his father's private house. His mother was so upset over his injury. She continued to dote on him as though he had done nothing to disgrace the family name.

Lionell sat on an ironwork bench and put his head in his

hands. *Do the others really realize what tonight's events could mean to them?*

There was a hush suddenly among the voices at the gate, and Lionell looked up. One of the soldiers was starting across the courtyard toward the baron's quarters with a sullen expression.

"What is it, Marcus?" Lionell asked him.

"The mercenary, Samis, has come to see your father."

"Alone?"

"It appears so."

Lionell shook his head. The man was bold. Surely he must understand that the baron would not be in good temper right now.

"Did he tell you why?"

"He claims he has a worthy plan."

Lionell snorted. What need did they have of more plans? They had gained only trouble by them so far.

"Why would he come to Father with it?" he wondered aloud. "I would expect the man to be angry for the loss of his prisoner."

"He is," the soldier said. "I can tell it. That is why I will ask the baron before opening the gate to him. They are both in foul moods tonight. They might kill each other."

Lionell stared at him in surprise and could not suppress his smile. There might be a way to save his future after all.

"Bring him in, Marcus," he told the soldier.

"Excuse me, sir?"

"Bring him in. I want to talk to him."

"But he is a dangerous man, sir."

"And we can be just as dangerous, with our numbers of soldiers within the gates. I don't fear him. I would hear him out before he troubles my father again."

"Are you sure?"

"Of course I'm sure! Show him here!" He watched the soldier walking away, shaking his head. *Our men have little confidence in us lately,* Lionell thought. *They have had good reason to doubt, but that will change.*

He started thinking about what he might say to the mercenary to encourage a duel. But the soldiers had no good feelings for Samis, after his men abandoned them in the press of the crowd at Onath. It was doubtful they would honor his victory in a duel with the baron. And even though the baron might actually consider such a thing, Lionell's mother would surely change his mind. Lionell sighed. If a duel was impossible, there must be some other way.

Marcus was returning quickly with the old warrior, and Lionell didn't think he looked so dangerous. *He's an old man who thinks the world should revolve around him. Just like my father.*

He had once been strong, no doubt about that. Lionell had heard enough about him to know he was formidable as a friend or a foe, not someone to be taken lightly. But in the pale moonlight, he was looking old, his graying hair dampened by beads of sweat though the night was increasingly chilly.

"I am favored to meet the young Baron Trent at last," Samis said.

Lionell didn't answer for a moment. That title would not be appropriate for him until his father's death. Still, it was a civil greeting, and it surprised him. Marcus stood behind Samis, the distrust obvious on his face.

"You may leave us, Marcus," Lionell told him.

"Sir—"

"No. Do not argue. I am sure Mr. Samis knows that any guest who seeks to do us harm will not leave here alive." He smiled. "He *is* within our gates, after all. Go on, Marcus. I will take him to Father myself if he has something of importance to tell him."

Reluctantly, the soldier left them alone.

"You are a bold young man," Samis told the Trent heir.

"You are far bolder, to come here tonight. Surely you realize that my father is not happy with your services."

"My services have not been the problem. The folly is in him."

"To my face, you call my father a fool?"

"You know it to be so!" Samis blurted. He leaned one arm against a tree and took a deep breath. "You know the trouble he has caused all of us. It was his responsibility to consider consequences. He is more than a fool. The snake sought to blame me for his stupidity! Then he took my prisoner for his scheme and accomplished nothing but endangering the lives of his men. You, young baron, should understand what he has cost me. I needed Tahn Dorn dead. And I need my reputation cleared of this mess."

"Why are you telling me this?"

"My quarrel is not with you. I tell you plainly that I came here to ask your father to face me in a fair fight, if he is man enough!"

Lionell could not suppress his pleasure, but he tried not to appear too forward. "Marcus told me you would relish the opportunity for a duel."

"Indeed. No one crosses me so. Not even a nobleman who has paid me well."

"As though you bore no fault, mercenary!" Lionell exclaimed. "There would have been no Triletts to stir up Onath if your men had done their jobs. You were responsible for that."

This time Samis smiled, but there was something sinister deep in his gray eyes. "You are bolder even than I thought."

The young man squirmed, suddenly painfully aware how well armed this man was, while he himself wore no weapon. *He has come to kill Father,* Lionell understood. *He has come without fear, completely confident of his ability to get it done. So let it be. I'll not be an obstacle in his path.*

"Mr. Samis," he said, "I have no quarrel with you. I know

my father made a grave miscalculation to attack such a popular rival. The House of Trent may never recover its honor in the eyes of the people. Father has done me a terrible disservice." He smiled suddenly, an idea forming in his mind.

"You do not protest my challenge of him, then?" Samis asked with a searching look that betrayed his satisfaction.

"I don't, no. But my mother will, and she will convince my father not to fight you, regardless of his anger. Because he is injured, he will listen to her. And our soldiers do not appreciate you, sir. If you kill him openly, even at a duel, they would not be pleased to let you live."

Samis didn't seem the least bit concerned by that. "You have a reason for telling me this?"

"I want the House of Trent to own the respect it deserves. That is no longer possible under my father's leadership."

Samis laughed. "Kill him yourself, then! There is no one worthier."

Lionell scoffed. "I would not estrange my mother so. The poor soul *loves* him! No, my father has brought death upon himself. Let his own dagger kill him."

Samis narrowed his eyes and stared at Lionell. The sweat now rolled down the mercenary's cheeks. He looked deathly gray. *Perhaps that is part of the reason he is so feared,* Lionell thought. *Samis, the corpse who kills.*

"I will give you an opportunity with my father alone," Lionell told him. "Choose daggers, and do not cut him until he is down. Use his own weapon and leave it in him. Then I will shut his doors till morning and see you out in peace. Tomorrow, Mother shall mourn what will appear he did to himself in his despair."

Samis shook his head. "I came to kill him. I want it known that I did."

"I will pay you well for your loss of fame. You know I will have his riches. Tell your own men, or your women, if they love such things. I will give you one of his rings to prove you have been here. Only let the masses shake their heads at such a dishonorable death."

"The young serpent is a venomous one."

"I think of it as realistic, sir. When he sent his men to drag the Triletts out of a church, he doomed himself to disgrace. What choice have I? Live and die with him in the wrath of our countrymen? I shall not! In a couple of days, when I have recovered somewhat from the shock of my father's suicide, I shall send Benn Trilett a careful letter of apology for my father's behavior and a plea for peace between our great houses—that should placate the other nobles. Father can carry the blame to his grave. And you, sir, may comfortably do as you wish with the rest of your days."

"It must lie in your blood to scheme."

"You know this can be successful. Even if I am found out, only Mother would chastise me. All the world would see my reasons."

"Your mother must eventually sleep, boy. Why don't you do the deed yourself then in secret?"

Lionell bristled at being called a boy. He was twenty-five. But it was a valid question requiring a truthful answer. "Mr. Samis, you have *craved* to do it. And I need peace with you as much as with everyone else to recover the standing that *I* crave! I do not wish your grudge against him to follow me about like a shadow. For the opportunity to part as friends, I will compensate you generously."

"Very well," he said. "If it please you, I would be of service to the new baron as I was to the old. Perhaps you shall appreciate me more."

"You can be sure of it. I will not repeat his mistakes."

19

Tahn tossed on his bed of blankets. He dreamed of Samis, fiery and younger, chasing him with the terrible sting of his whip. With a cry, he opened his eyes. He was still in the old church. A strange man sat beside him.

"Deep breath now," the man said. "Slow. It will be easier."

He tried to obey. "You're the healer?"

"No, son. I am the priest."

That surprised Tahn, but it was comforting. "Thank you for allowing me here. I am indebted." He tried to look around him, but every movement hurt. This room was small and dark, and he could hear voices nearby, but he saw no one else. "Where's Vari?"

"The boys are sleeping, I think. He is the oldest, yes?"

"Yes."

"He went to check on them. I expect he'll be back, though it would do him good to rest."

It was no surprise to hear of Vari's watchfulness. "He is becoming like me for worrying. But there has been reason."

The priest laid a warm hand on Tahn's shoulder, but the troubled thoughts poured over him regardless. "The baron won't be pleased losing his prisoner," he breathed out painfully. "Nor Samis. He won't stop. And I fear I will be of little use to you if we are attacked."

"Do not fear. Almighty God will protect us. You can have faith in him."

Tahn tried to move, and groaned with the pain. "I have little experience at faith," he admitted. "But I know Samis well. He won't give up. Not while he lives. The little ones—"

"Stop," the priest told him kindly. "It is in God's hands."

"I—I may have to kill him, when I'm able. God help me! I don't want to kill again, but . . . but he—"

"No, son. It is in God's hands. You must leave it there. He will take care of you and your children."

"The Triletts!" Tahn suddenly remembered. "Does the lady's father know what he's up against? Are they safe here?"

Father Anolle smiled down at him. "They are safe. Can you let it go from your mind? Can you trust God and relax?"

He gasped again in his pain. It was so hard to lie here unsure if he could even get up. "I will try to trust. I told you I worry. But not without cause."

"Do you thirst?"

"Yes, sir."

The priest helped him drink and then laid his head down gently. But thoughts of Samis's whip entered Tahn's mind again. Back then, he couldn't escape it. He had sunk to the floor with arms over his head, a child of Doogan's age, bearing the awful blows. He started shaking, took a deep breath, and struggled to speak. "I know what he would do with me. He said he would burn me alive. But it is the children—"

"Please, son. You need to rest and—"

"Trust God—I know. But Jesus, help me! Let Samis never take another child!"

"Netta told me you had called on his name," someone spoke from the doorway.

With painful effort, Tahn turned his face to the new voice. It must be the lady's father. "Yes, my lord. But . . . but I never got to properly tell her."

The priest put a hand again on his shoulder. "He is troubled for your safety, Benn."

"I heard."

"And he has a heart for the orphans, truly, as Netta said."

"You do not need to sell him to me, Father," Benn said gently. "He can speak for himself."

Tahn looked up at him and swallowed tensely. The Trilett patriarch had a right to be suspicious of him. "It's all right, good priest," he said. "I need to face him." He struggled to sit up but collapsed back in pain, suddenly ashamed of his weakness. It plagued him that he could not give Netta's father the courtesy of a bow. "Forgive me, sir—"

Benn walked toward them. "Please. Rest easy." He knelt at Tahn's side. "You trouble me, troubling yourself so. You have no cause for concern from me."

"God has touched you, son," the priest added. "Let him give you his peace."

Tahn closed his eyes, wondering at them. How could they speak to him this way? He could have expected any number of things, but not their acceptance.

"Did he wake up yet? Is he all right?" It was Vari, and Tahn opened his eyes to greet him. The youngster smiled immediately. "Don't tell us it was foolish," Vari said. "You're worth every risk we took."

Tahn had to return the smile. "You were worth the risk back then, friend. No matter what I said. But I don't know how you got me out of that crowd." He paused to catch his breath. The weakness seemed suddenly consuming, but he fought it. "Surely . . . a miracle . . ."

"We will explain it," Benn said. "In time. Can we bring you food?"

"No." He took a deep breath. "But please . . . post a watch."

"The villagers have done that for us," the priest said. "Trust now."

"Villagers?" He turned his eyes to Lord Trilett, remembering the cries of the crowd.

201

"They are your friends now," Bennamin told him. "Though I understand that would seem a miracle to you. We told them you saved my daughter's life. They are indebted."

It was an amazing thought. Too much to take in. "More water," he asked. "Please."

"Of course," Father Anolle said, and began to lift him. But Tahn moaned with the pain of the movement and sunk in the priest's arms. "Benn," Anolle whispered as he lifted the water, "he's so weak. We've got to let him rest."

"Yes." Benn stood and extended his hand to Vari. "Come with me, son. Father Anolle will care for him."

Vari glanced at Benn but turned to Tahn again. "You'll be all right if I go?"

Tahn nodded. "Sleep."

"Yes, sir."

They left together, talking in low voices. Tahn coughed, and the priest eased him carefully back down to the blankets.

"You also should try to sleep now," Father Anolle told him. "That is the best way to regain your strength."

But his mind would not rest. "Long ago Samis saved my life," he said, his voice barely audible. "Why does he value it so little?"

"Shhh—"

"I would have died in Alastair. It would have been better, in some ways—"

"Peace, now."

"I don't know what Rane did with the whip. I've been glad not to see it again." His voice broke, and he struggled with the words. So weary tonight, so sore. But he couldn't let it go. "I—I felt it more than once by Samis's hand. But the little ones must never—"

"Holy Savior hold you," Anolle said and touched his head. "Son, you need to forgive the man."

Tahn started shaking again. "I can't. Not yet."

"Peace, then," the priest said gently. "Our Lord will give

you all the time you need. Sleep now. God be with you in sleep."

Tahn closed his eyes and let the priest's soothing words flow over him. Peace. Indeed there was peace, knowing he would never be alone. The priest had said God would protect them. Surely it would be so. And Samis would never touch them again. Father Anolle was praying, but the words slipped past Tahn as he drifted away into calmer dreams.

20

It was almost sunrise, and Samis was running his horse toward Jura with smug satisfaction and money in his bags.

The old baron had been easy to better. The best part of it had been when he'd seen that his own son was privy to his blood. That was, after all, why Samis had agreed to the young man's scheme. Just a fight would have provided no such cruelty. Better that the baron die knowing his disgrace, knowing that he was despised by his own heir.

Samis lifted his arm to wipe the sweat from his brow. Once again, his heart pounded heavily in his chest. Such a hot night! He pulled at his collar.

"Slow down, Leviathan." He reined in his horse and pulled a bottle of liquor from his coat. He chased one long drink down with a second one and looked at the fiery glow in the east. The trees blurred together in the orange haze, and he was suddenly dizzy.

"Hold, Leviathan." The horse obediently stood still as Samis looked down at the liquor in his hand. Drink had never affected him so. But he could barely discern the shape of the bottle. And he could barely keep himself in the saddle. The very ground now was swirling. The bottle dropped from his hand, and he clutched at the saddle horn and tried to dismount. But before he knew how it happened, he landed hard in the dirt.

***

Hours later at their appointed place, Lucas stood among a restless band of warriors.

"Where is he?" Donas was the first to ask. He stood taller than most of them and was one of the oldest.

"I already told you what I know. He went to see the baron."

"Maybe he's been bought again. Maybe they're drunk together and stuffed with a feast." Donas had a look of utter disdain. "And we hurried here without taking time for breakfast."

Lucas pulled a biscuit from his pocket and tossed it to him. "Here!" The others were watching him, and he was not comfortable with that. "He was in no mood for feasting," he told them. "He would sooner kill the man."

"Maybe the baron has killed him, with his soldiers," offered Toma, a dangerous sixteen-year-old.

"We should be so lucky." It was Lorne who dared such an opinion, and everyone looked at him. The quiet teenager did not back down. "Who would mourn him?" He turned to Donas. "Would you? He paid my father a scrap of money for me and told him his son would become a worthy soldier. Sure, he gave my family one less mouth to feed, but they don't know the shame he's brought them!"

"Bold words from such a timid little devil," Donas answered him. "You'll be bowing to him again as soon as he comes riding up."

"No. I don't choose to be here to find out what's delayed him." Lorne stood and started walking for the horses.

"Leaving's not the smartest thing to do," Lucas told him. "Look what happened to Tahn."

"That's the point," the young man answered. "He's one of us. We have nothing against him, no reason to want him destroyed. We're just slaves. And the Dorn is the smart one. He's still alive, after all. I think leaving's the only option. Hunt me if you want to. I don't care anymore."

He went to the horses and took the reins of his own.

Toma stared at him and suddenly smiled at his boldness. "You're right," he declared. "What will the old man do with

205

a lot of us missing? Let him search! We can overpower him if we have to. By now we know how he thinks. I'm coming with you."

"I'm going to find my family," Lorne told him. "Maybe I can find decent work to help them, if they'll have me."

"Joram, right?"

"Yes."

"There's got to be women in that town."

Lorne gave him a hard look but said nothing.

"Anybody else man enough to be your own man?" Toma challenged the others.

"You're crazy," Lucas told them.

But Donas suddenly laughed. "No we're not! *We're* his strength! He relies on us to keep each other in line. We've all expected the rest of us to do what he says. But if we go our own ways, he's got nothing." He laughed again. "I'm going to Tamask. There's a barmaid there who'd be tickled to see me again."

"Even if all of you go, he's still got Dothe and Mattius. And the three we left at Valhal," Lucas warned. It seemed foolish, but he felt he must try to hold them together. It was the only life he knew.

"They'll be awfully busy dealing with the bunch of us and Tahn too," Donas maintained. "I'll take my chances."

"Does your pledge of service mean nothing?" Lucas asked, knowing it was too late to stop them.

"Are you kidding?" Toma scoffed. "You think your life means anything to him? Why should we care about our word?"

"It wouldn't take him long to hire more men," one of the others said. "Maybe we should wait till we know what happened."

Lucas faced Toma and Donas. "He'll be here soon enough or send one of the others with new orders. We should stay and do what the master says. You make trouble if you do otherwise."

"You're cowards!" Toma yelled. "Be his slaves if you want! But if you tell him where we're headed, I'll kill you myself."

He mounted. Lorne was already riding away from them in silence, and Donas and eight of the others were soon on their horses as well.

A man called Kent looked over the line of men who hadn't moved. "We'll be our own from this day on," he said. "Let us respect each other's choices because we've been brothers. We will not turn and fight you. You will not give chase and fight us. Let the man die who doesn't abide in that."

They rode off, leaving Lucas and the others standing and staring after them. *Now what?* Lucas wondered. *Samis charged me to gather the men. He could ride in any minute, and here I stand with some of them gone. Toma said we were cowards. But I am the brave one, staying here to face him this way.*

The men around him were silent. He knew that none of them really loved the master, but many had enjoyed at least part of their tempestuous lifestyle, riding about for secret schemes and exhilarating fights, inspiring dread and awe. He shook his head. Things were changing, and he couldn't be sorry. But he wondered if the future might not be even worse.

It was evening before a rider finally neared them. Some of the young men watched from a hill. They had no trouble recognizing Samis's big coal-black stallion, the envy of many a horse lover among them.

"It's Leviathan, all right," one of the warriors said. "But the rider doesn't ride like Samis."

"He's hurt, you idiot!" chided another.

Lucas looked at them and then at the approaching figure. Could it be possible that Samis had taken the poor end of a fight? But if it were so, how had he gotten out alive? Lucas scrambled down the slope and hurried to meet the master.

Samis seemed slumped in the saddle. He must have been

wounded. Lucas took hold of Leviathan's bridle and led him among the other horses.

Samis was studying him oddly. "Which one are you?"

Lucas turned and stared at him. Which one? Something was very wrong if he could not tell who stood before him. "Sir! What happened? Where are you hurt?" There was no blood on him anywhere, but he had a deathly gray pallor so unlike his usually robust complexion.

He knew the other young men were gathering behind him and, strangely, he wished they wouldn't. It didn't seem right to have a strong man's weakness suddenly on display.

"Lucas!" Samis spit out. "Help me down!"

He jumped to help him, glad to be recognized. Maybe he'd been in a shadow or something. "Where are you hurt?" he asked again.

"Sore from the fall, that's all," Samis grumbled, the words coming slowly. "Bring me a drink!"

All the men were staring at him as Lucas brought him to the side of an old stone building and helped him sit on a log. He leaned back weakly and eyed the men.

"Did you fight the baron?" one of the warriors asked.

Lucas could see the restlessness in their faces, the lack of pity, and especially, the lack of fear.

"I killed the snake!" Samis boomed. "Got paid well for it too. His own blood. Long live the scheming baron. Hah!"

The words made little sense to them. Who would pay him? Long live the baron? The one he said he'd killed? Samis had never looked old like this before. What was he talking about? Even his voice was strange, as though forced with great effort.

"What happened, sir?" Lucas asked as he held the water steady for him.

"Lionell," Samis said and coughed.

"Lionell Trent?" Lucas asked. "He hurt you?"

Samis narrowed his eyes and swore under his breath. "He paid me to disgrace his father. He'll say it was suicide."

An amazing turn of events. His words were understandable now. But it was no explanation for the shape he was in. He had started sweating suddenly, though he sat still and the evening bore the crisp cool of autumn.

"Are you ill?" one of the men asked bluntly.

"I'm fine!" he roared, though he should have known they wouldn't believe him. "Let me get some sleep!"

"Get his bedroll," Lucas commanded.

The other men just looked at him for a moment. Finally one of them went to Leviathan for the pair of blankets Samis carried.

"Let me get you inside," Lucas was saying. "It could rain again."

He started to pull him up, but Samis shoved his arm away. He stood and walked on his own, but he was limping. Lucas followed him inside and watched him select a spot in the abandoned shell of a great stone house.

"How far did you fall?" he asked. "Where?"

"From the horse."

Lucas knew the men outside had heard, and he would have expected Samis to consider that before he spoke. To fall from a familiar mount was worse in their eyes than losing a fight. No matter how strong Samis showed himself to be tomorrow, his status would never be the same. He'd be just a man. Powerful, perhaps. But subject to defeat, just like anyone else.

Lucas waited until Samis slept and then went outside again. All the men were gathered under the trees. "Something's wrong with him," one of them was saying.

"He fell," Lucas said. "He's hurt."

"He fell off his horse!" A big man named Burle laughed. "He's finally become an old man."

"He killed the baron," Lucas reminded him.

"He couldn't now! We could easily best him. He didn't even notice that some of us are gone. I say we kill him and be done with it. We can draw straws for the horse and what's on it."

"No." Lucas faced all of them. "Samis may deserve death. I know it as well as you do. But could you feel right about slaughtering an old man while he sleeps?"

"I could," Burle maintained. "Why not? He would do it, wouldn't he?"

"That's not the point. He's weakened right now. If you want to be free of his hold, you don't have to kill him for that."

"But what if he recovers quickly?" fifteen-year-old Marcus asked. "If we don't kill him, he may be the same as before. I don't want to miss this chance."

Lucas well understood his desperate expression. Marcus had been a captured street boy like himself and some of the others. Who could blame him for wanting to be free? He sighed. "Don't miss your opportunity, then. Leave now. You have a good chance he'll not find all of you. And we'll be bound by Kent's words. Agreed?"

Marcus looked at him as though he longed for some more tangible assurance.

"I'm going to take him back to Valhal," Lucas continued. "I'll stay at his side. The rest of you should do what you need to. But you're not going to kill him, and you're not going to take the horse."

"Why not?" Burle demanded.

Lucas met his eyes, knowing he would not hear any plea for the master's sake. "If you would start a new life," he said, "you might as well begin it clean."

Marcus stepped forward and extended his hand. "I'll agree."

Lucas shook his hand and smiled. "You'll be a good man one day," he told him. "Go and find a place where you can forget what you've learned."

"I think you're a fool," Burle told Lucas sharply. "Bet-

210

ter not to forget. The sword can serve us well, away from Samis's yoke."

Lucas ignored him. "How many of you are leaving?"

"What will you tell him of us?" asked a short young man.

"Nothing," Lucas promised them. "Hide or leave the country, I don't care. He'll be sore a few days. It will give you time to get where you're going."

Marcus and one other young man were already starting on their way.

"You *would* be the only one to stay with him," Burle taunted Lucas. "We know what you're like, waiting on Samis hand and foot. You're like a wench, trying to be the old man's favorite."

"If that's what he wants," one of the other men said, "I say he deserves it."

Burle laughed. "Hear that, Lucas? You can follow the old man around and lick his wounds for him if you want. But we'll be free of him. There are plenty of good horses out there for the taking, and anything else we could want. We'll not be bound by anyone's orders. You stay and be the dog that follows the master. You deserve him, Lucas. Who else would feed you?"

"Just take your horse and go," Lucas told him, more wearied than angered by his words.

"You can be sure I will." Burle laughed again. "Come ahead, men! We can be a band to be feared without Samis over us. Let him and Lucas get a taste of each other alone! Which would be worse? Knowing you have only one pathetic servant left, or being the wretched beast?"

Lucas was not surprised by Burle's taunting. He'd grown used to it over years of bad feeling between them. He just shook his head and stood watching the men saddle and leave. Some went off alone or in pairs. But most followed Burle, who would be looking for goods to plunder everywhere he went.

He turned back to the old stone house where the master slept. But he stayed outside, silent and alone. Maybe the men could conceive of nothing more than becoming bandits. That would be better in their eyes than where they'd been. Samis was a heartless beast who cared for no one, not even those loyal to him.

Why do I stay, Lucas wondered, *when all the others have the sense to get out while they can?* He sighed. The dog following the master. Wretched indeed.

PART TWO

ISSUES
OF
HEART

21

Tahn leaned against cushions in the little room, listening to the noises of people entering the church. It was the Sabbath, and Father Anolle was proceeding with morning worship as usual. It sounded like a huge crowd, as though all the town had come out to see the Triletts.

Netta suddenly appeared in the doorway with a smile and in a beautiful dress a friend had brought. She looked so splendid that he turned his eyes away quickly, ashamed to be admiring her.

"Are you sure you don't want us to move you to the sanctuary, Mr. Dorn? You might enjoy the service."

He sighed. That was an alarming thought, to say the least. How would the crowd react? "No, Lady. Not with so many people. Take the boys, if you're sure it's safe. Might be good for them."

"I'm sure it's safe. Even if an enemy came in, we're surrounded by friends and in God's house."

He was staring out the one window to the west. "We should be leaving soon."

"I'm sure the other little ones are fine."

"We need to get them," he insisted. "I need to know for sure."

"Tomorrow then. We can go. Vari and I."

Tahn looked at her with surprise. "You? And bring them here?"

"Yes. You're not strong enough."

"With a wagon I can make it," he determined. "We can get

215

to the cave all right. These are . . . your people. We shouldn't be staying."

"Don't make that decision yet. Not until you speak of it again with my father, please."

"We can't hide in this church forever. The cave is sound and harder to find."

She smiled. "Perhaps things have changed. I need to join Father before the service begins, but we'll be in when it's over. He has something to tell you. I will have one of the boys stay with you in case you need anything."

He watched her turn and go out with a swish of her full velvety skirt. Then he took a deep breath and shook his head. *Such a woman. God, why have you made her so fine? I need to leave here. No question about it.* He looked out the window again and asked the Lord's help for the coming days. In the sanctuary, music was beginning.

"Sir?" It was Stuva, shyly standing in the doorway. "May I stay with you?"

"Come ahead. Sit down."

"The lady told me you shouldn't be alone. I was glad. I don't like so many people in one room."

"I don't blame you. But I think they're here to worship. They should be harmless."

Stuva sat beside him and started fiddling with the corner of a blanket. "Can I talk?"

"Indeed. Don't be afraid of me, all right?"

The boy smiled. "I'm not. Not like I used to be."

Tahn leaned his head back. He couldn't recall ever seeing Stuva smile before. Things had truly changed.

"I miss Duncan, sir," Stuva told him. "And I think they must be awful worried."

"I know. We'll go back soon. Tomorrow."

"Can you ride?"

"I'll manage."

"Will we ever see the lady anymore?"

"I couldn't say. Maybe when we know things are safe, you could visit her. She'll probably miss you."

"I like her lessons."

Tahn nodded. "She's a good woman. I thank God she's got family again."

"What did God do to you?" Stuva's eyes were full of the question, but it seemed to embarrass him and he lowered his head.

Tahn looked at him for a moment, thinking how to answer. "You mean I seem different?"

"Yeah. I know you was bad hurt, but there's more than that. You're not angry no more."

"Stuva, God took away an awful burden. Do you know what that means?"

"I'm not sure."

"If I was angry, it was because no matter what I did, there was no way out. I didn't think God would have me, Stuva, not ever, because of the things I'd done. A life full of blood, then some painful death, and then the fires of hell. That's all I ever saw."

"You're really for sure he's real, then? I mean, I try, but I still don't know sometimes."

"I'm sure. You will be too. He'll show you, like he did me. He loves us. I can't say why, but he does. He'll give us better things than we've known. I know it, even when I worry. And we've got heaven when we die, Stuva, where nothing hurts anymore."

"All of us?"

"I trust it will be so. The lady taught you to pray, didn't she?"

"Yes, sir, but it's hard. I can't see him. And I'm not sure why he'd want me anyhow."

He smiled. "You sound like me. I'm not sure either. But I'm glad he does. Maybe we're not used to the idea of being cared for. That'll change for you, though."

"Our father didn't want us."

217

"It was his loss. A man ought to be proud to have you."

The boy was looking at him so strangely. "Are *you* proud of us?"

"Indeed."

"Are you going to stay with us, then, and not just leave us sometime?"

It was a hard question. He couldn't imagine leaving them now, but it was still just as unimaginable that they would really want him. "Stuva, you won't always need me."

"Yes, we will! You've been good to us."

"Not good enough to keep you from fearing me."

"It's different now. None of us are scared of you. Even when things are all safe, we want to stay with you and the lady both."

That struck him deep, and it hurt. "You can't have both, Stuva. Lady Trilett belongs here with her family. We can't just claim her."

"She said she loved us, sir. She can't just forget us, can she?"

"She won't. But that's not the same as living where you live."

"They're rich, aren't they?"

"They were. I expect they will be again, once they don't need to be hiding."

"You'll miss her, won't you, sir?"

He didn't quite know a safe way to answer that. "We'll be busy," he finally said. "Stuva, I need some water."

"Yes, sir." The boy jumped up for the pitcher and cup the priest had left on a table by the door. "You hurt a lot, don't you?"

"Not like I was."

"I thought we'd lost you, sir."

"God gave me my life again. I pray he helps me use it well."

Tahn could hear little of the worship service, but he knew it was over when the sounds changed to a low chatter of voices. Father Anolle was the first to come to him. He stood in the doorway for a moment and then stepped forward, extending his hand.

"Mr. Dorn? Permit me to pray a blessing for you."

A blessing? Tahn was not completely sure what the priest meant. "Sir, I—"

"God knows your heart, son," Anolle said. "And I believe he would have you know more of him."

I don't understand you, Lord, Tahn was thinking. *I don't understand you at all, but I thank you for your love and your good people.*

Just as the priest was finishing his prayer, Jarel Trilett came in with Vari, Doogan, and Tam.

"I guess a lot of people love God," Doogan said. "And a lot of people love you and the lady's family too."

Tahn assumed he was talking to the priest. He watched the elderly man in his long robes straighten himself and turn toward the doorway. How could Anolle possibly accept him the way he did? This holy man could put him at ease more than any of the Triletts, more than anyone in his life ever had, except perhaps Vari, whom he counted his best friend.

"Benn will be coming soon, Mr. Dorn," Anolle said. "Jarel, help me bring some of the food. We can eat together what our friends have shared."

"Church was strange," Tam said as soon as the priest was gone.

"It was okay, though," Vari added. "I think the lady will be safe here. Those people won't let anything happen to her."

"The Triletts truly have friends," Tahn told him.

Benn entered in time to hear it. "We are not the only ones. The people are asking about you."

That made Tahn uneasy. He didn't like their whereabouts being so widely known.

"Father Anolle told you to trust," Benn said. "It is sound advice." He sat down beside Tahn as Netta came in behind him. It was very clear she'd been crying.

"Come here, little girl," her father said, and Netta sat on the floor beside him in her fine dress and put her head on his shoulder.

Tahn leaned forward, gripped by her tears. "What's wrong?"

Benn put his arm around his daughter. "She is missing my brother, my sister, the rest of our family," he said. "Their presence was sorely missed in our gathering this day."

Tahn could not help watching her. What must it be like to have had a loving family surrounding you all of your days? And suddenly many, he didn't know how many, were ripped away. *Dear Lady,* he thought. *It's a pain I don't understand.*

"I'm sorry I couldn't do better for them," he told her sadly. "Forgive me."

She looked up at him and burst into tears again. "You did what you could, Mr. Dorn! It's not your fault."

Benn hugged her, his own eyes brimming with tears. "We shall see them again. We take peace in that." He kissed Netta's hair and then looked up at Tahn. "Our friends have brought us news, sir. I should not wait to tell you that Baron Trent is dead. They say he took his own life. Apparently, he did not know how to save face for his deeds, God rest him."

Netta's father had bowed his head, and Tahn was stunned more by him than the baron. "How can you speak so kindly of him? God rest him?"

"He was not my friend. I have not always felt so kindly. But we do better not to speak our feelings sometimes."

"It was him that died? There's no mistake?"

"No mistake, Mr. Dorn. I know he doesn't seem the sort. I wondered myself, but it is true. His son found the body yesterday."

"Lionell."

"Yes. Do you know them?"

"The deeds of the father. Not the son."

"He is baron now. And perhaps it is a mercy. He cannot

share his father's war on us without it costing him dearly among the other nobles. He is intelligent enough to know that. It will not be easy for him to restore the Trent honor after what has been done. I don't think he will be willing to risk confrontation."

"Then are they safe, Tahn?" Vari asked.

"The baron may be gone. But there is still Samis."

"You said the baron financed him. Perhaps with his source of income gone, he will leave us all alone," Benn suggested.

"He may leave *you* alone," Tahn told him. "But his quarrel with me is not for money. It would be better for all of you if I were not with you."

Netta shook her head. "You can't go anywhere. Not while you're weak. Especially not alone."

"She's right," Benn said. "And we want to help you. From what I understand, it is time you had the support of friends."

The words scared him, but he wasn't sure why. Friends? It didn't seem wise. The more people really know you, the more chance some of them could get hurt. "Please, sir—"

Father Anolle and Jarel returned at that moment, arms laden with dishes. Tahn was glad for the interruption.

"Is anyone hungry?" Jarel asked. "We have a feast here."

It did seem a generous supply. Bread and honey, roast beef, plums, and pie.

Doogan couldn't keep his fingers away from the honey. "This is a lot of food."

The priest smiled. "There's more we couldn't carry."

"Gifts," Benn explained. "From our friends today."

"You have kind friends." Tahn saw that Netta was still looking at him, and he lowered his eyes.

"They wish to be *your* friends," her father told him. "Many of these gifts are for you."

"For me?" He looked up at him in shock, and his stomach knotted. "Why?"

221

"An effort to make amends, I think, toward the man they wronged."

Tahn was speechless for a moment. Amends? A strange tension filled him. Despite the pain he was in, he almost wanted to run. He shook his head. "No. They thought I killed you! They didn't wrong me to be grieving you so." He could only think of the sea of faces and their angry shouts. His hands started shaking. He couldn't blame the crowd, but he wanted no part of them seeking him out, no matter what their reason.

Benn leaned forward and took his arm. "We all wronged you, including myself, to judge you without pure evidence."

Tahn was still shaking his head. He tried to get up, but the movement hurt so badly. Somehow he had to get out, away from all of this.

But suddenly Vari was at his side. "Tahn! How long since you had good beef? We might as well eat it, don't you think?" He put his arm around him, and Tahn breathed a sigh.

Vari, you always know how to cut through whatever possesses me. God bless you! He looked down at the food. "They just didn't know. It isn't right—"

"They are basically good people, sir," Benn said. "It would be a blessing to them if you would accept their gifts and their apology."

Tahn lowered his head. "Maybe we should eat, then."

"There's always a first in your life, friend," Vari told him. "Even for apologies. Feels good, doesn't it? Knowing they're not waiting with rocks outside?"

"May it bring healing to you," Netta said softly.

Tahn looked at her and knew she wasn't speaking only of Onath and the physical pain. Somehow she understood Alastair and his fear of crowds, good or bad.

Father Anolle was watching him. "You will permit me to bless the food?"

Tahn could only nod.

When the prayer was finished, the little boys ate hungrily.

But Benn first prepared a plate for Tahn. "With an enemy gone and friends around us alert and asking to help, we are far safer. I am hoping with God's help to make a home for us again soon. We own other property. The springhouse might be suitable, when the time is right."

Doogan looked at him in surprise. "You have a house just for spring?"

"No, child," Netta explained. "It's built next to a spring. It was my grandmother's once. Her place to get away, she called it. But it stands empty now."

"I hope your friends will keep their watch for you there," Tahn told them. "Though I pray it is a new day and you will prosper again."

"They will help us when we are ready," Benn said. "There's no question of that. But I want you to consider coming with us. And I mean all the children."

All four boys looked at him in amazement, but Tahn shook his head. "I won't consider it. Not if we're still hunted."

Benn's face seemed to tense, and his eyes were sad and stormy. "Netta told me about the cave and your efforts. Forgive me for saying this, but you're scarcely more than a youth yourself. You've done the best you could, but you can't continue like that."

Tahn steeled himself against persuasion. "Better than death for any of us, or any of you."

Father Anolle gave a deep sigh. "It is one man—the root of the threat that remains?"

Vari nodded. "Samis, sir."

"God answers prayer, children. We have already prayed for your safety."

Tahn bowed his head. "May the Lord grant me your faith."

"It will come in time," the priest told him. "As you decide for it, again and again."

Tahn understood that. And he remembered the confidence

he'd had in the face of Samis's ranting, that no harm would come to the lady or the children. It was true. He could decide to believe it. The God who'd spared him from hanging and from a pot of boiling water could continue to perform such miracles. For the little ones, surely he would.

"Son," Anolle continued, "you will need the help of your new friends to care for the children, at least until you are strong. I am confident it is God's way and that he will protect you."

Stuva gazed at Netta in wonderment. "Does that mean after we go get the others we'll be coming back to stay with you?"

She looked at Tahn. "Will you let us bring them to you and care for them?"

"I can manage the trip."

"Not yet, son," said Anolle. "Not if you would heed what the healer had to say."

"Would you rather wait and bring them later?" Benn asked.

"No. I don't like not knowing about them."

"Then let *us* go and get them," Netta said. "Vari and I can do it."

Benn looked at her with some concern, and Tahn shook his head. "There is no way I would have you do this. Nothing should take you from your father's side again."

Vari crossed his arms impatiently. "Tahn, it's no big job. I can handle it without either of you."

Tahn pulled himself forward to sit straight. "Not alone. We don't know where the warriors might be. I'll come and—"

"No." Jarel finally spoke. "I'll go with him. I can take Tobas and the Clareys. It shouldn't take long."

Benn nodded. "He speaks of capable friends, Mr. Dorn. I think it is a good plan."

But it was not an easy thing for Tahn to consider. Should he trust men he barely knew? Could he actually allow the Triletts to do as they proposed? He felt that it had all gotten out of his hands, and he didn't like it. But something the priest had said stuck with him. God's way. Trust. "As you say," he finally answered. "You'll lead them, Vari."

"Can I go?" Stuva asked.

Tahn considered how Duncan might feel if he didn't. "Yes. But Doogan, Tam, you stay with me."

Father Anolle smiled. "Your lives have forever changed. It is time for the blessings of God to be upon you."

The next morning was sunny and warmer than it had been in days. Netta stepped outside, looking for Jarel. He, Vari, and Stuva were ready with the Wittley's wagon and three strong men. Netta gave her cousin a hug. "Why are you going with them?" she asked him. "Such a venture seems unlike you."

He smiled. "They touched you so much. Maybe I'll learn why."

"You will, Jarel. They'll have your heart."

"There's a Scripture verse about that you would do well to remember." He looked past her to where Father Anolle and Amos Lowe stood in the church door supporting Tahn between them.

Netta turned to see them and beamed. "It's the first he's been up."

"Keep your heart with all diligence," Jarel said with a frown. "That's the Scripture. Meditate on it for a while."

Netta stared at him in surprise and pulled him away from the others. "What is wrong with you?"

"I think of your future, cousin. You can be grateful, yes. And help the children. But don't think too much of him. He's like a caged animal. You should have seen the way he jumped when Amos returned this morning. He could still hurt someone."

Netta shook her head. "No. Amos must have touched him without warning. Was he asleep?"

"It seemed so, yes, but—"

"Jarel, he can't help it! He's been hunted all his life by threats of some kind. But he's so much better now. I would trust him with our lives. He needs our prayers, and time. Weren't you jumpy in hiding? Can you imagine living with that danger every day?"

Jarel turned toward the wagon. "I'd best be going."

"Blessed are the merciful, Jarel."

He sighed. "I love you as a sister, Netta. I thank God for using this man to keep you alive. But his method was not exactly kind, and I don't want to see you hurt now."

"Let Father and our Lord take care of me, will you?"

He started to walk away and then turned back to her. "I'm sorry I caused you so much grief when we were little."

She waved her hand dismissively. "You were a child. They do childish things. Keep that in mind as you travel with these."

Vari jumped to the wagon. "We'll be back tomorrow if we can, Tahn," he was saying. "They'll be glad to see you."

"Don't push them too fast. Give the Wittleys my thanks."

Vari nodded. "Don't worry about us. God's hands are big enough."

With the healer's help, Tahn lowered himself to sit on the church steps. How life had changed, just as the priest said.

Stuva put his arm around him. "I'm going to tell them the good part of what happened to you. I'm going to tell them the Dorn loves us with Jesus now!"

Tahn tousled Stuva's hair. "You do that. I would not have them fear me anymore."

As he said it, Jarel was walking past to his horse and looked up at him soberly. *He's the only one*, Tahn thought. *The only one that doesn't have more confidence in me than I deserve.*

22

Lucas rode northward at his master's side. Samis held himself in the saddle stiffly. He seemed a little better but was seething angry that the other men had left.

As they traveled, Lucas was seeing signs that at least some of the men had gone ahead of them to Valhal. What the men would do when they reached the stronghold he didn't know, or how they'd react to Samis's arrival. But still, he pushed on. Samis had taken him from a life of hunger. The master hadn't been kind, not by a stretch of the word, but something constrained him to stay anyhow.

No one met them at the gate. No one was in the front courtyard. Lucas left Samis sitting in his chamber and went to look around. The reserve horses were gone, and virtually everything of value. The three men that had been left to keep watch had disappeared too. Probably they were afraid to face Samis after the other men came to rob the place. And it was probably Burle and his friends. It would be like him to take what he could.

He walked back gloomily to give Samis the report and found him standing in the sparring room.

"There's no one here, is there?" the older man asked.

"No, sir."

"Why would the guards leave?" he raged.

"Some of the other men have been here. They have taken all the stores, and they've been in your treasury room."

"Curse them! Why would they do this to me?"

Lucas sighed. How could he not understand the thoughts he inspired?

"What about you?" Samis demanded. He leaned back against the wall. "What are you waiting for? To put a knife in me? You think you'll gain their fear? Is that what you're about? Or do you want the horse, or this place, for yourself? Tell me, Lucas, and we'll fight it out now!"

He shook his head. "I'll not fight you."

"You're a coward! You're waiting till my back is turned."

"No, sir. I'll give you my back. Call for me if you need something. We have plenty of water but supplies for maybe two days." He turned around and walked slowly back out to the courtyard.

Samis sunk to the floor. All of this he'd seen coming when Tahn had betrayed him. Everything but that strange spell in the forest and this accursed blurred vision. Somehow he'd managed to keep from the men how poorly he was seeing. But one turncoat leads to another, and they were just waiting for an excuse. The Triletts' God might be against him. But never mind any of it!

"I'll not be stopped!" he shouted at the ceiling.

I'll find the men who stole from me, he thought. *I'll kill every one of them! But first I'll kill Tahn Dorn. All of this is his fault.*

He pulled himself up and limped to his bed in the adjacent chamber. Then he dropped to the cushions with a grunt and lay staring at the wall.

To think that all these men could walk out on him, after what he'd given them. He had made them soldiers and taught them the skills they needed to survive and prosper with the sword. Many he'd taken from the desperation of the streets, and he'd always made sure they had food. That alone should have mattered to them. Without him they would be nothing but street rats, beggars, and thieves! Yet not one of them thanked him.

And Tahn! Of all of them, he should have been most

grateful. He'd brought the boy here when no one else would help him with his burns. Samis churned it about in his mind. He'd even paid for a healer's help when he should have put the cursed child out of his misery.

He rolled onto his back and sighed. *I made of Tahn such a good killer,* he thought on. *But he is flawed. I tried to groom the bitterness in him, to use the hate I knew must be there, but he would not hold on to it for very long. Toward anyone but me.*

"Die, ungrateful traitor!" Samis shouted and then moaned. *I will make him fight me. And I will use his weaknesses to kill him!*

But not yet. He would rest first. It was good to give them a few days to let their guard down.

It was evening. Vari was on horseback now, just ahead of the wagon driven by Tobas and Stuva. Jarel rode at the wagon's side, and the other two men followed along closely. They were only a few miles from Merinth.

Jarel cleared his throat and turned to Stuva. "Was your master hard on you boys?"

Stuva answered, sounding reluctant. "You mean Samis, sir? I never owned him my master, though he would have had it so."

Vari knew that wasn't what Jarel had meant, and he glanced back at them. Jarel was looking at Stuva in surprise. "No. I meant Mr. Dorn."

"The Dorn is our teacher," Stuva answered him. "We don't call him our master. He don't favor the term."

"But he made you fear him?"

"We did at first. I don't guess he made us to, though. Sometimes you just do, without thinking much on it, you know?"

"I understand," Jarel told him.

"I'm proud to have him," Stuva continued. "He could have left us at Valhal easy, but he came back to get us out."

"I've heard the story. But I wonder—if he helped you, why did you fear him, even at first? How did he treat you? Did he hit you?"

Vari almost wheeled his horse around when he heard such an accusation against Tahn. But he constrained himself. The question had been for Stuva.

The boy took his time answering. "In lessons, yes," he finally said. "Everybody's got to learn to block. But he never beat us, sir, and he could have done whatever he wanted."

"Please don't take offense, young man," Jarel said. "The longer we have him around us, the more we need to know. If you ever have a problem, you can tell us and expect to get help."

"Thank you, sir," Stuva said rather coolly. "I'll remember that."

"Netta feared him too, didn't she?"

"For a while. But a couple of times she stood up to him better than I would have dared."

"What did he do?" Jarel pressed. "How did he treat her?"

"Seems to me you should be asking her that, sir," Stuva replied.

"Her father and I have discussed it all with her already. I thought it might be helpful to hear other views."

"He never hurt her, sir. And I wouldn't lie about it. I like the lady. More'n I like you."

Tobas the craftsman laughed. "I believe you invited that, Jarel," the big man told him. "How would you feel if I came asking the same questions about your uncle Benn?"

"It's a different situation."

"Not to these young ones it's not. He's the one they've relied on. If you act like you're digging dirt against him, they're liable to shove your face in it."

Vari laughed. He liked Tobas.

"Stuva," Jarel asked somberly, "please accept my apology."

"I do. But if you've got something against the Dorn, you ought to face him with it when we go back. He won't kill you."

They were on the main road to Merinth, surrounded by trees. It had been a quiet journey. But from the wooded hill to their left came a sudden shout. "Vari!"

They all stopped. Vari's heart pounded as he turned in the direction of the familiar voice. But he saw no one. "Get out of the clear," he told the others hastily. "In the trees, hurry!" With his own mount, he retreated with them.

"Vari!" The shout was repeated.

But he wouldn't answer.

"You know the man?" Tobas asked him.

"One of Samis's. But he's not much older than me." He looked out and saw the thin figure now standing in plain sight on the slope.

"Vari!" the youth shouted again. "I'm alone! Please let me talk to you!" He raised both his arms above him. He was not holding weapons.

Vari looked at Jarel Trilett and the men beside him. This could be a trap. Or a genuine plea.

"I'm coming down to you!" the youthful warrior yelled.

Vari knew it was Marcus. And he was a stronger fighter, though Vari was bigger.

"Vari! Don't run off! Tell your men I don't want trouble!" There was a strange desperation in the voice, and Vari made a quick decision.

"Leave your sword on the hill if you want to see me!" he shouted. Then he turned to Tobas. "I have to know what he wants. Unhitch the team so you and Stuva can leave the wagon and get out of here fast if he's not alone."

Still on his horse, Vari left the shelter of the trees and returned to the road.

Marcus came down the hill quickly and stopped at the edge of the trees. "I don't mean you trouble, Vari. I hope

231

you believe me." He lifted his hands again and anxiously looked at the trees behind Vari.

"What are you doing out here? What do you want?"

Marcus took a step closer and lowered his hands. They were shaking. "Does the Dorn give you your measure?" he asked. "I was hoping you'd share."

"I don't use the stuff no more, Marcus. What happened? Why are you alone?" He studied him carefully. It was no ploy. The young man was hurting badly for his opium.

"I was such an idiot. I thought I'd be okay. I didn't think about this when I went off alone."

"You ran from Samis?" Vari was more than surprised. Marcus had obeyed Samis's every word. One whipping had been enough to keep him deathly afraid of the slightest infraction.

"He's sick. A lot of us took the chance, Vari. He hasn't many men left."

Vari dismounted and walked toward the young warrior slowly. "What kind of sick? How many's he got left?"

Marcus was shaking and suddenly sunk to the ground. "I don't know what's wrong with him, but he looks bad. He fell off his horse. And he's lost a lot of the men. I'm not sure how many. When I left, some were still there, but they weren't thinking too good of him." He looked up with fear in his eyes. "I wish you could help me, Vari. I need it bad."

Vari squatted beside him. "God helped me be done with it forever. Will you ask him to help you?"

"I can't just quit! Don't you know somebody? Please!"

Vari glanced behind him where he knew the others were watching.

"How long's it been since you ate?"

"I'm not that kind of hungry, Vari."

"You're a sight, brother." He shook his head. "You're bad, all right. Where's your horse?"

"Tied on the slope."

"Just happened to see us?"

"I followed you. But I can't take it anymore."

"You'll have to, Marcus. Closest tincture's in Merinth, and I'm not sure I can get it in my present company."

"Please, Vari. I'm not your enemy! I took a pledge, even, that we don't fight each other."

"That one's new to me."

"Kent's idea, before he left. Lucas and me, we're bound by it. I'm not sure about the rest. Who's with you?" He was trembling all over now.

Vari sighed. "The Dorn's friends. Wait here." He stood and walked back into the trees toward Tobas.

"He needs help getting to Merinth," he told the craftsman.

"What's the problem?" Tobas asked.

"Who is he?" Jarel questioned. "You said one of Samis's men. He's one of those killers?"

Vari glanced up at him, knowing he wouldn't understand. How could he, considering what he'd lost? But Vari could relate to Marcus so well, he had to try to help. And it seemed best to tell things as they were. "He's in a bad way for a tincture of opium, sirs. He's already hurting and pretty scared it'll get worse. And I don't want to leave him out here alone."

Jarel protested. "How can you trust him?"

"He left Samis. He's on his own, and he's not a threat by himself. I want to take him to town and get him some help."

Tobas nodded. "We've got room in the wagon, Jarel."

"And then what?"

"I'll be honest with you, sir," Vari told him. "I know you're carrying money. I'd be grateful if you'd part with a bit of it for me."

"For opium? For one of the cutthroat mercenaries? Was he one that raided our home?"

"I can't say, sir. I wasn't in a position to know who did

what when that happened. But it wasn't his idea, nor to his liking, I'd wager."

"I'll not be a part of giving him any drug. What would he do once he got it?"

"That's not up to me. I'll be telling him more about God, though."

"What would happen to him without it?" Tobas asked.

"If he doesn't have Jesus's help with it like I did, he'll likely be past himself hurting for a while, sir. He won't care a thing for eating or drinking nor have much mind for his own safety or anything else. If you can't see clear to help him, go ahead on. Stuva knows the way. I'll catch up."

Tobas smiled. "I don't think your Dorn would much appreciate me losing sight of you." He turned to Jarel. "The Bible tells us to help the needy, Jarel."

But the nobleman shook his head. "This is not like feeding the hungry."

"He's that too," Vari pointed out. "Only it's not foremost in his mind, but I'll persuade him to eat."

"Something could befall him if we don't help," Tobas told Jarel. "I'll pay for his needs of my own pocket. Perhaps the good deed may persuade him toward our Savior. Let us pray it for him."

Vari smiled his relief. "Thank you, sir," he told Tobas hurriedly. Then he went running back toward Marcus.

When Vari reached him, the young man struggled to his feet and watched the bushes behind Vari nervously. "What'd they say? I don't want trouble from them, Vari, please! I swear I'll not try nothing!"

"It's okay, Marcus. We'll help. We'll put you in the wagon, and then you tell me where your horse is."

Marcus looked so scared, like a cornered rabbit. Vari grabbed his shoulders. "They won't hurt you," he told him.

"You're not sore for vengeance, are you?" Marcus asked. "Nor the Dorn?"

"We're not out for anybody. You have my word."

One of the Clareys helped Vari get Marcus into the wagon. The boy was exhausted. He seemed to fall into a fitful sleep almost as soon as his head was down. It didn't take long for Vari to retrieve the horse, which he tied to walk behind the wagon. He had also found Marcus's sword.

"I'll keep this for him," he said.

"We should leave it," Jarel told him. "No telling what he'll do with it when he's able."

"He might need it to stay alive," Vari reasoned. "Samis isn't dead, and I don't know what it will mean to have men running loose of their own accord. Some of them'll make good, but some are bound to be trouble and wouldn't mind keeping the younger ones for a following."

"You're saying a scourge is loose on our land." Jarel shook his head in dismay.

"It always was. It's just changed. Can't predict them now. But we ought to thank God Samis hasn't got the same power."

"What happened to him?" Stuva asked.

"I don't know, but I can see a day when we won't be looking over our shoulders. Maybe I'll have a bunch of sons, and we'll put in some field, and then lay on the grass and look up at the sky without a care in this world."

Tobas smiled largely. "Let's go. We can praise God as the wheels turn, boys."

Jarel was watching Marcus tossing and jerking in the wagon. He looked over at Vari as they continued down the road. "Did you say you went through this?"

"Not like that. I said I had Jesus's help." He glanced down at the sword across his lap, remembering the night Tahn had rescued him. "It *was* bad once. I thought I'd die, but the Dorn helped me till I was ready to give it to God. Now I can help Marcus this once. Maybe he'll be ready one day too."

"Are all of Samis's men drugged killers?" Jarel asked with a scowl.

"Yeah. I guess so."

"So does Mr. Dorn use the drug too?"

Vari looked at him in surprise. Why hadn't it occurred to him to wonder about that? "No. He's not had any. And it's been too long since he was caught. We'd have seen sign by now. He must have been through it before we found him." He shook his head. "I wish I could have helped."

"Could he be hiding it?"

Vari stopped in his tracks. "No, sir! He wouldn't hide it from me."

Jarel turned his head, but Vari wasn't finished. "You may never love him like I do, Mr. Trilett, no matter what he's done for you. But you can at least have some respect for him or I'll have you off your horse in a minute!"

The Clareys rode closer, but Tobas waved his hand at them.

"I did not mean any insult," Jarel said.

"Yes, you did! He saved the lady's life, sure as we breathe, and probably her father and you too. And he saved mine, and the little ones. It should matter to you, especially since he follows Jesus now. But you try to make him a vile thing so you can be better than him. I heard what you told the lady. And you're nothing in my eyes till you can see a man for what he is." He kicked at his horse and glanced at Tobas. "Let's get going. I need to be done with this trip."

<hr/>

With Tobas's money, Vari purchased a bottle of tincture from the seller Tahn had told him about. Marcus had woken, and he reached for it greedily.

"Take it easy," Vari cautioned. "You may want to keep your head about you."

Marcus sipped and capped the bottle. "Thank you, Vari. I'd fight a demon from hell for you right now."

"You got your own demons. You need Jesus. He took the tincture out of me, Marcus. Without the struggle. I just didn't need it anymore. He'd do the same for you."

Marcus scoffed. "You always had some of God about you, Vari. Rather die and meet him than kill for the master. But I've given him no cause to care about me."

"He needs no cause. He made us. And he cares, no matter what we do. That's just the way it is. He loves you. I think that's why he had you meet up with us. So you'd know it."

"Hard to believe."

"I know what I'm talking about. I think he *likes* to forgive people, if they'll give him the chance. You don't have to keep on like you are."

"I'll find work or something."

Vari looked over to the rest of his group. "You could come with us. If you understand we're all Christians and you'd have to keep in line with that."

Marcus shook his head. "I'm fearing the Dorn right now. Your word and his aren't the same thing. He knows what I've done, better than you do. I'm going to stay here a while."

"You ought to come to him. He won't hurt you. He won't turn you away, either. You know what he did for me."

"I'm not cut out for that, brother."

Vari sighed. "My friend will give you a little money and some food. Getting work's a good idea. If you have trouble, you know I'll do what I can for you. But this is it for the tincture." He glanced at Jarel for just a moment. "I'd feed you anytime, but I won't get you another bottle. When you're ready to get free of it, you come to me. I'll be with the Dorn and the Triletts, and we'll help you. You'll see how much better things are when you've got God's help."

Marcus was looking at him in wonderment. "Why are you doing this?"

"I know what it's like. And none of us is cut out for this world on our own. Remember what I told you. Talk to God, all right? He knows you're scared. He'll help."

"Thanks, Vari. You're better than I expected. Will you give me my sword back?"

"If you pledge to me you won't use it unless you have to. Don't hire out with it, and don't become a bandit, Marcus. You come to us first."

"I never had no father, Vari. It wouldn't be you if I did."

Vari understood the defiance in his words, but he didn't let it trouble him. "If you want your sword, you'll give me your word."

"Why do you think I'd keep it?"

"Because I helped you. And I'd help you again. And you don't have nobody else you can count on."

For just a moment, Marcus's eyes misted, but he fought it away and stood up. "All right. You got my word. I'll find decent work. I'll figure something out." He opened his bottle and took another sip.

"Stretch it out as long as you can," Vari advised him. "The more you drink, the harder it is when you haven't got it. Go easy. Make it hurt a little every time. Maybe you'll get the will to get rid of it."

Marcus took his hand. "I don't know where you're going with your friends, but I owe you now. You go on. I'll be okay."

"God be with you," Vari told him and placed the sword in his hand.

Marcus sheathed his weapon, took hold of his horse's lead rope, and walked away.

23

Netta sat quietly in a back room of the church with a collection of psalms on her lap. Tahn was stretched out on his blankets. It was good to see him sleeping so peacefully. But she couldn't concentrate on reading with her mind returning to Jarel's words. *"Keep your heart with all diligence."* She looked at Tahn again. *Lord, am I wrong to appreciate him so? I thought he was a monster, but instead I find in him rare bravery and even kindness. But such need. I still find myself longing to help.*

Father Anolle stepped in quietly. "He sleeps, daughter?"

"Yes." She looked up with a grateful sigh, hoping for the chance to speak to the priest.

But Tahn rolled to his side and opened his eyes.

Anolle moved immediately toward him. "I'm glad you have woken. A stranger has come asking for you. He said that he knows you but that you would not recognize his name. He's not armed."

With a groan, Tahn struggled to sit. Still he was so sore, so bruised.

"Is he alone?"

"Yes, son. And I don't believe he's a threat."

"Then I will meet him, sir."

Netta laid the psalms aside and stood.

"No, Lady," Tahn told her. "Stay here, please."

Benn had come in behind Anolle. There was a depth of compassion in his expression. "One of our friends is with the man outside," he said. "He told me his business. I am comfortable to allow him in. Shall I bring him to you?"

239

"No. I'm coming out. I should meet the man before he enters your refuge, sir."

Benn stepped forward and took Tahn's arm. "Let me help you, then."

Together they went out, and Father Anolle followed. Tahn leaned on Benn and a staff the priest had given him. A tall man in common dress stood with one of the villagers in the churchyard, and his large horse grazed behind them. The stranger looked up at them and immediately approached. At the base of the steps, he made a quick bow.

"Tahn Dorn, I thought you were dead. When I heard what happened here, I had to come."

"I don't know you."

"You know my work. My name is Marc Toddin. Your former master hired me to track you."

Tahn looked away. "You did a good job of it, sir."

"Perhaps so. But I owe you an apology. I didn't know the true color of what was going on until they kidnapped the girl."

"I wanted to free her." Tahn bowed his head. "Did they take her with them?"

Toddin smiled. "No, sir. I did."

Tahn looked up at him.

"When you told her to run on and leave you, I took her on my horse in the woods. Two of them chased us a while, but I lost them over time. I took her to her home."

"Sir! With all my heart I thank you!"

Benn looked at the singular relief in Tahn's face, knowing it was for a girl whose name he didn't know. The nobleman bowed his head. There was something very humbling about this Mr. Dorn. Triletts had the reputation, but not such heroics.

"I wish I could have done something for you then," Toddin was saying.

"You did."

240

But Toddin fidgeted a bit. "I went home with my pay. My wife was in need of about half of it, and I figured it her due for my absence. But I brought you the rest. I don't like being part of wrongdoing." He took a bag of coins and set them on the steps at Tahn's feet.

But Tahn protested. "You're worth your hire, Mr. Toddin. You can't be blamed. I can't accept your money."

"I wish you would. It doesn't feel right in my pocket."

Tahn was quiet for a moment. "I can't take a man's pay. If you can't keep it, maybe it can go to a needy soul."

Toddin looked to the priest. "May I put it in your hands to be used where you see it right?"

"Yes, son," Anolle told him. "And God bless you."

"You're certain your wife will not lack for it?" Tahn asked.

"We have enough. I'm certain."

They clasped hands. "I live in Alastair, sir," Toddin said. "If you ever need my assistance."

Tahn nodded. A friend in Alastair. That was beyond mortal arranging. "Thank you, sir."

With another bow, Toddin turned to go.

Tahn watched him. It was a wonder the man would come. It was an equal wonder that he'd gotten up to meet a stranger with so little question. That was almost careless. But it had been right.

Toddin was already halfway down the street. Everything was so quiet now. Tahn looked at the peaceful shops and suddenly saw a man's face appear in the upper window of the building across from them. The face disappeared almost instantly, but not before Tahn recognized it as familiar.

"My lord," he said to Benn, "have you known any of the baron's men to be about?"

"No. And I don't expect any open trouble from them now."

"Have the people reported to you any of the mercenaries?"

"No," Benn answered, following his eyes. "Is there a reason you are asking now?"

"One of them is in the room above the shop there," he said, gesturing with his head.

"Mercenary soldier?"

Tahn nodded.

"Could he be dangerous to us now?"

"Any of them could be. Have I another pie among the gifts?"

"Yes. You have." He looked at him with question.

"Could you call two of your friends, fighting men if there are any, and ask them to take it to the man there watching?"

"You would win an enemy by feeding him?"

"If there have been no others about, he has probably been left alone to his post. He will be hungry by now."

"You have a large mercy, Mr. Dorn."

"I've received mercy. I can afford to extend it. Perhaps he will hesitate at causing us harm."

"And if he doesn't welcome the offering?"

"I think he'll not hurt your men if they are careful. If it were his orders to attack, he'd have done it by now. He's here to watch. So they'll know if I leave."

"You expect he's alone?"

"I hope so. I hope there wasn't another now following Vari. That troubles me."

"No one's been seen. And I assure you this town is watching. There are capable men with your boys, as well."

Tahn nodded. "Tell them to ask him to come and speak with me." He looked up at Father Anolle, who hadn't said a word. He didn't need to. Trust. That's what he'd say. We are all in God's hands.

They had not gotten into the church before a rider came swiftly toward them.

"My lord!" the man called and stopped his mount at the

base of the steps. "Josef tells me there are four men with the insignia of Trent entering the town."

"Thank you," Benn told the man. "Watch them but do not interfere."

"Yes, sir. And if they come here?"

"Let them come. They'll not get this far without drawing attention."

"Yes, sir." The man took his leave of them, and Benn turned back to Tahn, who was leaning on the stair rail with a frown.

"They'd not be in Onath if they weren't coming here," Tahn told him. "You can't trust them, even with the baron dead."

"I know that," Benn assured him. "Let me help you inside."

Lionell Trent's messengers made their way through the quiet streets.

"You're not welcome here!" someone shouted.

Most of the people who saw them watched in silence. But slowly from out of shops and houses, men began to follow the riders on foot. Whatever their business was, they would not be left to it unwitnessed.

"They've got sticks and such," one of the soldiers whispered to his companion, their captain. "You suppose they'll let us leave?"

"We've come in peace," the man replied. "They'll be all right when they see that."

"I hope they see it before we get to the church," the youngest soldier said. "They're liable to kill us if we try to go in."

"Leave that to me," the captain told them. He stopped his horse. "Citizens!" he called out. "Tell me if the honorable Lord Trilett may still be found in your esteemed holy church!"

"Go home!" a man front and center in the crowd told him.

The captain bowed to him. "We cannot, sir, until we deliver a message personally from the young Lionell Trent. He wishes to express his regret for the actions of his departed father. He has sent us in peace. Please, good men! Help us to deliver our letters and we shall go with our gratitude."

The man in the crowd picked out a sturdy teenager from the group. "Run ahead and tell the guards at the church to alert our lord. We'll escort them."

Then the man turned his attention back to the soldiers. "Give us your weapons. Peaceful messengers don't need them. You'll have them back when you leave Onath."

One of the soldiers began to protest, but his captain immediately stopped him. "Of course, sir. They are but a traveling precaution."

When the soldiers had given over their weapons, the group of townsmen surrounded them as they progressed to the churchyard, where more men were waiting. Benn Trilett and Father Anolle came out together.

The captain immediately dismounted and bowed himself to the ground at the base of the steps. His men followed him. "Gracious Lord Trilett," the captain said. "I beg you to receive us in peace. We come with letters from your countryman, Lionell Trent, who continues in mourning for the breach his father caused between your noble houses."

The captain looked up at Bennamin Trilett's face, which at that moment looked as immovable as stone. "We are his humble servants, Lord, and yours," the soldier continued. "Allow us to present his message."

Lord Trilett did not move from his position on the highest step. He did not give them the customary greeting or the courtesy of a more private audience. "Proceed, sir."

The captain removed two rolls from the pouch at his side and took a step forward. But Benn Trilett nodded to one of his guardsmen, who took the papers from the soldier's hands and carried them up the steps to him. The crowd waited in silence as Benn read both messages.

"He has acknowledged the wrongdoing," Benn addressed the people. "He says it was his father's alone, not his. He sends an apology and his sympathy for our loss. He pledges peace and asks for it in return. And he mentions a gift for our rebuilding."

One of the other soldiers pulled a box from a saddlebag. The guard brought it to Benn's hands. It was full of gold coins.

"I do not wish his money," Benn said and closed the box.

"Sir!" the captain exclaimed. "To refuse a gift is an insult."

"You are right. Let us not insult the young baron. I will give this to the church to finance the repairs of the rectory."

The captain frowned.

"Thank you for your labor," Benn told him. "The people will allow you to go in peace."

"Have you no word in return for our lord?"

"Tell him I received his message. I thank him for his expression of sympathy. And he can expect peace."

"You will not put it in writing for our hand, Lord?" the soldier asked with some surprise.

"No. Your mouth will be sufficient. You have no interest in poor relations between your lord and me, I trust."

"None, sir. Of course not."

"Very well. I would be grateful if you return my answer swiftly. Extend my condolences to the Lady Trent in her grief."

"Yes, sir." All four soldiers returned to their horses.

"Cabot," Benn spoke to his guard. "See that they have provisions for their journey."

Benn and Father Anolle watched the soldiers leave with their reclaimed weapons.

"You may have insulted them," Anolle told him, "by refusing to entertain them in the ordinary fashion."

"I have little stomach for custom today," Benn answered. "Let Lionell understand that ordinary relations are not won back so easily. He can take some time at earning that. It will not hurt the Trents nor their soldiers to wear humility for a season."

"You don't believe him innocent then?" Anolle asked at a whisper.

"I know the young nobles of our land. Until the cost became too great, he enjoyed his father's ambition."

When the soldiers were gone, Benn drew the people's attention again. "Publish it about," he told them. "I will hire honest men to be soldiers in my service. I am grateful to you all beyond words. You are my dear friends, but you have families and other labors you must return to."

"Benn!" Anolle exclaimed. "The House of Trilett has never kept soldiers."

Lord Trilett looked up to the darkening sky. "And we have not had the power to prevent the evil of those who have, Father. There's not even a just and organized law in our land anymore! We can do more for our countrymen than pray for them only."

He bowed low to his people and went inside.

The following evening, Netta finally got an opportunity to speak to Father Anolle as they both entered the sanctuary alone.

"Father, I am troubled," she began. "I need to speak to you about Mr. Dorn."

"Yes?"

Netta fidgeted with a dress ruffle. "I—I respect what he's done for us. And I rejoice at his salvation."

The priest looked confused. "Then why are you troubled, daughter?"

She burst out with the words before she could think better

246

of it. "I don't want to think too much of him! It concerns Jarel. He feels I could become too attached. Am I being unwise to care about him?"

"You would be un-Christlike if you did not care."

"But do I care too much, Father? Or inappropriately?"

Anolle smiled. "You'll find your heart."

"Jarel says he could be dangerous. And I had such a fear of him before. But I don't see it now. What do you think? Is he yet dangerous?"

"I have no doubt, daughter, that if you were in peril, he would be dangerous to your assailant."

Netta shook her head. "Not only me. He would help you or anyone else, surely. You don't think he has a special care for me, do you? Vari thinks he does, but Vari's a bit of a dreamer."

"It will take him some time, Netta, to know his heart and accept it. He does not see himself in the light others see him."

"What do you mean?"

"We see the lives he's saved. But he sees himself as a man struggling for a footing in faith, with no special virtues to his credit."

Netta stared at him. "No virtues? He has such strength! To survive, and to reach out—"

Father Anolle smiled.

"Oh!" She shook her head in embarrassment. "You must think Jarel right, how I talk! But I never expected to find good in such a nightmare."

"Peace, child. There is no harm in gratitude nor in admiration."

"But—"

"Love is of God, Netta. You'll have to sort out your own heart and trust what you find there. And that is not Jarel's job to do. Your father would appreciate you sharing your feelings. But he will not be too greatly troubled, I think.

247

He accepts Mr. Dorn as an honorable man with a captive past."

"Father! I expected your caution. Similar to Jarel's, to say the least."

He stood. "I hope I'm no disappointment. But your father taught me something yesterday. Our hearts can convince us of need, and it is more important that we obey than do what our tradition tells us is proper."

Netta looked to the cross at the head of the sanctuary. *Lord, help my heart! Tradition would have me protesting even the priest's words. I should not even think of a man not of noble birth. But wherever the Dorn may go, I shall not be able to forget him!*

Suddenly her thoughts were interrupted by the excited sounds of children. She jumped up. "Father! They're back! They're here!"

She ran out in time to nearly collide with the group of little ones on their way in.

"I *told* you!" Vari yelled with disgust. "Walk in quietly and decently. He might be asleep!"

Netta laughed as Temas and Rane hugged at her.

"We missed you, Lady," Briant said with the decorum of an adult. "How is Teacher faring?"

"He's much improved. He's been expecting you."

Duncan and Stuva came in behind Briant. "We can go back and see him, can't we?"

But Tahn suddenly appeared in the doorway at the back of the sanctuary. "No need."

They all looked up. He walked to them on his own, leaning on the staff first, then the church pews. Netta knew it was difficult for him, but he scarcely showed it.

"I am pleased to see you all healthy," he said. "Even taller, it almost seems."

They just stared at him, unsure what to expect or how to respond.

"I'm not fragile." He smiled. "Temas," he called the little girl and opened his arms to her. "I believe I owe you first."

She burst into a wide smile and raced forward into his hug.

"You didn't hate it?" she asked. "When I hugged you?"

"No, child. I didn't know how to take it. No one had ever—"

He hadn't finished before Duncan, then Doogan, Rane, and the rest crowded in to share the embrace.

Netta stood back with tears in her eyes. Vari walked up and put his arm around her. "They've been praying for all of us to be a family. They want you and the Dorn both to continue as their teachers. They want us all to stay together."

She looked at his youthful eyes and knew that he, like them, would not understand if it could not be so. She thought of the Dorn, but it was not him only that drew her. She could gladly give her heart and her life to these children. They should have the security of a fine home, and she would love to have a part of it. In truth, she wanted their happy dream as much as they did.

Then she looked up to see Jarel standing at the outer door and watching the scene. He turned abruptly and went back outside.

24

Tahn was glad to hear the report Vari brought him of Marcus's words, and he knew he was not the only one. Such news added to the Triletts' growing sense of security. And with the threat of Samis diminishing, the children were beginning to relax and be children.

But Benn was still cautious. He had plenty of men with them two days later when he decided it was time to take everyone to see the springhouse estate on the southern edge of Onath.

Once again, Tobas went with them. He drove a wagon with Tahn seated beside him. Benn was leading them. Vari pranced ahead toward him on a horse.

"He's a good boy," Tobas told Tahn. "But he thinks he's a man already. He did the young warrior a good turn, but I'm not so sure about the farmer's daughter."

Tahn was surprised at his words. "You mean Leah Wittley?"

"Yes. They were kissing when I went to the Wittleys' barn for our horses. And it was not the kiss of children."

Tahn looked up at Vari now riding happily alongside Benn.

"I don't mean to cause him trouble, sir," the craftsman said. "But it concerned me. She's a young thing."

"Thank you for telling me. She's almost his own age, I expect."

"And how old is he?"

"Thirteen."

"Lord above! I would have guessed him at sixteen and thought then he acted too old for himself."

Tahn sighed. "Never had a father's guidance. I'll talk to him."

"I meant him no trouble, now."

"You've not caused it."

They had barely left the homes of Onath when Benn stopped and pointed. As the wagons caught up, he turned and looked at the group with a smile. "There she is!" At the end of a lane stood a beautiful two-story house of white stone with a railed roof garden.

"It's big!" Doogan exclaimed.

But Tahn's heart fell within him. Why hadn't he realized where they were going? He shook his head. "No."

Netta was suddenly beside his wagon, but he couldn't look at her. He could barely speak. "Why didn't you tell me?"

"I told her not to," Benn said immediately. "I wanted you to see how it can be made secure. You said you thought it unwise to leave the safety of such good friends. We are near town here. Our cottage at Fjord is much further out, and smaller."

But Tahn shook his head again, imagining Karll's blood to be staining the roof tiles still. "I can't believe you would want me here."

"I knew it might be hard for you," Benn told him. "But I hope you agree it's sensible. Our horses and men will require the space. We must return to a more normal life, and your children need to experience one. This place has all we need. We can rebuild our primary home, but that takes time."

"How can you stand it, Lady?" Tahn asked, still unable to look at her.

"There is more to this house than the tragedy," she said with tender voice. "Please, Mr. Dorn. It *is* home."

"She's right," Tobas said. "Practical men do what is practical." And without another word from Tahn, he drove the wagon swiftly through the gate and down the pebbled lane.

The rest of the children were soon running about, exploring the spacious courtyard. But Vari waited with Tahn, who sat on the wagon watching them. They looked so happy.

"Let me help you down," Vari offered.

"I need to go back to the church."

"Tahn, they've laid down the past. It'll be all right."

Jarel glanced at them and then at his uncle. "When will Hildy be here?"

"She should be already. Go in and check the kitchen. I asked her to prepare us a meal."

Jarel went in through wide double doors that opened to a grand entryway.

"Do you think we can live like this?" Vari asked in a whisper.

"I know I can't." Tahn looked across the yard to a sudden commotion. Duncan and Tam had scared a group of chickens out of their coop. Just past them, Rane was on his way up a tree.

"I'll be lookout!" the little boy yelled.

They deserve a decent home, Tahn was thinking. *Which is something I can't provide.* He turned and watched Benn's men moving in different directions. Some took the horses to the large stable. Others, presumably, would watch the road.

He looked around him. Benn was right. The place could be carefully secured. Alone in his silence three years ago, he'd had little trouble at his task, at least on the way in. But the lack then had been for watchfulness. That would not be a problem now.

He turned his head and saw Temas pulling Netta toward an apple tree. The lady looked like she belonged here, with her lovely dress and regal manner. But strangely enough, so did the children, who were so immediately comfortable. Netta glanced up at him, and he averted his eyes.

"Come on," Vari urged. "Let them put up the wagon. It won't kill you to stay for a while. They're good people, and they don't hold anything against you. God doesn't either, remember." He took Tahn's arm and helped him to the ground just as a robust woman came charging out of the house with a delighted squeal.

"Benn!" She hugged Lord Trilett with a motherly fondness. "I was thrilled for your message! How we've prayed for you. Thank God you're spared!" She turned her attention quickly. "Netta! Netta, let me look at you! Are you all right, child? Come here!"

She started for the yard, but Netta ran to meet her. "Hildy! A blessing to see you!" Their embrace was a familiar one, and Tahn supposed she must be a trusted servant of years.

"We're so glad to be back!" Hildy was saying. "Ham's gone for feed for the horses, but he'll not be long. I've got you a feast. Come ahead. My, all these children!"

Tahn turned away and seated himself on a bench beside a pillar. He set his staff between his boots and looked outward toward the pond behind the house.

"Netta, dear," Benn said, "take the children with Hildy and let her feed them. Show them the house. We'll be in soon enough."

Vari stood in silence, watching Tahn.

Benn put his hand on the boy's shoulder. "Go with the others, Vari. It will be all right. I'll talk to him."

"Maybe you could keep the little ones," Vari offered. "He and I could stay together and . . . maybe visit."

"I want you all to stay," Benn told him. "I have lost much of my family, and now God has given you all to me. Pray for your friend that he may see that."

"All of us? Not just the little ones?"

"Vari, you and your teacher amaze me. I would be honored to have you both. You inspire me to look past myself."

Vari smiled.

"Go on. I will speak to him alone."

Tahn heard the footsteps behind him and knew it was Benn. He bowed his head. "You have a good home. The children are already happy here."

"You are content that it can be safe?" Benn sat beside him.

"I think so. Once you have men organized to their tasks."

"I would like your help with that. I know you are uncomfortable, but we can forget what is behind us, friend. Whether here or elsewhere, I would like you to stay, not just till you're stronger. I want you all to be a part of my family."

"They are a lot of children to take on, sir. And they know not the way of fine houses."

Benn smiled. "I would be pleased to adopt them all, with your permission. I always wanted a houseful of strong sons. I had one boy, but he died as an infant. I had nephews, but now only Jarel is left. We have plenty to give them, Mr. Dorn. You don't need to worry for their sakes."

Tahn sighed. It made sense. Benn Trilett could provide for them and keep them safe, once he had his standing soldiers. But Tahn could not see himself in the picture. He knew it was the answer to his prayer for the future of the little ones. But it hurt terribly, like he was losing his family. "I will stay long enough to see to their safety," he said slowly. "And then I will grant you your wish, sir. You are right. They should not have to steal for food anymore. They can become good men. And you can help them more than I can."

"I don't think you understand me. I want you to stay as well."

Tahn looked down at his boots and shook his head. *Dear Lady Trilett! There will always be blood between us.* He glanced up at Benn. "I can't live off the kindness of you and your friends," he said, unable yet to voice the rest.

"I need you," Benn told him. "I will have men coming

who are untrained and untried. I would hire you to help me mold them to our needs. We have resources. I can pay you well. You would be protecting my family, and yours."

"It would be robbery to ask you to pay me for that."

"Why, Mr. Dorn?"

"Because I would do it unbidden. It is my heart." His voice broke, and he turned from him. "But you have many men willing, sir. You will not need me, and I don't belong here."

Benn placed a hand gently on his shoulder. "If you will not work for me, allow me to adopt you as I would the children. Let me claim you to my house."

"I am not a child as they are."

"That is not what my daughter tells me. She says you are a brave child who carries far too much pain."

Tahn tensed at the words. He whirled around. "Did she also say I am a man who terrorizes her? She knows it is true!"

Benn nodded, but there was a softness in his eyes. "You did terrorize her once. You hurt her terribly with the death of her Karll. And I am glad to see how deeply you realize that. I couldn't trust you if you didn't."

Tahn took a deep breath. He leaned down for his staff and then stood and took a step.

Benn was immediately at his side. "Let me help you."

"You brought me here unwarned to test my heart."

"No. I brought you unwarned because otherwise you wouldn't have come."

Tahn limped toward the pond, refusing Benn's arm. "I don't belong here, sir. Grant me permission to visit the children. In a few days, I will be much stronger, and I will go."

"You don't hear what I'm saying?"

"She does not need a reminder before her daily."

"God rest your heart, Mr. Dorn. I want you to stay. My

daughter respects you deeply, and she has forgiven you for what happened."

Tahn only bowed his head. *She said that once,* he remembered. *But what of the thoughts I think of her? Surely such thoughts would frighten her. And I am not worthy.*

"You know God has forgiven you?" Benn asked gently.

"Yes, sir." There was eternal peace in that. Tahn looked up at the hazy sky.

"It is time you forgave yourself, then, son." Benn stepped in front of Tahn. "We need you here. I have never had a standing army, but I must protect my family. I want you to train the men I hire to be honorable guards for us. You know you are able. And your family is here. None of the children will want you to go."

"You don't understand." He swallowed hard. He would have to tell it plainly and perhaps become abhorrent in this nobleman's eyes. "I care for your daughter, sir." He took a deep breath. "I should not be here to trouble her with such a thing."

But Bennamin only smiled. "I have no fears in that. She's an intelligent woman. She will know her own heart. And how to manage yours."

Tahn could not have been more shocked. He trembled. "You don't object to my feelings?"

"I couldn't very sensibly, could I? If you did not care for her, I would not have her with me, alive and well."

"But, sir . . . I—"

"I understand what you meant. And I will leave the matter between the two of you and God." He must have noticed Tahn's trembling, because he helped him to a rock to sit down.

"I will never hurt her again," Tahn told him, struggling to speak past the lump in his throat.

"I know that, son."

He looked up at Benn, still unable to believe the nobleman's reaction. "If my heart troubles her, I will leave."

"Or at least we will come to manageable terms. I will build you your own quarters, separate from the house."

"You are sure, sir?"

"I have seen enough of you to be sure. You belong here." He knelt and put his hand on the younger man's shoulder. "The Bible says God puts the solitary in families, Tahn. May he give your heart peace and help you to accept us so."

25

Lucas filled a pitcher from the stream by the millhouse and carried it to Samis's room.

"Sir, I can't put it off any longer. I'm going down to Alastair for provisions."

Samis coughed and sat up in his bed. "Alastair? No, no. We've got to get back to Onath. It's time we settled our business there and then went looking for the rest of the traitors."

Lucas shook his head. "I don't think you're ready. I'm going to Alastair. I'll be back in a few hours."

"I give the orders!" Samis stood up but leaned quickly against the wall. "Whistle for my horse!" he commanded.

"No, sir. You're not well yet. I wish you would let it go and leave Tahn to whatever life he's found." He turned to walk out.

But Samis lunged toward him and grabbed his arm. When Lucas turned around, Samis struck him in the face. "You will not defy me!" he yelled. "As long as you're here, you will obey my orders!"

Lucas pulled away from his grasp. "Or what? Will you kill me, Master? I don't fear it anymore."

Samis's face reddened. "You have always feared me! You are still here because you fear me. And Tahn fears me too. He knows I will come for him. And I will not disappoint him."

Lucas sighed. "You're not as strong as you were, Lord. What would happen if you got to Onath? Tahn would either kill you quickly or walk away in pity and leave you to whatever it is that ails you."

"I know his weaknesses," Samis replied. "I can defeat him. And even if I did not, what better way to die?"

Lucas looked at him in surprise. He had never before heard the master concede the possibility of defeat. *Perhaps it is really over,* he thought. *Perhaps he knows that he will not recover from whatever grips him.* "Sir," he said sadly, "before anything else, we must have the provisions. I am going to Alastair as I said. Rest until I return. We can speak of travel then, if you insist on it."

Samis sat on the edge of his bed and glared at the younger warrior. "I don't need you. You don't think I can manage, but you're wrong about me. I could kill you if I chose to. But you've been loyal. It's the others who've earned death. I will find them. But first the Dorn."

"Whatever you say," Lucas muttered. He left the room as Samis lay down again. Shaking his head, Lucas went out and mounted his horse.

"Come on, Danger. Let's leave him to himself for a while." He spurred the horse and parted Valhal's gate for the path to Alastair.

<hr />

Samis lay on the bed, waiting for nearly an hour, then pulled himself up slowly. Leviathan would be in his usual place. Lucas would know better than to meddle with such normalcy. He must take water, of course. His knives and sword. He dressed quickly and concealed the knives in his clothes. Then he strapped on his sword and looked across the room at the table beside the far wall. Another sword lay there flickering in the light of the oil lamp beside it. It was Tahn's. And the time had come to return it to him.

He walked slowly across the room. The dizziness was not so bad as it had been, and the blurred vision was gone. He lifted the sword.

Tahn! So often I saw it in you. You would have loved to

259

fight me if only you'd had the proper chance. Now I will give it to you, and you will not be able to turn it down.

With Tahn's sword in hand he pushed himself through the chamber door to find Leviathan. Tahn would fight him. Surely there was no Name he could now call upon to erase the anger in his heart. Samis smiled, remembering Tahn at seventeen shouting his hatred through locked doors.

"Some day I'll kill you!" he had raged. "I'll kill you!" His failure with Netta Trilett had caused his punishment then, just as it had again. The boy should have learned his lesson.

He will have to fight, Samis reasoned. *And if I cannot best him, I shall win over him another way. He can't escape what I've made of him. He must kill me or die. And because he thinks he's changed, my blood will haunt him forever.*

Hours later, Lucas returned with his bags full. He had taken some of the money Samis had gotten from the young Trent. Why steal if it wasn't necessary?

But it was a troubling trip. Burle and several men with him were drinking and creating havoc in the town. They bragged openly about stealing from the mercenary on the hill. Valhal was probably not safe anymore, and Burle and his friends had so quickly become a rogue gang of hoodlums and thieves.

He entered Valhal's gates quietly, struck as he had been before by the barrenness of the place. There was not a sound. *Perhaps he is sleeping again,* Lucas thought. But Samis's room was empty. His weapons, and Tahn's, were gone.

Lucas ran to Leviathan's stable. The animal was gone too. Lucas spat into the hay. He had hoped to put off this trip, but the master had a bullheaded determination. He would be on his way to Onath already. And there was only one thing to be done now, like it or not.

Lucas went back to his horse and swung himself into the saddle. He'd have to follow. Burle and his men might kill Samis if they found him alone, and he still couldn't let that happen.

He hurried through Valhal's gate again, perhaps for the final time. It made no sense to him why he continued to help the man who had hurt so many. Or why he did not want Samis murdered. If ever a man deserved it! He shook his head. It was a mission that compelled him without reason, but he would obey it until the man was finally dead and he was free of him forever.

26

All of the boys except Vari gathered with Temas in Netta's room on their second night. The little girl was afraid to have a room alone, so Netta had set the child's bed beside hers. Now both beds were full of children, and Netta sat at her dressing-table chair.

"Teacher walks better, but he still hasn't given us a lesson in all the time we've been here," Doogan pointed out.

"Everything is new," she told them. "It will take some time to get lessons sorted out."

"Do you think we won't need lessons anymore?" Rane asked.

"You will still need lessons. But they will be different, I expect."

"Why did he go to the guardhouse again to sleep?" Doogan pressed. "Why won't he come inside?"

Netta tried to smile reassuringly. "It's only been two days. Give it time."

"Do you think he's avoiding us?" Stuva asked.

"No, dear," Netta answered honestly. "I think he's avoiding me."

Temas looked bewildered. "Why would he do that?"

Netta shook her head. "I can't explain that very well tonight."

"But he hasn't even seen our rooms!" Duncan exclaimed. "I want him to see my real bed and everything!"

All of the children were nodding their heads in agreement, and Netta smiled. "Why don't you go and tell him?"

"You mean right now?" Doogan questioned.

"Sure. You all know the way to the guardhouse."

"Come with us!" Temas urged.

"No. This is for you to do."

For a moment they just looked at her.

"He won't bite," Briant put in shyly.

Giggles swept over them, and they were soon on their feet and running down the curved oak staircase to the main floor.

———

At the ruckus, Hildy dashed from the kitchen in time to see them pouring out the front door. "How good it is to have this place rocked with children!" she laughed. "It is almost like Netta and her so many cousins all over again."

She turned and saw Jarel standing at the top of the stairs.

"One little girl and a crowd of noisy boys, Hildy? Is it just the same?"

"Oh, Jarel." She stepped toward him. "I'm so sorry. You must miss them terribly."

"I just don't understand why of the five boys I'm the one who lives."

"God has kept you for his purpose, Jarel. I thank God you're here! Please, join me as I finish up for the night. It's not good for you to stay to yourself."

"You love to mother everyone, don't you?"

"The lot of you need it! Even Benn. And what better calling in life. Now come on, and I'll spice you a bit of cider."

———

Vari sat cross-legged on the floor of the guardhouse entry. Tahn, also on the floor, leaned his back against the wall near him. He knew he needed to discuss Leah, but with the Wittleys in Merinth, there seemed no hurry for that. Vari had other things on his mind anyway.

"You're better about this place now?" the youth asked.

"Better. You deserve more than a cave."

"You do too, Tahn. But Jarel doesn't like us very much."

"He has nothing against you. He liked his family the way it was before, and he can't be blamed for that."

Vari suddenly had a sober expression. "After we met Marcus, Jarel asked me about you and the tincture. Was it hard, Tahn, getting clean?"

Tahn stared at him a moment and suddenly felt like shouting. He'd forgotten all about it!

"Vari, God spared me! Like he spared you! To such an extent, I didn't even notice. I didn't feel a thing!"

Suddenly there was a clamor of children outside. They came bursting through the doors in the dim light and nearly tripped over Vari.

Tahn pulled himself to his feet. "What is it? Is something wrong?"

"Nothing's wrong, Teacher," Rane told him. "We came to get you!"

"Come see our rooms!" Temas begged and reached her little arms around his waist.

"You ran over here in such excitement for that?" Tahn questioned.

"Yes, sir," Stuva told him with reserve. "You haven't been in the house. You don't even know what it's like."

He looked at their faces with genuine surprise. "It's that important to you?"

"We don't want you to leave us," Temas said, clinging to him still.

"It's because of you we're here," Tam added. "But you don't even eat with us now."

It was true. But it was certainly not their fault. They'd been served in the dining room, which was more than Tahn could take. He sighed. "All right," he told them. "I'll come. You show me your rooms."

But it was a struggle. The house was a painful reminder. Anywhere else, even on these grounds, it was not so bad. But the house had been the abode of newlyweds. He could imagine Lady Netta as haunted as he was by the memory.

264

But Temas and Rane had his hands, and he walked with them across the wide lawn.

"Why don't you stay with us tonight?" Tam asked. "You can have my bed."

"Or you can have our whole room," Doogan offered. "We can go in with Duncan and Stuva if you want to be alone."

Tahn smiled at their fond efforts toward him. Without even trying, somehow he'd gained their love. Another gift from God, the eternal, merciful Giver.

He stopped and hugged the nearest of them. *You've given me love for them, Lord. How warm and wonderful it feels. Like being alive from the dead.*

Tahn did stay in Doogan and Tam's room that night, but he was far from alone. All of the children, even Vari and Temas, crowded in, and they camped out together on the floor, their new pillows all in a line. Well after midnight, Netta looked in and found them. Quietly, she sneaked in and covered the little ones with blankets. Then she sneaked out again with a smile.

It was a busy day that followed. Tahn knew that Benn Trilett was receiving messengers from the other noblemen of the land. Sympathy for their loss. Gifts for rebuilding. It was as though the rest of the nobility followed Lionell Trent's lead and gauged the Trilett heart toward them by Benn's response. In addition to that, the people of Onath had spread the word far and wide that Benn was gathering soldiers. Men came every few hours to offer themselves for the post.

But different guests drew attention in the late afternoon. Kert Wittley and three of his children came rumbling up the lane with their farm wagon laden with goods.

As Netta greeted them with appreciation, Tahn stepped

forward from beside the pond, followed closely by a dripping wet Vari, who'd been swimming.

Kert Wittley gave Tahn a quick bow. "Mr. Dorn, my friends I told you about—they and I—we felt badly that we couldn't come in answer to the children's plea for help. We owe you an apology, sir. We did nothing but pray for you. I hope you forgive us for not taking to arms. A hard thing it is, fearing for the wives and little ones."

Tahn shook his head. "You cared for my children. You owe me no apology. I thank you for the prayers. They did me more good than your arms could have. I owe you my gratitude."

Kert gestured to his wagon. "Well, anyway, we all—and that's about six families—we wanted to do something for you. Thinking of all of you in a cave! Lord o' mercy! We've been poor but not that bad off. And Lady Trilett, how she lost her home and such! We can't do so fine, you know, but we all sent what we could just to make the way a little easier."

"Sir!" Netta exclaimed. "We have enough!"

"I couldn't have rested, ma'am, thinking about the children! I couldn't have rested not knowing for sure. Your men, they said they'd be fine, but you know how men are sometimes. Wouldn't admit to a need if it bit 'em in the face! And besides, I felt guilty not coming to help the young man when God knows I could have."

Netta was looking at the wagon with its array of garden produce, butchered meats, and woven wool. "Sir—"

Wittley looked at Tahn. "I'd be obliged if you'd take 'em. Take a load off my conscience, if you know what I mean."

Tahn nodded to Netta. He knew what it meant to the man, though the rural families, facing winter, surely had a greater need for such goods than the Triletts did.

Netta looked from Tahn to the farmer for a moment. "All right," she finally said. "I'll go get Ham to help us unload."

Tahn would have suggested Vari's assistance, but when he turned toward the boy, he stopped cold. Vari only had eyes for Leah. And Leah made no secret of how she felt.

"So good to see you again," she told Vari with a smile far from timid. "I have prayed every day for your safety."

Netta was back quickly with the faithful servant couple. "Stay to dinner with us and rest the night," she told the Wittleys. "And allow us to return a gift to your families as a thanks for your generosity."

Kert gave her a quick smile. "I welcome your hospitality, ma'am." He went around the back with Ham and the wagon to unload.

"You can come with me," Hildy told the three Wittley youths. "Be a couple of hours before dinner, but anyone that's been traveling has need of a good bite to tide them over till then."

Vari moved to go with them, but Tahn caught his arm. Now that the girl was right in front of their faces, he'd have to say something while he had the chance.

"Vari," he began when the others were gone. "About Leah—"

"Pretty, isn't she?"

Tahn cleared his throat.

At that moment, a guard came running to them from the gate at the head of the lane. "Mr. Dorn! Sir!"

Tahn tensed immediately, knowing there was worry in the man's tone. "What is it?"

"We've caught one of the mercenary men come looking the place over. He says he's alone, but I don't believe him. Armed to the teeth, he is! And I knew his face myself as one that was with the baron's men searching the countryside after Benn Trilett's head."

"What have you done with him?"

"Nothing without your word or Lord Trilett's, sir. And he asks for you by name. But then they all know you, don't they?"

"I'll speak to him."

"You want me to come?" Vari asked. "It might be Marcus."

"No," Tahn said immediately. "Stay with the children. It might not be Marcus."

As quickly as he could manage, Tahn went with the guard to the trees by the gate. Three of the Triletts' men were gathered around a young blond man slumped beside a tree. His hands were tied behind his back. As Tahn approached, one of the guards struck the prisoner in the face.

"Stop," Tahn told them. "Let me talk to him."

The young warrior looked up at him. It was Lorne.

"He fought us," one of the guards explained. "As soon as we got close."

"He's not fighting you now," Tahn said, but he could see that Lorne still wore the garb of the dark angels and had been armed as the guard had said.

"He was on the wall, sir. He might have been in the yard in seconds. You warned us about such attacks."

"I wanted to see if you were here, Tahn," the young prisoner said. "That's all!"

"He fought us off like a demon!" a guard argued. "He had more in mind than a look!"

"I was afraid!" Lorne admitted. "I knew I wouldn't have a chance if you weren't here. I thought they'd kill me, that's why I fought! I never should have come."

Tahn lowered to one knee. "Why did you?"

"I—I need decent work, so I can send money to my family. They sorely need it. I thought to offer myself to the Triletts' service. But it was a foolish chance to take—an enemy coming back. I shouldn't have done it!" He stopped and swallowed hard. The desperation was clear in his eyes. "Please let me go, Tahn! I swear I'll not trouble you. It wasn't to my liking what they did to you and what we did to these people. You know I didn't want it! Now I can hardly—"

268

One of the local guards cut in, glaring. "You admit you took part in the Trilett murders?"

Lorne bowed his head. Tahn knew the truth. He could do nothing but own to it. "Yes, sir."

The guard scowled. "Onath may yet have its hanging." He grasped the prisoner's arm roughly. "Shall I call for Lord Trilett for this judgment?"

"No!" Lorne cried. "Tahn, please! My mother's got a hope in me. They need my help. You weren't the right one to hang, I know that, but—"

He stopped when he saw Tahn's eyes, so dark and distant.

"Oh, God." There was a tremor in the young man's voice. "No." He hung his head again. He seemed to sink before them, broken.

Tahn was remembering when he'd first met Lorne and how hurt the boy had looked when he knew he was being sold by his own father. Yet he'd gone back to his family now. And for them, he'd come to him for help.

"Lorne." Tahn lifted the young man's face and saw the anguish in his eyes. He moved his hand to his shoulder. "There'll be no more talk of hanging." He turned to the guard. "Let him go."

"What? Sir! The Lord Trilett—"

"I'll explain this to him myself. Let him go. He came looking for a job, and that is exactly what he'll get from us."

The guard frowned. "How can you trust him?"

"I know him," Tahn answered without hesitation. Lorne was telling the truth, he knew it beyond doubt.

"But he is a killer! We must consult Lord—"

Tahn looked at him with impatience. "Then go tell him now! I'll bring the young man to him as soon as he is ready for us."

As one guard hurried away from them, Tahn pulled the knife from his belt and cut the prisoner's bonds himself.

269

Lorne looked at him as though he could scarcely believe it. He rubbed his right wrist.

"You're all right?" Tahn asked him.

"Yes, thank you."

Tahn looked around them at the guards who still watched. "They have a zeal for Benn Trilett," he explained. "It is a thing to admire."

"I understand."

"You're on your own?"

"Yes."

"What do you know of Samis now?"

"Nothing. And I hope it stays that way. I rode off when we were waiting at Jura. About ten of us left him, I think."

Tahn smiled. "Our second report of such good news. Marcus said he is sick."

"I hope it's true. He chases me in my dreams."

"You're not alone in that. Do you have a large family?"

"Yes. Six sisters and four brothers. Most of them younger. My grandmother and a widowed aunt are with them too."

"They have nothing?"

"Almost nothing. My father can't work. He can't even walk anymore. The others try, but—"

Tahn held up his hand. "I'll ask an advance in pay for you. If Lord Trilett agrees, you can take it to your family to ease their burden. Stay with them a while, and come back when you are ready."

"But I haven't earned—"

"You've earned a bit of peace, don't you think?"

"No. I haven't earned it."

"Then count it a gift from God. I have a wagonload for them, no matter what Benn says about the pay. You'll take it in the morning, won't you?"

Lorne closed his eyes against the moistness in them. "Are you sure he'll let me go?"

"I trust it, Lorne. He understands now what sort of army

we were. It can't erase the hurt, but he won't be able to hate you."

Bennamin met with Tahn and Lorne, and the three of them went walking around the pond. In the kitchen of the house, Jarel looked out at them from the window. "Another rough sort," he said with a sigh.

Hildy looked up from her cutting board and saw his displeasure. "The world is full of those, Jarel. God help them."

"Does my uncle have to entertain them so close to the house? He trusts Mr. Dorn too much, being alone with them like that! Something could happen too fast for a response."

"He trusts him, all right. But he trusts God more."

Jarel bowed his head. "God does not always prevent tragedy, Hildy. We know that plenty well."

The cook looked at him, searching for whatever words he might need.

Jarel left the window and picked up a large spoon. "Mind if I stir the pot?"

"No. You know I've always loved your tinkering. Go on. Spice it up if you want."

"I don't understand it, you know, Hildy—how he could accept Dorn so easily. I heard what he's been through, but the man was a murderer. I know people can change. I know God has reached him in some capacity. But I'm just not sure this is wise."

Hildy nodded with compassion. "You remember the prodigal son, don't you?"

"Yes, Hildy. But that's different. He really was a son. He wasn't going into a home where he'd never been a part."

"Jarel, what do you think of that little boy, the youngest one, Duncan?"

"I don't know, Hildy."

271

"Would you put him out because he wasn't born a Trilett?"

"No. I guess I couldn't. Not in his circumstances."

"Benn has seen another side of life, Jarel. You may not be able to stop him from reaching his hand to every poor child or rough sort he finds."

"There are too many of them. More than we realized."

"It's time you realized. I used to tell Benn about the poor. He gave to his church, he said. Well and good that was—the church has been a blessing to Onath. It is a truly blessed town to have the Trilett money and favor. But go elsewhere and you see the drunken men, and the children in the streets. It's time you looked further."

He stared at her a moment in silence. "Then that is the good in our tragedy? That he extends his hand to the hopeless?"

She saw the pain in his eyes and immediately moved to hug him. "You may never understand the reason for it, Jarel. But we find good where we can."

"Like Tahn Dorn? What do you think of him?"

"I've hardly spoken to him. He'll barely let me feed him!"

"I know you, Hildy. You don't have to do either to have an opinion."

"Right now he seems a lot like you."

Jarel bristled. "What do you mean by that?"

"I mean that you're both trying to sort through what's happened and find the best way to face the future."

"Oh, Hildy. Everyone does that."

"Not with the same intensity, Jarel. Or self-doubt."

"Self-doubt? That makes no sense. Dorn's already started telling the guards what to do. He acts like he knows better than we do what's best for us. As for me—" He stopped.

Hildy looked at him kindly. "Yes?"

"I'm the same as I ever was, except that I don't have my . . . mother or father or—" He stopped again, his eyes filling with tears. He turned abruptly away.

"You've got to cry, Jarel," Hildy told him. "Don't try to stop it."

"What good will it do?"

"Benn told me, dear one, about the nights you spent under that church, staring at the wall and not shedding a tear. I know you're a man. And a Trilett, at that. But your two brothers, Jarel. Your aunt Ariole and both her boys. Your parents. Gone in a night! Jarel, dear, I've seen Benn and Netta cry, both of them, more than once. But you're the one who worries me." She left her work and went to put her arm around him again. He let himself be drawn into her hug, still fighting off the tears.

"Hildy, I know the children had nothing. I can see that they need us. But I don't like having so many in our house. It's no substitute. It just makes it harder."

"They aren't here to replace our loved ones," she said softly. "No one could do that."

He seemed pale, and he was quiet a long time before he could speak again in a voice low and earnest. "I miss Mother the most, Hildy. Can you imagine, for all we fought?" He leaned his head into her shoulder.

She felt the shudder run through him and held him tightly. Finally, Jarel was crying.

Out the window behind him, the blond stranger was on his knees by the pond. His weeping was obvious, even at the distance. Bennamin appeared to be praying with him. And Mr. Dorn stood leaning on his staff against the reddening sky with his head bowed low.

Tahn stayed the night with Lorne under the stars while the Triletts entertained the Wittleys in the house. Lorne was ready to go at the first hint of light, and Tahn helped him with the wagon goods so he would not have to disturb Ham or any of the others. They parted with an embrace and a prayer at the front gate, and then Tahn turned to the house. It suddenly occurred to him that he should find Vari before everyone was stirring. He didn't expect the Wittleys to stay long, but it would be best to use this chance to speak to Vari anyway.

He walked back, his eyes on the big old house, when he thought he saw the flutter of a skirt and long flowing hair disappear over the hill beyond the east porch. It could only be Leah. Netta's hair was lighter with a hint of red. Leah might be going to the stable, but why?

The wounds of his leg and back still prevented him from moving very quickly. He went for the stable, and as he got close, he began to hear giggling. He knew what he'd find before he went in, but he went in anyway, without warning.

Vari and Leah were in the hay. She jumped to her feet at the sight of him.

"Good morning, Miss," Tahn told her. "Your father'll be rising early. You'd best be in the house when he stirs."

"Yes, sir." She gave Vari a quick glance and then ran out the door.

Vari lay in the hay, completely unfrazzled. "Good morning," he told Tahn.

"Vari, you're too young for that."

"I'm older than my years. You should know that."

"About you, perhaps. But not your friend. She's a child. You should not fail to treat her like one."

"She'd be insulted. I can't do that."

"You will, or you will not see her again."

"Tahn!" He sat up, clearly surprised by his friend's reaction.

"You have the honor of Christ and the House of Trilett to uphold. Let the girl become a woman first and then court her with the proper restraint."

Vari's look was close to defiant. "You're being my father?"

"You need one, don't you think?"

"Benn Trilett may be the one, for all his talk of adoption."

"Go ask him about my words, then."

Vari smiled and shook his head. "That's all right. I'll hear it from you. I can see her, though?"

"If you can control yourself. Keep her brother along."

Vari laughed. "Didn't you ever have a girl affect you like that?"

"No."

Vari looked at him in surprise. "Really?"

"When was I ever around girls who were not afraid of me?" Tahn answered with some impatience. "I never left Valhal without an order. And I can't imagine that anyone would have wanted my company."

"That was then," Vari maintained. "But the lady's not afraid of you. She doesn't seem to mind your company, either."

Tahn suddenly paled in front of him.

Vari grinned. "You really do love her, don't you?"

He shook his head, but he knew he couldn't deny it. "Don't tell her, Vari, please."

"I think I already did."

"No." His heart pounded.

"It's okay," Vari told him. "I don't think it's bothering her any."

"When did you tell her?" Tahn asked, wondering how he could possibly face her now. This kind of thing would not be fair to her. He would surely have to leave—for her comfort's sake. "Was it today, Vari? Yesterday?"

"No." Vari couldn't help but smile to see the Dorn so nervous over this subject. "It was back at the cave when you disappeared."

His brow furrowed in disbelief. "And she agreed to come after me anyway?"

"Yeah," Vari nodded. "She did."

"She loves all of you," Tahn decided. "There's no doubt. She would have to help you."

"She couldn't let a good man die, Tahn. She's a good lady, and she's an adult too. You'll court her, won't you?"

275

"No, Vari." His sadness was obvious.

"Tahn! Why not?"

"You and Leah are both innocent children with a love for the land. The lady and I have nothing in common."

"Yes, you do! You've got us. And Jesus."

He started to turn away. "Just remember what I told you about Leah. Or if you question me, ask her father's opinion."

"Tahn, you can't ignore your heart!"

"That's enough of that. Get back to the house and get your brothers around. See that your rooms are straightened before breakfast. We don't want to make work for anyone."

"Are you going to come in?"

Tahn just shook his head and walked away.

Benn and Netta exchanged glances when everyone was seated for breakfast and it was clear that Tahn wasn't coming.

"Perhaps he's still with the young man he helped to draw toward God last night," Benn suggested.

"His friend's already gone, Uncle," Jarel told him. "I saw them. Mr. Dorn seems to prefer to be a loner."

"I hope he's not offended at me," Kert Wittley said. "I meant to come and repair any such thing between us."

"I'm sure it isn't that," Netta explained. "He's only eaten with us once, and that was in the courtyard. We were just hoping, because Father invited him again last night."

"He's a loner," Jarel repeated.

"Well, if we don't see him before we leave, Vari, son, do tell him how well his horse is mending. Meant to say something about that yesterday. We'll bring you the animal, lest you plan to visit."

"I'll visit," Vari volunteered.

Leah looked at him across the table with a gleaming smile, but Vari ducked his head.

Netta looked at the food and sighed. "I'll take him a tray as soon as we finish."

"No," Jarel told her. "Let me."

Netta and Benn both looked at him with some surprise, but Benn nodded.

"He's by the pond again," Vari told them. He was looking at Netta. She was nearly as pale as Tahn had been.

27

Tahn was in the woods, sitting with his back to a tree, when Jarel found him.

"It's a quiet place," Jarel interjected. "Good for praying."

"Yes, it is," Tahn said without looking up.

"I brought you some breakfast."

"Not very hungry right now, but thank you."

Jarel laughed. "When are you ever hungry? It's no wonder you're small."

Tahn sighed. "Some habits are hard to change, I guess."

"Not eating is a habit? You do come from a strange world." He set the tray down beside the tree. "Still, that's a better habit than some to keep, I'm sure."

Tahn looked up at him. "I'll return the tray myself in a while."

It was a dismissal of sorts, but Jarel ignored it. "If you're not going to eat anyway, would you want to go riding?"

Tahn studied him a moment. Such an invitation was the last thing he expected from Jarel just then.

The young Trilett smiled. "You don't trust me? Come on! What would I do? Try to lose you someplace?"

"I don't think so."

"You think you could take the saddle very well yet?"

"I would manage."

"Well, then, do you want to come with me to the stable or shall I bring you a fine beast where you sit?"

"You don't want to ride with me. What do you really want?"

278

Jarel laughed again. "I used to ride with my brothers, my cousins, my friends. Why wouldn't I ride with you? Just last night Hildy asked me why I haven't been riding. Maybe I don't want to go alone."

"The boys would be delighted for the opportunity. Stuva or Doogan, in particular."

"I'm not looking for the company of boys right now."

Tahn knew there was more to his message. He pulled himself to his feet. "All right, sir. But I should greet the Wittleys again before they go."

"I'll meet you in the stable then."

After Tahn had seen the Wittleys off with their wagon newly laden with gifts, he and Jarel rode into the wooded hills beyond the springhouse estate. Jarel stayed ahead until they were more than a mile out. Then he turned his horse and stopped. "Did you ever know your parents?"

Tahn walked his animal closer. "I don't know. One man I remember slightly, but I don't know if he was kin."

"Was he good to you?"

"I don't remember. I only know it was upsetting to see him hanged."

"He must have meant something to you, then."

"Evidently."

"I lost my parents to your mercenary brothers," Jarel said.

"I know, sir."

"Let's go." Jarel stirred his horse to a run again, and Tahn followed.

It was a long while before Jarel stopped, and the surroundings were beginning to be unfamiliar to Tahn. "Are you sure you should be so far out from your soldiers, sir?" he asked. "And only one man with you?"

"I'm not the important one," Jarel answered. "Benn is."

"I don't think he would agree with that."

"Of course he would. He knows he's important."

279

Jarel was dismounting, and Tahn did not even try to answer.

"Need some help, Mr. Dorn?"

Tahn swung his leg over and lowered himself to the ground. Oh, Lord, how it hurt! This was harder than he'd thought.

"You'd better sit a minute."

Tahn didn't hesitate. He lowered himself carefully against a tree.

"You'll manage?" Jarel asked.

"Yes, sir. Just a moment, and I'll be ready to get you back home."

"I'm not ready. Not yet. Who would trouble us? The baron's men are bound to peace, and the mercenaries seem to be your friends."

Tahn looked up at him, knowing there was a challenge in his words. "We can't put confidence in either of those ideas."

"Can I put confidence in the Dorn's protection, then? My uncle seems to think so."

Tahn sighed. "I appreciate his trust. But I am not as able right now as I hope to be."

"And what do you hope for, when you're fit and able? You've made a lot of progress. You get around pretty well now."

"Jarel, why did you ask me here?"

"Answer my question, will you? What do you hope for?"

Tahn bowed his head. He was not welcome in Jarel's eyes. Netta's cousin would like nothing better than to have him gone.

"Well?" the young Trilett pressed.

"I don't know, sir. I haven't thought much further than safety for the children and for your family."

"You expect me to believe that's all that occupies your

mind? What interest do you have in my safety? I think not! I think your interest is my cousin."

"We need to go." Tahn started to get up, but Jarel shoved him down again.

"Don't do this, sir," Tahn pleaded.

"What? Don't get you angry? Is that what you mean? What would you do?"

Tahn turned his head away in silence.

"You might be able to kill me, even at less than full strength, but you'd never explain going back without me, would you? There are no tracks of any horses but ours, no black-garbed warriors dropping from trees to explain it away!"

Once again, Tahn tried to get up, but Jarel pushed him harder, into the tree. To the young Trilett's surprise, Tahn let it happen again and sunk meekly to the ground.

"I don't want an enemy," Tahn said. "If you can't stomach my presence, I will go."

"And leave Netta?"

"Yes, sir." He turned his face away, afraid of what Jarel might be able to see there.

"Fair enough. You've got a good horse. I'll give you money right now. Will you ride on out, once you've rested?"

Tahn took a deep breath. "No, sir. I would see you back to your home and not have you ride the distance alone. I have that obligation to your uncle. And I would think it cruel not to tell the children good-bye."

Jarel stared at him, not sure how to respond. "You would go, then, once your details are taken care of?"

For the third time, Tahn pulled himself to his feet. "I think that I am ready now."

Jarel didn't push him down this time, and Tahn took a step toward the horses, knowing that these wouldn't respond to his whistle.

"I don't think I'm finished," Jarel said, his voice much quieter.

"It seems that I am." Tahn took another limping step.

"Mr. Dorn, do you think my uncle would let me run you off like this?"

"You're family. You'll come to terms."

"Sit down."

Tahn turned and looked at him. "I will not create a war for myself or anyone else. If my presence does that, I'll have to leave." He turned away again quickly.

But Jarel had seen his eyes. "Do you love her?"

He couldn't answer. He took another step, but felt Jarel's hand suddenly on his shoulder.

"I asked you a question."

But he pulled away and took the horse's reins.

"That's what you've wanted all along, isn't it?" Jarel demanded. "A chance at fair Netta, to do what you will?" He slapped his hand down again hard on Tahn's shoulder.

It was a reflex. Before he could think about it, Tahn had whirled around and knocked the young Trilett to the ground. Both horses skittered away from them.

Jarel looked up and shook his head. "I knew I could get a reaction. Now that I'm down, what do you do?"

Tahn turned away again. He wanted to leave this difficult soul in the woods and flee, but he knew he couldn't do things that way. "I'll not fight you, sir."

"That's not how it appeared just now."

"I'm sorry." He slowly sunk again to the base of a tree. "I'll wait here until you're ready to go back. Forgive me."

Jarel sat up and looked at him. Was he serious? He had not expected such meekness. But he knew he'd struck a nerve, a deep one. Could he dare probe it further? "Mr. Dorn, do you know what you are to me?"

"I can only imagine."

"A vexation! My uncle respects your opinion in our situation more than mine. And my only surviving cousin would rather have your company, though you entertain men who have slaughtered all my immediate family!"

"I am sorry. Please believe me. I am sorry."

"I wasn't sure today if you'd kill me or if I'd manage to kill you. But you're not being very cooperative."

"I won't hurt you, but you shouldn't put yourself in danger. You're important to a lot of people, whether you know it or not."

Jarel stood. "Karll was my friend, Mr. Dorn. Perhaps the best friend I ever had outside of the family that's gone now too."

He couldn't answer. Jarel's pain justified his words, his actions.

"I've wanted to hate you, Mr. Dorn," Jarel admitted. "But Benn and Netta do not make it easy. Nor do you. Why couldn't you just be the foul murderer they claimed? We could have let Onath hang you and be done with it. But you aren't blamed for Karll, because now you've saved lives. You aren't blamed for kidnapping Netta because you helped her. You've a collection of orphans to win the heart of the hardest skeptic. What am I to do with you? It's no wonder Onath is willing to hail you now!"

"No, sir," Tahn spoke quietly. "I'm no hero. I don't want your town's attention. And if I am not to be blamed, it is because of Christ's mercy. I've got no other claim. I well know the darkness that was in me."

Jarel turned toward him. "What kind of darkness? Can you answer me honestly?"

Tahn sighed. If there were any practical way out of this, he'd have taken it. "I will try," he said. "But God is my Savior. I'm not what I was."

Jarel smiled. "That's exactly what I'm trying to determine here. But you may have had that figured."

A test. Tahn thought of Samis, dagger in hand. "*Let me test your mettle, boy!*" he'd taunted. Tahn shook the thought from his mind and turned his eyes to Jarel.

"If you're a deceiver, you're the devil at it," Jarel said. "Uncle Benn trusts you with his life, and Netta's willing to cry tears over your miserable past. I know it's true to a point,

283

but I need to know how deep it goes, Mr. Dorn. Could we count on you if you had to stand against your mercenary friends? Or if you never had a hope of Netta's interest? Please answer me."

"I've already stood against them, and I expected nothing but your cousin's fear when I kidnapped her."

"What about now?"

"Were she as bold as you, perhaps I would face *her* hard questions."

Jarel laughed again. "What do you think she'd ask you?"

Tahn swallowed. "If I had it to do again, would I yet spill Karll's blood?"

"Would you?"

"Not as a Christian. But if I was still living under Samis's power, I don't know. I had no strength to resist in those days."

"So did you like it, the killing?"

"No. Can we not return now?"

"You said you'd wait till I was ready. I know you're uncomfortable. That's exactly what I wanted."

"If you had found the villain you were looking for, sir, you would have put yourself at risk. Don't take such chances."

"Are you telling me not to be alone with you?"

"A man's instinct is a good guide," Tahn told him. "I'm saying that if you don't trust a man, no matter who he is, don't be alone with him."

"A little late for that now."

"But easily remedied."

"It's you not wishing to be alone with me."

"I'll not deny it."

Jarel smiled. "You may think me a pig, but Netta is worth that to me."

Tahn nodded.

"You didn't answer me before," the young Trilett pressed. "You think you love her, do you?"

284

"I would not wish to put her in such a spot."

"But what about you? Are you in that spot already? Has she got a fire lit in you like the farmer's daughter has in Vari?"

Tahn looked up at him in surprise.

"Oh, I see a lot. They can't very well hide it, can they? You, on the other hand, are trying very hard. You can't move too quickly, of course, without ruffling Benn a bit."

"Jarel, sir—" Tahn took a deep breath. "Your uncle was not distressed by my feelings. But I'll never pursue them. Neither God nor the lady would have it from me. I wouldn't trouble her for all of this world, but I can't deny that I care for her. I think you know that already."

"How do you expect to live with it and not act on it?" Jarel questioned.

Tahn sighed. "Elsewhere, truly." He lowered his head to his hands. "I'll go, sir. You are right that I should."

Jarel looked down at the figure before him. *He's like a whipped pup*, he thought. *A wounded child, just like Netta said. What might I have been like in his place?*

"Mr. Dorn," he said with quiet voice. "Perhaps we've been gone long enough. Can I help you up?"

"I'll manage, sir." He stood carefully and turned toward the horses again.

Jarel put out his hand toward Tahn's shoulder but drew it back, uncertain. The man's limp was worse. He seemed to be carrying an extra weight. "Can I help you mount?"

"No, sir—"

"You'll manage."

"Yes."

"But how will *I* manage if you leave us now?"

Tahn stopped. Whatever could he mean by that?

"Everyone in the house is rather fond of you," Jarel said. "I don't need them angry at me. Things are hard enough already."

285

"Maybe you don't realize how they value you, sir. I can't imagine any anger there."

Jarel met his eyes. "You've leveled with us completely, haven't you?"

"As best I know how." He knew Jarel's stricken look but not the reason for it. "Sir, I'm sorry about Karll. I'm sorry about your family. I can't change the past, and I can't excuse what I did. But I hope you'll forgive me one day."

He turned back toward the horses, but Jarel quickly stepped in front of him. "I came out here wanting to condemn you, Dorn. I should ask *you* to forgive *me*."

He shook his head. "There's no need. You have a right—"

"No. Not to throw my hurt onto you. You've got plenty of your own. You've been beaten enough, haven't you?"

Tahn couldn't meet his eyes this time. Something inside him was shaking.

"This may be the safest home you've ever had." Jarel sighed. "You shouldn't leave it on my word."

But Tahn only reached for the horse's bridle and with great effort pulled himself into the saddle.

28

Lucas rode through the foothills north of Joram. A farm boy had said he'd seen an old man riding a black stallion not long before. Samis might be close.

He kept considering what to do when he found him. He remembered the master steadying himself against the wall in his chamber. Something was wrong with him, more than soreness from a fall. How long would he be able to pursue his vengeful ideas? They should shelter somewhere and get a healer before things got worse. But going back to Valhal might not be wise. Burle still claimed more than a dozen of Samis's men and posed a threat in that area. It was hard to say where Samis would be safest. Any of the men might be pleased to pay him back for the pain he'd caused them. He must find the master before they discovered him alone.

The scolding call of a bird interrupted his thoughts. He looked around him at the nearly barren trees. It had been autumn like this the first time he'd ever traveled this way—with Tahn when they were twelve and thirteen. By then, many of the men had thought Tahn mad because of his fearsome screams at night and his unpredictable manner.

But Lucas knew him better than most, and traveling alone with him had been a welcome relief from Samis and his ruffians at Valhal. He'd never felt threatened by Tahn, except when the man was asleep.

And that was something he still felt guilty about. Because they'd shared a room as young boys, Lucas had been the first to learn about Tahn's dreadful dreams. It scared him, and he'd gone to the master with it hoping for a remedy.

But God Almighty! Lucas cried in his heart. *Why haven't I killed Samis by now?* The horrible man had only used Tahn's torment to torture and bind him, piling scars on top of the ones he'd already had. *Why haven't* you *killed him, Lord God?* Lucas questioned. *Why would you let a man like Samis steal our lives from us?*

He shook his head in derision at himself. That was a poor excuse for a prayer! He could still remember the grand cathedral at Alastair and the glorious prayers floating from the lips of the priest. He'd been a street urchin then, sneaking into the back pew every chance he got. To think he'd actually dreamed of becoming a priest!

He sighed. The best he could hope for was to find a back pew again some day, just to take it all in one more time.

Lucas stopped at a brook to let his horse drink. He was about to cross the water when he looked down and saw the print of a horseshoe in the soft bank. *Maybe Samis has been here,* he thought. Leviathan was shod, unlike many of their mounts.

He turned in the direction of the track, following the stream, and eventually found another print in the mud. *Oh, let it be him!*

Lucas shook his head. *There I go again! Feeble prayers fall from me like an incessant drip. It must be irritating indeed to the Almighty. He couldn't possibly take me seriously, a lone fool out here hoping to help a merciless killer live a bit longer. I can't even take myself seriously! God, help me ride off and let him die!*

But suddenly he saw movement in the trees ahead. Leviathan. Unmounted. The big horse ignored him on his way back to the stream for a drink.

"Master!" Lucas yelled. He hurried to search in the direction that Leviathan had come.

─────

Samis lay on the ground in the midst of the trees. The dizziness had come over him again, with a crushing headache, but this time he managed to leave the saddle without falling. The pounding in his head was already fading. Soon enough he would get up. But he knew he could not gather men again. Strong men only follow a strong leader. He could not even hunt down his deserters with this curse of heaven striking at him without warning.

He closed his eyes and cursed the fate that brought him this humiliation. But he would not let it get worse. He no longer thought of how many villagers there might be with Tahn at Onath. It didn't matter. He would find him. And there would be victory, regardless of the outcome.

Lucas found Samis beneath a fir tree and dismounted anxiously.

But the master's eyes popped open, and he looked up at the young warrior with a frown. "What the devil are you doing here?"

Lucas sighed. "Are you all right, my lord?"

"Of course I'm all right! A man's got to rest, you know! I've come quite a ways." He sat up quickly.

"Are you sure you're feeling all right?"

"What's the matter with you?" Samis snapped. "Just waiting for me to die, are you? Well, you can just wait! I'm fine, and I have no need of you running after me!"

"I beg your pardon then, sir. But I . . . I thought I could be of assistance to you."

"Really? What would you do?"

"Anything you say. I didn't think you should be alone."

"You're an idiot!" Samis declared. "I'm better off alone than with your help. I can't expect you to be worth your spit fighting Tahn! You've always been too afraid of him for that."

"Fear is not my reason, sir."

"Yes. You actually *liked* him, didn't you? You were always the worst sort of fool. You fancied I'd be your father. You remember that? And that he'd be a brother to you, he and

289

the others. You were the only one soft enough to hold that fantasy for long. You've always been soft. You'd be worthless entirely if you didn't make yourself so handy. Get my horse, will you? I'm ready to go."

Lucas stood and stared at him. He remembered very well how he'd wanted a father. But Tahn *was* a brother. There was no way he would be able to help Samis kill him.

"Have you eaten?" he asked.

"Didn't you hear what I said?"

"Yes, sir. But there's no hurry. You might as well eat for strength."

"I have plenty of strength!" Samis pulled himself to a stand against the trunk of the nearest tree. "No hurry? You're the poorest excuse for a soldier I ever trained. Except that idiot Vari. Wouldn't kill a dog if it bit him." Samis laughed. "What brothers you'd make! Have you yet got any kills under your belt, Lucas?"

"I don't know." He fidgeted uncomfortably. It was true. He'd fought alongside the others, and he'd caused enough injuries. But he'd never been able to stand there and finish it. Instead he always walked away, not knowing whether those people had lived or died.

Samis was still laughing as Lucas turned away.

He whistled the three brisk notes Leviathan would recognize, and the horse ambled toward them obediently. "You wanted your mount, sir."

"Indeed. I'm ready to see Tahn again. You should watch me face him. Now that's a fighter! You might learn something before he dies."

Lucas watched Samis pull himself into the saddle, and then he sprang to his own horse's back.

"You with me, are you, Lucas?"

"I want to know something, sir." Lucas swallowed hard and mustered his courage as he moved to Samis's side. "Why is the Dorn so important to you?"

"Important? Bah! I'm about to kill him! Unless you wish the chance."

"No. But I know he *is* important to you, sir. You were hard on all of us. But then you let us go to our own style, or lack of it, so long as we obeyed you. You never let up on him, though. You made him be more disciplined. You got excited at his successes. And the one time he failed, you cut him down more than you would have anyone else with as true an effort."

"I expect more when I see talent." Samis kicked Leviathan to a trot.

Lucas kept up with him, suddenly determined. Most of the men had considered Tahn the handpicked favorite, precisely because of the intense way he was treated. Now Lucas wanted an explanation. When Samis finally slowed, he persisted.

"You *made* him be talented. He had to be good to survive you. For me, willing to take the orders and fight was good enough. Why?"

Samis laughed. "You're not worth the horse you're sitting on."

"I know that. But why was Tahn worth more?"

Samis stopped and stared at him, suddenly serious. "Perhaps I'll tell you sometime."

He rode in silence for a while as Lucas stayed close. They went through a beautiful meadow and onto a rocky hill. Finally, when Samis spoke again, his voice sounded far away, and Lucas had never heard him that way before.

"I used to ride with my father like this—just the two of us. Of course, I was younger than you are, then. He was such a cutthroat! And a worthy deceiver. But he never dreamed of the power I've known. He died alone in a drunken stupor, so they say."

Lucas didn't dare speak a word. He had never heard Samis reminisce about anything. Any interruption might be dangerous, or might prevent him from learning something important.

"I left him to join up with the king's soldiers at Alkatel. Such a good training there. But I was already better than the best of them at fighting sneaky, fighting dirty. We were good for each other, those men and I!"

He stopped and looked at the scene ahead of them for a moment. When Leviathan went on, it was at a walk, and Samis sighed.

"Father was dead by the time I got around to looking him up again. He was a good bandit, but he never cared if I ate or not, you know. I thought he'd have a stash and I'd get one last good meal off of him, after all those years. But I found out he hadn't been traveling alone after I left. I had a half brother. He took my father's belongings with him, so I looked for him."

He turned to look at Lucas. "But you know, they hung him at Alastair for killing some woman. He was traveling with a little mite of a kid. That was Tahn—you remember what a runt he was? I was sure he was my brother's boy. My own nephew. I spared him because of it. And I had hopes for him. But, of course, he might just be some misbegotten imp my brother was using for the sympathy. Hungry kid, sad eyes. It takes the ladies, every time. My brother would have known that. Father certainly did. It was a game we played often enough when I was a mite. I swore I'd never do it. And I haven't, have I, Lucas? I always fed you well, never put you on display."

Lucas stared at him, stunned. It was strange to think of Samis as a vulnerable child. He waited, but Samis said no more.

"Did you ever tell Tahn?"

Samis scoffed. "No! I didn't want him going soft toward me. It might have ruined what he was becoming."

Lucas shook his head. "You might have been a family. You might have been friends."

"What good have such things ever done you? You weary me with your softhearted talk. One would think you were a woman."

"God help you both." Too late, Lucas realized he'd said it aloud. And to his surprise, Samis did not react angrily.

"Well! You still believe in that after all these years? I'm surprised you've kept that much of a mind of your own. I thought you were a spineless thing by now, swaying whichever way I command you."

Lucas felt an odd satisfaction. It was the closest thing to a compliment he'd ever gotten from the man.

29

It was a cool, starlit night. Tahn sat alone on the bench by the pond. Netta stepped from the house in her coat and saw him there looking out over the water. He'd been so withdrawn since his ride with Jarel. She wanted to talk to him, but she wasn't sure how to start. A chilly breeze swept over them, and an owl called somewhere in the trees.

She moved toward him slowly at first, hesitantly, hoping her intrusion would not be unwelcome. But he must have been deep in thought. She was less than ten feet away before he heard her.

She jumped when he whirled around so suddenly. For just a moment he looked at her with stormy eyes before turning around again.

"I'm sorry, Lady, for frightening you. I'm so sorry."

Netta hung her head. She should have been more careful. "No, Mr. Dorn. You didn't frighten me. I am sorry. I shouldn't have surprised you so."

"You should be at ease at your own home, Lady."

"It would be good to see you more at ease too. I am hoping you will learn to relax. We are guarded, and we are in God's hands. No one will hurt you in this place."

"That does not concern me so much as the thought that I might cause hurt." He rose and started in the direction of the guardhouse.

"Jarel's thought?"

"My own."

"You'll not hurt me. You only turned to see who was behind you. I would have done it myself!"

"That's not what I meant." He was walking away, and she followed him.

"It is very late, Lady."

"I know that."

"I should get some sleep. Your father asked me to meet with some of the guards again in the morning."

"I'm glad you decided for that," she told him.

He kept right on walking, and there was a strange tension in his voice. "I need to settle my heart that you are secure. It'll be a couple of days only."

"Days?" Suddenly she was worried at his meaning. "Then what?"

"Then I'll tell the children good-bye."

She stopped, feeling as though her heart had ceased along with her feet. "Why? You can't leave them! You know how they feel about you!"

"I will visit them. I expect they will insist upon it."

"And you haven't told them this yet?"

He turned and shook his head. "I've not been strong enough so far. God help me."

"God help us, indeed! Why would you go? Why, Mr. Dorn? You are welcome here. You are needed here. What do you have elsewhere? Please, explain this to me!"

"I am like a rat in a den of rabbits, my lady. I'll never fit in."

"I think that in Christ there are neither rats nor rabbits. We are all one."

He smiled. "A kind thought. I thank you." He turned away again.

"Mr. Dorn! I am quite serious. God's blessings are not for heaven alone. You can receive some of them now, including a home with people who care about you."

He stopped. "Do you mean you would want me to stay?"

"Of course I would. Did you think not?"

He only bowed his head, but his relief did not escape her.

She smiled. "We would worry if you weren't with us. We would wonder if you'd eaten, if you had shelter, or if you'd run into trouble. We are all God's family, and you are a part of that. You always will be, Mr. Dorn. May that thought ease your mind."

She started to reach for his hand, but there was yelling suddenly from the north wall, guards ordering back some unwelcome stranger.

And then came a wail, a shout, of utter desperation.

"Vari!"

Tahn looked toward the sky with a gasp of recognition. "Lady," he said, "go and wake the boy. Tell him to hurry."

"Vari!" the stranger screamed again.

"And don't worry," he told her. "Tell him it's Marcus." He hurried toward the wall with his limping gait, and she turned and ran inside.

<hr>

"He's drunk!" one of the guards complained in disgust.

Tahn brushed the comment aside.

"Marcus?"

A boy's face emerged from the shadows of the trees for just a moment and then drew back, tainted with fear.

"What do you want with him, sir?" a guard asked. "He wouldn't be chased off. Is he dangerous?"

But Tahn ignored the guard. "Marcus," he said calmly, "I have sent for Vari. He told you truly that you need not fear. Come ahead and let me talk to you."

"It's the Dorn, isn't it?" the boy was saying with shaky voice.

"Yes. You know I'm Vari's friend. And yours if you want one. But I can't help you if I can't see you."

"I had a hold of him," one guard said. "But he slipped my grasp, and Josef said it was better to run him off, a drunken kid unarmed."

Unarmed? That was strange, Tahn knew. "Marcus, has something happened to you?"

"Don't hurt me, sir. Please just let me see Vari. Please!"

"I told you he's coming. He'll be quick enough. Just relax. I'll not hurt you. Are you all right?"

"I'm hurting bad."

"The tincture?" Tahn was walking slowly and silently into the trees toward the voice.

"I had another sip or two. But they took it."

Tahn stepped from around a tree, and Marcus screamed.

Tahn took his arm. "Sit down before you fall," he said. "You're safe. You have my word."

Marcus sunk to the ground. He was shaking badly. "I can't do this! Vari said he'd help, but I can't take it!" Marcus's clothes were torn, his belt was gone. He had a painfully obvious black eye among a collection of other bruises.

"Marcus, who did this to you?"

The boy didn't answer. He was suffering a violent tremor and cried out again.

From somewhere behind them came the sound of running footsteps. "Tahn?"

"Over here."

Vari was at his side in a moment. "Thank God, Marcus! Hold on."

"Vari! Vari, I need a measure! Please!"

"You know I can't. You're going to be glad I won't."

"Oh God!" the young man shrieked. "Somebody kill me! Dorn—"

"Take a deep breath, Marcus," Tahn told him. "Breathe slowly. Try to relax. If you can sleep, it'll go faster."

"I can't sleep!"

"Probably not," Tahn conceded. "Unless God would give it to you." He was suddenly aware of another presence. He looked up and saw Jarel standing in the trees, watching.

"Marcus, God will help you," Vari was saying. "He did it for me and for the Dorn."

"He—he wouldn't help me! Not after—"

"It doesn't matter what we've done," Tahn told him. "He wants to forgive. He *will* help, if you will have it."

Marcus sat up, breathing in hard gasps. "I'm going to die! Vari, don't leave me out here to die!" He was shivering.

"Can we get him to the house?" Vari asked with concern.

Tahn looked up at Jarel and shook his head. It was too much to ask to bring another of the mercenaries under the Trilett roof. Especially one unconverted and beyond his senses right now. "We'll go to the church." He turned to one of the other men. "Can you go and beg Father Anolle's permission? If he agrees, then bring us a wagon."

The young guard looked up at Jarel in question. "Sir?"

"Do as he says," Jarel told him.

The young man hurried into town, and Jarel stepped closer. "He's one of whatever you were."

"Right now he's hurt," Vari answered impatiently. "And I gave him my word I'd help."

"I'll not stand in the way."

Marcus gave a sudden cry, his eyes wide with terror. Tahn took hold of his shaking arms. "Breathe," he said. "Think about your breathing. Close your eyes, Marcus. Ask God's help."

"Vari!" Marcus screamed again.

"No, brother." Vari shook his head. "You've got to listen to Tahn. Call on Jesus. He's your only help."

Marcus reached out for Vari and fell against his shoulder. Vari cradled his head as he lay against him and began to gently rock. "Jesus," Vari said again. "He already paid for this. He already took care of it. Just say his name, Marcus. Believe it."

"Jesus." It was Tahn's voice, soft and distant. "Lord Jesus."

Jarel looked long at the Dorn and then down at Marcus. God had lifted a killer out of the darkness. Now here lay another soul in need. Suddenly it didn't matter so much what role this boy might have played in what had happened. He was a lost child, and Jarel wanted him to respond, to whisper the blessed Name and know peace. He wanted to witness such a transformation before his own eyes and be a part of it. He knelt down next to Vari and began softly singing his mother's favorite hymn.

"Almighty God of majesty high, walked on this earth, and came to die. Bore on his back the weight of our sin. Beaten and bruised, the Savior of men. Such love as this, I cannot tell! He gave me hope, released me from hell! Holy Redeemer loveth my soul! By his stripes healed! In his blood made whole!"

There was a hush over them all.

"Jesus," Marcus whispered. "Jesus." He sunk into Vari's lap, and the shaking stilled. By the time the wagon arrived, he was asleep.

"Bring him to the guardhouse," Jarel told them. "He'll be much closer for you to watch over."

The next day, Netta had all of the children in new clothes and gathered them on the east porch for a reading lesson.

"Don't we look like haughty beasts?" Stuva remarked. "If I saw me riding by in Tamask, I might throw rocks at myself!"

"One can dress as a gentleman and keep humility, child," Netta admonished. "I'll not have a haughty spirit from any of you. I'll be the first to inform you of the error if ever I see it."

"Yes, my lady," Stuva answered.

Netta smiled and shook her head. "I told you about that already. All of you still calling me Lady! Or Miss, for goodness sakes!"

"Isn't it proper?" little Temas asked, finally looking feminine in a ruffled dress.

"Of course it is. But I have a name, and I like to hear it sometimes."

"It seems rather strange to call you Netta," Tam told her. "Makes you like one of us."

"That is the point, isn't it?" she asked.

Tam wrinkled his brow and looked down at his new shoes. "I think that when you were in the cave puttin' on Vari's clothes, you were still a lady. And I suppose that we're still the same bunch we ever was."

Bennamin had stepped out behind Netta. "You are very right, young man," he said. "Men consider the outward things, but God sees to the heart. What is inside us defines us. And you were all worthy gentlemen—" he bowed to Temas, "and a lady, when you were hungry, or homeless, or locked within a tyrant's gates. We are all God's children."

Doogan was fidgeting in his seat. "But what if we can't be like we should? Scares me I might make you wish you hadn't took me in."

Benn smiled. "I have just that problem. I pray God that I may measure up to what you deserve. And it will take his help, no doubt."

Most of the children sat there stunned. It was hard to imagine the powerful man saying such a thing.

"We will all pray for one another," Netta told them. "God's love molds us together already."

She looked out over the yard, following her father's eyes. Tahn was walking toward them, his limp nearly gone.

"How is our guest?" Benn called out.

"He is hungry." Tahn smiled. "A pleasant surprise born in God's grace."

"And yourself? I don't recall if you ate a bite yesterday."

"I will today. With your permission, I'll ask Hildy for a tray for us, and Vari as well."

"Of course." Benn laid a hand on Tahn's shoulder as he

stepped to the porch. "Has he told you what happened to him?"

Tahn looked at the children but decided to proceed. "Six of Samis's men have banded together near Merinth under Donas, one of the eldest. They wanted Marcus to join with them. When he would not, they beat and robbed him."

"They are very dangerous, then?"

"Not like they were under Samis. They let him live. And they have not the numbers nor the organization they had before, my lord. They will be bandits, no doubt, but no more threat to you than to any other man of means."

"How many were there, organized before?"

"Nearly forty."

"And does he say they are all scattered now?"

"We expect so, sir. It seems only one man had a heart to remain with the master when they saw him weakened."

"Let us pray for them, shall we?" Benn abruptly asked.

But Tahn felt a sudden churning in his stomach. Pray for who? The scattered soldiers? Or Samis? He reached his hand to the porch rail to steady himself.

Netta stepped forward. "Are you all right, sir?"

He held up his hand before she could touch him. "Yes." He looked at her and then at Benn. "Forgive me. It is not an easy thought, to pray for my master. It is a good idea, though."

"It seems it would help you," Benn told him gently. "You are in God's hand, but Samis still bears a hold. He is not your master, son. Christ is."

"I know it," Tahn answered almost angrily. "I know what I've been given. I know what I've left behind." He was suddenly uncomfortable that the children should see him so unsettled. He nodded quickly to Benn and to Netta. "Please excuse me." He turned from them to the yard again and walked away.

"I'll bring a tray shortly," Benn called after him. "Thank you for the report."

Netta was dismayed for him. "Father—"

"Leave him be, for now," he told her. "He's all right. I have the same struggle toward the man who took so much from us. We will grow past it together, perhaps, Tahn and I. It is not always easy to forgive."

30

When afternoon came and the children were either playing nimbles or climbing like monkeys in the trees, Netta sat alone on one of the porches, with the psalms once again in her hand. But she couldn't concentrate on the reading with Tahn Dorn on her mind. She thought of what his presence had been like for her at first and how completely her feelings had changed—from terror to deepening admiration. She knew she was getting more sensitive to his struggle and more attached to his humble smile. When he said he was leaving, it had rocked her horribly and forced her to confront her own emotions toward him.

He was a puzzle of strength and vulnerability. Before he had whisked her out her window, she'd never known anyone so deeply needy. And yet he'd taken immense responsibility on himself, even before he knew God's mercy for himself. Jarel could be right. He might still be dangerous. But only in an extreme circumstance, which was all he seemed to know before. Now he was a man who knew mercy and was willing to share it. And Netta found that very easy to love.

"Love is of God," Father Anolle had said. *"Sort out your own heart and trust what you find there."*

Netta looked out at the leaves scattered across the yard. Soon it would be winter. Karll came courting for the first time in winter. It had been a stormy day, and he'd lingered and gotten snowbound at their estate. Father had said he surely planned it that way.

She smiled for a moment and then glanced over at the guardhouse. She wasn't sure if Tahn were there with Vari and his guest or not. They were so different, Karll and Tahn. But alike in some ways too. In other circumstances, they might have been friends.

She looked up at the clouds and wondered what Karll might be thinking of her now. Surely in heaven, he understood and had forgiven. But how would he feel, now that she found herself desiring to be courted again?

Lord, am I a fool? She rose to her feet, her heart full of questions. *It seems crazy to feel this way, but I can't deny what I come back to again and again. What would he have without us? What would I have without him?*

She hugged her arms to herself and bowed her head. *Jesus, you redeemed a dark angel to become a man of your light, and now I find that I love him. Help me! I want him to be free, yet he tries to hide himself so much. Help him to give you all of that hurt. And guide my steps and my heart.*

The rest of the day afforded no opportunity to talk to Tahn. Supper was busy with the chatter of children. Vari was with them for the first time all day. But not Tahn.

"Is Mr. Dorn with your friend tonight?" Netta asked him casually.

"Yes," he answered between bites of Hildy's pudding.

"Ask them both to join us for breakfast," Benn told him. "If young Marcus is up to it."

"He will be. I asked him tonight, but he didn't expect he'd be welcome. He can't really figure why you'd let him be around."

"I am pleased to learn he hungers for more of the God who gives him rest. He's about fifteen, you would say?"

"We think so. It's hard to know for sure."

"I want to talk to him about his future, if he has any special plans."

"He does, sir. He heard about Lorne, and he's hoping you'll hire him too, though he's got no family to support."

"I am willing to consider it. After we talk."

Vari smiled. "I knew it! You're God blessed, sir!" He ate

heartily, triple helpings. When the meal was finished, he promised the younger boys he'd join them overnight and then took a tray back to the guardhouse.

Benn went to his study, and Netta followed him.

"Father, may I talk—" She stopped suddenly, seeing Jarel in a chair.

"Of course, daughter." He sat down. "Jarel was just suggesting to me that we support some sort of plan to help the poor of other towns as we have in Onath."

"A wonderful thought," Netta agreed, turning to Jarel with a smile. "I'm pleased. I think of it when I see these children. How many more are out there?"

Jarel stood. "Do you want me to step out, cousin?"

She hadn't considered Jarel's presence, but she shook her head. He was family, after all. "No, it's all right." She clasped his hand for a moment and then turned again to her father. "I'm concerned about Mr. Dorn. He is so withdrawn."

"Between young Marcus and beginning his work with the guards, he's been occupied," Benn tried to assure her.

"You know it's more than that. He spends almost no time at the house, Father, even for the children's sakes."

Benn sighed. "Netta, dear, I don't think he counts himself worthy of us yet. He carries himself toward me like a bound servant, though I try to treat him like a son. I told him this afternoon that we are all made worthy in the love of God. He understands, in his heart. But his mind still tells him he does not belong here."

"How can we help him?"

Jarel cleared his throat quickly. "There's only one way to help."

Benn and Netta both turned to look at him.

"You're the problem, Netta," Jarel said. "He's so afraid of insulting you that it's breaking his heart."

She was so stricken by the words that her hands shook. "Insulting me?"

"Of course. A street rat turned killer—the killer of your

305

own husband, even—daring to think as he does of the Lady Trilett. What would you have thought a year ago?"

"None of us are as we were a year ago."

"True enough. But I found out how vulnerable he is. I asked him about you. I was hard on him. And he very nearly left then. If he ever gets the idea he bothers you, cousin, he'll be gone. And I'm not sure he would recover from it."

She turned to her father with her heart pounding. "What should I do?"

But Benn took her into his arms. "We trust him in Christ's hands, my child. If there is to be more than that, God will guide your heart."

The next morning, Vari and Marcus joined the Trilett table for breakfast, but Tahn was not with them. It was too much for Netta. She excused herself quickly and went outside.

He was not at the guardhouse or anywhere by the pond. She went to the shelter at the gate.

"He was by the wall to the west a short time ago, my lady," one of the guards told her. "He was walking the perimeter. Is he needed at the house? I can find him for you."

"No. No, thank you." She turned from them and looked out across the estate grounds. Was he still by the wall somewhere? She started out to the east, praying that God would give her the right words to say.

Where the north and east walls met, there was an old willow tree with branches drooping nearly to the ground. Tahn was sitting there, his back to the tree and his head bowed. Before she could speak, he looked up.

"Lady." The title hung in the air for a moment. He stood, glancing past her, and realized she was alone. He stared down at the dirt. "You've walked far. Is there something I can do for you?"

"I wish to speak to you, if it is all right."

"Of course, my lady." He ducked his head like a shy child.

She smiled. "I have told the children to please call me Netta. I would like it of you, as well. And I am not greatly fond of continuing to call you Mr. Dorn. Might I please call you Tahn?"

"Yes." He spoke quietly and with difficulty, without looking up. "Whatever you wish, Lady. I will answer to it."

"Tahn, you are not our slave. You do not need to be afraid to meet my eyes."

"I can't hide what is in them, Miss. And I don't want to frighten you. I swore to your father I would never hurt you again."

She stood for a moment, wondering how to respond. It surprised her that he would be so straightforward.

"You won't hurt me, Tahn. I know you better than that by now."

He sighed. "You don't understand. I wish you a safe and prosperous life. But I don't fit with that, Lady. It is better that I find another way for myself. I was thinking to go after Smoke and then—"

"What? Where would you go? You've become important to me. And to your little ones. You can't leave!"

He shifted uncomfortably and looked at his boots. "Lady Netta . . . forgive me. I—I need to be honest with you." He took a deep breath and suddenly seemed almost frail.

"I care for you," he said with quiet voice. "Deeply. You are a saint. A loving teacher. A precious jewel. I can't stay here. I can't think these thoughts."

"Leaving won't stop you from thinking, my friend." She took a step toward him, but he shook his head and turned to walk away.

"Tahn!" she called after him. "Please—why are you punishing yourself?"

He stopped for a moment, and his shoulders seemed to shake. But then he went on from her with quick steps.

"Tahn!" She ran after him.

He was going through the trees, toward the stable, but

finally as they broke into the clearing by the pond, she caught his arm. "You should know us by now! If you go, Vari and I will come after you. We will find you and bring you home."

She stepped in front of him and saw the depth of pain in his eyes.

"I have never had a home," he said. "Except in heaven now."

"You have a home here. With us! We want you here."

He shook his head again. "I am not Lorne or Marcus. Your father expects something different from me. But I look at myself, and I know I don't belong."

She took both of his hands. "Tell me, Tahn, when God looks at you, what does he see?"

He bowed his head. "A sinner—a man of blood—that he graciously saved from eternal fire. May I never shame the gift."

"Yes. But there is more. He sees his *child*, Tahn! And he loves you dearly. The only blood he sees now is that of his own Son, and it gives you all the favor of heaven."

"But what about you, Lady? Do you not see Karll when you look at me?"

"Not anymore. I see Vari sometimes. Or Duncan, or some other little child. Or the weight of a man named Samis who haunts you still. But mostly I see the love that is in you—"

He started to pull away, unable to bear it.

"Wait! Let me finish! You love all the children. You love me, and my father, the priest in town, even Jarel. I rejoice that you received God's love for salvation! But please, receive our love too, Tahn. Let us care for you. Let me care for you!"

He stared at her with fear in his eyes. "But I'm not—"

"Don't say you're not worthy! Jesus counted you worthy of eternal life. Of his love! How could you not be worthy of mine?"

He saw the tears now spilling down her cheeks. And

something inside him seemed to melt away. "Netta . . ." He spoke with trembling voice.

"Yes?"

"I thought I would frighten you. But right now, I am the one afraid."

"I know." She smiled. "I like to tell the children how good it is to hug one another. But we have never . . . dared. Do you think we could?"

He looked like he might flee. But he took a deep breath and nodded. She took a cautious step, and he pulled her into his embrace. She could feel him trembling in her arms.

"You have no obligation to me," he said. "I would be pleased to call you my friend."

"I will always be that." She held him tightly, hoping he could put aside his doubt. "Thank you, Jesus," she whispered, petting his hair. "Thank you, Jesus."

"I loved you before I kidnapped you, Lady," he said softly. "The night your husband died, when I saw the angel standing between us, I wanted to know a person God loved so much as that. I think I fell in love with the idea of it."

She pulled from him just enough to see his face, but he turned his eyes away again.

"I never thought I could touch such things. God, and you, were out of my grasp. But when I knew God . . ." He shook his head again suddenly and tried to pull away.

"Tahn! Please finish!" She touched her hand to his hair again. "Please. It's all right."

"I can't describe what happened when God touched me, Lady! I never thought he would ever have me! I cried and I danced like a fool. I have never been happy like that. All of my days I will praise him for it. His love *was* within my grasp, because he was reaching for me! But you—"

"You never thought I would?"

"Never, Lady. And I'd never been more sure of anything. But it is not so bad. To have the love of heaven is an unspeakable gift. And I am used to not being loved in this world."

"Oh, Tahn! Can you forget the past?"

"Without it, I would have no identity at all. Except as a babe in salvation."

"That is all you need, don't you think?" She smiled.

She had such a beautiful smile. How he'd longed to see it so, without a trace of fear. It brought his smile in response, and he moved to hug her again but then hesitated. Would it really be all right with her? "Lady . . ."

"Yes." She understood the question before he spoke it. "Of course you may." She held him tightly and felt his strong arms encircle her again. *God, fill him with the peace I feel,* she prayed.

"Perhaps you're right," he told her. "I told Tam we just go on from here. Yesterday is like the wind that is blown past us."

"You will stay with us then, won't you?"

He met her eyes for the first time and nodded. "I would not put you to the trouble of seeking me. And Vari has enough to think about."

"I am so glad!" She laughed and hugged him again. "It would be terribly hard to find another suitable trainer for our men."

He looked at her oddly and saw the gentle tease in her eyes.

"I would have missed you greatly, my friend," she said and gently touched the scar on his face. Then she reached and kissed his cheek.

He looked as frightened as he had before, but he lifted his hand to touch her hair.

"Netta . . ." Slowly he leaned and kissed her lips. They were so warm, so inviting, that he abruptly turned away from her again.

"Tahn." She reached for his hand before he could get away and held on to it tightly. "Will you join me for our next meal? Please? We all think you need to eat more, and certainly not alone."

"You are reaching for me too," he said with tears in his eyes.

"I can't help it. God has placed you in my path, no matter which way I turn."

He lifted her hand and kissed it softly. "I would be honored to join you for dinner, my lady."

She suddenly looked up at the gentle slope behind him and laughed. Lined up behind a bush were Duncan, Rane, and Temas, watching them. Tahn turned and saw them. "You did mean the table for everyone, didn't you?" he asked.

"This time. But tomorrow, or soon, we could picnic, if it is all right with my father."

He didn't know what to say. Her acceptance—what could it be but another gift from God? He felt suddenly lighter, like he could float right into the clouds above them. Who could imagine that even God could conceive such a thing? This beautiful soul, willing to love him!

It was a glorious day, the only damper on it being the thoughts of Samis that crowded his mind as he instructed new guards. Samis was like the devil, still out there somewhere, hoping to find a way to destroy the good Tahn had found.

Since hearing that Samis might be sick, Tahn had not known what to expect. But now he knew he was coming, as sure as if the voice of God had told him. Samis would not give up, not till one of them was dead. And he would go to any length to get here for the opportunity to face Tahn again. It was just a matter of time. Tahn taught the soldiers with that in mind. They might as well be prepared right along with him to finish it as quickly as possible.

But it was not hard to lay down such thoughts while in Netta's company. It was a pleasure to accept Benn's suggestion that the two of them take the children riding. Such a troop they made, seven little ones in hats and coats, trotting along so happily. It was like an incredible dream that life could be so good.

He spent the night again in the house with all of his boys and dreamed he was in the church listening to Jarel's hymn.

The next day was unseasonably warm, and they had their picnic. Tahn fell asleep on the blanket outside and woke to the snuggling of children beside him.

"I love you, Mr. Dorn," Temas whispered.

"I love you too, child." He looked up at the blue sky and smiled. Such a gift was love!

"We're glad you took us from Samis," Rane added. He looked so serious for a six-year-old. "He might have killed us by now."

"He won't ever find us, will he?" Temas looked suddenly worried, and Tahn sat up and put his arm around her.

"You'll never see him again. You have my word."

"Can I tell you something?" Rane asked. "I threw your whip away in the rocks when you went back for Vari. I was scared you might change your mind about it. You weren't mad, were you?"

He pulled the boy to him and hugged him along with Temas. "I was delighted to have it gone. You did me a favor."

"I'm not sure I understand that."

"It plagued me to see the thing," Tahn told him. "I can't bear a whip, not even for a horse."

Briant had walked up beside them and sat down. "Did you get it from him a lot?"

Something still shook inside Tahn when he thought of it. "Too much," he answered soberly.

But Rane took his hand. "That's why you helped us. I wish someone had been there for you."

"God bless you, child," Tahn answered softly. "The Lord was there, I expect. I just couldn't see him for the darkness."

It was a peaceful evening, and cooling considerably. After dinner in the house, Netta wrapped a cloak around her and asked Tahn to join her for a walk.

He was hesitant. It had been another wonderful day, but was there such a thing as too much pleasantness? And being alone in the lady's company made him anxious. He well remembered their kiss and feared there could be another one.

But he would not refuse her. With his heart pounding, he left the house with her, well aware of her quiet thoughtfulness.

"Why do I make you nervous?" she asked.

"I'm not used to this."

"Nor am I. Only once before did I ever really love a man this way."

He stopped and stared at her, his feet suddenly itching to run. But she took his hand.

"I need to talk about it, Tahn," she said. "I know it is hard, but it will help us. If we can talk about him, there'll be no barrier there."

"I'm sorry." He hung his head. "That's all I can say."

She lifted his head again gently. "You're like him. So sensitive to my feelings. So gentle at heart."

"I've never been called gentle."

"You've never been understood, then. Even by yourself. It hurt you to hurt him, didn't it?"

"I would not let myself think about it."

"What would have happened if you had?"

"I don't know, Lady. Insanity, probably." He sighed. "I don't think I can do this."

She hugged him quickly. "Tahn, two days before we were married, Karll told me our life together might not be long or easy. He gave me a chance to walk away, knowing he had enemies and something might happen. But I couldn't leave him, regardless. And I think my father has always felt guilty that we were not guarded more carefully."

"You had guards," he said. "They just weren't expecting anything."

With her hand in his, he walked to the pond and then around it toward the east wall.

"Karll would be pleased with what you've become," she told him suddenly.

"I can't grasp how you could say that, Netta."

"He loved God. He hated the thought of anyone suffering wrongly. If he had known of you and what you were trapped in, he would have longed to help."

"A terrible loss I gave you and your people." He looked up at the gathering clouds.

"I'm not trying to make you sad, Tahn. I just want you to see that I have peace with it now. I will always love him, but I know I have the blessing of God to have you here." She stopped and took his other hand. "God wanted you in the Trilett house. He wanted you to have my father's authority behind you. And you are a warrior for a reason. In God's hands now, you will be a blessing in justice for people in need. You already have been." She kissed his cheek softly and then released his hands. "I had to tell you that. Do you want to continue our walk?"

"I think so."

She smiled, and they walked together along the eastern edge of the quiet pond.

31

In Onath, Samis and Lucas acted the part of common travelers and stopped at the shop where Mattius had stayed to watch the church. He was gone, and it seemed he had been for days. They asked an old man sitting outside where they might find the saver of Triletts to bear him a gift. The old man gave them the directions without a worry. They probably seemed harmless enough, just an elderly gent and his rather distracted son.

Samis was in a good temper as they left the houses behind them. He began to sing, a melody familiar to all his men from the times he'd been drunk or celebrating some special victory. Lucas rode in silence behind him, thinking he'd lost his mind. There was no way a man of any sense would ride up to the Trilett estate like that. But then he realized Samis didn't care if he had the element of surprise. Maybe he didn't even want it. He wanted Tahn's attention. He seemed to think the rest would take care of itself.

By the willow tree again, Netta was talking about the church and Father Anolle's hope that Tahn and all the children would choose to worship with them.

But Tahn was suddenly quiet, and he turned his head toward the wall at the north, listening.

"Tahn? What is it?"

He held up his hand. She watched him in tense silence, wondering what he might have heard.

"Go inside," he whispered.

"What's wrong?"

"Please, Netta, go to your father."

But she lingered, seeing something frightening in his eyes.

"Samis is here," he told her. "I know I heard him. And I don't want you out here." He turned toward the gate.

"Where are you going?"

"He's come for me. And I might as well go and greet him."

"No, Tahn!" she cried. "There are guards if he tries to enter! Let them take care of this!"

"I can't, Lady. It's my responsibility."

She was suddenly afraid of what he meant by that. "You don't have to do this."

"Yes. I do." He reached and touched her cheek. "I don't expect you to understand. But please, Netta. Go. Trust God for me."

He was walking away from her, despite her protest, toward the gate and what would have to be a wrenching meeting for him. Something about his look terrified her. She knew he was prepared to fight. But the tyrant mercenary would mean it to the death. Surely he knew that!

"No, Tahn!" she called after him.

He turned and looked at her with compassion. "Don't, Lady," he said. "Your father says he still has a hold. I have to face him."

Dear God! her heart cried. *If I cannot prevent it, surely you can!*

But Tahn was already out of her sight. She turned to the house as he had said, but she could not bear to obey him. She dropped to her knees on the spot.

Father Almighty, protect his life again. Strengthen him to do what he must, but give him the courage to let it rest in your hands, not his own.

<hr />

At the gate, a guard stood to his post, looking out over the wall anxiously.

"Samis is here," Tahn told him in a quiet voice. "Go quickly and alert the others. I will see him first. But no matter what happens, he must not be allowed to escape."

As the first guard departed in obedience, two others approached. "Be prepared," he told them. "We can't be sure he's alone."

He stood at the gate for a moment and looked out, marveling at how dark the night now seemed when only moments before with the lady it had been so much lighter. Every sound had stopped. But Samis would still be there, waiting. And Tahn refused to hide. He pulled open the gate and stood clutching an iron rail.

"Samis!"

Netta jerked her head upward at Tahn's voice, her heart pounding thunderously within her. *He thinks he is prepared to kill Samis tonight,* she realized. *By his own hand, or that of our guards. But I know it is not really what he wants, not even for this villain. More blood now, even such guilty blood, will plague him. There is surely another way, dear God, to be free of the man!*

Tahn waited in silence, knowing one shout would be enough. He'd be there in the darkness, there was no question in his mind.

"Well," the voice finally came. "You make yourself a handy target, standing there in the gate alone."

"You've no archers today, or I'd have known already."

"You're not thinking," Samis scolded. "I could have thrown my knife."

"It's not your way. Not until you've railed at me first."

There were men now behind Tahn, and men coming on the wall. Soon there would be men outside the gate, circling behind Samis, searching for others, and closing him in.

But the old man seemed to understand that. "Tell your

guards to relax," he said. "I've come to bring you something. You can receive a guest without supervision, can't you?"

"They will do nothing beyond my say," Tahn told him.

"How coldhearted you can be. I've earned no audience with you? Even though I saved your life and gave you sixteen years of my own to make you what you are?" Somewhere in the darkness he laughed. "Ah, Tahn. You will always hate me. To the day you die."

"You came for a reason," Tahn replied. "You might as well show yourself and let us be done with it."

Again he laughed. "Indeed! We have been bitter long enough. It is time this foolish feud was ended, as it should be, just you and me. I am brave enough. Are you?"

Samis stepped from the shadows toward Tahn. He had a slight limp and was looking strangely gray. "I am alone," he said. "And I brought you an old friend." He tossed Tahn's sheathed sword carefully so that it landed a few feet in front of him. "Now you are ready to fight me honorably, if you have it in you."

"You're not well," Tahn told him. "I would kill you easily."

"Perhaps not. You're not that good, and you're still weak. I can tell it in your stance. But if you did manage it, isn't that what you've always wanted?"

Tahn's stomach was a knot. He *had* always wanted it. He had waited for the day. But that was before. Now, he remembered his prayer that God help him not to shed blood again.

But the guards were ready. He could accomplish the deed with his hand or with his word, and it would be almost the same. And this was not just anyone. This was Samis. They would never be completely safe as long as he was alive.

"You try my patience, boy!" Samis yelled. "Pick up your sword like a man. This has been a long time coming. We have both known it!"

Tahn looked down at the weapon at his feet.

"You never wanted anything more than this," Samis taunted. "You remember, don't you, three years ago? You told me then how you longed to face me down. After you killed that wretched worm in this very house! Now there you stand as if you owned the place. Haughty devil! You think tying your tail to Netta Trilett has gained you something? But you know she has caused you nothing but pain. What a fool you are to think they would accept you. You're just a useful slave to them until they tire of you and throw you out. You're nothing! I put up with you longer than anyone else ever could. Fight me, Tahn! We both know it is what you want!"

Netta's heart pounded. She was close enough to the wall to hear the awful words. But she ran to the gate, needing to see Tahn, praying that he could bear this as God would see it best.

With a steel he hadn't expected, Tahn leaned slowly down and lifted the sword. He could see Samis step closer with a gleam of expectation. Surely he knew what he was up against with the guards standing by. He must have come knowing it would be the end, wanting it to be.

Tahn looked up at his teacher with turmoil in his heart. It would be easy to finish and easy to justify. But that prayer, his own prayer, would not let go of him.

"Draw the blade, Tahn," Samis told him coolly. "You will appreciate the feel of it in your hand again. It is part of you, isn't it?"

Tahn shook his head. "You gave me this sword when I was ten," he said. "You can have it back." He hurled the weapon through the air, and it landed in the dust at Samis's side.

"You wish to carry your hate for me burning in you to your grave, Tahn? I have offered you the opportunity to purge it and avenge yourself of me! Would you walk away from the one thing you've wanted most in your life?"

319

Tahn took a deep breath. "What I wanted most was the peace God has given. I wanted to be loved, and I found that with him too. You need God now. You have nothing else."

"They've filled you with a lot of drivel, haven't they? You will see one day how much God and the Triletts really care for you. You remember the pain the lady caused you, don't you? You were days at it, weeks, weren't you, Tahn? You remember!"

Tahn stood still, watching him. It hurt to let him go on and not silence this monster with his own hand. Indeed he did remember. Everything. And it made him shudder.

"There will only be more of it, Tahn," Samis continued. "Your friends will betray you as you have betrayed me. And you will deserve the knife in your back!"

"I've heard enough," Tahn told him. "Leave us."

Samis laughed. "You're afraid of me still! You are a coward not to fight me. And so dishonest. You know you want it."

"No," he said slowly. "I want to forgive you and go on with the life God has given."

"You talk like an old woman! Fight me, boy, or I shall kill you, I swear it!"

Tahn shook his head. "God take pity on you," he said. "Just let him leave," he told the soldiers and turned back to the gate.

But Samis was not to be denied so easily. He pulled the knife from his belt and flung it at Tahn with all the strength he could muster. It struck him at his left shoulder.

Tahn clutched the rail and cried out with the sudden pain. He could hear the soldiers rushing at Samis.

"Stop!" he told his men. "Let him go!"

He turned and saw Lucas for the first time, standing beneath a tree, watching. Suddenly Lucas was raising his arm and bowing his head in salute.

"Come and take him," Tahn told him. "And be gone from here."

The soldiers stood in disbelief. Why would he let them go?

Lucas rushed forward and lifted Samis from the ground where the soldiers had knocked him down. It was clear then that Samis was weaker than he acted. He looked truly old. He was muttering as Lucas led him away toward their horses.

Netta ran to Tahn and lended her arm for support.

"I told you to go," he said, suddenly exhausted.

The guard named Josef was at Tahn's other side, and Netta looked up at him. "Help me get him to the house."

But another soldier approached who thought the lady's presence might be the reason for Tahn's behavior. "Shall we follow and overtake them?" he asked.

"No. I said let them go. It's over." He took a deep breath, realizing suddenly that he'd reached a hand to Samis when he told him he needed God. *Let him hear it,* he prayed, *before it's too late.* God would be willing to reach out his own hand, even to Samis. *He did save my life once,* Tahn thought. *There must be something in there somewhere to redeem.*

"Just keep watch," Tahn told the soldiers. "In case he returns."

Josef pulled Samis's knife free and threw it on the ground. Netta held the wound with her fine lace kerchief. "Tahn," she said softly. "Let us take you to the house."

<hr />

Lucas led his master through the trees, but he stopped and offered him water when Samis suddenly started sweating. He was panting for breath. But the soldiers hadn't hurt him, Lucas knew that. This must be something else.

"He's no different than I am," Samis was mumbling. "He's a killer at heart. It's his hate of me, that's what it is! He won't accept any plan of mine. But he'd fight me when my back's turned. If he knew I didn't want it. Curse him! I'll find a way."

"No!" Lucas told him. "Don't you know when it's enough? We are lucky to be leaving alive. He should have told his men to kill you on the spot."

Samis stared at him and clenched his fists. Lucas was right, of course. Tahn could easily have had him killed. Why had he not?

Surely it was what Lucas had said at Valhal, that Tahn would either kill him or walk away in pity. Pity! The thought enraged him. "Curse you, Tahn Dorn! May your friends destroy you!"

Lucas just stared at him.

"Get out of my way, you fool!" Samis yelled. "You're just like him! You're enjoying this. That's why you've stayed with me. You want to watch me waste away. I curse you! I won't have your pity. Leave me, or I will kill you in Tahn's stead!"

In a fury, he shuffled away from Lucas as quickly as he could move. There was such a pounding in his chest, such a terrible headache again. The night was whirling around him, and he hated life and the thought of death. There must be victory to be found in this somewhere. There must be!

He had known where the horses were, but now he couldn't see them. He pressed on past them through the trees, cursing under his breath.

"Samis!" Lucas called, intending to direct him.

"Leave me alone!"

His breathing came hard now. The weakness and dizziness rushed over him mercilessly, but he wouldn't give in to them, nor to Lucas's call. He walked on with faltering steps. He didn't see the old tree he'd come to until he fell against it, suddenly too weak to stand. He grasped at the trunk for a moment, pain tearing at his skull. Then his right arm gave way, and he sunk slowly to the ground, now drenched in sweat.

"Sir?"

It was Lucas, following as usual. He stood there, just watching. What he must be thinking! There the old man goes. Another spell. Let him die in such misery.

He wanted to yell at him again, but he could not find his

voice. Even his body betrayed him. Even his face felt like it was tearing away and leaving him. He could not make his mouth form the words he wanted to use.

"Samis, sir, what has happened? Can you get up?"

He tried. Oh, how he wanted to prove he could do anything he set his mind to. With his left arm he could grasp at the air, but his right arm hung limply and would not respond. He could shift his left leg wearily, but he could not make the right one move at all. He knew he could not get up this time. He stared up at Lucas, suddenly aware of his own trembling.

"Sir? Speak to me!" The younger man actually looked afraid.

Fool! Samis's mind cried. *You're a fool, Lucas!* He struggled again to speak, but he could not make it work. The effort left him gasping for breath.

Lucas straightened Samis's limbs on the grass and covered him with his coat. "Lay calmly, now," he said with fear in his voice. "I'll get help. Tahn showed you one mercy tonight. Surely they will tell me where to find a healer. I'll be right back. Stay calm."

Lucas left him at a dead run, and soon in the distance Samis could hear his shouts. *A good thinker, Lucas. If he runs up unannounced, he could get himself killed. To think he would go back to Tahn at the Trilett house. For another mercy! To beg me a healer!*

It was too much. He could imagine them laughing together and then watching him linger for days in an agonizing death. A finish in fighting would have been honorable. That was why they would so carefully deny it him. *But they will not have their laugh!* he raged. *I will not amuse them so!* With his left hand he fumbled about in his clothes until finally he found the handle of a concealed blade.

I will not live needy in their care. I will not die helpless under their gaze. I have yet some strength. Let me die strong!

323

Netta was glad that Benn had met them as they came to the house. They had their entry well lit with oil lamps, and Jarel was outside now, speaking to Josef. Thankfully, Vari and Hildy were with the children. *Let them not know it was Samis here,* Netta thought, *till he is long gone.*

She held a cloth to Tahn's bloody shoulder.

"Are you sure you're all right?"

"It will heal, Netta. I think it did not go too deep."

"Do you expect him back?" Benn asked.

"I don't know. He's weakened."

"If he returns," Benn said, "I will have to apprehend him."

"I would expect that." Tahn looked up at the Trilett patriarch. "Thank you for not rebuking me."

Netta touched his head. "I believe God honors what you did. But what did he mean, that I'd caused you pain?"

Tahn looked out the open door. "There's no truth to it."

"But he meant something. I saw it affect you."

"He punished me, Lady. That's what he meant. For my failure to kill you with Karll."

Benn laid a hand on his daughter's shoulder.

Netta thought of all Tahn had told her about that night. It was a devil's world he'd come from. Because he hadn't slaughtered them both, he went home with wrath to face? Had he ever known a kindness?

"It wasn't your fault," she whispered. Carefully, she helped him remove his shirt, and for the second time, she saw his scars. "Oh, Tahn." She ran her hand gently over the stripes on his back. Tears filled her eyes. "Is that what these are?"

Tahn didn't answer. He was listening again suddenly, to a new commotion beyond the wall. He pulled away from her and stood.

"What is it?" Netta asked with fresh tension.

"Lucas, I think. With the guards again."

"He wouldn't come back for you, would he?"

He shook his head. "Not Lucas." He was in the doorway before she could stop him.

"You're not going out there! What if there are others?"

"Something's wrong, Lady, or he wouldn't be back." He saw the fear for him in her eyes, but he went for the door anyway.

"Father?" Netta turned to Benn.

"I'll go with him. It's all right, little girl."

Josef and Jarel went for the gate as well, but Tahn was ahead of them. The guards were sounding angry, but there was desperation in the other voice.

"Let me see the Dorn!" Lucas was pleading. "All I want is a healer!"

"A healer?" one of the guards questioned. "Go to the town for that!"

"Lucas?" Tahn called out.

"Tahn! Help me!" the warrior yelled in response. "The master is fallen!"

Tahn pulled open the gate. Three guards had hold of Lucas, one of them with a drawn sword.

"Mr. Dorn, sir," said one. "You told him to be gone. It's trickery, I say."

"Release him."

At the nod of Benn Trilett behind Tahn, the guards shoved Lucas roughly away.

But the warrior turned back. "We need a healer. Please."

"What happened?"

"A spell—I don't know. But it's worse this time."

Tahn's heart suddenly was pounding. Instead of gladness at such news, he felt heaviness. He had prayed that Samis somehow hear the words of God calling to him. Now there seemed to be very little time left for that. He turned to Benn. "Please allow us to send for the healer quickly."

"You're sure you can trust these words?" Benn looked at Lucas skeptically.

Lucas turned to Tahn without a word spoken.

"He would not lie to me, sir," Tahn said. "It is an old understanding."

Benn sighed. Such a world he couldn't grasp. If the stranger valued his own word, then how could he value his conscience so little that he continued to ride with a cruel killer of men, women, and children?

"He will die," Lucas said solemnly.

"Take the guards with you," Benn told Tahn. "Josef, go and find Amos Lowe." He turned back to the gate, leaving the matter in Tahn's hands.

Tahn looked gravely at Lucas. "Show me where."

They went together into the trees with guards following.

"He couldn't stand," Lucas was saying. "He couldn't speak." He hurried through the woods, but when the old tree was just ahead of them, he slowed, suddenly afraid of what he might find. Tahn took his arm and pulled him forward. Together they found Samis lying almost as Lucas had placed him. But blood still oozed from a wound to his throat. The knife lay across his chest, and the bloody left hand was back at his side.

"No." Lucas stared down at him. He had thought to protect him from others, but it was Samis himself to do the deed.

"He's gone," Tahn said, the words soaking over him like water.

"He shouldn't have done this! I would have cared for him."

"Surely he knew that."

"But he didn't want it!" Lucas shouted in anger. "Just one man serving him willingly! I tried to do him good! And he didn't want it!"

"Lucas—"

"He would rather have dragged me here as a slave, unwilling. He would have rather beaten me into doing the things that I volunteered to do. He loved it when we feared him. He couldn't stand me just to offer my hand." He turned away.

Tahn bowed his head, understanding his pain too well. "I remember when we were small. We wanted to call him Father, you and I. We wanted to love him, from the start. I never managed. But you did."

Lucas shook his head. "He called me the weakest sort of fool."

"We were all fools in such a godless daze." Tahn put his hand on Lucas's shoulder. "But you were not the weakest sort."

The warrior looked at Tahn and then down at the body at their feet. "I don't want to take him to Valhal, or anywhere else. I don't want to travel with the body."

"We'll bury him here, then. You choose the place. I will gain Benn Trilett's permission."

Lucas swallowed hard. "Right here. Right where he lays." He knelt.

"I'll get the diggers in the morning."

"No," Lucas told him. "I'll do it. As soon as I have a shovel. And don't tell me you'll help. I know you're hurt."

"I have a friend—a priest," Tahn ventured quietly.

"It's too late for that now."

"I didn't mean for Samis," Tahn told him. "I thought he might talk to you."

Lucas looked up at him and their eyes met. Suddenly Lucas's brimmed with tears. "You never forgot?"

Tahn reached his hand to the man's shoulder. "The little boy who idolized the priest at Alastair? And went to sleep with the Lord's Prayer on his lips? It was torture to me! How could I forget that?"

"I outgrew such things," the warrior said with a sigh. "And I hear that it is you now who speaks the holy Name."

Tahn smiled. "I thank God for it, Lucas. You know what he saved me from. And I know what your childhood dream was, before you met this dead man. The priest is Father Anolle. He and his merciful God have embraced this once-dark angel. They have room for another."

Lucas stared at him. "Send a man for a shovel."

Tahn turned to the guards. He nodded, and one of the men left for the tool.

"By the time you're finished, you'll need breakfast," Tahn told Lucas. "There's a pond, with benches not far from here. And a woman named Hildy who would be pleased to bring us a hearty tray."

"I can't fathom your reasoning, Tahn. But I tell you, I will not stay."

"Then allow me to be your brother before you go."

Lucas buried Samis's weapons with him, and his own. "Do not mark the grave," he said. "Let his memory be in the wind."

He accepted the offer of food and gave Benn Trilett his thanks when he learned he'd agreed to let him leave.

Tahn and Lucas walked together to the horses. Leviathan stood pawing the ground.

"I guess he's yours now," Lucas said.

"No. You have the right."

"I don't want the awful beast."

"Then we'll sell him," Tahn offered. "And the money is yours."

"All right."

Tahn took a deep breath. "You'll not be alone. Remember that."

"You really think God's still with me?"

"Yes. Just waiting. And nothing's holding you back now."

"You're incurable, Tahn," Lucas told him. "I never imagined such an outlook from you. Those nightmares—are they gone?"

Tahn smiled. "Yes. I dream of my family here. Even the church."

Lucas looked past him, toward the morning sun. "You are proof there is a God." He smiled. "And maybe you're right.

Maybe I'm not alone. I should have been dead by the master's hand years ago. I was nearly as useless to him as Vari."

Tahn clasped his hand and then hugged him.

Lucas stiffened. He would never have expected an embrace from Tahn. Not in a hundred years. "Or *you* might have killed me in your sleep," he said quickly. "I used to think you surely would."

"Forgive me for that torment, my brother," Tahn told him.

"I'm just glad it's over. I should be going."

"Where, Lucas? You're my friend. I'd like to know where to find you."

"Alastair. It was home once. But I know you, Tahn. You'll not be visiting me there."

Tahn bowed his head. "I'd like to keep you here."

"That won't happen."

"Let me get you the money for the horse, then." Tahn was troubled for Lucas, but he knew he couldn't hold him. When Lucas had provisions and the price of a strong horse in his bags, Tahn hugged him again before he mounted. "You told me about Burle, but you left your sword in the dirt with Samis. Are you sure you'll be safe?"

"I don't really care right now."

"At least promise me you'll go to the church if you get in trouble," he told him.

But Lucas only saluted him and rode away.

When he was gone, Netta put her arm around Tahn. "You're all right?"

He nodded. "More than that, Lady. I can see how richly I am blessed."

32

A week later, they were all at the site of the Triletts' first estate. Netta had filled a wagon with bundles of dried flowers and twelve carved angels.

Hildy and Ham walked with the children as Benn and his daughter and nephew moved in silence over a row of seven stone crosses marking the graves of their slain family members. Just beyond those were five more, servants and friends who fell the same night. They decorated each of them with Netta's flowers and a single wooden angel.

Jarel hugged his cousin and then turned away in tears. Benn went after him, and they walked together the entire way from this place of memories to their current home. Netta watched them leaving but turned to find Tahn. He sat alone against a piece of the damaged wall he'd once so easily climbed.

"I am sorry," he told her as she approached him. "Would God that I had known a way for all of them!"

She took his hand and knelt at his side. "They are rejoicing," she said. "They know the bliss of our Holy God. And you, Tahn, are part of the blessed gift that he gave me in their stead."

She touched his cheek with a gentle smile. "We will live our lives now to honor him, my friend. And join them in heaven one day."

He leaned and kissed her softly. In a moment, he helped her to her feet. Seven little ones and a boy now as big as a man clustered around them. And together, they went home.

L. A. Kelly is a busy Illinois writer who is active in the ministries of her church. She works at home in order to spend time with her husband and two beautiful children.